MURDER WEARS MITTENS

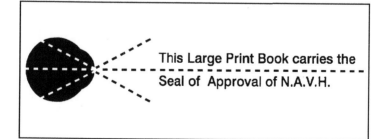

This Large Print Book carries the
Seal of Approval of N.A.V.H.

SEASIDE KNITTERS SOCIETY

MURDER WEARS MITTENS

SALLY GOLDENBAUM

KENNEBEC LARGE PRINT
A part of Gale, a Cengage Company

Farmington Hills, Mich • San Francisco • New York • Waterville, Maine
Meriden, Conn • Mason, Ohio • Chicago

Copyright © 2017 by Sally Goldenbaum.
Seaside Knitters Society.
Kennebec Large Print, a part of Gale, a Cengage Company.

ALL RIGHTS RESERVED
Kennebec Large Print® Superior Collection.
The text of this Large Print edition is unabridged.
Other aspects of the book may vary from the original edition.
Set in 16 pt. Plantin.

LIBRARY OF CONGRESS CIP DATA ON FILE.
CATALOGUING IN PUBLICATION FOR THIS BOOK
IS AVAILABLE FROM THE LIBRARY OF CONGRESS

ISBN-13: 978-1-4328-4064-8 (softcover)
ISBN-10: 1-4328-4064-9 (softcover)

Published in 2018 by arrangement with Kensington Books, an imprint
of Penguin Publishing Group, a division of Penguin Random House LLC

Printed in Mexico
1 2 3 4 5 6 7 22 21 20 19 18

CAST OF CHARACTERS

The Seaside Knitters

Endicott, Nell: Retired nonprofit director, lives in Sea Harbor with husband, Ben

Favazza, Birdie (Bernadette): Sea Harbor's wealthy, wise, and generous silver-haired octogenarian

Halloran, Cass (Catherine Mary Theresa): Co-owner of Halloran Lobster Company

Perry, Izzy (Isabel Chambers Perry): Former attorney, owner of the Seaside Knitting Studio; Nell and Ben Endicott's niece; married to Sam Perry; toddler daughter, Abby

The Men in Their Lives

Brandley, Danny: Mystery novelist and son of Archie and Harriet Brandley; Cass's fiancé

Endicott, Ben: Nell's husband; Charlie and Izzy's uncle

Perry, Sam: Izzy's husband; award-winning

photographer

Sonny Favazza: Birdie's first husband, now deceased

Friends and Townsfolk

Adams, Willow: Pete Halloran's girlfriend

Anderson, Mae: Izzy's shop manager

Brandley, Archie and Harriet: Owners of the Sea Harbor Bookstore; Danny's parents

Brandley, Marian: Librarian

Brewster, Jane and Ham: The Endicotts' oldest friends; artists and cofounders of the Canary Cove Art Colony

Cardozo, Dolores Francesca Maria: Sea Harbor resident

Chambers, Charlie: Izzy's brother; nurse practitioner at Sea Harbor clinic

Danvers Family: Laura, mother of three girls; **Elliott,** Laura's husband and owner of Danvers Family Bank; **Daisy,** 11-year-old daughter

Duncan, Marlene and Joe: Neighbors of Dolores Cardozo

The Fractured Fish band: Andy Risso (drummer); Pete Halloran (guitarist, singer); Merry Jackson (keyboard, singer)

Garozzo, Harry: Owner of Garozzo's Deli

Gibson, Esther: Police dispatcher

Halloran Family: Mary, Pete and Cass's mother and secretary at Our Lady of Safe

Seas Church; **Pete,** Cass's brother and co-owner of lobster company and singer in the Fractured Fish band; **Sister Mary Fiona Halloran,** Mary's sister-in-law and Pete and Cass's aunt.

Hartley, Elizabeth: Friend of the police chief

Jackson, Merry: Owner of the Artist's Palate Bar & Grill; singer in band

Mackenzie, Glenn: Family doctor

Marietti, Gabby: Birdie's preteen granddaughter from NYC

Northcutt, Father Lawrence: Pastor of Our Lady of Safe Seas Church

Palazola, Annabelle: Owner of the Sweet Petunia Restaurant

Perry, Abby: Izzy and Sam's daughter

Pickard, Shelby: Owner of Pickard's Auto Repair

Pisano, Mary: Newspaper columnist; owner of Ravenswood-by-the-Sea

Pisano, Richie: Reporter and distant relative of Mary Pisano

Porter, Tommy: Police detective

Purl: The yarn shop's calico cat

Risso, Jake: Owner of the Gull Tavern; Andy's father

Russell, Claire: Manager of Lambswool Farm

Sampson, Ella and Harold: Birdie's housekeeper and groundskeeper/driver

Stewart, Kayla: Waitress at the Ocean's Edge Restaurant; Christopher and Sarah Grace's mother

Swenson, Hannah: Director of the Seaside Initiative nonprofit organization

Thompson, Jerry: Police chief

Virgilio, Lily, MD: Ob/gyn

Wooten, Don and Rachel: Owner of the Ocean's Edge Restaurant (Don) and city attorney (Rachel)

CHAPTER 1

Kayla Stewart leaned against the old tree. Its gnarled branches, shaped by decades of ocean winds and nor'easters pounding the miles of shoreline, creaked menacingly in the cold wet wind. She glanced across the yard at the gray Cardozo house as if she were seeing it for the first time. Two long windows stared back at her — glaring, judging, as if they already knew why she was there.

She turned away, dismissing the image, and looked around the property — the scrub bushes, a tree hugging the corner of the house, a narrow walkway. And acres that wound back to the dense woods and beyond.

The familiar terrain calmed her. A patch of garden was just visible along one side of the house, wedged between a gravel path and the gray siding. A row of nasturtiums Kayla had planted last spring outlined the walkway. She remembered tossing the seeds on a whim, willy-nilly, thinking a little color would provide a good vibe for the house. But it had surprised her when something beautiful came from her random gesture, the scattered seeds turning into leafy crimson and yellow plants. It had made her smile, and unless she had imagined it, had softened the homeowner's lined face, too.

Dolores Cardozo's face came to her now, the familiar lines and wrinkles etched in her mind — a face so dark and weathered from the elements that Kayla wasn't sure what nationality or race Dolores would claim as her heritage. When she asked her about it one day, Dolores had chuckled, the ambiguity seeming to please her. She never answered.

Was that face peering at her right this minute, as Dolores stood in the darkness, looking at her from one of the windows, her long white hair pulled back in a ponytail, or maybe loose, falling over her shoulders? Was she wondering why Kayla was standing in the wet chill of the day, no bundle of food in her arms?

The first day Kayla had made her way out to the Cardozo property, driving her old beat-up Chevy along the rutted roads, she had gotten lost, in spite of the clear directions given to her. A wrong turn had taken her to a patch of gravel, a parking spot alongside the road that led to several hiking paths. Kayla had parked the car and walked along one of the paths, long and narrow, curling through the woods until suddenly it all opened up to a vast clearing — a silent quarry filling the space. She had stood at the edge of the once active granite pit and stared down at a bottomless pool of water held intact by massive slabs of granite. The day had been crisp and clear, with sunlight reflecting off the water so white and bright she had to squint her eyes. It was one of the most beautiful sights Kayla Stewart had ever seen. She'd stood there for a long time, mesmerized by the black water, the sky above, and the air, crystallized into tiny diamonds.

Lucy in the sky with diamonds.

The song had hummed in her head that day. A good day. A new chapter in her life.

From then on she had welcomed the solitude that always met her at the Cardozo place. Her body would loosen, her shoulders relaxing and the tight kinks giving away to the space around her. It was a meditation, helping her think about her life as it slowly reassembled itself little by little, the pieces shifting and turning until they fit together

11

in a comfortable way.

When she had shared the thought later with Sister Fiona, the nun had nodded in that way she had, and Kayla had seen the satisfied look on her face as if she were the one who had put the thought there to begin with. And then the slight lift at the corners of her wide mouth brought on by the incongruous thought of Kayla meditating at all.

On one of her trips to Dolores's home, she realized that next to the solitude and the woman in the small house, it was the unlocked doors that she liked. Unlocked doors and wild and free land with a silence so profound that she could hear her own heartbeat when she walked through it.

Peace.

But tonight it was hard to hang on to that peace. It was flying around her like loose feathers, difficult to grasp.

The late afternoon shadows felt ominous with creatures crawling out from behind the trees, rattling Kayla's resolve. They fueled the burning in her chest, the discomfort, the distaste that coated her tongue. She wanted to be home cleaning up the kitchen. Reading *Where the Red Fern Grows* to the kids, all of them huddled together beneath a blanket, the soft warm bodies of Christopher and Sarah Grace making Kayla's heart hum.

Soon she'd be there. This wouldn't take long.

She forked her fingers through her short-cropped hair, then tugged a baseball cap on, frowning as spokes of black hair poked out. It had been a mistake to cut her hair so drastically. Sarah Grace had cried when she saw it. She said that she missed the long hair Kayla would let her twist into braids and tie ribbons around. She said it made her mother look like a boy.

She'd done it impulsively, the day she'd seen the photo in the paper. A picture of *her.* Her long black hair framing her face. The waves she could never control touching her cheeks. Thick, shiny black hair. The kind people wanted to touch. *Striking,* people said. *Distinctive. Memorable.*

All of the things Kayla didn't want to be. She didn't want anyone to remember. Ever.

But cutting her hair hadn't worked, and she had promised her daughter that she would let it grow. *Hair grows fast,* she had consoled Sarah Grace as she wiped away her tears.

The wind picked up and Kayla pulled the edges of her jacket tight. She wrapped her arms around herself. Some of the waitstaff at the Ocean's Edge Restaurant had told her she'd love September and October in Sea Harbor: late summer blooms, leaves beginning to turn, and most of all, the space that opened up in the town when summer people went back to Boston or New York or somewhere. The streets became their own again, the restaurants less crowded, the beaches wide and welcoming, the cool sand soothing.

But today had been damp and cold, not at all what had been promised.

Kayla rubbed away the bumps beneath the thin jacket fabric and tried to ignore the headache that began to pinch her face, tugging at her forehead and narrowing her eyes. She rubbed her temples, knowing before the headache took hold completely why it threatened. Favors tethered you to people, you *owed* them, no matter what. And what they'd ask of you in return could ruin your life.

The day Kayla turned eighteen, she had celebrated her birthday by running away from her last foster home in North Dakota. It was in the middle of a North Dakota snowstorm so blinding no one could have found her even if they had tried. She had vowed that day never to be dependent on anything or anyone again. Dependency brought pain and deception — and it eroded the bubble she tried so hard to construct around herself.

Depending on others wasn't necessarily a bad thing, she'd been told. *Ask and you shall receive, Sister Fiona always said.* Kayla had cringed at the words. She knew about favors — favors that beget favors, that stole her body and soul.

She admitted to herself there had been decent people along the way, like when she ended up in Idaho and a woman a few years older than herself had helped her out. Her name was Angel. *Angel!* Kayla had ridiculed the name, scoffed at it. But Angel had been tough, her life once a mess, just like Kayla's. Later on, Kayla came to understand that "Angel" had been a perfect name for the tough girl with the purple hair who believed anyone could pull themselves together if they decided to do it.

And sure, Sister Fiona, as bossy as she could be, was a part of the whole life raft deal. Maybe she was better than okay. Maybe she and Angel had saved her life.

After all, Fiona had brought her to Dolores.

Sea Harbor, Massachusetts, was a place for living, the nun had told Kayla. Sea Harbor was where problems could be

15

solved. Where kids could thrive. Where pasts could be buried.

So she swallowed her fear and her secrets, buried them deep down inside her where no one would find them.

But someone had.

Kayla took a deep breath, curled her fingers into a ball and stared at the house. It was now or never. She needed to tell her what she had done. And then to beg . . .

She blocked from her mind what she'd do if it all fell apart.

And then, with steely resolve, she walked along the path, past the nasturtiums and the darkened windows, to the back door.

The door she knew was never locked.

CHAPTER 2

The wind slammed the door shut behind Cass Halloran as she walked into the Harbor Road Laundromat. She bunched up a fistful of unruly dark hair, damp from the wet, salty air, and bound it with a scrunchie she pulled from her wrist.

Beneath an old sweatshirt, her stomach complained, reminding her that it had been hours since she had eaten. *Quiet,* she murmured. *Nell's homemade lasagna is just minutes away.* At least that's what her friend Izzy's texts had been promising her for the last hour. And that made the hunger bearable at least. *Homemade.* Even the lasagna noodles would be made from scratch, a fact that still puzzled Cass. Noodles were like crackers and baked beans. They came in boxes, cans, or bags. No one made them. But much to Cass's sublime happiness, Nell Endicott had proved every one of her assumptions wrong.

Earlier that day, Cass had made her own plans for the evening. She'd finish the company laundry and race home, out of the chilly night, to a waiting Danny Brandley, who would warm her up nicely in the cozy seaside house where they *co-lived,* a term a relative had recently — and pointedly — coined. Her fiancé would massage her feet while she'd stretch out in front of a fire he'd have laid. A fire in September, unheard of, but it sounded perfect and wonderful and there was plenty of cut wood out near the garage.

She was bone weary. Probably, she told herself, because it was Saturday — a day off — and instead she'd spent the day putting out fires. Everything seemed to have gone wrong at the Halloran Lobster Company that day — including a breakdown of the commercial washer and dryer they used for nets and sweatshirts, towels, and all things smelling of fish. Which was nearly everything. So she had dragged them all to the Laundromat, then run errands while waiting for the machines to do their thing. She hoped the bad day wasn't an omen. Nor the reason her weariness had a touch of worry attached to it. Silly. All would be better once she got home.

And that's when her friend Izzy's texts

started messing with her plans.

Nell is cooking lasagna. Says we should get over there ASAP. There'll be champagne. Pick me up at my yarn shop.

Danny followed up with

Hey, babe. The Endicotts are feeding us. I know you were dead set on my grilled cheese. I'll make it up to you.

So Danny was headed to Ben and Nell's, too. It was all about homemade lasagna and champagne.

The group of friends had missed their usual Friday night dinner at Ben and Nell's because the couple was out of town for the day. Friday night dinner was a ritual born when the Endicotts had retired and settled permanently in Sea Harbor. It had become a comforting staple in Cass's life, right along with the older couple themselves, more family now than friends. Maybe that's what this was about — Nell feeling guilty, knowing that none of them took canceling dinner on the Endicott deck lightly. It was therapy and friendship and amazing food all mixed up together in one bundle — something they all held sacred.

Sure, that was it. And that was fine with Cass. Few things outdid Danny's foot massages, but Nell's cooking might be one of them. Champagne? she texted back to

Danny. You're kidding me? Her fiancé knew she hated champagne, but the thought of lasagna caused her stomach to dance.

Danny sent two kissing, carefree emoticons back.

She stuck her phone in her pocket and set her laundry basket beneath the round door of the dryer, pulled it open, her mind still on the lasagna. And beer. Ben would most certainly have beer. Who drank champagne with lasagna?

She pulled out a damp towel, grimaced, and tossed it back in. Next she felt something fuzzy and pulled out a small pink sweater, its buttons caught in a ratty fisherman's net. She pulled them apart and stared at the clothing. It was soft and pretty and tiny. Nicely hand knit.

Cass frowned, then reached in and pulled out another net, this one tangled up with a small plaid skirt. Cass leaned over and looked in, then pulled out a pair of boy's jeans and several other small garments.

She glanced around the room. The harsh fluorescent lights lit up every corner. She was completely alone. Even the girl who usually worked nights was absent, most likely having a burger and beer across the street at Jake Risso's tavern.

Cass felt a peculiar twist in her stomach,

20

an unexpected pang that something was wrong. Then just as quickly, realization dawned and she tried to lighten up. Well sure. A busy mom ran out of change and found a creative solution — Cass's dryer was going strong so she had tossed in her own items, probably thinking she'd be back before Cass. *Creative,* Cass thought, something she herself had done once or twice in college. But the poor woman was in for a surprise if that pretty pink sweater ended up making her daughter smell like a lobster.

The imagined scenario somewhat easing the tension she felt, Cass mounded all the damp clothes back into the dryer and slipped a couple more quarters into the slot. She listened for the familiar tumbling of the net hooks against the dryer drum, and stretched her toned shoulders back, working out the kinks. Though Cass did little exercise, lifting lobster traps and machinery kept her lean and trim — and strong — a fact new members of her crusty fishermen crew figured out quickly when they'd find themselves misled by her lovely Irish face with its long lashes and prominent cheekbones. She headed for a chair across the room and sat down, stretching her legs out in front of her. *Buy new jeans,* she thought, the permanent saltwater stains at the edges of her jeans looking shiny in the glare of the fluorescent light.

A large clock near the washing machines reminded her of how late it was. They'd all be as hungry as she was. She sent Izzy a message to go on without her, but her friend refused.

Don't be a martyr, Izzy replied. I'll wait. Birdie's coming too, and bringing wine and Ella's brownies. Something about a surprise.

Ella's brownies? Cass's stomach reacted instantly. *Buttermilk, Valrhona chocolate, rich, gooey frosting.* Birdie Favazza had stopped cooking long before her seventy-fifth — or was it her eightieth? — birthday, but her amazing housekeeper, Ella, spared no calories or expense in making perfect brownies. Only when Cass had exhausted the mental taste of the brownies did she consider the rest of the message.

A surprise? What is that about? Good news, she supposed, which would account for the champagne, though Izzy seemed slightly rattled, if one could be rattled in a text. Maybe she was just hungry, too.

Cass stretched her legs out in front of her, leaned her head against the wall, and closed her eyes briefly, her attention going back to the noisy dryer and the delicate sweater inside, vying with the menacing lobster nets.

22

She had a sudden urge to take it out, rescue it, keep it safe for a little girl who liked pink. Then she rolled her head against the wall and scolded herself for conjuring up a story about nothing.

Outside branches slapped against the front windows. Cass looked over, hoping to see a woman in exercise clothes race in, maybe leaving a kid in a soccer uniform sitting in the back of the car. She'd scoop out her clothes and head home to the rest of her family. The thought comforted Cass briefly, but she couldn't completely push away the irrational worry that the sweater was lost, tumbling around in a stranger's dryer.

And the troubled thoughts wouldn't go away. Would a mother come all the way to the Laundromat with so few clothes and on such a crummy night? And all kids' clothes, no tights or underwear or . . .

Still she hoped for the mom, but no one rushed through the front door settling Cass's crazy thoughts. All she saw through the windows were swaying branches on the pear tree at the curb and a flickering of lamplights.

She glanced again at the clock and thought about her waiting friends. *Okay, Halloran, think about surprises, not some stranger's laundry. What surprise is huge enough to explain the flurry of texts?* Her mind went blank. It wasn't that they didn't have their share of good news — even some that merited bubbly beverages. They'd had champagne when Danny sold his first mystery, when Cass opened her new lobster warehouse and office. When Izzy's yarn shop had its first profitable year. And other times, too.

But none of those events were actually *surprises* — simply celebrations of good happenings. In fact, she couldn't remember the last surprise any of them had pulled on the others — unless it was that December night not so long ago when she had knelt down in a patch of snow and proposed to Danny Brandley in front of her friends and practically the whole town. All of them had been surprised that night — even the one who did the proposing, Cass admitted.

The hollow sound of the wind, chilled air, and the slamming of a door jerked her from the flood of memory. Next, footsteps and the click of nails on the linoleum floor echoed in the large room. Cass opened her eyes and sat up. A slender figure came into view behind the line of vending machines. *The mom,* Cass thought, surprising herself at the relief that swept through her.

But when her eyes focused, it wasn't a

24

woman — or a dad. It was a young boy — followed closely by a shaggy wet dog. The boy was focused, his eyes straight ahead. Strands of wet hair fell across his forehead and he looked cold in a thin T-shirt, no jacket.

There was only one dryer with clothes in it — hers — and Cass watched as he headed directly for it. He jerked the door open and leaned in, elbow deep, then pulled out a handful of clothes and roughly separated his own from Cass's tangled towels and nets, throwing those back inside. The dog sat at his side, keeping guard.

Cass glanced through the front windows, squinting to see a car parked at the curb, headlights on and the engine running, a mom behind the wheel waiting for her young son. But all she could see was the silhouette of an old bike leaning against the glass.

She felt the twist in her stomach return. *A cold black night. A dog, a bike, and a kid.*

She started to get up, the movement immediately turning the dog's head toward her. One ear stood erect as its eyes locked into hers. It assessed her with a soft growl, throaty and not very threatening, much to Cass's relief. The boy, intent on his task, seemed to not have noticed.

Cass took a deep breath and started to get up again, slowly and quietly, not wanting to scare the boy. She wanted to assure him it was okay to use her dryer — she'd done it herself once or twice. *But hey,* she'd tell him, *she had a truck parked in the alley. How about a ride home? The dog, too? No problem.*

But at the movement the dog bounded across the room in a blur of gold, its nails clattering on the linoleum floor, until it landed squarely in front of Cass.

The young boy dropped the clothes and stared across the room.

Cass let the dog smell her hand, then spoke softly to it, its floppy tail assuring her they could be friends. But her eyes were on the frightened boy across the room, his dark eyes staring, his mouth set. A deer in headlights.

Finally, the boy broke his stare and looked at the clothes he had pulled out of the dryer drum, then back to Cass. His brow was furrowed now, his thin body stretched tight.

Cass stood up, leaning over slightly as she kneaded the dog's ears. "Hey," she said, her voice friendly, nonthreatening. "It's cool that you used the dryer. Not to wor—"

But the boy seemed unmoved by her smile or affection for his dog and turned abruptly back to the dryer, pulling out a few more pieces of clothes.

"Let me help," Cass said. *Help? She wasn't sure how or what kind. There was something* desperate *about the boy.* "I could —"

But the end of her sentence fell flat as the boy stuck two fingers into his mouth and whistled to the dog, then shoved the clothes into his backpack as if his life depended on it. He turned once more toward the dog, yelled, "Shep, come," and headed toward the exit.

Before Cass could react, he disappeared through the open door, the dog at his heels.

Cass yelled after him as she ran, too, then tripped over her clothes basket. She regained her balance and caught the door a second before it closed. Stepping on to the sidewalk, she peered down the street.

But all she could see was a disappearing backpack strapped to a boy's shoulders as he pedaled wildly down the Harbor Road sidewalk. The dog kept pace, a tail flying in the wind.

"Stop!" Cass yelled. But her words were blown away by the wind as a boy and a dog were quickly swallowed up by the dark night.

Fleeing whatever danger they might have imagined they'd left behind.

CHAPTER 3

"About time."

Sam Perry was waiting at the front door of the Endicotts' home, one foot holding it open, a bottle of Sam Adams in one hand and the other pulling Izzy into a hug. He had a strange grin on his face.

Izzy slipped from beneath his arm and took a step away, examining her husband's face. "Okay, you, what're you up to? What's with the big surprise? Cass and I are starving."

Her teasing voice wasn't entirely pleasant. The weather had been weird, the shop busier than usual, and Sam had texted several times that their daughter, Abby, had been fussy all day. The two-year-old was the peaceful heart of the Perry family — but for some reason, as if expecting strange things to be happening, Abby had been as unpredictable as the weather.

Before Sam could answer, Cass stepped

inside and pulled the door shut behind her.

Sam looked at her. "You're a mess, Cass. The polar plunge isn't until January."

Cass looked down. Her jacket was soaked, and wet strands of hair fell across her face. She'd started down the street after the boy, instinctively afraid. But she had no idea of what, so she'd finally gone back inside the Laundromat and tried to think ahead to brownies and lasagna.

"It's nasty out there," was all she said to Sam. "So what gives around here? Surprises usually herald nine months without wine. You pregnant, Sam?"

Sam laughed. "Not after dealing with our angel baby all day, while Izzy here fiddled around in her yarn shop, free as a bird. Ten-minute nap, that was it. But she's asleep now in Nell's guest room — so don't either of you gals go hootin' and hollerin' and waking her up."

"My goddaughter, Abigail Kathleen, is perfect." Cass shook off her jacket and hung it on a hook beside the door. "But there's a strange vibe in the air today along with the crappy weather. There was this kid — I can't get him off my mind —"

Sam interrupted. "I agree. Crazy vibes. Strange things are happening here, too. Just you wait."

Cass looked at Izzy, then back to Sam. She forced her own worry aside. "What?"

"Okay, out with it," Izzy said. They both looked down the hallway toward the back of the house.

The house was unusually quiet, but they supposed people were talking softly for sleeping Abby's sake. In the distance, music was playing, but not as loud as usual. Some Phil Collins or Stevie Wonder eighties music — which meant Sam had plugged his music in first.

"Come on, come, come," Sam urged. They followed him through the entry that opened up into the long airy room running along the entire back of the Endicott house. It was framed in windows and French doors and filled with comfortable slip-covered furniture around a fireplace at one end. At the other was an open kitchen with an enormous island that seemed to center their lives and hosted important announcements — good and bad.

Tonight was no exception.

On the island stood the bottle of champagne, with glasses neatly lined up around it. A stack of dinner plates behind it, the smell of lasagna wafting from the oven. And standing center stage — flanked on either side by Ben and Nell, the diminutive,

31

silvery-haired Birdie Favazza, and Danny Brandley — was the surprise.

"Hey, beautiful ladies," the tall, floppy-haired man said. "Long time no see."

"Charlie!" Izzy dropped her bag and flew across the pine floor. Charlie Chambers's arms opened wide to embrace his older sister. Izzy squeezed his broad shoulders hard, and when she finally released him, Cass moved in and did the same.

"Wow. Now this *is* a surprise," Cass said, and pummeled him with a tumble of questions: "How long are you staying? When did you come? Why didn't you let us know, you big jerk?"

"You look great," Izzy finally said, her voice husky. She grabbed a tissue from the counter.

Charlie brushed a thick strand of dark blond hair off her cheek. "Hey, you too."

Nell watched her nephew and niece's reunion with a flood of memories — summers on the ranch watching them squabble and giggle with their older brother, Jack — the three Chambers kids running wild, their skin turning bronze beneath the Kansas sky. Charlie always had a football in his hand those long-ago summers, Jack a book, while Izzy was more interested in horses and not having to wear a dress for three months.

But the Chambers's only daughter had eventually shed her pigtails and grown tall and graceful, heading off to an east coast law school, impressing her professors and associates who remembered Isabel Chambers long after meeting her. Maybe not her name, but they remembered the enormous brown eyes that filled her face, the dimples that punctuated a wide smile in her fine-boned face, and the tall figure of a woman whose slightly irregular features fit together in an intriguing way.

Charlie, the family jock, had taken a different path, dropping in and out of the family's life for a while. But he'd come back a while ago, and now here he was again, standing right in front of them. Safe and whole.

Cass was the first to move beyond the welcome. She eyed the champagne, then looked at Charlie. "Hey, this is a great surprise, Charlie. But a champagne surprise? You don't even like champagne."

"You think maybe I'm just a beer-level surprise?" Charlie asked.

"Something else is going on here, dude. I know you too well. Out with it." Cass stuck her hands on her hips, her eyes holding him to an answer.

Charlie's head fell back and he laughed.

He looked across the island. "Aunt Nell, if you drag this out any longer, it may backfire. They may all send me back."

Ben stepped up, his glass held in the air. "Hold up your glasses, folks. Charlie's here to stay." It took less time than it did to down the champagne to explain that Charlie'd be working for the town's family practitioner, Dr. Glenn Mackenzie.

Nurse practitioner extraordinaire was how Nell put it. "That's what Glenn was looking for. I saw the ad and e-mailed it to Charlie, knowing he was the perfect person to fill the bill."

Charlie got the job but had asked Ben and Nell to keep it quiet. Just for a while, he'd said.

The reason for keeping it a secret, they'd both suspected, was so their nephew could change his mind, a possibility not entirely out of character for Charlie.

But he hadn't.

"He's here to stay." Nell walked over next to him, looking less tall next to her ex-football-playing nephew. "It's permanent," she added, one hand resting on her nephew's arm. She felt Charlie's slight shiver at the word *permanent.*

And that news, they all agreed, *did* deserve a celebration. Even champagne.

Followed by happily filling their plates with cheesy lasagna and hunks of warm Italian bread. They moved around the family room and settled wherever legs could be stretched out, plates balanced on laps and the square coffee table.

Charlie sat quietly in the middle of it all, his fingers wrapped around a bottle of stout.

Nell watched from her chair near the fireplace, her mind wandering back over the years of her nephew's life. Things hadn't been as easy for Charlie as they had been for Izzy and their older brother, Jack. An accident to a fellow player on the college football field had sent Charlie into a tailspin, one compounded by bad decisions, bad circumstances, bad company. But the most difficult person Charlie had had to deal with had been Charlie himself.

And it looked like he had done it, defined himself, his goals. At least for now.

When Charlie looked up, their eyes met. Nell smiled, her hopes for Charlie as clear as if she had spoken them out loud. Happiness, for starters. Some peace in his life.

Charlie lifted his bottle in a silent toast and managed a smile back.

He hoped the same.

CHAPTER 4

It was at Cass's request — more of a command, Izzy said — that the women meet for breakfast the next day.

The Sweet Petunia, she had texted. *We can talk there.*

Cass had been distracted the night before, but when Nell had asked her what was wrong, she had shaken her head and turned her attention back to Charlie. Cass loved her best friend's brother almost as much as she did her own. And it was clear she wanted it to be a celebration about Charlie, so Nell had let it rest.

They all agreed to meet at the restaurant. Annabelle Palazola, the restaurant's owner and chef, made the best omelets on the North Shore — certainly an added impetus to show up.

Cass was already camped out at her favorite table when the others arrived — an end table on the deck that ran the length of the café. The view of the Canary Cove Art Colony below was partially hidden today by trees just beginning to release their leaves.

"What is that you have there, Catherine?" Birdie asked, sitting down across from Cass. She slipped on her reading glasses and reached over with a crooked finger to touch the tiny plaid skirt that Cass had laid out on the table. A little girl's sweater was beside it.

Izzy sat down next to Cass, crossing her long legs out beneath the table. She leaned back and smiled up at the waitress while she poured coffee all around.

A basket of warm fried biscuits and pot of apple butter appeared next.

Izzy looked at the clothes and asked, "Did you save your grade school uniform, Cass? That's sweet."

Cass didn't laugh or tease her back. Instead she folded the skirt and sweater and slipped them into her backpack. Her blue eyes lacked the laughter usually held there. Cass was serious.

Birdie broke the silence, a kindly fan of wrinkles spreading out from her clear gray eyes. The oldest member of the knitting group — no one knew for sure how old — Birdie easily brought focus to conversations. "All right, Cass, dear. You have our attention. Now tell us why you brought a child's school uniform to breakfast."

Cass wiped a dollop of butter from the corner of her mouth. "Thanks. So I would have said something last night, but it was Charlie's homecoming — a great surprise, by the way. But Nell, you do know that Charlie dislikes champagne as much as I do, right?"

Nell laughed. "It's symbolic, Cass. She pushed her sunglasses into her salt-and-pepper hair. "On with your story — you have worry written all across your face."

Cass took a drink of coffee and began, relieved to have the chance to talk about the boy who had troubled her dreams the night before.

"The thing is," she said, as the story wound down, "it was nasty out last night — you all know that — and too late for a little kid to be out doing laundry. His T-shirt was torn, and he didn't even have a jacket on. It was just him and his dog." She tried to lighten the mood and looked at Izzy. "A cute dog, though. He looked like you, Iz. His fur was wild and crazy, all different colors. Yellow streaks with some brown tossed in."

Izzy shook her golden streaks proudly.

"Anyway, there wasn't anyone waiting for

him, no car, only a bike. There was something about the whole thing that wasn't right. He pedaled away like a madman, as if he thought I was going to call Tommy Porter and have him arrested for using my dryer or something. He was clearly afraid of me. Or of something. I can't get him off my mind."

"I've seen kids in the Laundromat before, helping their moms —" Izzy began.

"Sure, me too." Cass interrupted. "But there was no mom last night. That's the point. He was alone. But anyway, the kid ran out so fast he left these things behind. I want to return them. It's the same uniform I wore a thousand years ago. Our Lady of Safe Seas Elementary School. I used to get in trouble when I wore the wrong color sweater or pinned my skirt up too short. His sister will need her uniform."

"His sister?" Nell asked.

Cass welcomed the waitress's interruption and sat back as the young woman placed heaping plates of omelets in front of each of them.

"Annabelle said this is what I should bring you," the waitress said, new to her job and clearly uncomfortable bringing a meal that hadn't been ordered.

Birdie smiled away her discomfort. "Annabelle always knows *exactly* what we want.

39

This is perfect. Thank you, dear."

The waitress smiled gratefully, refreshed their coffee, and disappeared.

Cass eyed the omelet. There was always some amazing surprise folded into Annabelle's eggs — Gruyere cheese, herbs, pine nuts, even spinach could be transformed beneath her masterful hands. Unable to wait, she scooped up a forkful and murmured something indecipherable. Then she got back to business. "Okay, so about this little boy —"

"Have you seen him before?" Nell asked. She'd seen Cass deal with poachers and recalcitrant fishing crews with a single glance. Seeing her now so suddenly taken in by a child's lost clothing was curious.

"I don't think so. All I know is the dog's name is Shep. He shouldn't be hard to find, though. His mom wrote initials on the inside of the clothes, just like my ma used to do on mine. That'll help."

"Wouldn't Father Northcutt know? Or maybe Sister —" Nell paused.

"You can say her name out loud. Sister *Fiona.* It won't make me lose my appetite." Cass took another biscuit and broke it apart while she talked. "And you're right. My Aunt Fiona knows everything, so I called her, but she wasn't answering her cell. She was probably still in church lighting candles for me. But somehow we need to figure out where the kids live so we can return the clothes."

"All of us? They're that heavy?" Izzy's fork wiggled midair.

"I know it's crazy, but I have this weird feeling that something might be wrong. The only way to get rid of that feeling is to take the clothes back, have the boy's mom thank us, and be on our way. But if there *is* something wrong . . ."

Nell put down her fork and wiped a trace of sour cream from the corner of her mouth. "Cass, it isn't like you to worry about something like this."

"I know. Crazy, huh? But it doesn't matter. The clothes still have to go back. And your clear thinking is why I need you all to go with me. If his parents are home when we drop off the clothes and none of you sense any kind of problem, then I'll forget about the boy and his dog and move to easier problems — like finding out if the dagnabbit engine on the new trawler needs replacing. But at least the kids will have their clothes back and they won't have to face Sister Mary Fiona Halloran's wrath at being out of uniform tomorrow morning."

Birdie chuckled, then said gently, her

41

silver cap of hair moving with her words, "Your aunt isn't a bad person, Cass. She's doing wonderful things for the parish. I've known Fiona a long time. She's a good woman."

Nell held back a smile, knowing Cass's complaints about her aunt were strictly personal and the kind only one family member can give another.

"So she wants you and Danny to get married," Izzy said, hitting at the heart of it all. "That's not such a bad thing."

Cass glared at her.

Birdie and Nell listened without offering opinions. Mostly because they wouldn't mind at all if Danny and Cass got married. But they understood Cass's emotional reaction, too, especially after they heard Sister Fiona tell her niece one day that long engagements were the work of the devil.

"Back to the business at hand," Cass said. "So let's find out where the kid lives and be on with it." She looked at each of them over the rim of her coffee mug.

"I think the answer to that just walked onto the deck." Nell lifted her chin and looked over Cass's head. She lifted one hand in a wave.

A round, ample man with thinning gray hair, his shoulders slightly hunched, followed the hostess onto the deck. His gait was slow but his blue eyes sparkled as he greeted parishioners along the way. He caught Nell's wave, and returned it.

"Sunday Mass must be over," Nell said. "Our font of information has arrived."

They paid their check and walked to the other end of the deck, gathering around the man who had been Our Lady of Safe Seas's pastor for as long as any of them could remember. Cass pushed aside the salt and pepper shakers and spread the uniform skirt, the sweater, and the jeans on the table and waited while he perched his glasses on the end of his bulbous nose. He checked the black markings inside the clothing while Cass explained how they'd come into her possession. The priest's head nodded as he looked at the initials inside.

He held up the delicate pink sweater and looked at Cass. "We used to only allow navy blue sweaters, remember that, Catherine?"

She nodded. "It was okay with me. Pink was never my color."

"Well, this little skirt and the sweater belong to Sarah Grace Stewart. I believe Sister Fiona said she and her mother knit it for the little girl. And the jeans must belong to her brother, Christopher." Father Larry smiled. "She's mighty fond of those two little ones. Sure and they're lovely children. Christopher can be a bit rambunctious at times, but it's understandable, considering the li—" the priest paused for a minute, then shook away the rest of his sentence and took a bite out of his second fried biscuit. "Their mum will be grateful to get these items back, I am sure of it."

He pulled a church bulletin from his pocket and scribbled an address along with squiggly lines. "Your good mother and Sister Fiona will be joining me shortly," he said to Cass.

With that, Cass brought the conversation to a swift close and headed toward the parking lot steps. The others urged Father Larry to order Annabelle's Sunday special, and quickly followed.

"He rode all this way?" Cass said. She was sitting in the backseat of Nell's car, watching the blocks go by. She had taken the scribbled map from Nell and checked for the next turn.

"I sometimes run over here," Izzy said. "There are a couple shortcuts he probably took. But you're right. His parents must have been worried about him."

"I wonder if they knew he was gone," Nell said.

Birdie glanced out the window. "I don't think the lad would have been sneaking out to do laundry without his mother's knowing it, do you? But no matter, I'm sure everyone will be happy to have the clothes back. It's thoughtful of you, Cass."

Cass leaned back into the seat.

Izzy looked at her sideways. "You still think something's wrong, don't you? Is there something you're not telling us?"

"No, nothing. So I'm crazy, right?" Cass said. "But there's this irrational prickling I get on the back of my neck sometimes. It's probably nothing. Maybe I just looked scary and that's what caused the look on his face."

But she didn't convince anyone. They believed strongly in intuition — and that included strange pricklings at the back of a neck. And they knew such things could trump reason in a big way.

Following Cass's directions, Nell made a right turn onto Elm Street into a quiet residential neighborhood. Covering most of the corner was the old shoe factory that now housed at least a dozen affordable apartments. Across the street several teenagers pitched to each other on a dusty diamond. Two dogs circled a screaming gull near a half-eaten sandwich until it finally abandoned its prey and flew off.

In the next block a row of small houses lined each side of the street, each one identical to one on either side of it, distinguished only by the toys in the yard, the color of the door, or the numbers on the mailboxes. Modest and tidy, the houses had small front porches and square patches of yard separating them from the sidewalk and the neighbors.

It was a pleasant sight. Doors and windows were wide open, catching the breezes. Children played on front lawns and the sounds of cartoons, lawn mowers, chattering voices, a baby waking up all blended together and wafted across lawns.

Normal. It all seemed normal. Lazy Sunday living. Certainly not fearful.

A group of teenage girls, their young bodies clad in identical skinny jeans and tees, was gathered around a telephone post, laughing and tapping into cell phones.

"It's on the left, near those valley girls," Cass said from the backseat.

"The one with the bright green door," Izzy said in her best Father Larry imitation.

Nell slowed and pulled over to the curb, turned off the engine.

The teenagers glanced over at the car, then quickly lost interest at the sight of four women and went back to their phones.

46

They looked up at the house with the green door.

It looked like all the others.

But yet was different.

This house had the same patch of lawn, a narrow walkway leading to the front steps. One small tree with a homemade wind chime hanging from a branch.

But on this bright Sea Harbor day, with sounds of life rolling up and down the street, this house sat as lifeless as a tombstone. The porch was empty, the windows were closed, and heavy blinds kept out the sunshine and brisk breezes.

"I think we're out of luck," Nell said. "No one's home."

Cass nodded, her disappointment clear. "I suppose. But we should check, just in case." She picked up her backpack and climbed out of the car with Izzy close behind her.

"I really don't think there's anyone here, Cass," Izzy said. Her voice was almost a whisper, as if the house in front of them demanded quiet. "It looks deserted. Maybe for the first time in his life Father Larry was wrong. This doesn't look like a kid house. Maybe he gave us the wrong directions."

Nell and Birdie stood on the sidewalk looking up at the closed door.

"It could be the right house, but they're

simply not home," Birdie said. "But Cass is right — we might as well have a look as long as we're here. I thought I saw a curtain move, but then these eyes sometimes play tricks on me."

She wound her fingers around the railing and walked up the steps with the others following. Several knocks on the door were met with silence.

Cass walked over to the front window and cupped her hands against it, peering in. "I can't see anything through these drapes. They must be an inch thick. It's like a barricade."

Cass leaned over the side of the porch. "The bike is here. At least it looks like the one I saw last night."

Birdie turned the knob. "It's locked," she said.

Izzy walked over to the door, her almost five-feet-ten advantage bringing her eye level with a small window near the top. "The hallway's empty but there's a room at the end. I can see something back there. It moved. And I hear something."

And then they all heard it, the loud click-click of paws, followed immediately by rapid barking and a thud as loud as an earthquake hitting the front door, clamoring for it to open.

"Shep, quiet!" It was a boy's voice, followed by the soft pad of sneakers racing down the hallway.

The four women waited, but the dog had gone quiet and the only sound coming from behind the door was the tugging on a collar as a dog was reluctantly being pulled away.

"Hey, Christopher, wait," Cass said loudly, her voice carrying down to the curb, where the girls stopped talking and stared up at the women.

Birdie smiled and waved at them, effectively dismissing their interest.

"It's me," Cass went on. "The lady from the Laundromat. You forgot some clothes there last night and I thought you'd need them."

Silence.

Cass shrugged to the others, then tried again. "You know, for school tomorrow? I used to wear a uniform like this and Father Northcutt had a fit if we came to school in plain clothes. And that Sister Fiona? She can be a grouch, right?"

At the mention of the priest's and nun's names, the lock slowly turned and the door opened a crack. The boy looked surprised to see the four of them on the step and started to shut the door again, but Cass's foot moved faster.

"They're my friends," she said. "They know Father Larry, too."

"Chrissie, my uniform," a small voice squealed from behind the boy.

They all looked down into the smiley face of a curly-haired girl who had wedged herself in between the dog and the boy. Her missing two front teeth accentuated her grin. She pushed the door open wider.

"Are you Sarah Grace?" Birdie asked, her gentle voice doing magic.

Sarah Grace's head bobbed in agreement. "I wear a uniform," she said, reaching out for the skirt. "It's for kindergarten."

"I used to wear a skirt that looked exactly like yours," Cass said.

Sarah Grace looked at her own skirt, then back to Cass, a puzzled look on her face. "How did you fit in it?" She pressed one finger against a dimple in her cheek.

Her brother glared down at her. Sarah Grace had pulled the door wide open. She nudged her brother aside and said to her new friends, "You can come in if you want."

Birdie looked at Cass, then the others. And then she looked down at the little girl and asked, "Why don't you get your mother instead? Maybe she would rather talk to us out here on your porch. We'll wait right here." She looked over at Christopher, not

50

much shorter than herself, waiting for a response.

He met her eyes.

"Why don't you tell her that we're here, Christopher?" Birdie said. "We will wait on the porch —"

"And, buddy," Cass said, "you're not in trouble, honest. I'd have done the same thing if I needed some dryer time. It was cool."

Christopher caught his bottom lip between his teeth, but his eyes remained on the small woman with the silvery hair and map of wrinkles defining her face. Finally, he stuttered, "It's just that, well, she doesn't wanna see you. Not right now. She's . . . she's really busy. She's —" But the end of his sentence fell to the floor, lost in a choking odor that rolled down the hall like a tumbleweed. In the next second an ear-piercing alarm filled the house and sent Shep howling in distress.

Christopher spun around and raced back down the hall. Four women, a dog, and a tiny blond girl with her fingers stuck in her ears followed close behind.

Nell rushed past Christopher to the stove, where a scorched griddle belched smoke into the kitchen. Coughing, she turned the burner off, grabbed a hot pad, and lifted the heavy pan into the sink, piled with cups and plates.

Izzy dodged a pile of toys on the floor and threw open the back door.

"Where's the smoke alarm?" Cass yelled.

Christopher pointed back to the hallway ceiling, and in less than a minute Cass had pulled a chair from the kitchen, climbed up, and disconnected the batteries.

The young boy watched her silently, his eyes damp. A shock of dark hair fell over his eyes. He stuck his hands in the pockets of his jeans.

"Chrissie was making me grilled cheese," Sarah Grace said. "It's my favorite. It burned."

"You have a good brother," Nell said. "We kept him talking at the door too long and the butter got too hot."

Sarah Grace shook her curls. "Mommy won't like it."

"Are your mommy and daddy here?" Birdie asked, leaning down until her face was eye level with Sarah Grace.

The answer was obvious. Nell looked around, scanning the refrigerator and the counter for a calendar or family schedule that might give them a clue, but all she saw was a pile of envelopes and papers at one end of the counter. Just like home, she thought, checks and bills in a heap.

Sarah Grace looked at Birdie. "My daddy?"

"Hey, I can handle it," Christopher blurted out, silencing Sarah Grace. "It's okay. It's cool. Thanks. I can clean the pan. I clean up all the time."

Birdie started to say something but stopped short when Sarah Grace's face broke into a brilliant smile. She and Christopher were both looking beyond Birdie toward the hallway, and for the first time, a small grin lightened the young Christopher's face, too.

"Hey, kids," a voice bellowed from the hallway. "What's going on here? This place looks like the wreck of the Hesperus."

CHAPTER 5

Cass spun around. She stared into a set of piercing blue eyes that looked remarkably like her own. "What are you doing here?" she asked.

Sister Mary Fiona Halloran nearly filled the entry. She stood tall with her hands on her hips, her large feet apart, and her clear eyes taking in the messy kitchen, the smoke-filled air, the toys scattered everywhere — and the four women in the small room.

Shep bounded over to her, licking an outstretched hand, then settling himself happily at her feet.

Sister Fiona looked around the room, greeting Nell and Izzy, then Birdie in turn. And finally her niece. But it was clear her attention was on the children, her face softening as she assessed them from a distance. They were standing still in the middle of the messy kitchen, seemingly unsure of the mood among the women surrounding them — or the formidable woman in the doorway.

"Hey, Sarah Grace. Christopher," Sister Fiona said, her voice soft with affection and her hands outstretched toward them.

In an instant, as if released by the smile and the sound of their names, both children flew over to her. Sarah Grace nearly tumbled over Shep as she vied with the dog to be closest to the nun.

"Like I said, what brings you here?" Cass asked.

"Father Larry told me you were here." She mussed up Christopher's hair and smiled down at Sarah Grace. "He thought you might need some help."

"Help doing what?" Cass asked, but her voice had softened, her eyes, too, as she looked at the kids.

Her aunt dismissed the question. She reached down and kneaded one of Shep's ears, then looked again at the mess in the kitchen.

Nell followed her glance as it continued into the adjoining room, where a rug and sofa were littered with popcorn. Blankets and pillows were piled on the floor in front of a television.

Sister Fiona's smile dimmed but her voice was considerate, careful. "Where's your mom, Chris?"

"Running errands." Christopher's answer came quickly, as if he had been rehearsing the line. He glared at Sarah Grace, sealing her lips with his look.

Sister Fiona accepted the boy's answer. Then she gave Christopher an encouraging nod and suggested he and his sister go into the living room for a while to watch cartoons.

Surprised, he poked Sarah Grace in the shoulder and ran off, eagerly following the suggestion. Shep bounced along behind them.

As soon as the children were out of earshot, Sister Fiona looked at Cass. "So, what's going on?"

Cass explained the Laundromat incident to her aunt. "It was nasty out. Not fit for a young kid. Something didn't seem right."

Sister Fiona was quiet.

"So that's it. I was concerned, that's all," Cass finished. "I figured they'd need these. Wouldn't want a cranky principal to wonder why they were out of step with the other kids."

That drew a half smile from her aunt. Cass went on, "We expected to hand them over to a parent and be on our way. But that didn't happen, and from the looks of the house, these kids have been alone for a while. The place was like a fort when we got here, everything locked as if they were protecting themselves from the enemy."

Nell and Izzy had busied themselves cleaning the stove, putting dishes in the dishwasher, and rummaging around for more bread and cheese. But their ears were tuned in to the conversation.

Birdie walked over. "You seem to know this family, Sister," she said. "The children are clearly fond of you."

Sister Fiona Halloran made a tsking sound with her tongue, her cropped dark hair shaking with the sound. "Birdie Favazza, since when are you formal with me? You've known me all my life, for better or worse. Let's leave the 'Sister' moniker to the kids and their parents. Keeps them just enough afraid of me to do what I say."

Birdie laughed. She glanced into the living room. "I was trying to show respect in case the kids heard me. And I haven't seen you much since you've been back in town, Fiona."

Fiona's laugh was robust. "You thought I was turned into a proper nun, you mean? No, I'm as ornery as I ever was." She looked at Cass and lifted one brow. "And no lip outta you on that topic, Cass Halloran."

Cass managed a smile. "Wouldn't dream of it. But back to what Birdie was saying — what's your relationship with these kids? Just the school?"

Fiona mulled Cass's question over for a minute. Finally, she said, "Yes. I'm the cranky principal. Both kids go to Our Lady of Safe Seas, but I'm sure you know that from the uniform. Same one you wore. The Stewart family moved to Sea Harbor late last year."

"So you know their parents, too?" Cass asked.

Fiona looked into the living room, satisfied when she saw the kids laughing at a purple creature bounding across the television screen, totally oblivious of any adult conversation. "There's only one parent. The mother. And yes, I know her. She works hard for her kids. A good lady, good mom."

"Where is she?" Cass asked.

"You heard the little guy. She's running errands."

"Was she running errands all night?" Cass's voice had a slight edge to it, but she quickly took it down a notch. "All I'm saying is that it doesn't look like she's been around for a while. These kids are little. Who's responsible for them?"

Fiona gave her niece the look that probably worked like a Taser on eighth-grade boys.

But Cass was reluctant to step down completely. "I was worried about Christopher last night. He's so young and he looked scared, like he was doing something he shouldn't be doing. And riding his bike in the dark? What was that about?"

"Wasn't Shep with him?" Fiona leaned down and scratched the dog's head. He was still leaning against her leg, and if dogs could smile, Fiona had enticed one out of Shep.

"Shep? So you're saying dogs can parent now?" The flush in Cass's cheeks deepened to the color of Izzy's crimson blouse.

Nell broke into the tension from the stove, "A fresh batch of grilled cheese sandwiches are almost ready for the kids. Anyone else hungry?"

Sister Fiona looked relieved at the interruption. "Thanks, Nell. That's exactly what the kids need. Food." She turned to Cass. "I appreciate what you've done, Cass. You're just like your dad. A good heart. My big brother would go out of his way to help anyone, even knocked around a few bullies who picked on me. He was the good kid in the family. Me — well, not so much maybe, but I do have a little of his protective

59

instinct in me."

She started to say something else but thought better of it. Instead she lightened her tone and said, "Those sandwiches smell great. Who wants to pour the milk?"

The four women left soon after, nudged out the front door by Fiona, who stayed behind. She was staying there with the kids until their mother came home from running her errands.

"She works hard for these two. Loves them like the dickens." Then she thanked them sincerely for their help and stood at the door, waving good-bye while they walked to the car. Her message was clear that she was in charge now. They were no longer needed.

Nell started to open the car door, then turned back, the keys dangling from her fingers. Fiona was still standing in the open doorway. But her eyes were no longer on the four women whom she had politely expelled from the small square house on Elm Street.

Instead she looked off into nothingness, or so it seemed to Nell. Her confident, take-charge demeanor was less pronounced, and her shoulders were slightly slumped. But it was the look on the nun's face that Nell couldn't dismiss. The confident smile had faded and been replaced by something she herself was familiar with: a deep worry that holds one prisoner, squeezes one's heart until it has been resolved. The kind of worry that tells you everything is really *not* all right, no matter what words come out of your mouth or what face you put on to cover up the emotion.

Nell stood in a circle of moonlight, looking through the bedroom windows. In the distance, the sea pounded the shore, a rollicking tide erasing the beach, lap by lap. She could still hear signs of life, a group of teenagers on the beach, music blaring, neighbors sitting on porches having a nightcap. She and Ben had decided to retire early, Ben weary from a day of sailing with friends, Nell exhausted from things she couldn't put her finger on.

Across the room, Ben was already in bed, his reading glasses at the end of his nose, a sailing book resting on his chest.

He had listened thoughtfully as she had replayed her day over dinner, explaining about the children, about the vague feeling that something wasn't right in that house. "It's probably much ado about nothing," she'd said finally, following her words with a forced chuckle.

Ben had nodded and agreed, all the while knowing that while it was probably exactly that, his wife didn't believe a single word of the quote.

Nell rested her palms on the windowsill now, still niggled with uncomfortable thoughts. She knew it was because children were involved. And that look on Fiona's face. *Much ado. Sure, it could be nothing, and yet . . .*

And yet what? She looked over at Ben again. He was already lost in the world of the sea, vicariously sailing around the world with the intrepid Joshua Slocum on his wooden sloop.

She envied his ability to disengage from an event or topic or conversation and totally immerse himself in something else. It was a gift. Ben didn't hang on to things like she did. Disturbing thoughts didn't linger in his head long, not unless there was a reason for them to stay there. *Let it go, Nellie,* he would say to her gently.

Just minutes later she heard the sounds of Ben dozing off, his book sliding to the floor, his breathing slow and rhythmic.

She took a deep breath, matching his breathing, feeling her tangled thoughts dissolve. *Let it go, Nellie.* She walked over to the bed and the warmth she'd find curling up next to him.

She rested her head on the pillow, her eyes closed. One arm looped comfortably over Ben. And then her eyes opened wide.

At first the sound was undefined, and then quickly became familiar as sirens and horns filled the night air.

Sounds that in Sea Harbor could mean something as simple as rescuing a cat caught up in a tree.

Or in the darkness of night could take on another tone completely.

Sounds that could signal lives changing in a single instant.

CHAPTER 6

For Cass Halloran, Mondays were sacred: her day off, free of lobsters and broken trawls and billings. It almost always began with an espresso and chocolate éclair on Coffees' patio with the *Boston Globe* smoothed out on the wrought iron table. Izzy usually joined her before heading down Harbor Road to open her yarn shop; sometimes Birdie or Nell or other friends would stop by, knowing where Cass would be. And on some days everyone left her alone, which was always fine with Cass.

Today her thoughts were still lingering on the two kids, wondering if their mom had ironed the uniforms she'd pulled from the dryer. Wondering if they'd made it to school okay. Wondering why Fiona hadn't called to let her know everything was fine.

"Hey, Cass." Izzy sat down. She dropped her bag on the floor. "You're a million miles away. Where've you been, girlfriend?"

"Sorry. I'm back now."

"It's the Stewart kids, isn't it? They've gotten to you."

"I think it was the uniforms. I had a dream last night of me and my brother running around like demons while our ma ironed the life out of those uniforms, then sewing patch after patch on the knees and seat of Pete's pants. In the dream he pulled on the threads of the patch until the leg of his pants fell off on the playground. So, yeah, I guess I was thinking about those two kids getting off to school today, just like we used to do. And hoping it all went okay."

"And that no pants fell off?"

Cass laughed. "Yeah. I hope they're okay."

"Why wouldn't they be?"

Cass shrugged.

Izzy pointed to Cass's phone, sitting on the table between them. "Just call your aunt. She'll tell you the mom came home with groceries, the kids arrived at school safe and sound, uniforms clean and neat, and you can smile again, easy peasy."

Cass looked at her phone. "You're so smart, Iz. Must be that Harvard law degree. But for your information, I tried her earlier — and I went to Salem State. But I'll try again." She picked up the phone and tapped in the number. This time a live voice answered.

Izzy listened discreetly, picking off more of Cass's pastry as she leaned in.

Cass spoke quietly, explaining she was just wondering if the kids got off to school okay.

There was a pause while Cass listened, her frown deepening. It was replaced a second later by a puzzled look and the phone being shoved back into her pocket. "She hung up on me."

"No she didn't. I heard her talking."

"Maybe. She sounded rushed, and her voice competed with wind or something, like she was in her car. She pretty much said, 'Of course the kids are fine — why wouldn't they be?' But she couldn't talk. She was needed somewhere else — an emergency. She had important things to do. And that was it. No good-bye."

Izzy took a drink of coffee. "Well, my grandma Chambers never said good-bye. Some people just don't."

"Fiona sounded odd, though. She said the word *emergency* as if she meant it. But she probably just wanted to get off the phone."

"Maybe there was something urgent," Izzy said. "Maybe not. Sometimes when Fiona comes into the shop for yarn, she acts that way, like getting the right yarn is an absolute emergency. I think she accomplishes as much as she does because she treats everything that way — everything is important, an emergency."

"Maybe," Cass said, her voice muddled with distracted thoughts.

"But she didn't connect the kids to the emergency, right?" Izzy asked.

Before Cass could answer, Birdie and Nell walked out of the coffee shop patio door carrying mugs and knitting bags. The *Sea Harbor Gazette* was tucked beneath Birdie's arm.

Before they were barely seated, Birdie had smoothed out the folded paper.

"Have you read this?" she asked.

Cass tapped her own paper, the *Boston Globe,* which was anchored to the table by a heavy coffee mug. "Danny subscribes to this one now. We're big-time."

"Snobs," Izzy said.

"Yep. That and it provides more grist for the mill — for his mysteries anyway."

"He couldn't find enough murderous ideas from our paper?" Nell asked.

Birdie made a clucking sound that brought their attention back to her and her finger tapping on the paper. "He shouldn't be so hasty. Look at this. I'm sure Danny could easily turn this into a mystery. It's already a mystery to me." The finger landed on a block of text down in the corner on the front page.

They all leaned over their hometown paper, with its hometown way of saying things. Nell slipped on her glasses and read aloud:

NEWS FLASH
Dolores Francesca Maria Cardozo, long-time resident of Sea Harbor, has died unexpectedly. Dolores was 76. Details of her death will be released soon.

"Who's Dolores Francesca Maria Cardozo?" Izzy asked. She looked around the table at three blank faces.

"A name like that would be hard to forget, right?" Cass said.

"It has a familiar ring to it, though," Birdie said. She stared off, forcing her memory to clear. "*Dolores . . . Dolores.* It will come to me. But no matter who she is, this is a peculiar way to announce her death."

Nell read it again. "It's almost an announcement. If it were the mayor or a prominent figure and the death had occurred unexpectedly, it might merit this news flash attention. But otherwise . . ."

"It's not exactly sinister, but it's sort of

mysterious. I wonder if my ma knows her," Cass said.

"Sure she will. Mary Halloran knows everyone, living or dead," Izzy said.

The slam of the wrought iron back gate interrupted and they looked over to see the *Sea Harbor Gazette*'s "About Town" columnist, Mary Pisano, stomping on to Coffees' patio as if she'd just been betrayed. She spotted the four women and dropped her computer case on her regular table, then detoured their way. A look of consternation pinched her small round face. "So you've seen it," she said without preamble, pointing to the newspaper on the table.

Shy of five feet tall, Mary Pisano nevertheless commanded attention. In addition to her chatty column in the family-owned *Sea Harbor Gazette,* she owned Ravenswood-by-the-Sea bed-and-breakfast. Together the two "projects" added legitimacy to her reputation for knowing everything that was happening — or ever *had* happened or *would* happen — in Sea Harbor and beyond. Ben often accused her of knowing the Patriot's score before the game started.

"Who is she, Mary?" Birdie asked.

"I know the name. *Cardozo. Cardozo.* It will come to me, but certainly not because of the information provided here." She slapped the paper with the flat of her hand.

Cass pushed her sunglasses into her mass of thick black hair. "Who wrote the announcement?"

"Hah. I know exactly who wrote it." Mary paused for effect. "Howdy Doody."

"The old fifties marionette?" Nell asked. "Shame on him."

"Richie Pisano — red hair and freckles, just like that wooden puppet. You've probably seen him around. He's been poking his nose into everything."

"Who is he?" Izzy asked.

"A distant relative, I'm sorry to say. Richie wiled away a few years in at least three colleges, then a stint in the service. His most recent venture is journalism, probably because his dad owns a dozen of our Pisano papers and Richie'd be sure to land a job somewhere." Mary paused for a breath, and then her face softened a little. "Anyway, his dad lives in New Hampshire and got him this job, probably to put some distance between them."

"How old is he?" Izzy asked.

"Twenty-nine, thirty. I know. It sounds like I was describing a kid. I was never that crazy about that arm of the family. He can be frustrating as all get out. But the *Gazette* editor says he's okay and can string sentences together. She did add that he sometimes oversteps his bounds." Mary pointed again at the newspaper. "Case in point."

"Why isn't there more information?" Birdie asked.

"Richie was probably on the graveyard shift — hanging around the police station or the hospital, heard about the death, and slipped it in quickly."

"The police station?" Nell glanced back at the announcement.

"Well, you know. Someone dies. An ambulance is called. It goes over the police scanner and, voila, there's a reporter hiding behind a tree who catches it all. But Richie will hear about this, I'm sure of that."

Sirens. Of course. The sirens that Nell had carried with her into sleep the night before. "Why did Richie think she was important enough to merit an announcement like this?" she asked.

Mary looked at Nell over the rim of her glasses, then stared at the paper as if the details had been printed in invisible ink and would soon rise to the surface. "That's a good question."

A shadow — tall and narrow — fell across the newspaper, blocking out the morning sun. It was followed by a distinct clearing of a throat.

"Hi, ladies. Sorry to interrupt."

Mary spun around and looked up — way up — into Hannah Swenson's clear brown eyes. "Oh, good grief." Her hands flew up to her cheeks. "I completely forgot."

"Don't worry about it." Hannah brushed away the apology. "You weren't difficult to find. It's Monday, and you have a column to write." She glanced down at the newspaper. "Is something going on?"

Mary glanced back at the paper. "We're not sure. Someone seems to have died last night and it made the front page of the paper. Do you know her?"

Hannah picked up the paper and read the announcement thoughtfully. As director of the Seaside Initiative nonprofit, she was well connected. She looked up. "You'd think I would. It's an elegant name. But no, I don't think so."

"Which," Mary said, "brings us to why I was supposed to meet Hannah this morning and completely and totally forgot."

Hannah explained. "Mary is helping me arrange a board retreat at Ravenswood-by-the-Sea. We're going to acknowledge some big donors and I figured if the board and I don't impress them, Mary's elegant bed-and-breakfast will."

"A perfect place," Nell said. "And it

sounds like things are going well at the Seaside Initiative. We've been to several of the recent fund-raisers — the last one was packed."

Hannah nodded. "And a good thing. We have lots of needs." Her voice showed the uncertainty that came with managing any nonprofit when public funds were tight and fund-raising was difficult. She added, "Hills and valleys. Always seeking new donations."

A retired nonprofit director herself, Nell understood. She'd been on Hannah's advisory board and knew of the difficulty in keeping things running. It was the plight of nonprofits, and even though the initiative did good work — helping other nonprofits along the shore, all the way up to New Hampshire, with workshops and joint purchasing arrangements and public policy work — it always needed money.

"But on a happy note," Hannah said, looking at Nell, "your old paperboy is getting ready for law school — hopefully at Harvard."

"That's wonderful," Nell said. "You should be very proud of Jason."

"I am," Hannah said, beaming. "He's studying for the LSATs as we speak."

Mary began thumping her sneaker on the flagstone patio, ready to move on to other things. "The day's getting away from us," she said. "Come, Hannah, let's pretend I didn't forget about you and we'll figure out this retreat in no time. It will be wonderful."

She gave a friendly but dismissive wave to the women around the table and motioned for Hannah to follow her, moving as quickly as an impatient preteen to the table beneath the maple tree. The About Town column would wait and the morning distractions would be set aside while she gave her full attention to florists, food, room assignments, and serving needs for a board retreat.

But Mary Pisano wouldn't forget the irreverent death notice, either. They were all sure of that. Richie Pisano was not about to escape his distant relative's disapproval, no matter how personable he was.

A short while later the small box on the front page of the *Sea Harbor Gazette* was almost forgotten as the four women cleaned the mess of crumbs from the table, returned their heavy mugs to the tray at the patio door, and went their separate ways to move on into their day: Izzy to her yarn shop to do some planning for a city-wide knitting project — the knitting of hats, mittens, socks, and scarves to keep all of Sea Harbor warm, come winter; Birdie and Nell to a lecture in Boston.

And Cass to help herself to another éclair, after which she would head out to do *nothing* — her favorite way to spend a day off.

But nothing could be *anything,* she reasoned, so when the faint sounds of recess at Our Lady of Safe Seas Elementary School reached her ears, Cass followed them, walking down the tree-lined streets, glancing up at the granite church tower, then slowing when she approached the school that Cass herself had attended. The playground looked the same, ringed by a chain-link fence, though colorful play equipment now stood where Cass remembered steel monkey bars and a giant metal merry-go-round on the asphalt-coated ground.

She stood outside the fence, watching dozens of small bodies in motion, whirling and twirling like whirligigs from a maple tree. On one side of the yard, a wide stretch of grass cushioned the knees of a group of boys kicking a soccer ball. With a twinge of relief, Cass spotted Christopher Stewart on the edge of the gang of boys. He was haphazardly kicking the ball when it came his way. She strained to see his face better. Chris was clearly not into the game, his shoulders slumped. *But he is here,* Cass

75

thought. So Fiona had told the truth.

On the other side of the playground, she spotted Sarah Grace's blond hair. She was playing with a group of equally pintsized girls, following each other up a climbing gym, then sliding down the slide, their laughter light and breezy and lifting Cass's spirits along with the sweet sound.

The scene was normal, ordinary. Cass shook her head. She was a crazy person for giving the kids' situation a second thought, for imagining a mother missing, defenseless kids with only a dog to protect them. For doubting her aunt's assurances. *What had gotten into her?* She had enough to worry about managing a company. There was no room for kids in her thoughts, no reason to suddenly let emotions take over her life.

Her mother would say it was because she was finally beginning to think about *building a nest.* A concept Cass readily disallowed.

Only birds build nests, she had told her mother.

But when Cass turned to walk away from the playground, she felt the emotion grow, as if someone had released a dozen butterflies around her heart.

She shook away the tangled emotions and looked back to the playground. The kids were starting to line up to go back inside, the youngest ones first, their innocence cloaking them in a protective halo.

A sound nearby caused Cass to look down the fence. She realized for the first time that she wasn't alone. A few yards down — partially hidden by a scrub tree whose trunk had grown in and out of the fence squares — a stranger leaned on the metal railing, body tight against it as if the galvanized mesh was the only thing holding the person upright. At first Cass thought it was a boy — short dark hair, slender and shapeless. But when she took off her sunglasses and looked again, the delicate features of a woman's face came clear. Large sunglasses covered nearly half of her small face, shadowing sharp cheekbones. A white headband spanned her forehead. Cass squinted. No, a thick piece of gauze, taped in place. A bandage.

The woman didn't move, not even when the last child had disappeared into the bowels of the old school. The teacher holding the door came back out and carefully scanned the playground, checking the yard for stragglers, then walked back in, pulling the heavy door tight behind her.

And still the woman stood there, her eyes scanning the playground as if it were still alive with young bodies whirling across the asphalt.

Finally, feeling as if she were somehow intruding on the woman's privacy, Cass turned away. Time to leave.

A choking sound, muffled and strained, stopped her.

Cass turned back quietly and looked through the knobby vines growing through the fence. The woman's shoulders were slumped, her glasses pushed into her hair now, her bandaged forehead low as she cradled her head in her arms. Her sobs increased, so fierce that the fence vibrated all the way down to where Cass's fingers still rested on a small square link of metal.

She began to walk toward the stranger.

Cass's nothing day had turned into something.

CHAPTER 7

"The traffic on 128 was a mess." Nell's words preceded her as she opened the back door and pressed the button to close the garage. "A long day and a nice one — a great lecture at the Stewart Gardner. But I'm glad to be home."

Seeing Ben's car in the garage had lifted her spirits. She knew before looking across the open living space where he'd be: sitting at the kitchen island, mail and books and papers spread on top. He'd be helping himself to a chilled Sam Adams, or, depending on the ease or unease of a day of city hall committee meetings, maybe slowly drinking one of his perfect martinis.

But the room was silent.

"Ben?" Nell frowned and dropped her bag on the bench beside the door. She looked out to the deck. Beyond the glass doors, the sky was pressing down on the day, bringing the line of solar lights around the railing to life. A sliver of moon peered through the branches of the maple tree that grew through the deck. But there was no Ben stretched out in his favorite chaise, looking for the first star.

She went back inside and headed toward the back stairs. But a light beneath the closed den door caught her attention. She stopped. Listened.

Doors, even Ben's den door, were rarely closed in the Endicott household. But before Nell could check, the banging of the front screen door, followed by familiar footsteps, brought Izzy and Sam into the family room.

"Hey, beautiful lady." Sam wrapped Nell in a hug.

"I thought you were headed to the Gull Tavern?" Nell said. "Game night?"

"The game is in Kansas City and got rained out or tornadoed out or something."

"But we didn't want to waste having a sitter so —" Izzy said.

"So here we are." Sam's grin was slow — the same one that had endeared him to Nell that day he'd walked into this same room those years before. There he stood — an award-winning photographer giving a lecture series at the art colony her friends Ham and Jane had founded. She knew right then that she didn't want him to leave their lives. Not ever. And he hadn't, marrying her niece Izzy to seal the deal.

Sam went on. "We thought we'd drop in to watch the stars come out. I'll get us a pizza later." He held up a six-pack of beer and set it on a table.

"Stars my foot," Izzy said. "He wants to talk to Ben about yet another sailing project — and he wants to be close to a television in case the game is resuscitated. And I want to knit with my favorite aunt." She glanced back toward the front door. "But are we interrupting something? Whose car is that out front?"

Nell hadn't noticed a car when she drove in, but before she could check, the den door opened and Ben walked out.

Behind him, getting up from a pair of wing chairs, were Father Northcutt and Sister Mary Fiona Halloran.

"I thought I heard voices," Nell said, clearly surprised. "But then, sometimes Ben talks back to his computer." She smiled, hoping it hid her surprise at least a little. Everyone knew the Endicotts' door was a revolving one, but there was something about the combination of Sister Fiona and Father Larry behind closed doors with Ben that didn't fit the usual gathering.

81

Ben kissed Nell on the forehead. "Hi, Nellie," he said. *It's all fine,* his tone and gesture relayed, but his somber face made Nell wonder.

Father Larry fared better. He readily apologized to Nell for the surprise visit. "There's been a bit of news," he said. He looked at Ben, smiled with his usual calmness, and then went on, his chins wobbling. "Sure and we should talk. Perhaps with a wee bit of aqua vitae, Ben?"

"Great idea, padre," Ben said, already moving toward a silver tray of bottles and glasses near the oversized island.

The others trailed after him while Sam began snapping the caps off the beer he'd brought.

Nell rummaged in the refrigerator, her thoughts scattered, half listening to the idle chatter behind her. Perhaps a dose of small talk would soften whatever Father Larry wanted to talk about. She knew Ben had spent the afternoon at city hall and wondered if that precipitated the den conversation. Somehow his retirement had morphed into his involvement in every aspect of Sea Harbor life. But it was a good thing, he always said. And the *Dream Weaver* — the sailboat he and Sam had invested in — was always there when days got too busy or stressful.

She pulled out packages of cheese, a jar of tapenade, a bowl of gherkins and olives, her mind mulling over the look on Ben's face as he'd walked out of the den. She closed the refrigerator and took a wooden platter from a shelf and began filling it with snacks.

"You have a nice art collection," Fiona was saying, glancing at the framed seascapes on the family room walls. But her voice was distracted, her eyes not focusing on art.

Sam pulled out a stool for her. "Would you like a glass of wine? Beer?"

She nodded with a grateful smile and reached for a Sam Adams.

Nell watched the exchange, wondering if the visit was somehow connected to the "emergency" Fiona had mentioned to Cass that morning. She set a stack of napkins on the island and looked around at the others. "All right. We're set here. Now what is up with the three of you?" She aimed the question at Ben, but made it clear she'd take an answer from anyone. One of them, however, had better speak up.

Izzy and Sam pulled out stools and sat on either side of Fiona and helped themselves to the cheese, listening.

Ben glanced over at the newspaper on the countertop. "So you've seen today's paper?"

Nell glanced at it. "Headlines, at least. And the odd box on the front page about the woman who died. Is that what this is about?"

Ben said yes.

"We all think we know her from somewhere," Izzy said. "But we can't place her. Maybe it's all those names. It makes her sound like nobility."

"Did you know her, Ben?" Nell asked.

"Yes, but only slightly," Ben said. "She lived on several acres out near the old quarry. Her property is prime land for development and a series of builders and investors have rotated in and out of our planning committee meetings at city hall trying to figure out how to get their hands on it. Their ideas are endless. I talked to her a couple of times about it. Davey Delaney tried to have the area rezoned so she might want to leave, but Miss Cardozo had absolutely no interest in the large amounts of money they were throwing at her." He looked over at Father Northcutt, who was busy smearing a spoonful of tapenade on a hunk of sourdough bread. "Larry, you knew her better than I did. Fiona, you too."

"She was a good lady," Fiona said. There was sadness in her voice that spoke of friendship.

"She was a parishioner at Our Lady of Safe Seas," the priest added, careful as he always was not to insinuate judgment on those who didn't belong to his church — or maybe belonged but attended infrequently. "Dolores was a good soul. I liked her. I think she preferred Sister here to me, though she tolerated me nicely and seemed fond of the food pantry, being a regular over there." He looked at Fiona and chuckled. "And of course she liked it even more once Fiona turned it into a five-star restaurant. Dolores had good taste. She also liked a nip of my Irish whiskey now and again, something some of my other Italian friends seem to think is next to heresy."

"Was she a volunteer at the Bountiful Bowl Café?" Nell asked. "Maybe I've seen her."

"No," Fiona said. "Dolores ate there." Fiona went on, correcting herself. "Actually, she usually had meals delivered to her. She'd check out the menu ahead of time, then tell me what she wanted. She didn't like crowds."

So Dolores was on food stamps, Nell thought. The situation was becoming more and more curious.

"I'm assuming you were surprised she died?" Sam asked.

Sam's question was logical, but Nell heard in his voice another question — the same one she and Izzy were toying with. *It was sad that the woman had died, but why were they spending all this time discussing a woman they didn't really know? And why all the worried looks?*

"No. Dolores was fit as a fiddle," Fiona said. "She walked every single day, no matter the weather. She walked all over Cape Ann — all the way over to Gloucester some days, up to Babson Quarry, Rockport, the library, always carrying her trusty walking stick."

"Wait, wait. Stop. Walking stick?" Izzy asked. Her face lit up and she slapped her hand down on the island, rattling a bowl of peanuts. "Of course. *The Wizard* — that's what we called her. Her walking stick was huge, just like that ornate thing the wizard Alastor Moody had in the Harry Potter books. Sure, that's who it is. *Dolores.*

"My running pals and I saw her all the time. She told us her name once, but it never stuck — she was always 'The Wizard' to us. Once we were running near the old quarry and ran into her, almost literally. We stopped to make sure she was okay. She overheard Laura Danvers or someone say the nickname 'Wizard.' I didn't want her to think we thought she was a witch or anything so I explained to her how it came about. She loved it. Clapped her hands and repeated the name in her gravely voice. She had read every Harry Potter book so knew exactly who Alastor Moody was, but she assured us that unlike that wizard, she still had all her body parts. And then she laughed some more."

Izzy was on a roll, her memories of the woman who had died coming back to her in waves. "She was strong and fit for someone her age. She walked straight, her chin lifted, as if she was taking the whole world in — and kind of meditating at the same time. She had this long white ponytail, and was almost as thin as her walking stick, but she never seemed out of breath. I'm not even sure why she used the walking stick, except she said she liked the feel of it."

"So that's who made the front page of the paper," Nell said. "Ben's right, then. That long white ponytail was a trademark. I often saw her walking the beach. *Alive* is the word that always came to mind, though she never stopped to talk."

Izzy was smiling. "One time, this was a while ago, I was jogging with Abby in her stroller and we ran into her. Where were we?" She tugged at a memory, then gave it up and took a swig of Sam's beer.

"Birdie will know her with this description," Nell said. "It was the long string of names that wasn't familiar. I was imagining a wealthy Italian dowager and couldn't come up with a single one in Sea Harbor. That's one mystery solved then. Are you planning her funeral?"

Nell looked over at Ben, who was strangely silent. "Ben?" she said.

Ben shook his head. "No. And I'm sorry for dragging this out. I just wanted to make sure you knew who we were talking about. Here's what's going on. The police got a call last night to go to her home. When they got there, they found her on the floor."

The sirens again, Nell thought. "A heart attack?" she asked.

"No." Fiona drummed her fingers along the island top, her square chin set and her eyes blazing. "Dolores was clubbed to death with her own walking stick. Some bloody fool killed her."

For a few moments the only sounds in the room were those of the wind picking up, rustling the leaves in the maple tree, exciting the gulls, and in the distance, beyond the Endicott Woods, the incoming tide crashing against the shore.

"Murdered," Sam finally said. "What?"

Nell looked over at Ben. He was unusually silent, and she could tell this wasn't finished.

Father Larry sipped his whiskey, his blunt fingers magnified through the crystal glass. "The announcement in the paper was a mistake and you can bet our Mary Pisano is pinning some young reporter's ears back."

Nell and Izzy nodded; yes, that was true.

"But whoever did it was correct in saying that there were more details to come. They'll be spreading through town by tomorrow. It's a horrible crime and the good people of Sea Harbor need to hear about it, it's their right. Right now the police are exploring all the things you'd expect them to be looking at, including the possibility of robbery."

"I've done a couple photo shoots out there," Sam said. "The neighborhood doesn't seem to be the kind that would attract a serious thief."

"Probably true. But Jerry Thompson doesn't want to rule anything out," Ben said. "I talked to the chief briefly. He said the house was sloppily ransacked, things in disarray."

"I guess that sounds like a robbery — but it still doesn't sit right. To rob one of those little houses — and then to kill the person?

To what end?" Nell asked.

"Dolores had some money stashed around her house. She kept it in strange places," Fiona said. "Cookie jars, under a mattress, in an old coal stove she didn't use. She sometimes joked to me about it. And it wasn't nickels and quarters. She preferred fifty-dollar bills, as neat and clean as if she'd minted them herself. The house may not have looked like much, but there was money in it."

They'd all heard about people like that — Nell had a great-aunt who died and left thousands of bills hidden in suitcases in her attic. But there was something more to this. A simple burglary in an eccentric woman's house — even a robbery that ended tragically in a death — couldn't be what had brought Father Larry, Ben, and Fiona together at their house, late on a Monday. The look was still there on Ben's face. The one that said there was more to say.

"Well, it's about more than the fifty-dollar bills," Ben said. "Elliott Danvers went to the police when he heard the news. He had a meeting scheduled with Dolores that she didn't show up for."

"Elliott?" Nell asked. "She was meeting with a banker?"

"*Her* banker. Elliott helped her with

money matters, and not the fifty-dollar bills stashed around the house. Dolores Cardozo was a very wealthy woman."

"Rich?" Izzy and Nell spoke in unison. It matched nothing that had come before it.

"Geez," Sam said.

"Sure, one doesn't have to look rich to be rich, but —" Izzy's words fell off and then she smiled at the image of her hiker friend and the secret she held tight to her chest.

Nell smiled, too. The thought of Dolores eating food from the Bountiful Bowl Café was somehow lovely. She was beginning to wish she had known Dolores Cardozo — and not at all because she was wealthy, but because no one knew it.

Everyone was still sitting quietly and Nell wondered briefly if she should order pizza for everyone, or if they were about to leave. She looked up at the clock.

Finally, Father Larry put down his glass. "Jerry Thompson, good man that he is, contacted me when the police were called to the house. He didn't know if Dolores'd be wanting the last rites, you see. The chief is considerate about things like that — he noticed the crucifix on her wall and maybe had seen Dolores at Mass now and then."

"Who was it who called the police?" Sam asked.

"Claire Russell," Ben said.

"Claire?" Nell said. Claire had suffered her own share of heartache over the years. A daughter dying as a teenager, losing her best friend and lover so recently. She didn't need this. Finding a dead body was an awful thing, one not easily put to rest.

"Yes. She was leaving Lambswool Farm after one of their sold-out farm dinners. She drives right by Dolores's house on her way home — a shortcut she discovered. Somehow she and Dolores had become acquainted in recent years. So when Claire saw a light on in the house, she decided to drop off some spinach and tomatoes that hadn't been used for the dinner. When Dolores didn't answer the door, Claire figured she was out walking, so she went on in to leave the bag on the kitchen table. That's when she found her. At first, she thought like you did, Izzy. That Dolores had had a heart attack. So she called nine-one-one, and the police called Father Larry," Fiona said.

"But before I even got there," the priest said, "they knew she hadn't died of a heart attack. *Blunt force trauma,* someone said. Awful thing. It was far too late for the last rites when I got there, so I gave Dolores a blessing and said a small prayer to send her

92

off in peace, dear lady."

Nell looked over at Izzy, knowing the lawyer gene in her niece was recording the details as they fell in place — as if it were important somehow for all of them to remember them. *Sunday night.* While she and Ben walked the beach, watching the tide — the miracles of nature unfolding in front of them — someone was murdering Dolores Cardozo.

"She'd been dead for a while," Fiona said, as if watching their minds trying to work out a timetable. "They don't know for sure how long, but the coroner said it could have been as long as twenty-four hours. They'll know more soon."

Sam frowned. "That's a long time. And no one knew?"

"Dolores wasn't exactly sociable," Fiona said. "I probably saw her as much as anyone. Well, no. Not as much as —" She stopped, considering her words. Then she reached for her beer and left the sentence hanging there.

"So you're saying it might have happened as early as Saturday, Saturday night? And the police didn't discover her body until yesterday," Izzy said, rearranging the order.

Nell thought back. They'd been dealing with their own mystery during some of that time. Two young children who lived on Elm Street.

Fiona was studying Nell. She nodded. "You had your own drama going on yesterday."

Nell frowned. She and Birdie often read each other's minds, finished sentences. But she wasn't at all sure how she felt about Sister Mary Fiona intruding on her mental space. But she nodded back, politely. After all, Fiona had been a part of it, too, in a way. But showing up Sunday surely wasn't what was on the nun's mind today, what brought her to their home. In fact, there was no reason to think about that incident at all. Not in the middle of a discussion about a murder.

She looked at Fiona intently, and wondered.

Fiona went on, talking about meeting the four of them at the Stewart home. She seemed to be digressing completely from the uncomfortable talk about a murder. But Ben and Father Larry made no move to pull her back. And the expressions on their faces suggested the others not do so either.

"Nell," Fiona said, "I know you suspected that I wasn't entirely sure things were okay in that house yesterday. I meant every word of their mom being a good mother, but I wasn't at all sure where she was. And I was pretty sure it wasn't running errands at Marshalls or Target or the Market Basket."

"Why is that?" Sam asked. "Izzy sometimes calls Marshalls her Sunday Church."

Father Larry chuckled.

Fiona kept talking, as if she'd never get to the end of the story if she stopped. "For starters, Kayla didn't have a car this weekend. It's over in Shelby Pickard's shop, waiting for some part that I had offered to help her pay for. Money is tight in the Stewart household but she needs her car. She's been getting around for a few days on an old bike I gave her."

"So where was she?" Izzy asked.

"I didn't know, at least not when I saw all of you. Scared me silly. Those two kids are Kayla's life. Her *whole* life. She would never have left them alone for hours if she could help it. Leaving them alone all night? Never, not in a million years would she do that. So I started calling around, waitresses at the Ocean's Edge, where she works. A couple babysitters she uses. Anyone I could think of. A waitress she works with had heard from her on Saturday but not since. She'd been looking for someone to watch the kids for an hour, the woman told me. A neighbor said the same, but they were leaving town.

95

The babysitters I reached said the same. She needed someone for just an hour but there was a big event at the high school that night and none of them could help. I suspect she even called me, but my phone had run out of batteries Saturday. She finally told Christopher that she was running an errand and would be back soon. She did that a few times, he said, like when she'd run to the grocery store for milk.

"Anyway, no one had heard from her since Saturday so I started calling clinics, ERs. The Beverly Hospital said a young woman fitting her description had been brought in."

The images of two beautiful children played across Nell's mind like a slow-motion movie. Her chest tightened.

"She's okay," Fiona said immediately, and Nell released the breath she didn't know she was holding.

"She had a bump on her head and a badly bruised forehead — as if she'd fallen and hit something. Apparently the blow to her head resulted in a concussion. But she'll be fine. Kayla Stewart is a very strong woman and has experienced far greater hurt than a bump on the head. When the doc heard she was riding a bike — Christopher saw her riding off on it — he said she could have lost control, maybe flew off it and hit her head on a boulder. He said accidents like that are a dime a dozen around here with granite boulders all along the roads."

But Fiona was using the same tone of voice she used to convince them that the kids were okay the day before, and that their mother would be back shortly. Kayla may be all right, but *something* wasn't. Nell watched the concern flooding Fiona's face as she continued.

"Kayla was found wandering around on a back road, not knowing where or who she was — which, of course, was why she didn't get in touch with me — or someone — to be with the kids. A man driving by spotted her weaving on and off the easement, right into the road. At first he thought she'd been drinking and might get hit, so he stopped. She couldn't tell him her name or address. She didn't have a wallet or phone with her. Nothing. Her forehead was bleeding, the blood running down her face — so he took her to the emergency room over in Beverly, where he was headed."

"Amnesia?" Izzy said.

"Yes. Temporary amnesia, the doctor said. I called a sitter for the kids and went over to the hospital." She took the thumb of whiskey Father Larry pushed in front of her and swallowed it down in a single gulp, as if the sting to her throat would bolster her to get the rest of the story out. "She knew I looked familiar when I walked in but at first she couldn't remember my name. She was fuzzy. The doc said her memory would come back, probably soon, but it was unpredictable. She had had a slight concussion and he was keeping her overnight. He suggested I talk about her family to try to pull her out of the haze.

"As soon as I mentioned Sarah Grace and Christopher, she went crazy. Frantic. Memories of her kids came back instantly. And she was wild with worry, pushing herself up and flinging her legs over the side of the bed, pummeling me with questions. Where were they? Had she left them somewhere? Were they all right?

"It was only after I told her several times that they were fine and healthy and safe that she began to settle down. She was insisting I find clothes for her and take her home. Finally, after promising I'd stay the night with the kids just like I'd done the night before, she settled back into the pillows. A nurse gave her a sedative. She was sleeping when I left."

"How awful for her, realizing the children had been alone for so long," Nell said.

Sister Fiona didn't answer at first. It was

clear she was playing the role of protector, not only of the kids but of their mother, too. Finally, she said, haltingly, "She remembered only bits and pieces — not that she had been gone overnight. She remembered that she had something she needed to do — an important errand that would take less than an hour. She couldn't remember what it was or where she was going — or how she had gotten out to that road where the man from Beverly found her. All I know is what I finally pulled out of Christopher after all of you left the house yesterday. His mother had made them an early dinner and told them she was going to run an errand. Christopher was in charge, she told him, and shouldn't let anyone in. She'd be home in time for dessert. The only reason he'd gone to the Laundromat that night was because Sarah Grace had spilled chocolate milk on her uniform and he wanted to surprise his mother so she wouldn't have to do it and they could go to the park on Sunday."

"And then what?" Sam asked.

"And that's it. She didn't come home. But she couldn't remember anything else, once she had gotten on her bike and headed out from home. She has no idea what caused the lump on her head."

Izzy, Sam, and Nell sat in silence, fragments of what they were hearing floating around in their heads.

It was Izzy, her desire for order and logic working overtime, who looked at Ben. "Uncle Ben, what are we missing? First we're talking about the awful murder of a woman we don't know well. And now, about the mother of two kids who had an accident. This whole conversation is disjointed. Why were the three of you sitting in the den talking about these two incidents — at least I presume that's what was going on behind the closed door?" She paused for a breath and looked at Fiona and Father Larry, then back to Ben. "Why? What's the connection?"

"Okay, you're right, Izzy," Ben said. "Here's what connects everything. When the police roped off Dolores's property, they found a bike leaning against a tree in her yard, not far from the house. The bike belonged to Kayla Stewart."

CHAPTER 8

Cass knew the instant Nell and Izzy told her about what had happened to Kayla Stewart's bike, the injury, the night in the hospital, she now had a face to go with Christopher and Sarah Grace's mother.

She sat in the cool sand near the wide steps of the Sea Harbor Yacht Club patio, facing the sea as she took in the news that hadn't made the morning paper. She had kicked off her Birks and was pushing her heels into the sand, her knees bent and her hands cradling her head as if holding in the chunks of the story she was hearing for the first time.

Behind her, Izzy, Nell, and Birdie sat in a semicircle of Adirondack chairs, coffee mugs from the club patio balanced on the wide arms.

The sun was warm, beating down on bare arms, the cool ocean breeze a soothing salve. Birdie's knitting bag sat opened at her feet, but her eyes were on Izzy and Nell as they repeated everything they knew about Kayla's missing two days. And a bike that was now in residence at the Sea Harbor police station.

The four women had planned to come together Tuesday morning — somewhere — to list community groups that might help with their new knitting project. The HMS project, Izzy's shop manager Mae called it. Hats, Mittens, Scarves. A community effort that would result in enough hats, mittens scarves and socks to warm anyone in need for the long winter ahead.

Nell suggested they avoid Izzy's busy shop and Harbor Road activity, retreating instead to the yacht club patio and beach. That area would be nearly deserted on a Tuesday morning, and the club's coffee was much preferable to what Izzy produced in her back room. They'd also avoid the storm that was sure to grow as more details of Dolores Cardozo's murder were passed around the town coffee shop, the deli, the bookstore, and along the sidewalks of Harbor Road.

But mostly it was the power of the sea they wanted, the calming motion of the tide that would cushion their thoughts and talk of Dolores Cardozo's murder and the mystery of where Kayla Stewart had been — and why.

They had all read the article in the morning paper, the earnest reporter fulfilling his promise to provide details of Dolores's death, although the article was once again scant in true details. The two-inch headline that covered the front page was nearly as big as the article that followed. Mary Pisano had clearly not corralled her reporter as adeptly as she had hoped. Birdie had brought the paper with her and read it aloud, puzzled by its brevity and tone:

Dolores Francesca Maria Cardozo met her untimely demise in the living room of her own home, a small woodstove-heated house on Old Quarry Road. She was killed by a blow to the head during what may have been a robbery gone bad.

The exact time the robber ransacked Miss Cardozo's home and delivered the fatal blow has not been determined. However, reports indicate that her body was discovered Sunday by a Sea Harbor resident delivering spinach to the victim, who was a vegetarian.

Birdie set the paper on the wide arm of the chair, absently smoothing it into a fold.

Cass's brows lifted. "A vegetarian? Good to know."

"It sounds like this Richie guy is pretty sure it was a robbery. I wonder where he gets his information," Izzy said.

"The police seem to be keeping information tight," Nell said. "Maybe the less people know, the less the disturbance to the town will be."

However, they all knew that people would be disturbed, no matter what was kept out of the papers. The sketchy details would gather momentum as the day wore on. Some of what was said and repeated, and repeated again, would be true, some facts would be embellished, and some would simply be made up to fill in the gaps.

It wasn't the anticipated rumors, however, but the details that had *not* made the paper that concerned the four knitters: a bike that had been found leaning against a tree near the victim's home. A blue bike. And the woman who had been riding it.

Jerry Thompson had held back about the bike and any connection between it and Kayla Stewart. She was a relative newcomer, barely considered a Sea Harbor citizen by some who demanded at least ten years' residency to qualify. And she kept to herself — two things that might make her a target for suspicion if the bike details were known around the town.

The chief was wise to contain the bike information. At least for now, Ben had said, and they all agreed. Although they had yet to meet Kayla, the faces of two small children were front and center in their minds.

They sat in silence, the sea breeze lifting their hair and cooling their faces, the cawing of the gulls cushioning their thoughts as they tried to process it all.

Finally, Cass said, "I saw her yesterday."

"Who?" Nell asked.

"Kayla Stewart." Cass explained about her trip to the school playground. "I didn't know it then, but now I'm sure that's who it was. She was alone, her body leaning against the schoolyard fence. She looked like her life was unraveling before her eyes."

"You went to check on the kids," Izzy said softly. But her voice wasn't teasing or judging; it was filled with empathy.

Cass seemed not to hear. "She'd been watching the same thing I was, the kids playing, laughing, kicking balls. The kids had gone back inside but she was still there. Still looking. She was roughed up, like she'd been in an accident."

Cass went on to describe the woman's short spikey hair, her slender, boyish frame.

"She had a bandage on her forehead, and her face looked blotchy, swollen."

"Did you talk to her?" Birdie asked.

Cass shook her head. "I felt like I'd be intruding at first — she thought she was alone." Cass thought back to the scene at the fence. "Maybe subconsciously I did, I don't know. I hadn't been able to get those two kids off my mind. And this woman looked so . . . I don't know, so unstable. If she hadn't had the fence to hold on to, a sudden breeze might have knocked her flat. And she looked really sad, like something terrible had happened. Finally, I started to walk over to her, just in case she needed help, but as soon as she heard the noise and realized she wasn't alone, she tore off in the other direction."

"Fiona had spent the night with the kids. She probably took them to school before she picked Kayla up at the hospital," Nell said.

"She'd have been desperate to see her kids." Izzy's voice was ragged.

"Fiona could have called me to help," Cass said abruptly.

They all looked at her.

"I mean, I could have helped out with the kids." Cass twisted her head around and looked into their surprised faces. She man-

106

aged a laugh. "I know, I know. I don't even know the kids. But I feel like I do. I feel — weirdly enough — kind of responsible for them." She waited for someone to tell her how ludicrous that was. All because she had found their clothes in her dryer?

Izzy nodded. "I completely get it. Remember when I found that abandoned car seat on the beach before Abby was born? *An abandoned car seat.* No baby. I felt the same way about that baby, and I never even *saw* him. But in my heart I had this connection, this emotional tug toward whoever he was, like I needed to protect that baby somehow because I had found the car seat. I even dreamed about him."

"So I'm not completely weird." Cass managed a smile.

"Well . . ." Izzy smiled, her brows lifting into scattered bangs.

"Of course you're not," Birdie said, reaching over and rubbing Cass's hunched shoulders. "You're simply compassionate and kind, Catherine, whether you like to hear it or not."

Cass brushed some sand off her legs along with the compliment. "So, is Kayla all right? What's with the memory loss?"

"It's not uncommon if there's trauma involved," Birdie said. "It will probably come back soon, the doctor in the ER told Fiona. Familiar things may trigger it. She recognized Fiona in the hospital room, and within a short time was able to put a name to her face."

"Fiona is going to stay at the house again tonight," Nell said. "Just as a precaution. She wants to be sure Kayla is okay and can handle the kids. They have an appointment with Doc Mackenzie to check her over. The piece of memory that hasn't come back — at least as of last night — is that chunk of time between leaving her house and ending up in the hospital."

"A big chunk," Cass said.

"Huge. It would include late Saturday afternoon to Sunday morning when she was wandering along the road," Izzy said.

"And even Sunday morning wasn't completely clear in her mind," Nell added.

Izzy pulled her tan legs up on the wide chair, crisscrossing them like a dancer. "That's a whole day to fill in. She left home. She rode her bike somewhere. And a day later she's in a hospital with a concussion. So she was unconscious some of the time, wandering around the rest of it."

And during that time, a woman was murdered.

"The doctor wasn't sure how long she was

unconscious," Nell said. "*If* she was unconscious. There are many unknowns." It was Ben talking through Nell, and they all knew it. The need to be circumspect and not let emotions color their perceptions.

"But surely, as soon as Kayla's mind clears, everything will be resolved," Birdie said.

Cass sat quietly, her eyes following a gull as it attacked a piece of toast marring the club's manicured beach. In the distance, sailboats silently rode the horizon.

"What are you thinking?" Izzy leaned forward, looking at Cass.

"I was trying to imagine what might have happened during the span of time that Kayla can't remember. We know her errand was important. Had to be, to take her away from those kids. So she was headed . . . somewhere. She hit a bump on the road and it threw her off the bike. She hit a rock. There're granite boulders all over those back roads. That would explain the cut to her forehead and the concussion. And when she came to she didn't know where she was."

"And her bike?" Birdie asked gently, treading lightly on what none of them wanted to address: Kayla's blue bike leaning against a tree. And a murdered woman found lying on the floor of a house, just a few yards away.

"Maybe she was near the Cardozo place when she fell. She wandered off and someone found the bike and moved it to get it off the road. They left it there so it could be seen when the owner came looking for it." She wiggled her mug back and forth, pressing it into the sand, as if making it steady would steady her words. "I mean, what possible reason would Kayla have had to go to the Cardozo home that night? We're old-timers here and we didn't really know the woman. How would Kayla, a relative newcomer, have known her?"

But even Cass was aware that her explanation lacked logic or believability, yet not one of her friends refuted it. Somehow, in the space of a few days, they were creating a strange shield around Kayla Stewart, protecting a woman they didn't know — and all because of two children and a dog who had inched their way into their lives. An unspoken alliance had them denying out loud at least one scenario, one that was probably a part of a police report somewhere: They knew from Fiona that Dolores had money around her house — did Kayla know that too? And Fiona said that Kayla was in need of money. She left home on a

110

bike that night, the same bike that was found leaning against a tree at Dolores Cardozo's house.

The same Dolores who was dead.

A half hour later, Cass reminded everyone that she had a job running a lobster company and needed to get back. "Pete's threatening to fire me," she said.

They laughed. Although Cass's younger brother was officially co-owner of the Halloran Lobster Company, Pete rarely stepped inside the office, leaving anything with numbers on it to his older sister and CEO. The boats; the sea; his girlfriend, Willow Adams; and his Fractured Fish band — those were Pete's passions. And not necessarily in that order, he'd be quick to say.

"Fifteen minutes, that's all I ask," Izzy said, holding her hands up to halt Cass's exit. "Mae will handle the nitty-gritty but we need to get it started." Izzy's shop manager could handle the world with one hand, they all believed. But she liked things handed over to her in decent order.

"Hey there, ladies." A faint but familiar voice floated up from the sand.

They looked down toward the water's edge, their eyes squinting against the sun as a runner waved at them in sweeping arcs.

"Hannah?" Nell said, cupping her hands

over her eyes.

Hannah Swenson had slowed to a jog, then walked their way, her body glistening with sweat. She stopped at the fan of chairs and leaned over, her hands on her knees as she sucked in lungfuls of air. "I thought I saw familiar bodies over here," she said between breaths.

"Bodies at rest." Birdie smiled. "Unlike yours, dear. You're putting us to shame."

"This is a great beach to run on," Izzy said.

Hannah straightened up and took a drink from a water bottle, her long, muscular body stretching in the sun. "I love running here. It's my therapy."

"It would put me *in* therapy," Cass said.

"My son's a runner, too. He coaxed me into it."

"I remember," Izzy said. "Jason and I did the Around Cape Ann race together a couple years ago."

Hannah smiled, then sobered as she spotted the paper next to Birdie. She pointed at it. "Now I understand why you looked so serious when I walked up."

"We're slowly taking in the news," Nell said.

"I was in a meeting with Mary Pisano when she got a call from her paper. Did you figure out who she was? The lady who died?"

"We realized we all knew her slightly," Izzy said. "I'd see her when I was running mostly."

Hannah said she'd seen her while running, too, although it wasn't until Mary identified her as the woman with the long white ponytail that she realized who she was.

A silence followed, along with a desire to set aside bad news.

Cass broke the silence, straightening her torso. She tucked some stray hairs beneath her baseball cap. "Hey, this is fate, or serendipity, or one of those things Birdie talks about."

Hannah's brows lifted, a guarded smile meeting Cass's words.

Nell caught on immediately. "Cass is a genius. Hannah, you know every group in town, you're a talented knitter on top of it —"

"And we need help with a knitting project," Izzy said brightly.

"Yep. And if you help us out, I can get back to work before my crazy lobster crew comes after me. It wouldn't be a pretty picture."

Hannah laughed, looking relieved that all they were asking of her were ideas.

"We just need a few minutes," Izzy said. "You already know about the HMS project."

Hannah nodded, and for the next fifteen minutes, talk of Dolores Cardozo was set aside and attention shifted to the fall knit-a-long project, with Hannah joining in and pitching dozens of ideas on how to meet the ambitious goal of filling the community clothing center with hats and socks and mittens and scarves: *HMS. No heads bare, no fingers blue* was Izzy's motto.

In short order they had listed more than a dozen groups to join in with the knitting, ranging from a group of incarcerated women that Esther Gibson, the police dispatcher, was teaching to knit, to book clubs and school groups.

For those who didn't know how to knit, Izzy was offering free classes. The town would be buried in soft luscious yarn — and hats, scarves, socks, mittens.

Hannah unfolded her body from the sand and stretched, looking down at all of them. "You four are great. A true society of knitters," she said.

"Along with running, knitting is a perfect panacea," Izzy said.

And definitely a welcome diversion from thoughts of murder.

Hannah continued her run, and Izzy left minutes later with Cass, knowing her shop manager, Mae Anderson, could handle any catastrophe, but it was bound to be a crazy day in the yarn shop. If any place in town was ripe for an analysis of everything from town politics to raising children, it was the group of amazing moms who met in Izzy's back room on Tuesday mornings. But on some days — particularly when the town had so recently been jarred by a tragedy — Mae might appreciate the owner's help in calming things down.

Birdie and Nell finished their coffee, returned the mugs to the club's patio bar, and walked slowly along the flagstone path to the club's parking lot. For a while they walked in that way friends do, silently, relishing the magic of the perfect Indian summer day. They were a duo in contrast — with Birdie's diminutive figure and her silvery bob barely reaching Nell's shoulder, and Nell's comfortably slender frame and still dark hair, highlighted with smooth strands of gray, walking tall beside her.

Above them, flocks of birds flew in erratic herringbone patterns as if wondering if heading south was really necessary.

Finally, Birdie brought them both back to real life. "I suppose it's because of all the unknowns," she said, waving to a neighbor heading down to the sailboat slips.

Nell knew she was speaking about Dolores Cardozo.

"The scenario you and Izzy mapped out has some curious elements that I'm having trouble wrapping my thoughts around."

"Which parts?"

"Fiona, for one. Her familiarity with the kids. Do you suppose Fiona is as familiar with every family at the school as she seems to be with the Stewarts? If so, I can't imagine her ever getting anything done. And from what Mary Halloran says, Fiona has her fingers in every pie — the food kitchen and clothing center, running the school — and if we can believe our dear Cass, trying to run her niece's love life. Mary Halloran tells me she even interferes in her job as parish secretary. And now Fiona is babysitting for a school parent? It seems excessive. Kind and generous, absolutely. But beyond the norm."

They had taken the path around the parking lot and headed toward Nell's car, parked adjacent to the main clubhouse entry. It was nearly lunchtime now, and the lot was filling up.

Nell rummaged around in her purse for her keys, thinking about Birdie's comment.

"Maybe it's just me," Birdie continued. "I gave up multitasking years ago. Maybe it's just the way Fiona is."

"I understand what you're saying. When we were talking last night, we took it for granted that Fiona knew the Stewarts from the school. She kept telling us what a good mother Kayla was, almost as if she'd had something to do with it. And the kids were clearly fond of Fiona; we saw that Sunday. There's a connection there, for sure."

Voices close by hushed their conversation, and they looked up toward the clubhouse doors, just as they swung open.

Father Northcutt and Chief Jerry Thompson walked out, heads bent in conversation. Elliott Danvers was a step behind them. The banker carried a leather attaché in one hand. His face was somber, matching that of the older men, as if the threesome had just come from a board meeting instead of lunch at one of the finest dining spots in Sea Harbor.

The men continued their conversation at the bottom of the steps, and the women continued toward Nell's car.

Finally, Father Northcutt looked up, rubbing his ample chin, his brow furrowed. It was when he lowered his chin slightly that his gaze fell on the two women walking to Nell's car.

Nell smiled and Birdie lifted one hand in a wave.

"Ladies," the priest called over, then began to walk their way, his arms already open in greeting. "And where will we meet next, Nellie?" he joked. "We seem to be stalking one another."

Nell laughed but the coincidence didn't escape her.

Elliott and the police chief dropped their conversation, looked up, then followed the priest across the drive, their expressions replaced with friendly greetings.

"I thought I recognized your car when I drove in," Elliott said. "It's last election's bumper sticker that did it, a clear giveaway, Nell."

Nell smiled and looked at the long black Eldorado parked next to her CRV. It hadn't been there when she and Birdie arrived earlier or she would have known Elliott Danvers was nearby. Everyone knew the elaborate Cadillac his father had given him when he took over the family bank. Nell suspected Elliott would have gladly given the car away in exchange for a small Ford if the gesture would not have insulted his father.

Elliott shook Nell's hand, then Birdie's, holding it a moment too long as he looked at her, opening his mouth as if to speak, then smiled instead.

Birdie broke the awkward moment. "I hope the food agreed with the three of you. The yacht club's chef usually sends diners out with a moonstruck look on their faces. I'm not seeing that today."

The police chief managed a chuckle. "Food wasn't a priority today. Liz Santos gave us strong black coffee, soup, and one of her meeting rooms. It's quiet here — certainly more so than a hectic police station or Elliott's bank."

"A secret meeting," Birdie said with a smile.

Jerry nodded. "Sometimes one has to get far from the madding crowd to get anything done."

"Things must be in turmoil over at the station," Nell said. "It hasn't been a good week so far."

Father Northcutt glanced over at the police chief's tired face.

"Not a good week," Jerry concurred.

Nell glanced at Birdie. There was a

strangeness about the conversation, the words stilted and the men uncomfortable standing there with them.

Elliott pulled his keys from his pocket, but his eyes kept going back to Birdie. He looked indecisive, as if he was playing out some kind of decision in his head, weighing the pros and cons.

It was Elliott who finally broke the silence. "We weren't expecting to run into you."

Nell felt an irrational need to apologize for something, although she had no idea what that would be. The yacht club was a popular place to go, and they often ran into friends there, though maybe not the police chief, their banker, and a priest, all at once.

But Elliott was focusing on Birdie. "I need to talk with you about something, Birdie. May I have my office call you to set up a meeting?"

"No, you may not," Birdie said. She frowned. "You can't say something so cryptic and then leave Nell and me standing here. We'd imagine wild tales."

Elliott tried to smile. "I don't mean to be secretive, but it's business, and we can talk better at the —"

Birdie interrupted, her small frame seeming to grow taller as she faced the banker. "Good heavens, Elliott Danvers. Nell is my dearest friend in the whole world. If her presence is why you're being evasive or subtle or whatever it is you're being, stop it right now. If, as my banker, you are trying to tell me my Sonny's fortune has somehow gone up in smoke and my house is in foreclosure, there's no one I'd rather have at my side to hear it than Nell Endicott. Besides, should I be destitute, she and Ben have a delightful guest cottage I quite fancy."

That drew smiles. Elliott shifted his briefcase and smiled at Nell in a kind of apology, then looked back to the small formidable woman in front of him.

"You're right, Birdie, of course you are. We'll still have to meet about this, but in a nutshell, Dolores Cardozo left a surprising last will and testament."

Birdie nodded. Of course she did. It's something any wise woman of a certain age would do. She looked over at Nell, who suppressed a smile, reading Birdie's thoughts: *I greatly admire these three lovely men — most of the time. But today they seem a bit daft.*

Elliott cleared his throat and tried again.

"Miss Cardozo's will has been written with careful thought and attention to detail. That includes her choice of executor. And that, Birdie, is you."

CHAPTER 9

Nell took a shortcut across the small park at the corner of Harbor Road. She had almost forgotten that she'd signed up for today's shift at the church's food pantry. She walked around to the side door of the church and noticed a large colorful sign she hadn't seen there before.

THE BOUNTIFUL CAFÉ, it read. WELCOME ALL! The sign was bordered in hand-painted flowers, birds, and bumblebees, clearly the work of spirited budding artists from the school.

She pulled open the heavy door and followed the sweet smells of cinnamon and coffee that wafted up from the kitchen below.

Once an all-purpose room, the space near the church kitchen had been completely redone and was now filled with white-clothed tables for four, creating a cozy restaurant atmosphere. On each plate was a typed menu, and each table held a slender vase holding a single flower.

Sister Fiona had insisted on the layout, as well as merging diners and volunteers into one harmonious whole with the diners taking turns waiting tables, lettering menus, doing dishes, right alongside the volunteers.

"I don't wait in line at a restaurant — except at Harry's deli— do you?" Fiona had demanded of Nell the first day she'd volunteered. And then she'd answered her own question. "No, of course you don't." Her voice was stern as if daring Nell to think any differently.

Nell wove her way around the tables to the stainless steel kitchen, now exuding delicious odors. The new layout had necessitated more volunteers — Fiona had insisted on waitresses for the tables — and it made more work for the cooks, but it was worth the effort to see the faces of the diners, folks from the hidden pockets of Sea Harbor and outlying areas. Folks who needed and deserved a good restaurant meal as well as anyone — and with their dignity intact.

Nell loved the cozy place, just as Fiona had told her she would on the day she had signed her up as a volunteer.

"Nell, over here." Laura Danvers waved at

her from behind the wide serving counter.

Nell followed the wave, greeting other volunteers as she walked into the kitchen and over to Izzy's good friend. "Corn chowder," Nell said, taking off the lid and leaning over a giant simmering pot. She breathed in the tantalizing odors — corn, turmeric and bacon, plenty of sharp cheddar cheese.

Laura handed her a spoon. "Taste it. Do we need more salt?" She added, "It's the Barefoot Contessa's recipe."

Nell took a taste. "It's delicious." She set the spoon in the deep sink and looked around the room. "Is Sister Fiona here tonight?"

"Nope. I'm in charge, for whatever that's worth. She had something else tonight."

The Stewarts, Nell supposed. Cass had said she was going to stay there another night. She leaned against the counter, watching Laura choreograph the dinner plans with a bevy of volunteers. The banker's wife was as dedicated to the project as Sister Fiona, Nell could see, watching her effortlessly pass instructions to the volunteers, check schedules, and in between tap messages into her phone. There was not a charity or benefit in town that Laura hadn't touched in one way or another. "But there's this whole other side to her," Izzy had said of her friend recently. "The simple, funny, unpretentious mom and loyal friend — and in addition to everything else, Laura is an expert knitter."

"Did you see Gabby?" Laura asked Nell, pointing to the other end of the kitchen where two young girls were slicing bread. "She and my Daisy are in charge of bread baskets and pots of Annabelle's apple butter that they talked her into donating. I'm putting them permanently on the donation committee. They're awesome."

Nell waved at Birdie's granddaughter. Gabby and Laura's oldest daughter were joined at the hip, the bespeckled, studious Daisy a perfect counterpart to her carefree Gabby. *Her* Gabby. The thought had slipped out. But she had become close to all of Birdie's close friends. Birdie's granddaughter was integral to their lives, as close and loved as any blood relative could be.

Gabby came charging around the long metal kitchen table and gave Nell a hug. "We get to waitress tonight," she said. "Who knows, maybe Daisy and I will sing. Singing waitresses, what do you think?"

Nell laughed.

"As long as you don't spill the soup," Laura called over from a giant bulletin board, where she was running a finger down the list of today's volunteers, checking off each one. "Did you see this article, Nell? We're famous." Laura pointed to a newspaper clipping that had been thumbtacked to the board.

Gabby pulled Nell over to see it. "Daisy and I are in it," she said proudly, then ran off to find her friend.

Nell scanned the article, a breezy human-interest article that detailed the Bountiful Bowl and its volunteers, and sure enough, there was a shot of Daisy and Gabby stirring a pot of soup, complete with chef's hats and a long caption about the girls' great work. Expansive. Lots and lots of adjectives.

"It must have been a slow news day." Laura laughed. "It continues on the inside."

Nell lifted the page and glanced at the next — more long sentences, more photos of the Bountiful Bowl Cafe. She let it drop back. "Who wrote it?"

"That reporter from the *Sea Harbor Gazette*. Richie somebody. The one who is probably on the outs with Mary Pisano and the *Gazette* editor for his announcement of Dolores Cardozo's death. Kind of awful, don't you think?"

"I heard about that. I suppose he meant well," Nell said.

"It was still awful. He's an opportunist. Makes nice to everyone, if you know what I mean. You wouldn't believe the time he spent here, interviewing everyone, featuring some of the volunteers, the people who eat here, exploring who they are, what they are all about. Some didn't like his questions and pushed him away, but others liked the attention. All for a little story that few people would read. Elliott said he's hanging around the bank right now doing the same thing, somehow trying to find a story."

"Ambitious," Nell said.

Laura laughed. "He's pretty chatty and has his nose in everything, schmoozing and asking a million questions. Elliott said he'd normally have given him a couple hours at most, mostly as a courtesy to the editor at the paper who's a friend of ours. But the office manager had set it up and he didn't want to embarrass anyone. Also the guy is funny and brings in donuts, so they let him hang around. He's kind of a flirt — I saw that when he was here. I think Elliott just goes up to his office and closes the door. . . ."

Laura's voice trailed off as she looked back at her list, hesitating at the last name. She called over her shoulder to her daughter. "Daisy, have you or Gabby seen Kay —"

Just then a figure raced through the restaurant area, heading their way. Laura grinned and grabbed an apron from the stack beneath the counter. She tossed it to the newcomer. "Great. Everyone's here."

She turned back to Nell. "Richie picked out favorites to focus on in the article, like Daisy and Gabby. I mean, who wouldn't? But I think he also had a crush on one of the volunteers." She nodded at the short-haired woman who was slipping a white apron over her head. "He gave her plenty of attention. In fact, it made me a little nervous."

Nell looked over, her eyes moving immediately to the woman's sweater. It was soft and slouchy, with a graceful fold in the front. Gorgeous and beautifully knit.

"If you'd give those pots a stir," Laura said, pointing Nell to the stove, where another pot of soup, this one filled with chicken, vegetables, and rice, was waiting.

Nell leaned over to adjust the flame. Out of the corner of her eye, she noticed Laura moving closer to the newly arrived volunteer with the beautiful sweater. Laura's face had a worried expression.

Nell stirred the pot, catching stray words

128

from Laura's direction. "Hurt . . . what happened . . . go . . . doctor . . ."

Diners were beginning to arrive and the kitchen came alive with bodies moving and voices colliding as fresh garden salads were tossed, pitchers filled with ice water, and small plates of olives, pickles, and raw veggies arranged on serving trays.

Nell continued to catch glimpses of Laura's worried face. She seemed oblivious to the activity around her, her attention riveted on the woman in front of her. Nell put the lid back on the pot and walked over. "Laura, is there anything I can do?"

Laura turned toward Nell, the woman in front of her looking up now, and Nell immediately understood Laura's concern. A thick gauze bandage covered the young woman's forehead, the ends frayed and yellowed where the adhesive had pulled loose. A pink stain discolored the bandage at one end.

"I'm fine, Laura," the woman said, ignoring Nell. Her voice was so quiet it was difficult to pick up the words.

"No, you're not fine," Laura said gently. "You need to see a doctor. I can take you over right now —"

Nell rested her hand lightly on Laura's arm to get her attention, knowing Laura was

129

much more necessary to the evening meal than she was. "If it would help, I could drive her to the clinic —"

"No," the woman said, more to Laura than Nell, giving Nell only a cursory glance. She turned her back to Nell, speaking softly. "It's not as bad as it looks. And I already have an appointment. It's taken care of."

Nell stepped away, reading the young woman's need for privacy.

And knowing, suddenly and surely, who the young woman was.

Although the bandaged woman didn't know it, Kayla Stewart was no stranger to Nell. Nor were her injuries.

She should have recognized her immediately — the short black hair, the slight, boyish figure. She matched perfectly the image that Cass had verbally painted for them, all the way to the ear pinna pierced with tiny rings. She looked tired, and Nell suspected she hadn't eaten in recent days. Her arms were wound around herself, the sleeves of the soft sweater curling over her fingers, as if that was all that was holding her together.

An hour later, Laura brought Kayla over to the stove, where Nell was stirring the last pot of simmering soup, adding cream and broth when the soup became too thick.

Laura introduced the two women and left Kayla there to help Nell refill bowls of soup.

For a while the two women worked quietly next to each other, passing and filling bowls, placing them on the waitresses' trays. It wasn't until the pot was nearly empty and desserts were being passed to the tables that Nell decided she needed to let Kayla know the connection between them. It felt deceptive, somehow, not saying anything. But she started by talking about the woman's sweater, the stitches even more admirable close up and the mulberry merino wool and silk yarn rich and lustrous. Nell fought to keep from touching it.

"Kayla, your sweater is absolutely beautiful. Did someone make it for you?"

Kayla looked down at the arms of the sweater, pushed up now to keep them clean, as if she'd never seen it before. Then she said matter-of-factly, "Thanks. I knit it a few years ago."

"I am very impressed. It's lovely."

When the conversation wasn't picked up by Kayla, Nell plunged in. "Kayla, I owe you an explanation."

Kayla touched the bandage lightly with her fingers, the frown beneath it tightening uncomfortably. "No you don't. I was the one who was rude. I just needed to talk to

Laura, that's all." She looked at the soup pot, not Nell, while she talked.

Kayla surely knew about the group of women who had come to her house. Fiona would have told her, knowing if she hadn't, Sarah Grace would have. But Kayla had a right to have faces to put to the visitors, especially if she had any lingering worries about it, which Izzy was sure she would have. "I don't mean that. I'm talking about last Sunday when you weren't home," Nell said.

Kayla's frown deepened. She fingered her ear, twisting the rings gently, large green eyes now focused intently on Nell. She was silent, waiting.

"My friend Cass Halloran found some school clothes that Father Northcutt thought belonged to your children. He gave us your address so we brought them by. You weren't home so we left them with the children. They're beautiful, by the way. I hope we didn't frighten them."

Kayla took a steadying breath. "So you were one of them. . . ." She spoke slowly, as if fitting a piece into a mental puzzle, matching a face to a story. Her shoulders relaxed slightly. "There were four of you. Sister Fiona told me about it. Who were the others?"

132

"Birdie Favazza," Nell began.

Kayla repeated the name, almost to herself, and said softly, "Sea Harbor's wise materfamilias."

Nell's brows lifted. "Do you know Birdie?"

"No. But a lady I know . . . used to know . . ." she paused for a moment and looked away, as if the look of sadness that shadowed her face was private. When she looked back it was gone. "She talked about the Favazzas once, Birdie and her husband. They were good people, wise and kind in the best of ways." Kayla's words were said more to herself, as if remembering counsel someone had once given her.

But Nell caught each word and tucked them away. "That's an apt description, although Birdie's husband, Sonny, died years ago."

Kayla stood silent, listening, waiting.

"We didn't intend to go inside your house," Nell went on. "Christopher was very clear about us staying on the porch. You've raised him well. It was sweet Sarah Grace and Shep who had other plans."

Kayla nodded, a slight smile lifting her mouth.

"Izzy Perry was with us, too. She owns the yarn shop over on Harbor Road. She would love to see that sweater sometime, by the way."

"I've seen her shop window," she said. "Gorgeous yarn. It makes me drool, but is out of my reach. Someday maybe I'll go inside."

"Cass Halloran was the fourth person. She was the one who found the clothes. She and her brother have a lobster company here in Sea Harbor."

"Do they keep any boats near the harbor pier?"

Nell nodded.

"Christopher loves watching the men unload their catch. He wants to be a fisherman."

"Maybe Cass could take him on one of the boats sometime."

When Kayla didn't answer, Nell figured she'd talked enough about Sunday's adventure. What Nell cared about was for Kayla to have real people connected to the women who had invaded the privacy of her home, who had talked with her children, who had walked through her house. She wanted her to be able to put kind faces on the intruders.

Kayla's narrow face had relaxed some, especially when Nell mentioned the children. She responded immediately to the mention of their names.

But mostly what Nell noticed — and what she'd think about later — was the look in Kayla Stewart's eyes. They were the color of the sea, startling in their brightness. Intelligent eyes filled with profound emotion. *A mirror to her soul.*

Later, as Nell helped Laura turn out the lights in the café, she thought about Kayla Stewart again. In spite of her injury, she had worked hard all night, laughing now and then when Gabby and Daisy broke into an impromptu dance or song routine.

"Kayla doesn't seem old enough to have two children," Nell said to Laura as they walked into the night, the sky lit by a sliver of moonlight.

"I know, right? She's twenty-nine, but she looks about nineteen. It's the hair, I think."

Nell nodded, wondering why she had cut it so dramatically. It looked like she might have cut it herself.

"Kayla shocked all of us when she cut her hair," she said. "She had hair to die for. The most gorgeous thick black waves you can imagine. Then one day she showed up looking like a tough kid, someone out of a Dickens novel. I guess she wanted a new look — sometimes we all do things like that. And, hey, hair grows back."

Nell tried to imagine Kayla with long hair. She had delicate features, but if she wanted to look tough, the choppy hairstyle had helped achieve it. Still, she had seen her earlier that evening standing alone, looking across the dining hall, her thoughts somewhere else. And Nell had glimpsed a beautiful, vulnerable woman hidden somewhere in the baggy jeans and apron.

"Do you think someone gave her a ride home tonight?" Nell had offered one, but Kayla said no, she didn't need one. And Nell hadn't pushed, slightly uncomfortable with the fact that she knew more about Kayla and her life than the young woman realized, including that her car was sitting in Pickard's Auto repair, waiting to be fixed. It felt sneaky somehow that she knew those things when she and Kayla were virtual strangers.

"I don't know. She's pretty self-reliant and doesn't accept help easily. I get the impression she's been around the block a few times."

"How long has she been volunteering here?"

"A while. Before the renovation, I think. When was that? Around Christmas, maybe. Kayla mostly does meal deliveries, taking food to people who can't make it to the cafe. The reporter seemed interested in the delivery program, too, and he glommed onto Kayla, asking her questions for his article. Following her around. He even went along with her on a couple of deliveries. Meal deliveries 'intrigued' him, he said — but we all suspected it was Kayla who intrigued him, since meal deliveries to folks who need them is nothing new at all. People do it everywhere. And that was before she cut her hair. She was a knockout and got second looks from lots of guys. Anyway, her car has been on the fritz so she's been helping inside the café lately."

"I'm surprised she has the time. I know she's a waitress at the Ocean's Edge, too. Not to mention caring for two little kids."

"Yes," Laura said. "She juggles it all. In my opinion, she should have been home tonight, lying on a sofa and taking care of whatever happened to her. Did you notice her forehead?"

Nell nodded. She had wondered the same thing, although Kayla seemed to handle it in stride.

Laura went on. "Sister Fiona is over there tonight, she said, so I guess that's okay. She did say Sister didn't want her to come tonight, but Kayla insisted. It seems important to her to keep things normal for the

137

kids. Anyway, Sister Fiona was bringing them ice cream."

Of course she was, Nell thought. They walked in companionable silence through the parking lot, stopping at Laura's car while she rummaged in her bag for her keys. "I assumed you knew Kayla, Nell. I guess because Gabby knows her."

"Gabby?"

"Gabby and Daisy. Kayla seems more comfortable around them than some of the others in the cafe. I think she likes their youth and uninhibitedness, if that's a word."

Nell chuckled. "Those two could make anyone comfortable. And I can understand it. Kayla seems so private, and Gabby and Daisy accept everyone exactly as they are, not probing, not expecting them to be someone else."

"That's it," Laura said. "You're spot on. I've known Kayla all these months yet I know little about her, and she probably knows I want to know more. I drop little questions here and there, just like you normally do when you're getting to know someone. I haven't made much progress, but the girls don't seem to need to ask anything. They tell her jokes, kid around with her. So you don't know her either?"

"No, I hadn't met her before tonight. But

I met her children the other day so I know *of* her. And I know she works hard to support them. Being a single parent has to be difficult, especially when you're relatively new in town and don't have a support system. I'm impressed that she carves out extra time to volunteer."

"Well, it isn't exactly her choice."

"What do you mean?"

"Kayla helps out because Sister Fiona thought she should."

"As a favor?"

"Not exactly a favor, I don't think," Laura said. "You know how Sister Fiona can be."

Nell wasn't sure which way to go with that. She said, "I know Fiona has a big heart. But I'm not sure that's what you're getting at."

"Yes, well, she is all that for sure," Laura said. She looked slightly embarrassed, as if she were saying something inappropriate. "She's encouraged lots of good people — you're a prime example — to volunteer for her endless projects. But she didn't really ask Kayla to volunteer. She *told* her to work here. She insisted on it. So Kayla's here once a week, without fail. And more power to her; she takes it very seriously and never misses a shift."

Nell didn't hide her surprise. "Do you

know why?"

"No. I try not to second-guess Sister Fiona. No matter how crazy some of her ideas are, she always seems to have a rationale for what she does. And for some reason — probably because Kayla isn't crazy about crowds — she wanted her to be a part of the team that delivers food to people in their homes. She even picked the person to whom she wanted Kayla to deliver."

"Dolores Cardozo," Nell said softly, the words slipping out without intent.

"Yes," Laura said. "How did you know?"

CHAPTER 10

One thing the *Sea Harbor Gazette* was known for was its effusive, elaborate obituaries of residents who had died. The smallest traces of goodness were uncovered and revealed in elegant and exaggerated prose, sending the deceased off in fine fashion.

And Dolores Francesca Maria Cardozo would be no exception, no matter that a peculiar announcement appeared about her death one day, and the manner of her death in frightening headlines the next.

"Dolores deserved to be remembered for living, not for the horrible way she died," Mary Pisano explained to anyone who asked. And on Wednesday, she practiced what she preached, and took it upon herself to honor the woman she'd been researching for the last many hours, and to send Dolores off in a fitting, if not surprising, fashion.

SEA HARBOR MOURNS BENEFICENT BENEFACTOR

Dolores Francesca Maria Cardozo lived a quiet life in a small, nondescript cottage bereft of worldly luxuries. She considered the beauty of nature, including the old north quarry at the far edge of her property, the sky, and the ocean breeze the only luxuries her soul and spirit needed to soar.

Dolores was seen daily by many, a fixture on our amazing landscape, but known by only a few. Dolores walked everywhere, every day, no matter the season or the weather. Sometimes she traveled as far adrift as Dogtown or Gloucester's Ravenswood Park, her strong, slender body and long white pony-tail recognized by all she passed, her only companion her signature hand-carved walking stick.

A generous and humble resident of our city, Dolores may be remembered best for her generosity to those in need and for her anonymous gifts, only in death becoming known to many of us. Few in Sea Harbor, whether knowingly or not, have gone untouched by Dolores's beneficence. Such humbleness of spirit is a legacy not soon to be forgotten.

Dolores was the daughter of Antonio and

Anna Cardozo. She followed in her father's footsteps, working as a brilliant accountant in a Sea Harbor factory. She maintained a residence in Sea Harbor all her life. A devoted member of Our Lady of Safe Seas Church, Dolores will be remembered and prayed for at a service to be announced soon.

"Mary has always been very good at headline alliteration," Birdie said.

She scanned the Endicotts' paper again, then dropped it on the coffee table in Nell's family room.

Birdie always read the paper before her early morning walk, but today had been an exception, a crowded day that canceled out both the early walk and the morning paper. "I don't know how Mary gets her information before other breathing souls, but she seems to be good at it. From what Ben and I learned today, most of what she said is accurate. Except for all the personal gibberish. If you ever let Mary Pisano write an obituary for me, Nell Endicott, I will haunt you the rest of your life."

"Then I'll be sure to do it so you'll be around forever." Nell smiled, but her thoughts were more on how tired Birdie looked than her threats from the grave. She seemed to disappear in the overstuffed sofa, her small head sinking back into the cushions. She opened the deck doors, ushering in a cool, late afternoon breeze. It brought some color back to Birdie's cheeks. She had read the paper early that morning and was still trying to make sense of Mary Pisano's words and innuendoes.

"So I can assume your meeting with Elliott Danvers was productive?" She looked from Birdie to Ben, who had joined them, stretching out in a well-used leather chair near the fireplace. He'd offered to give Birdie a lift to the meeting. *I'll be an extra set of ears,* he'd said.

I'd have dragged you along, had you not offered, Birdie had replied.

And if she hadn't, Nell would have urged him to go — Ben had been executor for more wills than she could count, and every now and then Birdie's hearing wasn't at its prime.

"We learned a lot," Ben said, but his tone indicated it might not have been as simple as he had promised Birdie it would be. "Dolores's will and testament isn't one of those complicated ones that create suspense in TV mysteries. It was done correctly. Uncomplicated on the surface. But Mary Pisano was on the right track: Dolores Car-

144

dozo was a millionaire."

"The food pantry millionaire," Nell said. "Such an irony."

"It's odd that so many of her meals came from there," Ben agreed. "But maybe she hated to cook and didn't like to go out at night. The Bountiful Bowl filled her needs." The thought was amusing to Ben, whose love for fine food was significant. "Think about it, she could have afforded a five-star dinner from Duckworth's Bistro every single night. And the chauffer to pick it up." He shook his head and laughed.

Birdie picked up her coffee mug. "Elliott has handled her accounts for years, and his father before him. Of course, it was all confidential so no one else knew of the wealth she was amassing, nor what she was doing with it."

"Did she inherit the money?" Nell asked.

"She was an accountant where her father had also worked. She started investing back when she was a young woman, and got a pension when she retired. She was an absolute genius with numbers, Elliott said — a human calculator — but also with an ability to assess and make enviable financial judgments. He'd have hired her in a heartbeat if he could have, he said. And she made all her own decisions. I suppose it's an understatement to say she didn't spend the money on herself."

"It's almost as if this woman is coming to life in front of us, layer by layer," Nell said. "Sometimes we think we know everything about everyone in Sea Harbor, and here's a wealthy financial genius, living in a small house on the edge of our town."

"She was definitely all those things, but like all of us, she had a few quirks," Birdie said. "Like the money stashed around the house."

"Some people find peace of mind in keeping supplies of water and dry food in a basement pantry somewhere, just in case of some catastrophe," Ben said. "Maybe Dolores found security in neat, banded stacks of fifty-dollar bills."

Nell sat down next to Birdie, still smiling at the thought of filling the beautiful pottery pieces Jane Brewster had given her with bills. "What about her family?" she asked.

"Her parents died when Dolores was in her twenties," Ben said. "It was a terrible accident after a company party, but wasn't anyone's fault. A tree fell across a road. There was a sister no one knows much about, but she died, too. Dolores's life was quiet, as we're all so aware of, and kind of a mystery. She lived in our midst, benefiting

146

our town, and we didn't know her."

"It's also a mystery why Dolores chose me as her executor. There's something back in the dark murky shadows of my head that tells me there's a connection but who knows if it will ever see the light of day? Elliott wasn't sure. He asked her once but all she did was mutter something about it being an appropriate decision, and *it wasn't any of his* — here Dolores added some colorful words — *business.* Of course Elliott, the gentleman that he is, backed off."

"That reminds me of something. I told you I met Kayla at the Bountiful Bowl?"

Birdie nodded.

"Well, I forgot to mention that she recognized your name when I told her about the four of us going to the house with the kids' clothes."

"Well, I suppose that happens. And I often eat at the Ocean's Edge, where she works."

"No, she said that someone told her about you. And about your husband, Sonny. She started to say a name, but stopped short of it. I strongly suspect it was Dolores Cardozo who told her about you."

Now she had Birdie's attention. She sat up straight. "Maybe Kayla misunderstood. Sonny has been dead for over forty years."

"I don't know, Birdie. Her hearing seems fine."

Birdie shook her head. "I can't worry about why that might have happened, not right now. What I know about Dolores Cardozo is probably more worthy of attention." Birdie pulled a file folder from her large bag and set it on the coffee table. She looked at it as if it were a living thing, about to pounce. "And this is it. Or at least what she wanted me to know, once she was no longer with us."

Ben sat quietly, rubbing his temples.

"But you said it's not complicated, isn't that right?" Nell asked Ben, who didn't look like anything about the afternoon had been uncomplicated. "It won't keep Birdie up at night?"

Nell's question hung in the air, unanswered.

Birdie looked up and checked the hand-carved grandfather clock near the fireplace. Elongated mermaids' fingers held the clock face lovingly. It was after five o'clock.

Ben nodded, reading her mind. "Would you like a glass of wine, Nellie? I'm thinking Birdie and I might like martinis. It's been a long day."

"Two olives, please," Birdie said. She leaned back again and closed her eyes, her

148

small, veined hands resting in her lap. The edges of her mouth lifted automatically into a half smile. No matter what swirled around her, the semblance of peace was always there in her expression, but today there was also concern.

Ben returned with their drinks on a wooden tray. He'd piled cheese sticks and crackers in a small bowl and added a wedge of Brie and bowl of grapes. "I've been trained well," he said with a smile at Nell's pleased look, and passed around the glasses.

Nell took a drink and was quiet for as long as she could be. She sensed Birdie and Ben's weariness, but her own need to bring clarity to the conversation was winning out. She waited until several cheese sticks had disappeared, a cracker or two smeared with Brie, and healthy-sized sips of martini taken.

Then she pushed for details. "Back to Dolores's will. The one that will not complicate Birdie's life and will not interfere with the knitting project awaiting us." She took a sip of wine and waited.

"Ah, that one," Ben said. He rubbed one finger along the edge of the martini glass, his mind humming along with the glass. "Under normal circumstances Dolores's last will and testament would be uncomplicated. She was precise and careful, listing

149

every material thing that composed her simple life. And she was on top of every dollar — every cent — even what was scattered around her house. She knew every transaction made to the nonprofits she gave money to. That, and the generous spirit with which she was 'relieving' herself of her money — that was the term she used with Elliott — was done in the most efficient ways of a well-written will, leaving the task of handling it relatively easy: beneficiaries would be notified, probate processed, and that would be that, as long as no one was contesting the will. Probably the most complicated part of the estate is the land. The house is worth nothing, but the land it sits on is more extensive than I realized and worth a big chunk of money. It's no wonder so many contractors have been interested in it. As for the rest of the estate, it's stocks and bonds and bank accounts, all listed in clear and uncontestable bequests." Ben paused to take a drink, then sat back in the chair, his hands clasped behind his head, and continued.

"But Dolores's death didn't happen under normal circumstances and that's where it all gets tricky. Not as far as Birdie is concerned. But because Dolores didn't die naturally, the will itself will be considered a part of the police investigation, and that complicates things."

"Why?" Nell asked.

Birdie leaned forward, her elbows on her knees. She looked at Nell, a small resigned smile on her face. "The police will want to look at anyone named in the will — especially if they are inheriting a sizable amount of money."

Nell hadn't considered that. Perhaps she should have. It was an uncomfortable consequence, but of course it made sense. "The beneficiaries become suspects in a murder," she said. "They have an automatic motive. Money."

"Hypothetically. At the least, they will be asked for alibis, accessibility — all those things we watch for on *Rizzoli & Isles* reruns," Birdie said. "Even though they supposedly didn't know they were in the will. Leaks happen."

They considered the irony of it all. The recipients of a woman's largesse, through no fault of their own, were now saddled with suspicion. An inheritance with a long, tangled string, and at its end might be something ugly: a motive for murder.

"Are there many beneficiaries?" Nell asked.

"There are two groups: individuals and

organizations," Ben said. "The organizations are all nonprofits and charities. And all but one are simple bequests with an exact amount stipulated. The odd one is a trust that Dolores established earlier this year. She gave it great thought and it's significant. It was clear from the way she handled her money that Dolores wasn't after praise or thank-yous for her generosity. For years the bank had been parceling out money to Sea Harbor organizations, always anonymously. That new roof the library got last year? *Dolores.* The new playroom the free health clinic needed? The expenses associated with turning the old food pantry into the Bountiful Bowl Café?"

"Dolores," Nell said quietly. "I wonder if Fiona knew that's where it came from. They were friends."

"Dolores was extremely private about her affairs. Secretive almost, and she seemed to take pleasure in that, almost like it was a game, so it might have been a surprise to Fiona. Dolores was adamant that the bank not reveal where the money came from while she was alive. She claimed she didn't want people traipsing around her property, pounding on her door and bothering her.

"Not her words, though," Birdie added. "Elliott said when she wanted to make a point, Dolores could match and surpass any fishermen talk rolling out of Jake Risso's bar on a Saturday night. She sent money out once a year and was clear about where it went, choosing the organizations, but only after she had carefully scrutinized them. And afterward she kept close tabs on how it was spent. She didn't tolerate people who were careless about other people's money."

"She checked up on the organizations?"

"She wanted to be sure the moneys were used fairly and appropriately, with the utmost integrity."

It took a while for the disparate images to settle in — the white-haired, ponytailed, taciturn woman with the walking stick accepting meals from the food pantry and this wealthy woman, seemingly wanting only to give it all away. And with the mouth of a drunken sailor, adding color to the portrait.

Ben collected glasses and was back shortly with refreshed drinks. He settled down and looked at Birdie's file of papers.

"So we know that plenty of organizations benefited — and will continue to, according to the dictates of the will. There are individuals in the will, too. People, I suppose — though no one knows for sure — who moved in and out of Dolores's life. Elliott said she didn't give reasons for her choices and refused to talk about it. His role, Dolores made clear to him, was to write things down, run the numbers, but not to have an opinion."

Birdie chuckled. "I *like* this woman, more and more. For being as reclusive as she was in life, Dolores Cardozo seems to be making up for it, reaching out to people from her grave. She sounds like a good soul. And a feisty one. I've a strong suspicion we would have been simpatico."

"It won't take the chief long to eliminate the people mentioned in the will as suspects," Nell said.

Ben took a long swallow, draining the last trace of gin. He placed the glass on the coaster. "It's the directors of the organizations that they'll talk to — reputable institutions, like the library, the community center, the free health clinic. They'll probably cross most of them off the suspect list after a two-minute conversation. Few people, as much as they might want their organization to thrive, would kill for it. Additionally, how would they know that their organization was in the will? Dolores liked to keep things private most of the time."

"Most of the time?" Nell asked.

Ben frowned and looked over at Birdie. "What did Elliott say about that? He wasn't clear, I guess. But the gist of it all is that Dolores liked anonymity."

"So why do you two look so worried then?" Nell asked. "You'll let the beneficiaries know. And the individuals. The police will do their job. And, hopefully, before the ink is dry, the real deranged person who took Dolores's life will be behind bars."

"That's the hope," Ben said. "But remember this is a murder investigation. Everyone who has or might have a link to Dolores becomes a suspect. People who wanted her land. Who might have had a grudge against her. Others we don't know about. And now those who are mentioned in her will, some who will get more attention than others. Maybe because they're guilty of something. The police will have to sort through it all."

"Were there surprises in the will?"

Birdie looked at Ben. She said, "In a way it's all a surprise. I suspect it will be for most of the people named in the will. There was one name in particular, though, that surprised the chief. It surprised us, too."

"Oh?"

"Elliott said it was the one Dolores was most adamant about getting right," Ben said. "She enjoyed giving money away, but didn't do it haphazardly. It was always done in an intelligent, thoughtful way and her will was no exception. But this last one, he said, made her positively joyful. It's a trust, different from the other simple bequests the organizations and individuals will receive that go through probate.

"She put it together for someone Elliott didn't even know. She spent days on it over the summer, he said, making sure all directions were clear, what moneys would go into it, how it would be handled, and the precautions needed to make it fail-safe."

Birdie took a last sip of her martini and set it down on the table. "Elliott didn't know her, but his wife, Laura, did. And we do," she said. "The trust is for Kayla Stewart and her children."

CHAPTER 11

Kayla Stewart sat on a chair in the cold kitchen, staring at the cracked Formica tabletop. She rubbed her fingers over the clean screen of a cell phone, shiny and bright, no game icons cluttering it.

The day wasn't really cold, despite the lower than usual temperature. It was filled with bright sunshine — a perfect late September day, just like the guy on the morning television show said it'd be. Sarah Grace had only needed her fuzzy pink sweater over her school clothes to walk to the bus stop. Christopher only his uniform — he was the tough guy. No jacket, just his white shirt and pants, looking so much like a little man.

Kayla's heart swelled at the image lingering there in the corner of her mind. Christopher and Kayla, climbing on the big yellow bus. Happy. Beautiful. Perfect.

She wanted to hang on to it, to preserve it forever. But the feeling circling inside her was blurring her mind's image, the sun's warmth mocking the icy feeling squeezing her chest.

She put the phone down and pressed her fingers against her temples. *Lapsed memory.* It'll come back. She remembered the doctor in the hospital, a young guy, younger than she was. But he was right about amnesia or whatever they were calling it. *It would come back.*

And finally, it had.

It was like that kind of clean air that a storm sometimes ushers in. It had happened suddenly, in the middle of a disjointed, unsettling dream, pulling her awake with giant creepy fingers. Something in her sleep had sucked away the fuzziness that had been filling her head. She had kept her eyes tightly closed, her head resting back into the pillows as her mind seemed to be acting on its own. And slowly, carefully, the images had begun to play across her mind. A movie, playing in slow, deliberate motion.

Making Christopher and Sarah Grace's mac and cheese dinner.

Giving strict orders to Christopher. No visitors. Lock the door.

Kisses, hugs.

More kisses, more hugs.

Promises.

I'll be back soon.

I love you.

She remembered the cold that tore at her bones as she rode along the narrow road, so vivid as she lay in bed that she pulled the bed blanket up to her chin. She remembered resting her bike against a tree, staring at the house, wondering if she should turn back, forget it all. Pack up the kids and move away. Surely there were other ways to solve her problem.

Most of all she remembered sucking in a lungful of air, clenching her fists, swallowing the second thoughts, and walking in through Dolores Cardozo's kitchen door.

She could see herself there, as if she were some ghost hovering above, watching it all. She was standing in the familiar kitchen. The kitchen was empty, one dim light left on above the sink. A pot of hot water on the stove, waiting to be made into that awful-smelling tea Dolores liked. Her eyes turned toward the stream of light pouring in from the living room, slanting across the black and white kitchen tiles.

She followed the light, and then she was there, standing over Dolores Cardozo, staring at a pool of blood, moving across the hardwood floor. Bending down. Her hands in it, her heart frozen inside her chest. Rising. Standing. Her scream catching in her throat.

Then darkness.

And Sister Fiona walking into a hospital room.

As she now sat at the kitchen table, she went over the moving images again for the umpteenth time, wondering if the video recording would change. But each time it was the same. Clear. Distinct. *Awful.*

And she didn't know what to do about it.

Kayla glanced at the clock on the stove. A doctor's appointment and picking up a new driver's license, although the old car she'd driven across the country was still sitting in Shelby Pickard's car lot, hoping for a miracle to get it running again. In a day or so, Shelby had promised.

She had lost her backpack that night, or had she even taken it? Surely she would have. Her phone was in it. A worn wallet with little in it but her driver's license and grocery store cards. A library paperback book and some school papers from the kids.

Sister Fiona had already replaced the cell phone. They'd stopped on the way home from the hospital. When Kayla had refused it, the nun had practically forced it into her hands, her voice commanding. "The kids," she had said roughly. "You need a phone for the kids. Don't be a nitwit."

But she needed far more than a phone. She needed a miracle.

How had it all turned around so quickly?

Things had been so good — she liked the town; Sister Fiona was right. The vastness of the ocean, the sound of the waves pounding the shore. Taking the kids to the beach, collecting stones and sea glass and wondering where they'd come from. Watching the smiles grow on their faces, day by day.

Even most of the people were okay. She'd learned early that not every smile meant "friendly." Some were Halloween masks. But so far, she'd met only one of those. At least one that she knew about.

There was the lady next door — what was her name? — who had brought cupcakes when they moved in, and her husband had fixed the toilet when Sarah Grace dropped a wash rag down it. The Ocean's Edge people were okay, even the owner, welcoming her. And the waitress who took her shift today so she could go to the doctor. She liked Laura, who sometimes was at the Bountiful Bowl Café — and those crazy, lively kids who volunteered over there, Gabby and Daisy. And then there were the ladies who brought the kids' clothes home. Who does that kind of thing?

161

But mostly, mostly she liked it because Sarah Grace and Christopher loved it here. They loved every single thing about Sea Harbor. Christopher still harbored a wariness of strangers, but even that was lessening. He laughed more. He loved the guys down at the lobster dock who had let him and Shep climb on their smelly boat. Most of all he loved that old priest from the church. Sometimes he'd be out on the playground with the kids, telling them jokes, kicking the ball to them with his big black shoe.

Christopher especially liked calling him "Father." The first man he'd ever known by that name.

She'd do anything in the world to protect what they'd found here in Sea Harbor — what had brought smiles to her kids' eyes and filled her house with giggles. She wouldn't let it be taken away from her, from *them,* no matter what it took.

For a brief moment, the resolve soothed her, broke her free of the icy fear that had hardened into a knot inside her.

But above all, Kayla Stewart was smart and realistic and rarely sugarcoated anything. Today she knew — now that her head was clear — she knew there was trouble ahead for her.

A sound outside drew her attention away from her thoughts. She looked through the window at a car pulling up to the curb, and her stomach knotted. And then she saw who it was and she breathed again. The car idled, the driver lightly tapping the horn. Kayla pushed back the chair and shoved the phone into the pocket of her jeans. A quick glance in the mirror brought her fingers to the bandage splayed across her forehead. She touched it lightly, resisting the temptation to pull it off and erase time along with it. She tugged on a strand of black hair like Sarah Grace did in her efforts to make her mommy's hair grow faster. What Kayla wanted was for it to disguise the wound. Neither of them had been very successful.

Kayla gave up and forked her fingers through the short cut to put some order to it, regretting the impulse she'd given into that day to cut it. Then she hurried out and locked the door behind her. A nod, a small smile, and she climbed into the front seat of Sister Fiona's small Kia.

The ride to the clinic was quiet, Kayla alone with her thoughts, undecided what she would do with the facts that were now echoing in her head. What to make of them. More importantly, who to tell about them.

"Dr. Mackenzie is a good man," Sister

Fiona said as they approached the family medical clinic.

Kayla didn't answer. She couldn't remember being seen by a doctor, except when the babies had come. All those hours bringing them into the world, and then the spectacular joy that she'd never before in her life experienced. New life. *Her* new life.

Fiona slowed down as she drove through a school zone. The clinic was just a couple blocks from our Lady of Safe Seas School and Church and Kayla strained to see signs of children as they drove by. Although the playground was quiet, her thoughts remained back on the granite building. She could almost see Christopher and Sarah Grace, sitting at small desks, their faces bright, soaking in some kind teacher's words.

Fiona glanced over at Kayla and noticed her faraway gaze. She held her silence and drove into the parking lot of the old sea captain's mansion that now housed two medical clinics, Dr. Glenn Mackenzie's family practice and Dr. Lily Virgilio's women's clinic. There were few, if any, Sea Harbor residents who hadn't at one time or another walked through the main doorway and into one of the clinics. And in either one they'd be welcomed like family.

"It's better to go there than back to the hospital," Fiona said, leading Kayla up the wide fan of steps into the gracious entry, its walls filled with paintings by the artists of the Canary Cove Art Colony. "You need that looked at, Kayla. You had a concussion. Concussions can affect moods and all sorts of things. You need to be healthy for Chris and Sarah Grace. Don't be fidgety. Nobody here bites."

Kayla followed the nun through the entryway and into the family clinic area. The waiting room was nearly full. On one side a toy alcove for kids was noisy and busy with children in for well-child checkups; intimate groupings of comfortable chairs filled the large waiting area, and a coffee and juice bar was positioned along a far wall. The sound of cartoons spilled from the children's area, and behind the reception desk, several people bustled about, tapping on computer screens and printing out files.

Kayla looked at Fiona. "Are you sure this is a doctor's office? Do they serve beer?" She sat down in one of the chairs, looking toward the coffee bar.

Fiona walked to the desk. She gave a pleasant-looking young woman Kayla's name, then returned to their seats with a clipboard and several forms for Kayla to fill out.

A short while later the side door opened and a woman holding a notebook computer looked around and called Kayla's name.

Kayla shot up from the chair.

Fiona was up, too.

Kayla turned and looked at her. She frowned. "I'm not a child," she said.

Fiona ignored her and followed her through the door and down the hall to an examining room.

Charlie Chambers rotated his shoulders. He'd been working nearly forty of the last forty-eight hours — three emergencies. Glenn Mackenzie wanted him to be an integral part of the practice — his second pair of hands, another mind to make important decisions. Charlie was flattered. And in spite of the aching muscles, he felt better than he had felt in a long time. He felt like he was home.

It hadn't been easy to explain to his aunt and uncle — and especially to Izzy — why he hadn't just stayed in Sea Harbor those months ago when he'd come to make peace with his sister. The volunteer stint at the free health clinic that winter had been satisfying and the town welcoming. He'd made some good friends. He had been content. But when his volunteer time had ended, something inside him nagged and a restlessness returned. A feeling that he didn't deserve to settle into his life — to plant roots — not yet. First he needed to sort through some things in his past, revisit people who had played prominent parts, sort through those years. Unfinished things, at least that's how they appeared in his own mind. Things that needed one more stab at resolution before he could put down roots.

His mother and father in Kansas City were part of it. He hadn't spent time with them except for brief weekends here and there. Not enough to make up for dropping out of their lives for a couple years.

There were others, too, people who had pulled him out of the darkness. Those who knew him during those years after he dropped out of college, months of a wild life that nearly destroyed him. He wanted to revisit some of those stops along that journey to offer a much belated thanks to people who had helped him along the way. The ones who had encouraged him. Like the woman out west, the one he had hung out with for a brief time. A wise and tough woman younger than he was, but far wiser. He would never forget the night she'd thrown a life raft at him. He was stoned, drunk, he couldn't remember. But he remembered how she had pulled him out of a bar, slapped him hard, then ripped into him like no one had ever done before. She told him boldly that he had two choices left: to kill himself or get his act together and begin to live. She'd help him with one; he was doing pretty well with the other on his own.

She'd saved his life. And he'd never thanked her for it.

It was partly selfish, this need to let people know that he had survived it all. That he even liked the person he'd become. Sometimes selfish things were fine. So he'd fixed up the well-traveled Bimmer and traveled from one side of the country to the other. Putting a period to some sentences, a thank-you to others.

He didn't set out knowing for sure he'd end up back on Cape Ann, but he had. The ocean's call was powerful — and he had answered.

Charlie took the file from the rack on the door, checked that the nurse had already recorded vital signs, and stepped into the examining room.

"Hi, Kayla," he said. "I'm Charlie."

Kayla nodded. She was leaning against the examining table, picking at a fingernail.

Charlie glanced at the older woman sitting on the chair in the corner. "And you are?"

"Sister Mary Fiona Halloran. And who are you?" Fiona stood up before he could answer. She walked across the room, her brown Birkenstocks squeaking on the oiled wooden floor. She stood in front of Charlie, leaning forward and squinting as she read the words on the white plastic name tag. "Charlie Chambers, RN, MN, FNP-BC." She looked up. "Good grief, what's with the alphabet soup?"

Charlie laughed. "I'm a nurse practitioner, new in this office. I don't think we've met but I'm going to make a wild and crazy guess that you're related to my good friend Cass Halloran. Everyone in Sea Harbor — at least anyone with an Irish name — seems to be. I'm Izzy Perry's brother, Charlie Chambers." He held out his big hand.

Fiona's face relaxed and she took it, shaking it warmly. "Well, sure you are. Though she's better looking. It's nice to meet you, Charlie. I heard you'd come back to town. Yes, I'm the aunt. And make no bones about it — and no matter what she's told you — I love Cass, even when we sometimes — well often, really — don't see eye to eye on things."

Charlie chuckled, knowing a little of the history between the two women. Then he turned his attention back to the slender woman with the tiny loops circling one ear. "I work with Dr. Mackenzie — he'll be in soon. But I'd like to check some things first. Would you mind sitting up on the table?"

Kayla wrapped her fingers around the edge of the table and pushed herself up, her face expressionless. She fiddled with a chain around her neck. "You don't look like a nurse," she said.

"Oh?" Charlie pulled a slender instrument from his pocket. "What do I look like?"

"A plumber or football player."

"Looks can be deceiving. I haven't played football in over ten years. Plumbing? Probably never." He fiddled with the instrument and started to lean forward, then stopped and stepped back again. He tilted his head, as if seeing something unusual on Kayla's face besides the bandage running the width of her forehead. "Hey, Kayla, we've met before, right? Somewhere. But I can't recall —"

Kayla stared at him, squinty, thinking. "No," she said finally. "I'd remember a football player acting like a nurse."

"Kayla is a waitress at the Ocean's Edge Restaurant," Sister Fiona offered from her

170

chair across the room.

"Nope, I don't think that's it," Charlie said. "I've only been in town a few days and I haven't made it over there yet. Soon, though. It's one of my favorite restaurants. A good place to have a job." His half smile was directed at Kayla.

"The answer's no, then," she said. "We haven't met." She put her palms flat on the table behind her, her elbows locked, her back rigid, and her tone telling him she wanted to get the examination over with as quickly as possible. *Cut the small talk,* her straight back said.

"I guess not, then." Charlie turned on the ophthalmoscope light, bending forward as he checked her pupils. He slipped the instrument back into his jacket pocket, made a few notes on a nearby tablet. He set it down and snapped on a pair of gloves, turning his attention back to his patient, moving her slightly to see the back of her head. There was still swelling at the point of contact, but it was receding nicely. He touched it lightly.

Kayla remained still.

Dr. Glenn had gone over the day's caseload with him before the office opened that morning, helping acclimate the new nurse practitioner to the clinic's patients. Kayla's case had risen to the top. *Concussion. Amnesia.* And the notes that had been added to her file after Glenn had talked with the police — and before they'd even met her as a patient.

The police report indicated the blow to the back of her head had caused her to fall forward. Injury number one. When she fell, she'd hit the edge of a table, and that was what caused the nasty wound on her forehead. Double whammy, the policeman had said to Glenn. But he'd refused to say more.

Carefully, Charlie began to pull the bandage loose from her forehead. He set it aside and examined the curled edges of the wound, probing them gently, checking for redness around the stitches. He felt a slight quiver beneath his fingers.

For all her bravado, tough Kayla Stewart was frightened.

Charlie moved his fingers even more gently, then stepped back. "It's healing nicely, but still has a way to go. We'll leave the stitches in for a few more days. Be sure you continue to take the antibiotics and keep it clean."

He applied a new bandage, keeping his voice matter-of-fact, his movements measured and assured. He felt instinctively that an unexpected gesture might send her flying off the table. Not that he could blame her. From what he'd been told, she'd been through a lot in a few short days. And from the looks of her, maybe before that, too.

He felt an unexpected urge to protect this woman from something. Maybe it was the fact that she looked so much younger than the age listed in her file — younger but shopworn at the same time. She sure didn't look like the mother of two kids, although he wasn't sure what that assessment had to do with anything. Nor was he an expert in the field.

Charlie knew about Dolores Cardozo's murder; everyone in town did. And he knew from Cass, Sam, and Izzy that somehow this woman and her kids had a connection to the murdered woman. He typed some notes into the tablet, then lifted his head and looked at her again. She was staring down at her hands, her fingers playing with one another. The white gauze pad was in sharp contrast to the slender face and the almost pitch-black hair, shorter than his own — though that didn't say much. His sister had told him daily since he'd been back to get rid of what she described as nearly ponytail length.

He stepped aside when the doctor walked into the room. Glenn Mackenzie greeted

Fiona warmly, then turned and introduced himself to Kayla, his pleasant manner seemingly lost on the patient sitting stoically on the examination table. Her legs just touched the floor, which is where her eyes were focused as she managed a hello.

It was when he asked about Sarah Grace and Christopher that she lifted her head, her face opening up just a bit. "I gave a talk over at the school one day," Glenn continued. "I remember your son because he was intrigued with some of the instruments I'd brought. He told me he was pretty smart and maybe he'd be a doctor someday. We settled in for what might have been a good long talk until Sister Fiona over there —" he nodded his head toward the nun as if he and Kayla were sharing a special secret from her — "pulled him away and suggested my time was up. Recess was calling, which Christopher was kind of into."

That brought a smile and a slightly more relaxed Kayla as he went over the notes that Charlie had added to the patient record. He looked up when he came to the kids' names, checked to be sure they'd stopped by the clinic for their vaccinations, and then suggested Kayla bring them in for annual checkups. He'd like to see them again. "Good kids," he said.

Charlie stood nearby, scanning Kayla's face as the doctor carefully examined her again. He was hoping to find something in her expression, although he wasn't sure what he was looking for. She had warmed up a little bit when the doctor mentioned her kids' names. Something he'd remember to do next time.

Charlie was terrible at names, but he rarely forgot a face, especially one as distinctive as Kayla Stewart's — sharp cheekbones, oval face, and a toughness that masked her emotions. Except for her eyes. Large, emerald green eyes — like the sea. Intelligent and wary. He probed his memory, scanning her face slowly. But his memory didn't clear, refusing to allow him to place this woman anywhere in his life.

Sometimes memory was like that. Evasive, playing games.

But no matter, Charlie was absolutely certain that he had seen this woman before. And he *would* remember, eventually. He, too, was good at playing games.

CHAPTER 12

"Rarely are people murdered who are one hundred percent kind and generous. I read that somewhere. Isn't there one person Dolores may have rubbed the wrong way? Someone who had a logical, if spiteful or hateful, reason for killing her?"

Cass was on her bandwagon, determined to come up with a logical reason for Dolores's murder. And to find the person who harbored that reason. But her ardor didn't fool any of them. She wanted to put it all to rest so a young mother of two sweet kids could go back to a normal life, the worry-free life that kids deserved.

Cass had gone soft on them.

Izzy watched her friend with interest. She was concentrating so hard on her conviction that she hadn't even stuck her finger in Nell's Thursday night casserole. Cass would know exactly what was in the casserole, of course: macaroni and chunks of fresh lobster from Captain Joey's tank — her favorite. Tonight the seafood and pasta were swimming in Nell's thick wine and cream sauce, with melted Gruyere crusting the browned surface.

The tantalizing odors were floating around Cass, making it hard for her to think. She picked up Purl, the store cat, and rubbed her silky belly.

"You're probably right, Cass," Birdie said. "I'm sure there are plenty of things about Dolores that the police simply haven't uncovered yet. But they will." It was Birdie's "glass is half full" response. But she was also practical, and it showed in the extras lines on her forehead as she set out plates and wineglasses on the old library table in the back room of the yarn shop. Her own thoughts matched Cass's closely. Somehow, in the space of a few days, they'd all become attached to a family they didn't know. And that family's ties to Dolores Cardozo — however fragile they might be — were troublesome.

Nell applied her own guarded optimism. "As frightening as a murder is in a small town, the fact that Dolores lived on the edge of Sea Harbor has somehow made people less fearful. Most people didn't know her, didn't belong to clubs with her, and that creates a separation. When commonality is lacking, it takes some of the intimacy out of it. Therefore, the danger is remote, not close to home. And the murderer, too." She carried a basket of warm rolls to the corner sitting area.

Izzy scoffed, "There's a horrendous fallacy somewhere in that argument, Aunt Nell."

"Of course there is. But if reasoning like that keeps people from drawing their curtains and double bolting their doors, it will do for now." She carried her plate across the room and sat in an old leather chair near Birdie.

"Missing premise or not," Birdie said, "it may be partially true. The working thesis is that this wasn't a random killing. Whoever killed Dolores meant to kill her, not anyone else."

"Which brings me back to my original point," Cass said. She had put Purl down and piled her plate so high with food that she was nearly hidden behind the golden chunks of mac and cheese. "What in Dolores's life could have provoked someone to kill her? We know now she was generous and all that — but what else did she do? What did she have in her life? Who was Dolores Cardozo?"

They were silent for a moment, thinking of the ordinary questions, but ones that took on ominous tones when the person in question had been murdered.

Izzy crouched down in front of the corner fireplace and poked at a small fire she had laid. "I know we don't need this fire tonight — it's for atmosphere. Knitting a zillion pair of mittens and hats for the clothing center needs at least the crackle and smell of a fire. Besides, talk about Dolores Cardozo's murder is chilling. It gets right into my bones, even with the positive spin you two manage to put on its quick resolution."

"You're right, Izzy," Birdie said. "The fire is lovely — and murder is most definitely chilling. It was a good idea."

Cass was quiet, her half-empty plate the reason why. She lifted her head and looked over at Birdie. "So what's going on with Dolores's estate? When does the will get read?"

Hearing that Kayla was mentioned in the will had upset Cass, even though Birdie had refrained from talking about it in detail. Cass remembered too clearly — they all did — how she had been in a similar position, having been named in an old fisherman's will a few years before. When it was determined the man had been murdered, Cass's own life had been turned on its head and scrutinized. Painfully. And, unlike Kayla, she had had an army of friends and family to support her.

"It's only in the movies that those shocking will-reading gatherings take place. Elliott, the lawyer, and I can decide how to distribute them — in person or by mail. But the police have suggested we bring folks together to distribute the copies. So we're going to do that. I suspect Jerry wants to see if he notices any strange behavior. For our part, Elliott and I would like to offer our help if people have questions. Since there are no living relatives and Dolores lived a rather solitary life, it will mostly be people with little connection to her — directors of the organizations included in her will. And then the people she singled out as beneficiaries. Most of whom will be very surprised, I suspect."

"There's something sad about having no relatives to mourn your death," Izzy said. She refreshed wineglasses and passed around the basket of rolls.

"I suppose it's sad," Birdie said. "Although I'm discovering that although Dolores could be blunt, she was definitely kind. People who felt that kindness while she was still alive are beginning to come out of the woodwork. Apparently her house was a favorite place to sell Girl Scout cookies or those huge candy bars to benefit some school drive. She bought dozens. No child was ever turned away."

"That jives with my encounters with her. She wasn't effusive, but friendly enough. And she had a sense of humor," Izzy said.

"Have you notified the beneficiaries yet about the meeting?" Cass asked.

"Elliott's office is contacting them," Birdie said.

Cass emptied her wineglass. "What about Kayla?"

"I will call her myself and let her know about it. She has so much going on, it seemed like it might be better that way. But I couldn't reach her today. Tomorrow maybe."

"You won't be a complete stranger to her," Nell said. She put her plate down and told them about meeting Kayla at the Bountiful Bowl Cafe. "Even without Laura Danvers's introduction, I would have recognized her. Your description was spot on, Cass."

"She volunteers over there?" Cass asked. "How does she manage that?"

"That was my question," Nell said. She held back the fact that Kayla wasn't a regular volunteer. The fact still bothered

181

her, and somehow repeating it without understanding it reduced it to rumor status. "I told her that I was one of the four women who invaded her home the other day. Hopefully, it dispelled any fears she had of strangers coming in when she wasn't there."

"That's good," Izzy said. "I'm glad you did that. The thought of four strangers coming into my house when I wasn't home is the stuff of nightmares."

"She was able to place each of you — Izzy, she knew about your yarn shop. She's an amazing knitter, by the way. She was wearing an old sweater she'd made — it was intricate and gorgeous. And she knew about Birdie, too."

Izzy pushed her empty plate aside and sat back. "And you'll meet her soon, Birdie. So I'm odd man out. Even my brother has met her."

"Charlie? How did that happen?" Cass asked. She reached down and pulled a ball of yarn and needles from her backpack.

"She had her stitches checked at the clinic. Glenn Mackenzie is throwing Charlie into the practice headfirst and he's loving it. He was interested in putting a face on what he'd heard about Kayla. He thought she was 'intriguing.' His word."

Intriguing. Yes, she was that. And the large

bandage across her forehead, frayed at the edges, added a Charles Dickens element to the young mother of two. "I'm glad she had that wound checked. She was looking a little wobbly at the food pantry," Nell said.

"How'd she get there?" Cass asked.

Birdie answered without really knowing. "Maybe her guardian angel? Your Aunt Fiona."

Footsteps and a loud voice followed Birdie's statement. They all turned and looked toward the archway that separated the main room of the yarn shop from the knitting room.

"Fiona what?" The words reached them before Sister Fiona herself did. She came through the opening and stopped on the top step, her formidable shape silhouetted against the shop light behind her. She looked at them all for a moment, then proceeded down the three steps in an urgent way, explaining as she moved that Mae, the store manager, was just leaving and had let her in. "No need to call the police."

"She's not supposed to let suspicious-looking strangers in, right, Iz?" Cass said, but she got up and pulled a chair over for her aunt.

"Strangers or strange looking?" Sister Fiona said, managing a half smile. But it didn't hide the worry pinching her face. She looked at their empty plates, then looked over toward the odors coming from the hot plate on the long table.

Nell got up and patted the nun's shoulder on her way to the food. "I insist you have some of this so it won't go to waste, Fiona. We're all stuffed." She threw Cass a glance to silence her from claiming the leftovers were hers to take home. In seconds she set a full plate down in front of Fiona.

The nun looked up gratefully. "You're an angel, Nell Endicott. I've completely forgotten to eat today." She looked around at the others and offered a slightly embarrassed smile. "I know this is your knitting night. And I'm sorry to interrupt it. Well, no, I'm not sorry. I needed wise, smart women to talk to tonight. So that's why I came."

Birdie poured a cup of coffee and set it next to Fiona's plate. "I don't know about wise and smart, but we're most definitely good listeners."

"I need to talk to someone about Dolores Cardozo's death, God rest her soul." She made a hasty sign of the cross over her chest that could easily have been confused with slapping away a fly. Purl thought the movement was meant for her and jumped up on the nun's lap, rubbing her head against

Fiona's ample bosom.

"Is there any news?" Cass asked.

"No arrests that I know of, if that's what you're wondering." She took a drink of the hot coffee as if to steady herself, then continued. "I'm concerned about the direction the investigation will take. Sometimes police are restrained by . . ." She paused, groping for a word.

The knitters knew exactly what she was saying. The police are sometimes restrained by *facts*. And it was true. Personality, emotions, being a mother or a father or even a nun — those things couldn't be allowed to influence the facts in a murder investigation. And yet they did. They were important. At least to the women sitting in the room, yarn and knitting needles in bags nearby.

"Surely the police will check out the development and construction firms that were haranguing poor Dolores to death, trying to wrest that property away from her," Fiona said. "It was pure harassment."

Fiona paused, aware of her awkward choice of words.

Nell said, "The police are aware of it. Ben mentioned the matter had been coming up in city planning meetings. Lots of heated discussions. I didn't realize it bordered on harassment, though." Nor did she believe it

— the Delaney and the Santos families were the two biggest developers in the area and she couldn't imagine either family resorting to murder to get a piece of land. Although, as Ben reminded her, everyone has to be a suspect at this stage.

Fiona swallowed a forkful of the casserole and acknowledged Nell's comment with a nod. But it wasn't developers who brought her to Izzy's back room.

"It's Kayla Stewart I'm concerned about."

Of course it was. They all knew that. The young mother was of greater concern than large, rich companies whose goal was to become larger and richer. They felt an intimate, albeit not entirely rational, connection to Kayla, too. And all because of a few pieces of forgotten clothing in a Laundromat dryer — and two sweet children with a friendly dog.

Something had been bothering Nell since meeting Kayla in the food pantry. "Fiona, how well did Kayla know Dolores Cardozo? Laura Danvers had the impression you wanted them to get to know one another, is that right?"

Fiona continued to eat, chewing and swallowing, her expression thoughtful. Finally, she looked up. "Dolores and I became friends. I'm not sure why or how but we got to know one another shortly after I moved back to town. She was a good woman who had experienced difficult times in her life. I thought it would be good for Kayla to meet her — I knew she would like Kayla. And although Kayla isn't an easy person to get to know, she let Dolores into her life. They enjoyed talking to one another — I don't know about what, but I think Dolores was kind of a mentor to her."

It was clear that was the end of the story for Fiona, although they all knew it wasn't really the end.

"Of course, now I worry about my own judgment, getting Kayla mixed up in a murder," Fiona said. "But who could have known that this was going to happen?"

"Finding Kayla's bike near Dolores's house is a worry, sure," Izzy said. "But maybe everything else can be explained away easily, even the bike, once she regains her memory."

Fiona didn't answer, and it was Birdie who filled in the silence. "There has to be a logical reason for the bike, for Kayla's injuries. It will be cleared up."

And hopefully without Kayla being accused of murder was in all their minds.

They waited, looking at the nun for affirmation that those were her thoughts, too.

187

But what they saw there were deeper lines, more worry, settling in on Fiona's face.

"It's back," she said quietly.

"What is?" Cass asked.

"Kayla's memory is back. And as much as I want what Birdie says to be true, it isn't necessarily going to be much better for Kayla now. It could be a whole lot worse."

At first her words seemed to suck all the air out of the room.

Finally, Birdie asked, "Kayla's memory about her injury, her disappearance — all that is back? She told you that?"

Fiona nodded. "She didn't tell me at first, not a word about it. I drove her to the clinic for an appointment and she was quieter than usual, didn't even talk about the kids. In fact, she didn't say much of anything. She was all curled up inside her own head. But I knew something was wrong, and later, after we left the office, I forced the issue. Finally, begrudgingly, she admitted that she was remembering things from that night, like riding her bike to Dolores's house."

"So it was her bike. She put it there —" Cass said, forced to give up her own explanation.

Fiona went on. "Things were still a little fuzzy, she said — like a dream that sometimes isn't in the right order — but the gist of that night is there. She knew where she was going, and she knew she got there. But then she stopped, and told me she didn't want to talk about it anymore."

Izzy had brought out more coffee mugs. She warmed up Fiona's and passed her the cream. Fiona cradled the mug in her hands. "So I said to her, 'What do you mean, you don't want to talk about it?' I tried to be calm, but sometimes that's difficult for me." She threw Cass a silencing glance followed by a half smile. "Finally, she added a few details. Basically that she went inside the Cardozo home and found Dolores on the floor in the living room."

Fiona's eyes focused on the table, the yarn, and then settled again on the dark coffee in her mug. *Knit Happens* was screened across the surface beneath a pile of yarn.

No one spoke, letting Fiona's words take hold. Izzy picked up the plates and put them on a side table. She replaced them with a wicker basket piled high with soft wool yarn. Birdie and Nell pulled bamboo needles and half-finished socks and scarves from their bags. It was the best remedy they knew for untangling thoughts and making order out of things. For arranging a barrage of questions that rose to the surface, the inconsequential ones sinking back down, the imminent ones lining up, all tangled with the image of a young mother face-to-face with a dead — or dying — woman.

Finally, Nell said, "It must have been a nightmare for her."

"It was horrible. She looked like she was going to be sick, remembering it all. She didn't want to tell me more, as if seeing Dolores that way had sucked her mind dry of everything. The only detail she would add — and that was because I pushed her — was that she heard a noise, stood up, thinking help was on its way, and then everything went black. And that was it."

"That was it?" Cass said. She began another row on her thick gray mittens.

"That was it."

"Geesh, she walked in on a robbery in progress, someone whacked her unconscious. She has a lump, a cut. She sure didn't do that to herself. How do the police explain *that*?"

Fiona sat still as the images played out around the table and Cass's words took hold, wanting to protect this woman from the scrutiny that lay ahead. Finally, she sat back in the chair. "When I called the hospital looking for her that night and finally found her, they told me to bring some clothes with me. They didn't say why, but when I got there, I knew why. Her jeans and jacket had blood all over them. And not all of it was hers."

"Dolores's," Nell said softly.

"And the police now have those clothes."

"Do the police know that her memory's back?"

"No. Kayla didn't think it was any of their business. Okay, it's a foolish statement — I know that and you know that. But she insisted that her trip out to Dolores's house had nothing to do with murder, and that nothing she could say would help the police find who did it. Therefore, anything else was of no consequence to anyone but her. It was personal and private, she said."

"That's naïve," Izzy said. "It will end up hurting her if she waits —"

"Yet the poor woman must be petrified," Birdie said. Her fingers worked as effortlessly and fluidly as a musician's, the yarn in her lap rising up to the needles and transformed magically into purl, knit, and slipped stiches, row after row, sliding from one needle to the next.

Fiona watched Birdie's nimble fingers, the small bulbs of arthritis ignored as they moved the needles in a mesmerizing rhythm. Finally, she looked up and nodded. "Sure it will hurt her. But I've become a nag, I think. Sometimes critical without intending to be. Maybe someone else will have a more calming influence right now than I have, and help her see the damage she could be doing to herself and those kids."

Fiona left unsaid her message for sitting there in the middle of a Thursday night knitting session, but they could read it in her face. For all her independence and stubbornness, Fiona couldn't handle this situation alone. She cared deeply about this family. And she needed help.

"The Stewart family means a lot to you, Fiona, I can see that. And you mean a lot to us. You know we'll do what we can to help," Nell said.

But all of the women sitting in front of the cozy fire knew that helping Kayla Stewart was going to require more than listening to someone who cared about her.

Fiona seemed to have gotten her second wind and sat up straighter in the chair. "I do want you to know this. It's the absolute truth or I wouldn't be asking you to get involved in this mess. Kayla Stewart is capable of many things, but murder is not one of them." She had switched to her Sister Fiona voice, the one that no grade school student would ever try to counter. "She absolutely, positively did not kill Dolores Cardozo."

"Fiona, do you know Kayla that well?" Izzy's voice lacked judgment, a simple question that any responsible lawyer would ask. "I mean well enough to be sure of her and what she could or could not do? It was clear on Sunday that those kids — even Shep the dog — think you're pretty great. So there's definitely a connection here. How do you know that Kayla is innocent? How do you know her — and her family — that well?"

Izzy asked the question well — and bluntly. They listened carefully, but Fiona's explanation was vague enough to be irrelevant.

"You're thinking that kids aren't supposed to like scary principals, I get that." Fiona shrugged. "Those two kids are different. Kayla and the kids didn't know a soul when they moved to Sea Harbor last year. The kids were new to the school. That's tough, any way you look at it. So I tried to make them feel at home, just like we do with new families. Like anyone would do. Father Northcutt did, too."

Izzy warmed up Fiona's coffee. She wasn't lying to them but she had skirted what they were really asking. She was holding something back that might help them get to know

193

Kayla Stewart. But for some reason she wasn't going to let them in.

Birdie had been quiet, her expression thoughtful. After Fiona was finished, she rested her knitting in her lap and pushed her glasses to the top of her head and returned to the pressing issue at hand. She chose her words carefully, posing the question that was missing from Kayla's story but loomed heavy in the room. Not a question about what happened next, nor about where the bike was parked or why the door wasn't locked, but something, perhaps, more critical to Kayla's story.

"Here's the great unknown. Why did Kayla leave her children home alone and go out to Dolores Cardozo's house that day? Why was she there? Was she angry with her? Did she need to settle a score? What was so important that it took her away from her children?"

Fiona's shoulders drooped, a slight sign of defeat. Then she shook her head and said simply, "I don't know why she went. She liked Dolores, just like I told her she would. They were good for each other."

"You didn't ask her why she went?" Cass asked, seeming to have stopped listening after the first sentence. Her words came out too quickly.

"Of course I asked her, Cass." There was a weary edge to Fiona's voice, but she softened it when she spoke again. "I asked and asked and asked, and I told her bluntly that I wasn't the only one who would want to know. A woman was murdered, for heaven's sake. But it was as if she had gone stone deaf. Nothing I said after that seemed to register at all. She refused to talk to me the rest of the ride home. When we pulled into her neighborhood, the kids were just getting off the bus.

" 'They had a half day today,' she murmured to the windshield, as if that was the explanation I was waiting for. Then, before I had brought the car to a complete stop, she opened the door and jumped out without a good-bye. I idled there, watching while she ran over, threw her arms around those two little angels, hugged them close as if a slight sea breeze would take them away from her, and she walked them on home."

Fiona shook her head, took a breath, and then went on, finishing what she had to say. " *Tomorrow,*' I called after her as loud as I could. But who knows if she heard me?"

For a moment, no one spoke. Then Birdie asked quietly, "And what are you thinking will happen tomorrow?"

Fiona focused on the brilliant array of

merino and alpaca yarn piled high in the middle of the table — soon to be knit into soft, comforting mittens, socks, hats, and scarves. Something to protect against the cold.

Finally, she spoke, a heaviness carrying her words.

"Who knows what I meant. That Kayla will answer my question tomorrow? That the police will come knocking on her door tomorrow? That somehow, whoever did this sinful deed will show up tomorrow at the police station, confess his crime, and we will all go back to our ordinary lives?"

She looked up, her eyes sad. "Who knows what will happen tomorrow?"

CHAPTER 13

Fiona left a cold empty feeling in her wake. A dozen questions spun around aimlessly, without anyone to answer them. And a sadness that none of the knitters were quite sure how to deal with — or even to figure out the source — floated softly on the air.

A young mom with two small kids was a suspect in a murder case. Someone they thought was innocent, although they barely knew her. And the only reason for their belief was in their hearts.

They sat in silence for a while, needles clicking, and the balls of yarn moving slowly as one row was finished and the next begun. All around the room, thoughts rose into the fire-warmed air, collided with one another, and fell to the ground, spreading out like a puddle in the shape of Kayla Stewart kneeling over the body of Dolores Cardozo. In a color as vivid as the crimson merino yarn hanging from Birdie's needles.

A jarring ruckus at the front door interrupted their thoughts and caused Izzy's knitting to fall, the beginning of a gusset in her Latvian mitten slipping from the needles before the soft wool hit the floor.

She was up and across the room in an instant, her heart pounding but her voice calm as she called over her shoulder, "Fiona must have forgotten something. No worries."

But when she unlocked the double bolts on the shop door and pulled it open, it wasn't a nun who lunged at her, nor an intruder or a stranger or even her husband, Sam, who sometimes had a theatrical way of greeting his wife.

It was a dog. Big, hairy, and . . . familiar.

As was the person behind the dog, holding its leash.

"Charlie, what are you . . . ?" Izzy stepped back and stared at her brother. Then in the next second, she yelped as the dog jumped up, his paws on her chest as it licked a drip of forgotten cheese sauce off her T-shirt.

"Watch your manners, dog," Charlie commanded with a lopsided grin. He tugged lightly on the leash.

Izzy stepped back, sliding the dog's paws to the floor and looking at him carefully. She frowned, then leaned over, looking directly into soft brown eyes. "I think we've met," she said. "Are you Shep?"

A tail thumped heavily on the hardwood floor.

Nell, Birdie, and Cass had joined the commotion, grateful for the interruption and a scene that was far more enjoyable than the thoughts and emotions they had left behind in the back room of the yarn shop.

"I think you're right, Iz," Cass said. She walked up beside the dog for a closer look, checking for a brown freckle near his nose that she had noticed the first time they'd met. She patted his head, whispered his name, and the tail now swept the hardwood floor with vigor and confirmation.

"What are you doing with this dog, Charlie?" Cass asked. Her fingers stayed entwined with dog fur.

"I didn't steal him, if that's what you're asking." Charlie looked down at the dog. "You and I are buds, right dog?"

"He has a name. It's Shep."

"Aha, Sam was right." Charlie scratched Shep's head.

"My Sam?" Izzy asked.

"Yep. Sam said if anyone knew who this dog was, one of you guys would. And it looks like he batted a thousand. You all seem to know him. So I'm presuming, as Sam also said, that you'd know his owner."

Izzy's voice was suddenly frantic. "Sam. Where is Sam? He should be with Abby."

"Don't get your bowels in an uproar, Iz. He's with Abby. I was, too. The three of us — along with Abby's happy dog, Red — I swear that old dog smiles. We went for pizza, then ice cream at Scoopers, and then we walked over to our Lady of Safe Seas school playground to swing a while. We set Red loose to lumber around while Abby played with Sam and me. She's crazy about me, you know." He grinned at his sister.

By now Shep had checked everyone out and was comfortably settled at Charlie's feet, his head moving back and forth along with the conversation.

"The dog, Charlie," Izzy said, pointing to Shep. "How did you get this dog?"

"It was Red who found him. Red may be the oldest golden in Sea Harbor but he was trying to run around the playground like a pup, spotted Shep here, and brought him over to us at the jungle gym. We couldn't find any tags, so here we are, seeking identification from the most amazing ladies in my life who know everything."

Nell chuckled. "Charlie, we're so glad you're back home."

Charlie got serious for a moment and gave

Nell a hug, his voice soft. "Me, too, Aunt Nell."

Nell hugged him back. "And now you've found a wonderful dog who needs to get back to his owner so two little kids will sleep tonight." Nell rubbed the top of Shep's head.

"Tell me who and where. Sam went on home with Abby but I will be happy to be the super-dog hero."

"He belongs to the Stewarts," Nell said.

"Stewarts?" Charlie said. "Who are they?"

"You know who," Izzy said. "Kayla. Fiona said she brought Kayla into the clinic. She's the woman we talked about the other night. . . ."

"You know," Cass nudged.

"Kayla," Charlie said, registering surprise and recognition at once. "Sure, Kayla Stewart. I didn't put the name with the face. This is her dog?"

"Hers and her kids', Christopher and Sarah Grace," Cass said.

Nell had disappeared down the back room steps and was back in a short minute, a wrinkled church bulletin in her hand. "I happen to have a Father Larry map right here. It's an original, so don't lose it."

Cass glanced at the paper, then looked at Charlie. "Hey, no problem, Charlie. I know where they live. I'll return Shep on my way home."

But Charlie had snatched the directions from Nell and was already heading for the door. "Nah, you go home to Danny, Cass. He gets cold without you. I can do this."

"Always wanting to be the hero," Izzy called after him.

"Always," Charlie said. He grinned at his sister, then disappeared into the night with a happy dog at his side.

CHAPTER 14

It was Ben Endicott who stepped in and insisted Kayla Stewart go to the police.

And it was his nephew Charlie Chambers who had urged him to get involved, and to give Kayla the sound advice she sorely needed. Few people ever felt threatened by his uncle Ben, and fewer still failed to be helped by Ben's thoughtful and wise help.

The situation evolved because of the dog, Charlie explained to his uncle and aunt the next morning. Shep, the Stewarts' dog.

He had returned the runaway to his home the night before, just as he'd promised Izzy and the others that he would do. He'd left the yarn shop and driven down Elm Street.

It's the house at the end of the street, Cass had said. *The one with the bright green door.* He spotted it easily. A dim light in the porch ceiling showed off the door and two rigid shadows standing in front of it. Charlie slowed, then started to pull up to the darkened curb, his eyes on the figures at the top of the steps. Just then one of the shadows turned abruptly and headed toward the steps, taking them two at a time, then ran through the shadows to a square car parked beneath a burned-out streetlight.

Charlie looked back at the figure at the top of steps. Kayla had moved to the railing, one hand gripping it, the thick white bandage across her forehead catching the porch light and turning it into a garish glow. In the background the grind of an engine and screech of wheels blurred the low growl beside him. Shep sat rigid, his eyes on the street.

Charlie sat there for a minute, the car still running.

Kayla seemed not to notice he was there. Her body was stiff, and her eyes were focused on the exhaust of the disappearing car.

Charlie looked over his shoulder as the tail end of an old Jeep disappeared around the corner. He looked after it for a minute, remembering doing corners like that when he was sixteen and inherited his older brother's car. About the same vintage. He turned off his engine and leaned through the open window, one elbow on the door frame, waiting for her to notice him so he wouldn't frighten her. She was in some sort of a trance.

The windows of the house behind her were open, and even from the curb, Charlie could hear the pitiful sounds of unhappy children coming through the screens. *Children calling for their mom, missing their dog.*

When minutes went by and Kayla made no move, Charlie opened the car door, swung his legs out, but before his feet touched the street, Shep took matters into his own paws. He pushed his furry body between Charlie and the steering wheel and raced across the yard and up the steps, throwing himself against the legs of a startled woman. In that instant, Kayla came to life. She crouched low to the floor, crying out the dog's name, her fingers and head buried in his fur.

Charlie closed the car door and walked slowly up the steps, not wanting to interrupt. But he went unnoticed as a small boy and girl pushed open the screen door and flew to the dog, their pajamas flapping and their small arms wrapping around the dog so tightly Charlie wondered if poor Shep could breathe. But the dog was happy enough, licking the kids and wagging his tail, and, as Charlie would later swear, *smil-*

ing at the family he'd briefly lost.

It was a scene, Charlie said, that almost made him a sentimental fool.

Finally, Kayla noticed Charlie standing there, his hands shoved in his jeans pockets. She immediately wiped the tears away with the sleeve of her shirt, but her eyes remained wary — and worried, Charlie thought later. In fact, her whole demeanor seemed a bit off kilter and he wondered briefly if the tears, too, might have been caused by more than a lost dog. A lover's spat?

"Who are you and how did you get my dog?" she asked, standing up. She leaned down once more and slipped off the choker collar — the only thing Charlie could find to bring the dog home safely.

Charlie wasn't sure if she was blaming him or thanking him, or neither.

He quickly ruled out thanking.

"We don't use this kind of collar with Shep," she said. "How would you like to wear one?" She handed the leash back to Charlie, lightly pressing a metal prong into his hand.

Charlie shrugged. "He's a great dog," he said.

"Shep sometimes pulls out of his collar," she said, as if an explanation was needed. She pointed to a leash with a collar attached that hung over the back of the porch chair. She looked down at the kids, still tightly attached to their dog. "We went for a walk earlier. And then the squirrel came out of nowhere."

"Squirrels do that," Charlie said. She hadn't recognized him from the clinic and that was fine with him. There was probably some clinic rule against showing up at a patient's home late at night.

"So, anyway," he said. He moved backward, stepping into the glare of the porch light. "He seems happy to be home. He's all yours."

Kayla looked at him more closely as the light defined his features, the strong nose and square jaw, slightly shaggy hair. She squinted. Then she stood back and said, "Oh. It's you."

He nodded. "I guess I could say the same."

"So I guess you fix kids' broken hearts as well as adult foreheads."

"I try." Charlie offered a half smile.

Finally, after a pause, Kayla offered a small one in return.

The awkwardness grew, and Charlie turned to go, his keys in one hand and the unacceptable leash he'd borrowed dangling from the other.

"Would you like a beer?"

Charlie stopped.

"Yes."

And he stayed.

"Sometimes it's easier talking to a stranger," Ben said, after Charlie had gone over the evening's events with his aunt and uncle.

He explained that he and Kayla had sat on the porch for hours, long after the kids and Shep had been tucked into bed.

"Talking to a doctor or nurse might be a little like talking to a priest or minister," Nell said. "Safe."

"That could be. The stranger thing works, too," Charlie said, slightly uncomfortable being put in the same camp as a priest. "Stranger," or "almost stranger" were better fits, even though he still had the sensation he'd seen the woman before. But the memory was not any clearer than when he saw her in the clinic. With a haircut like hers, he figured he couldn't forget so easily, but he had.

"How did the conversation go?" Nell asked.

"Awkward at first. I wasn't sure why I was there — except to return the dog — so I didn't say much. She talked about the dog at first. Then she turned the light out so it wouldn't shine in the kids' bedroom and the talk picked up. I think it was kind of like I wasn't there and she felt safe. She talked about her memory returning in the middle of the night, and then carefully, she repeated her actions that Saturday night, several times, step by step, almost as if she was trying to understand it herself.

"When she was finished, I told her I knew someone who could help with all this. I told her about you, Uncle Ben — that you would know the right thing to do, the right people and knew your way around complicated situations better than anyone I knew. Although I don't know the whole story, I know this is a mess for Kayla and I figured you'd be able to figure it out."

He looked over at Nell. "She mentioned meeting you, Aunt Nell. The food pantry or somewhere? Said you were nice. So that's when I asked her if I could talk with both of you today."

"And she didn't object?" Ben asked. They sat in the morning sun on the Endicott deck, the smells of fall and freshly brewed coffee mingling together, a brisk breeze sending orange- and crimson-colored leaves fluttering to the ground.

"She was okay with it."

The story Kayla told Charlie had matched Fiona's, although while Fiona had an outline, Charlie had the full report. Kayla had been less reticent with him, personal details filling in the basic facts: her hesitation as she stood near the tree, the uncertainty of going in; the horror of finding Dolores on the floor; falling down beside her, pressing her ear to the dead woman's lips, her fingers to her neck. Then hearing a sound, someone coming to help, she thought. She grabbed the back of a chair and pulled herself to her feet; next, a sweeping shadow emerged from nowhere, just a single second before the room went black.

"I think talking it through was a relief for her," Charlie said. "Like you said, Uncle Ben, I was practically a stranger. And I'd brought the dog back. Thanks don't come easily to this woman. She was about to explode, and losing her kids' dog may have been the thing that tipped the scales and allowed her to open up and talk about what she was holding inside."

"There's one huge piece that's missing from what she told you — and what she told Fiona, too. It leaves such an obvious hole," Nell said.

Charlie took a deep breath. "Yep, there sure is. I think it was the only question I asked all night. What was she doing out there? Why'd she go to the Cardozo place in the first place? She rode all the way out there on a bike on a nasty night — why?"

Ben and Nell waited.

He shook his head. "That's when she closed down. She said that it was none of anyone's damn business, that it was personal and it had absolutely nothing to do with the murder and I was a pretty nervy guy even to be asking it."

Ben looked off toward the sea, just visible above the tops of the trees. Then he took a deep breath, his expression grim, and said, "Charlie, Kayla is going to be pulled in for questioning soon. I think the only reason she hasn't been questioned already is because Jerry checked into her injuries and was hoping her memory would come back soon. Talking to her before that would have been unproductive, and, according to your boss, Glenn Mackenzie, pushing her could do more damage than good. Frightening people with amnesia — especially by trying to force them to relive the trauma they can't remember — can prolong it. When they confirmed that the bike they found was definitely Kayla's, Tommy Porter had gone by the Ocean's Edge and asked her to let the police know when her memory returned. Did she mention that?"

Charlie shook his head no.

"You know Tommy — he's the nicest guy on earth. Best detective in the department, the chief says. He would have been as un-threatening as a kitten. He said he told her she'd be a huge help in the investigation and that they would appreciate anything she remembered and could share with them about that night. The chief is a gentle guy, too, police chief or not. She's a young mom. Neither of them will scare her. But there's the bike, and Kayla's blood was found in the house. That's significant. And if she was actually the first person to see Dolores after she was murdered, talking to her could help the investigation greatly."

Nell was listening carefully, her heart heavy with what lay ahead for Kayla. Her mind was going in all directions, wondering about all the things they didn't know about the young mother. A week ago they didn't know she existed. And now, somehow, their lives were intertwined.

"I'm sure she could be of help," Charlie acknowledged. "She's aware of that in some vague way, but why she went out there? She's convinced — or at least trying to convince herself — that there's nothing she could add that would help the police. It's because of her kids, I think. She wants to protect them."

"Sure she does. But her actions may be doing exactly the opposite," Ben said. "She might be the closest person to the crime other than the person who did it. It'll be so much better for her if I let Jerry know she wants to talk to him, rather than Tommy Porter showing up in a squad car on her street. And sure, I'll give her a lift over to the station and wait while she talks to the chief." He checked his watch. "Do you know what her morning is like?"

"She doesn't work this morning and the kids are in school. I'm sure she's shaking in her boots and wondering if she really wants to go through with it, so I'd say the sooner the better." He handed Ben a cell number, scribbled on a gas receipt.

Ben took it and was up and walking inside while Charlie captured a stray thought and said to Nell, "She seemed afraid of something else last night. . . ."

Before he could finish his thought, Ben was back.

"It's all set. As soon as Kayla is ready, I'll pick her up."

Charlie and Nell watched Ben's efficient movements, the level tone of his voice. Tapping some notes into his phone. Canceling a sailing outing he'd scheduled. But efficiency was one thing, and they both knew that this morning that efficiency would be mixed with utter kindness.

Ben headed for the deck door, then stopped and turned back. "Charlie, you mentioned seeing a man outside her house. Did she mention him? A boyfriend?"

"I thought so, and that maybe I was interrupting something. I couldn't see the guy's face but his movements seemed kind of happy. But when I started up the steps I caught Kayla staring after his car. And the look in her eyes wasn't a look you'd save for a special guy."

Nell looked over at Charlie. "Oh?"

"It was a look you'd give to someone you'd like to wipe off the face of the earth."

After Ben left, Charlie and Nell sat with refilled coffee cups, not ready to move into the day. Their silence matched their relationship: comfortable and assured and respectful of the other's privacy. It was okay to talk. Or not.

As stone-faced as Charlie could sometimes be, his eyes were usually a giveaway. The gateway to what he tried so hard to cover up. For a moment she wanted to invade his privacy, to wrap her arms around him, to warn him of danger, to protect him like she did when he was a young impetuous boy in Kansas.

Though of course she never could. Not then. Nor could she now.

But she could see there was more going on in Charlie and she knew he was seeing more in Kayla Stewart than a mom who had lost a dog, or a brash young woman, one who needed help to cope with a difficult situation.

Charlie saw someone he was beginning to care about.

CHAPTER 15

Birdie was waiting in the circle drive of her sprawling estate when Nell drove up a few hours later. In minutes they were on their way out to Lambswool Farm, Nell to get fall vegetables for grilling that night, and Birdie to take some papers to Claire Russell, who managed the farm-to-table dinners and the working farm that Birdie owned.

Nell suspected mostly Birdie wanted to go along for a quiet time to talk. She knew she did.

Although there was a more direct route to Lambswool Farm, Nell took a turn that took them out near the old quarry. But it was the house that held their interest, not the quarry hidden back in the thick woods. Nell pulled over and stopped at the edge of the property, right beside the mailbox with Dolores Cardozo's name in gold stick-on letters. In the distance, a thick stand of trees swayed slightly, marking the beginning of the wooded area on Dolores's property. Several narrow pathways, overgrown with weeds, wound through the trees and brush to the quarry beyond. Straight ahead stood the plain house, quiet and serene, surrounded with yellow tape, a visual affront to the tranquil setting surrounding it.

Close to the car, a single wolf tree stood near the gravel drive, its branches bent and gnarled from years of battering sea storms. It stood guard, a lone sentry. And near the corner of the house, another tree — a tall thin pine, nearly leaning against the frame structure. The two women were silent, looking through the windows of Nell's car, imagining that night — windy, wet, and cold, a bike leaning against the bark of the old tree.

"If only bikes and trees could talk," Birdie said.

Nell shifted in the seat, looking through the back windows. "I never noticed how much property was here. I guess I never paid much attention to this land at all." Beyond the house, off to the left of the quarry woods, the property stretched long and skinny for as far as they could see. Behind them and across the road were several houses on small parcels of land.

"Someone's coming," Nell said, nodding

toward the street.

A tall, balding man walked across the road and around the car to the passenger window. His shoulders were hunched and a pair of binoculars hung around his long thin neck. In one bony hand he clutched a rifle. He didn't look happy.

Birdie lowered the window and smiled up into a weather-seasoned face.

"You need help?" the man asked. His voice was gravely, a smoker's voice with a wary cadence mixed in.

"We're passing through," Birdie said. She eyed the gun.

The man followed her glance. "Damn squirrels," was all he said.

Birdie smiled, gentle and soothing, just in case. "We stopped to pay our respects to the woman who once lived here."

The man hunched lower, peering in at the two women in the car. The fingers of one hand curled around the window frame. "The Cardozo woman is what you're meaning," he said. His head nodded with his words, his expression elongating into one befitting a death. "Why? Do you know her? Who are you?"

"I'm Birdie Favazza." She turned her head back toward Nell. "And this is my friend, Nell Endicott."

Their names seemed to carry enough recognition that the man relaxed slightly. There were few on Cape Ann who didn't know the Favazza name.

"Joe Duncan," the man said, pointing without turning to a house across the road. The house was similar to Dolores's — plain and small — except it lacked the acres of yard and woods and quarry that was unique to the Cardozo property. That, and a small porch tacked on the front, with two identical rocking chairs sitting side by side.

"It's a sad time for the neighborhood," Nell said.

The man nodded gravely.

"Were you friends of Miss Cardozo, Joe?" Birdie asked.

"Dolly — that's what we call her — didn't socialize much. But then, most of us around here don't. That's why we live here. It's quiet. Peaceful. It makes my Marlene happy not to have people around." He looked over at Dolores's house. "Or at least that's how it used to be. Now it's a wicked mess around here. Don't much like strangers." He shifted his gun under his arm as he spoke.

Birdie gave Nell a quick glance, wondering if the two of them were included in his statement.

Nell leaned across Birdie, coming closer to the window. "I suppose you've had your share of police traffic this week, Joe? It can't be pleasant for you."

Nell's expression of empathy seemed to relax the man's shoulders and his face became less somber. He nodded slowly, his narrow chin and the skin below it taking several shapes as it dipped low. "Yes'm, plenty of them. They upset Marlene no end, wanting to come up on our porch, then asking a million questions."

"I suppose they wondered if you saw anything, if maybe you could help them out," Birdie said.

"Yep. They wanted to know if we were home that day. Where would we go? I asked them, but then I remembered that it was a Saturday. We went into town. Well, I did, anyways. Marlene doesn't go out. I always go in on Saturday." He shook his head as if it had been the worst decision of his life. "Was late getting back. Had my oil changed that day. Ran into a mess of trouble with the truck. Marlene was mad as the dickens that dinner'd be late."

"And Marlene didn't see anything either? So it was quiet out here that day?" Birdie asked.

"Quiet as can be. Saw Dolly coming back

from a walk as I was heading out. She came back earlier than usual, if I remember right. Saturdays she usually went to the library."

"Do you know why she came back early?" Nell asked.

"Nope. Maybe she didn't go to the library that day. Who knows? What does it matter? Sometimes we get hikers out here in the fall, taking those trails back there along the road. Public access. So that's how they go. I heard one or two of them that day. Maybe a bunch. Can't remember. It was an ordinary day until the next one, when we found out Dolly was dead. The sirens nearly caused my Marlene to have a heart attack. And now, it's no better, with these dagnabbit curiosity seekers, folks just coming by to see what they can see. And then, sure, there's the usual hounds we've seen around here for months."

"Usual hounds?"

"A whole rat pack of 'em. My wife, Marlene, calls them the vultures. Riffraff, that's what they are. Damn riffraff. Some with fancy measuring tools. All computerized these days. They've been coming by for months. Dolly chased a couple away with an old BB gun she kept in her garage. That plus some salty words that sent my wife closing the windows. Dolly sparred with the best of them — and my Marlene don't like to hear that kind of talk." He chuckled. "There was no way in hell those fancy developers and construction workers were going to talk her out of her land, and we were behind her one hundred and fifty-two percent on that one. We had her back, she had ours. It's our land, that much is for sure. She'd never sell it."

Nell glanced up and down the road. She wondered if *our* meant the Duncans'. The nearest house was barely visible, all the way down the road and behind a tangle of scrub bushes.

"So that's died down now, I suppose," Birdie said.

"Oh, don't you believe it. It's a whole new ball game. With Dolly gone it's open season on this land. I hear talk of one of those big-box stores or a liquor store, a whole string of stores — you name it.

"But it's not going to happen," he went on. "Imagine what one of those developments would do to my birds."

"Your birds?" Birdie asked.

He touched his binoculars with an arthritic index finger. "I'm a birder. Been doing it for more years than you can count. Just this week I spotted a purple finch, Wilson's snipe, even a ruby-crowned kinglet.

Not many get by old Dunc. I love my birds. *And* my bins." He patted the rubber armoring on the binoculars hanging around his neck. Bird talk had added a whole spirited dimension to Joe Duncan.

Nell leaned over Birdie to look more closely at the binoculars. They were definitely high end, the kind Ben had been talking about getting for the sailboat. "Birding is a great hobby around Cape Ann, I hear. And those are fine lenses you have."

"Sure are. They're the best. Saved for two years to buy 'em." This time his laugh was more of a guffaw. "You'd be surprised what these beauties can see."

"Oh?" Birdie's smile came from her eyes. Intimate. A "tell me your secrets" kind of smile.

"Okay, I know you want to. Here, you take a look, Ms. Favazza," he said, pulling the cord over his head and thrusting the binoculars through the open car window. "It's not only birds this baby sees. Brings the whole world right into your head."

Birdie took the binoculars, adjusted them, and looked through the finely cut lenses. Dunc was right. It brought the world into your head. And along with it, the quarry trails and the trees, mailboxes — and nearly all the rooms of Dolores Cardozo's small house.

Lambswool Farm was busy, a John Deere tractor plowing a distant field, a riding mower creating neat grassy designs in a vast stretch of land that rolled all the way to the sea. Nearby, a flock of sheep settled in a field, ignoring an Australian shepherd practicing his herding skills.

The farm acreage had been in the Favazza family for generations — but none of the deceased would have recognized the post-card perfect land that had been recently transformed into a working organic farm, complete with chef's farm-to-table gourmet dinners served, in season, on long white-clothed picnic tables with a view of the sea. Although Birdie had handed over all responsibility for Lambswool Farm to Claire Russell and her staff, Birdie never failed to feel a swell of joy as she approached the farm. Her Sonny would have loved it.

Nell pulled in beside a truck and turned off the engine. "I know what you're thinking, Birdie. Coming out here affects me, too. Basking in the fresh air of Lambswool Farm is like taking a shower after walking through mud. It's pure magic. We both needed this."

They climbed out of the car almost forgetting the week that was, one they wanted to put as far behind them as possible.

Activity across the way from the working barn drew them toward a long table, groaning beneath the weight of multicolored squash, edamame, spinach and arugula, and vegetables they couldn't even begin to identify.

"I'm glad you came," Claire Russell called over to them, waving them closer. "Manna from heaven. Look at this windfall." She picked up a giant crooked-neck squash that looked more like a swan than a vegetable. She handed them each a cloth bag with a silk-screened image of the farm on the side. "Scavenge to your hearts' content. The rest I'll take over to the food pantry at the church."

Claire was dressed in her usual uniform: a floppy straw hat and jeans, a pair of gardening gloves sticking out of the back pocket, her fading brown hair pulled back in a ponytail.

Hiring a friend to accomplish that friend's lifelong dream had not only been a smart financial decision for Birdie — Claire quickly proved that her business savvy matched her gardening expertise — it had also given Claire a way to deal with grieving a dear friend who had died the year before.

Nell watched her as she broke into a ready smile, the well-earned lines in her face soft, the hollowness disappearing steadily. Lambswool Farm's magic and healing powers didn't discriminate; they were there for all who needed them.

The sound of giggles in the distance were familiar ones and the three women turned in that direction as Birdie's granddaughter Gabby and her friend Daisy climbed across a fence and started toward the barn. They leaned into one another as they walked, heads bent together in some secret girl talk. Gabby's uncontrollable blue-black hair fell over her eyes, and she brushed it back impatiently, her fingers pushing the thick curly mass over one ear.

When Gabby glanced up long enough to spot her nona, she changed directions and ran over, wrapped Birdie in a giant hug. The freckled preteen was now taller than Birdie by an inch, and proudly showed it off, standing straight as a reed, her arm around her grandmother.

"We're famous, Nona — again," Gabby announced.

Daisy grinned her agreement, her glasses slipping down her nose. "Or about to be anyway," she said. Her short hair bounced as she grabbed Gabby's elbow, pointing

226

toward the barn. "Gotta go. Interview time."

"We'll do autographs later," Gabby called out over her shoulder as they headed across the drive.

Claire laughed and filled in the blanks: "The farm is being written up again," she added in a plaintiff tone, her voice low so that the retreating girls wouldn't hear. The opening of Lambswool Farm a year before had presaged a flurry of media attention, from North Shore magazines to a few television appearances by celebrity guest chefs to a long article in the *Boston Globe*. And as wonderful as television cameras and reporters were for the business, it could be disrupting to the busy life of a working farm.

"The girls have become a great help out here — and they love it so much — that I thought they could handle this one. They know almost as much about the place as you or I do, Birdie. Besides, they have a zillion dramatic stories about lambs being born, saddling horses, meeting famous chefs, and riding on that John Deere. They'll bring a vigor to an article that yours truly might not succeed in doing. They're loving it."

"What magazine is it this time?" Birdie asked. "The *New York Times*?"

Claire laughed. "Well, not quite, it's —"

But before she could finish her sentence, a young man walked out of the barn, a camera hanging around his neck, striding toward one of the pastures. He was followed closely by Gabby and Daisy. The girls' heads were thrown back in laughter and Greta, one of Claire's Australian shepherds, was bouncing along behind them as if she were in on a joke.

"Hey, wait," Claire called out to them.

The trio stopped and turned around. Claire leaned toward Birdie and whispered, "If I'm going to exploit your granddaughter, you should probably meet the guy asking her questions."

The young man waved a hand in the air and headed their way with Gabby, Daisy, and the dog following.

Nell and Birdie stared at the man as he drew near.

"It's Howdy Doody," Nell said in a whisper so low only Birdie could hear.

"But better looking," Birdie whispered back. "I'm thinking he's more like a Jimmy Olsen."

Nell chuckled, and as the man came closer, she had to agree. He was a clone of the reporter from the old Superman movies. That sweet Jimmy Olsen — Superman's pal. Someone the young man walking toward them was too young to even know about.

Red hair and freckles; boyish in his jeans, cowboy hat, and boots — Richie Pisano was definitely every bit as distinctive as Mary Pisano had portrayed him. And his smile as wide and welcoming as if they'd known him for a long time. Perhaps from the old television days.

"Ladies," he said with fingertips to his hat and a slight tip of his head. Richie wasn't tall — just normal size — but one sensed a personality that made up for anything he might lack in other areas.

Claire made the introductions while Richie listened to their names, nodding, smiling.

Then he confessed, with a slight blush creeping into his cheeks, that he hadn't really needed introductions. "I spend a lot of time digging through archives at the paper. It gives me a good handle on what's going on around the town, knowing who's who. I know about your generosity to Sea Harbor, Ms. Favazza, your place in the town, your husbands." He added the last words with the suspicion of a wink that caused Birdie to frown.

Then he turned to Nell. "And you and your husband retired here from Boston, and became integral to this burg in all sorts of ways. Very cool. I met Mr. Endicott when I was covering a committee meeting the other day at city hall. He spotted my computer screen going black and gave me his cord. Saved my life, I swear. Good man."

Nell smiled, slightly embarrassed at the familiarity he was espousing. Someone knowing her from behind a curtain — without permission. Yet she'd done the same with him — and even more so with Kayla Stewart. It felt different being on the other side of it.

"Richie's the man who quoted us in the article about the food pantry, Nona," Gabby said, filling in a pause. "You know, the one on the fridge in your kitchen."

"Of course I remember, dear. I've only read it twenty times. It was a lovely article, Richie."

"Hey, thanks," he said. "This interviewing and writing for the paper has tapped into my hidden talent. And these two gals here helped me a lot, introduced me around that food place to everyone. I got to deliver some meals with one of their drivers, Kayla Stewart, too. Do you know her? It was cool. I found out lots about her. And to top it off, the café served me the best clam chowder in, well, maybe the whole world."

"Of course it was the best," Gabby said. "The Bountiful Bowl Café is a five-star kind of place."

Richie laughed. "Sure." He turned to Birdie and Nell. "Claire here has been great, too, letting me hang out and ask a million questions. This place is amazing. Must be worth a bundle."

It wasn't the way Birdie looked at Lambswool Farm at all, but she held a smile. "We all love it here," she said.

"It's been written up by the best of the best. I've read all of it. But I'm grateful for you guys letting a rookie like me give it my spin."

"We never turn down free PR," Claire said. Her voice was friendly but it was clear to her friends that Claire had far better things to do than accommodate yet another reporter, especially one who would be preaching to the choir. Everyone in Sea Harbor knew about Lambswool Farm — and they'd be the only ones reading his little piece.

Richie fingered his camera, smiling with pleasure.

"That's a nice camera," Birdie said, noticing the affectionate grip of his fingers on the Nikon.

"Yep. Makes me feel like a real pro." He

grinned. "Just got me this. Had a little windfall come my way. Now all I need is a plastic press card and wristwatch to call Superman like that kid in the old movies."

So he *did* know about his twin. That was a point in his favor. "Well, it looks like you're on your way up the ranks at the paper," Nell said.

"Nah. I'm good at this — it's easy. But reporting on a small rag doesn't pay much. You have to be innovative, keep your sights high, you know?"

"How high?" Birdie asked.

"Oh, who knows? Maybe I'll travel the world. Live the good life. But for today it's Lambswool Farm. And these two gals here have already tossed out my outline and replaced it with their own."

"Yours was slightly boring, no offense," Daisy said. "We'll show you the real Lambswool Farm. Just follow us."

They were off, this time Daisy and Gabby leading the way and Richie Pisano sprinting to keep up.

Nell watched them until they were out of sight. "Interesting young man," she said, more to herself, but both Birdie and Claire picked up on it.

"He's ambitious."

"Just like Jimmy Olsen," Claire said.

"I suspect there are some differences," Nell said.

"Yes," Birdie said with a smile. She shielded her eyes, scanning the horizon for Gabby and the others, who were quickly disappearing from sight. The sound of Greta's barking indicated their direction.

Nell watched Richie disappear, too, unsure of why she thought his disappearing might be a good thing. The fact that she knew little about him but he was learning all sorts of things about people she *did* know bothered her.

"You're wondering about him," Birdie said. "I see it on your face. 'Who is this Jimmy Olsen look-alike?' "

Nell laughed. "I'm exposed."

"Well, we know, or have heard, he's a hardworking rookie," Birdie said.

"Hardworking? Maybe. Rookie doesn't seem to fit."

"Is seasoned reporter better?" Birdie asked. "That doesn't fit in my mind."

"There's something about him that bothers me. I have the feeling that Richie Pisano has bigger fish to fry than those found at Lambswool Farm or food pantries or a newsroom."

And she wasn't sure she wanted to know what they were.

CHAPTER 16

"Is Charlie coming for dinner?" Nell stood next to Izzy at the sink, breathing in the loamy smell of earth as they scrubbed squash and potatoes and small sweet carrots, readying the late cultivars for the grill.

She and Birdie had taken Claire up on her generous offer and filled several bags with vegetables before calling it quits and heading back to town.

"I'm sure he's coming, Aunt Nell. My brother doesn't cook," Izzy said.

Nell nodded. Her mind was wandering, her thoughts scattered, the niggling feeling of leaving things unfinished. She thought about Richie the reporter — and wondered how many questions he had thrown at Kayla while they drove back and forth to the Cardozo house.

And she wondered if Kayla had answered them.

"I think Charlie's attracted to Kayla," Izzy

was saying beside her.

"Maybe," Nell said.

Izzy looked sideways at her aunt. "But . . . ?"

Nell gave a slight shrug and pushed the thoughts aside without answering. "Ben went to the station with Kayla this morning," she said, changing the subject. "Now that her memory's back, she might be able to help the police figure out what happened that night. She's a key witness —"

"Or chief suspect," Izzy said.

Nell looked at her, surprised. But she shouldn't have been. Izzy was seeing it without the filters of emotion. Exactly the way Jerry Thompson and Tommy Porter would be. The way a prosecutor would look at it. One who could even twist Kayla's injury and blacking out into something she'd done intentionally as a cover-up — or simply something that happened accidentally after the fact.

"I don't mean to sound callous." Izzy tossed the vegetables with Nell's basil and vinegar dressing and set the bowl aside.

"You couldn't be callous, not if you tried."

"Yes, I could. I was callous in the courtroom protecting my clients. *Icy,* a friend told me once. I told myself it was my job, it was the circumstance. I had to do it. And there's

235

some truth to that, sure. But we make our own choices. I wanted to get ahead in my law firm back then. Circumstances can drive people to do things in surprising ways. Maybe that's why I gave up my law practice. I saw it in others, too — not only people acting contrary to what their conscious tells them, but worse — seemingly good people doing terrible things. Even murder."

The rattle of the door disturbed the conversation, bringing in a gust of wind along with Ben, his arms loaded with bags. "Weather's supposed to pick up, but not until late. We'll be okay on the deck tonight." He walked across the family room and dropped his packages on the kitchen island, then moved to the sink to give Nell a kiss on the top of her head. He hugged Izzy, too, then shrugged out of his windbreaker.

"How did it go?" Nell asked, helping Ben unpack the bags.

"It went fine, actually. I took Kayla for coffee first. I thought it might put her at ease. But I also wanted to get to know her a little. And that was good. We connected. I like her." Ben pulled out some wine from one of his padded bags and lined the bottles up on the island. "She seems to be loaded down with too much baggage for a woman that age, but maybe that's beside the point."

"Maybe it's not," Izzy said.

"As for the police interview, Jerry was the gentleman you'd expect him to be. He tried hard to make Kayla feel like she wasn't under scrutiny."

Izzy rested her palms flat on the island and looked directly at her uncle, her eyes locked into his. "But she *is* under scrutiny," Izzy said. "She has to be right up there on the list."

Ben let Izzy's comment go unanswered and began pulling out fixings for the Friday martinis. "She's smart, Iz. And I think she's honest. She detailed everything she remembered carefully and articulately. The only glitch was the last question. And that threw a shadow over everything that had gone before. The 'Why did you go out there that night, Kayla?' That one didn't get an answer."

The conversation ended with the clamoring at the front door — not the doorbell, which none of their friends used — announcing the arrival of Cass, Danny, and the Brewsters, who filled the family area with voices and laughter and armfuls of side dishes and flowers. Jane and Ham Brewster were the Endicotts' oldest friends in Sea Harbor — the hippy artist couple from Berkeley who had traveled to the Woodstock

237

festival many years past, had stopped in Sea Harbor on their way back to California, and never left. And they almost never missed a Friday night gathering.

Before the first group made it to the kitchen island, Rachel and Don Wooten — the Sea Harbor attorney and her restaurateur husband — followed. Another group came in shortly after, the deck filled, the music was turned up, and the smell of Ben's grilled cod filled the air.

Nell moved in and out of the house, catching snatches of conversation, bits and pieces of Sea Harbor news — ordinary and pleasant. It was as if everyone was intentionally keeping it calm, and Nell was glad. They'd had enough commotion and an event with friends and little excitement was perfect.

"Charlie texted me. He's not coming," Izzy whispered in Nell's ear a while later. Around them people filled their plates and found empty chairs around the deck.

"Is he working? I know he's putting in long hours."

"Maybe you could call it work. He's over at the Stewarts'. Kayla's car broke down again." Izzy's brows lifted into sun-streaked bangs. "So what's that about?"

A call for dessert prevented Nell from pursuing it further, not that she'd have an answer. She had the same question.

The evening ended late, with music and conversation changing course as fast as they devoured the apple crisp Rachel Wooten had made. "And I didn't order it from Don's restaurant," she insisted as she carried the empty baking dish out to their car.

But a few stragglers, reluctant to give up the deck breeze and the starry night, had pulled on sweaters and sweatshirts and settled back on the deck. Ben brought out a tray with Scotch and some glasses, a pot of coffee and pitcher of cream.

It was the usual standbys who stayed, the knitters and Sam, Danny, and Ben.

"So," Izzy said, sipping Sam's Scotch, then scrunching up her face in a horrible wince and handing it back. "For a quick recap of the evening, Aunt Nell and Don Wooten only had one Mad Hatter encounter that I could see, Uncle Ben and Sam only brought up sailing fourteen times, and Birdie delightfully changed conversations whenever things turned to politics or a contentious pennant race."

"And my fair Izzy was her sweet, wonderful, adorable self," Sam filled in, wrapping one arm around his wife and pulling her close.

They all clapped and Izzy snuggled comfortably into Sam's side.

Footsteps on the deck steps broke into the quiet moment. Nell looked over, wondering what Ham Brewster had forgotten. The bearded artist nearly always returned shortly after leaving for his salad bowl, a sweater, or sometimes he'd forgotten to give his hostess a big bear of a hug.

But tonight the sound wasn't the familiar flop of Ham's Birkenstocks on the wooden steps, but a slightly firmer, quicker step.

"Hey, guys, guess I missed dinner." Charlie pushed a hank of hair back off his forehead and flopped down in a deck chair next to Ben. He looked tired.

His uncle immediately poured him a Scotch.

"You missed a mighty fine dinner, son," Ben said. "I hope it was worth it."

No answer. Charlie put his had back and looked up at the sky.

"It looks like you're trying to decide," Izzy said. "Speak."

"You're right, I'm trying to decide."

Nell had disappeared and returned before they knew she was gone. She handed Charlie a plate of crusty grilled cod, a dollop of lemon cream sauce on top, and long slices of roasted squash, sweet onion, and carrots with brown grill marks highlighting the tender flesh.

"You spoil him rotten," Izzy said.

Izzy sounded a bit like her mother, Nell's sister Caroline, who often accused Nell of the same thing. "Of course I do," Nell said, then settled down next to Ben and waited for Charlie to tell them why he'd come over so late.

He looked at the plate with longing. And then he dug in, his football appetite taking over while the others chatted, trying to ignore the speed with which he devoured the dinner.

When his plate was nearly empty, Charlie set it on a small table beside the chair and sat back, his eyes partly closed, but the look on his face was off kilter.

Nell watched him for a long moment. "Charlie, what's going on with you?"

He opened his eyes, as if expecting the question. His voice was strained and curious at once, as if he himself didn't understand what he was about to say.

"She doesn't know if she killed Dolores Cardozo or not."

CHAPTER 17

They sat in silence as Charlie's words settled around them. They waited.

Charlie took a deep breath and finally continued talking, his voice not as heavy as he tried to explain. "On one hand, she's convinced she didn't do it," he said, pulling at words that might make sense of it. "But I think the questioning has messed with her head. She's second guessing herself, wondering if she saw it right, the way she remembers it. Or if the concussion has screwed her up. Was Dolores already on the floor when she got there? Could she have done something, said something . . . ?"

"That isn't making sense, Charlie," Izzy said.

He looked down the length of his long legs, stretched out in front of him. "Maybe it doesn't. Here's how it played out."

He hadn't planned to miss dinner. He'd *never* miss an Endicott meal without serious cause. So here was the reason:

He had stopped by the Stewart house to drop off some free carnival tickets a patient had given the clinic. He and Doc Mackenzie thought the Stewart kids would like them. And Kayla could use something good happening. He had planned to leave them in the mailbox.

But Kayla was in the gravel drive of her house when he arrived, leaning under the open hood of her car. She was covered with oil and dirt and dust. The engine was dead and she was adamant that she could fix it herself. She'd promised to take the kids for ice cream and was determined not to go back on her word.

"It was as if getting them ice cream cones was the most important thing in her life," he said. "She was acting kind of crazy. I wondered briefly if it had something to do with the concussion, but I watched her carefully and decided it wasn't that. It was simply that she'd made a promise to the kids and was feeling that it was one thing in her life she could control."

"So you were the hero," Izzy said.

"Superhero, that's me. I played with the kids while she showered, then drove them all to Scoopers. It was late when we got back, the kids were tired, and the car was still broken."

"So you stayed and fixed it," Nell said.

"Yeah. It wasn't hard. She had done more to mess it up than solve the problem. But I don't think it's because she doesn't know how to fix cars. She probably does. She's tough, and seems capable of doing just about anything she wants to do. But like I said, she wasn't thinking clearly, at least from a mechanic's point of view."

"How are the kids?" Cass asked.

"They're great. She's a good mother, not that I'm much of a judge. The kids are happy. And the dog's great." Charlie swirled his glass of Scotch.

"Once the car was fixed and the sky was dark — she seems to talk better in the dark — she asked if I'd stay. I hadn't asked her about the morning meeting — somehow asking questions seems to shut her down. I wanted to, though, and hoped maybe she'd bring it up. So I stayed. And it turns out she did want to talk about it."

"Did she think it was a good meeting?" Ben asked.

"I don't think she judged it. But she thought that every word she had said to the chief was the absolute truth. I believe it. I'm not sure the woman can lie." He paused and thought about that. Then he said, "I don't know, maybe she'd lie for her kids, but I think it'd be hard for her. I've known a lot of liars, and I don't think she's one of them."

"But —" Ben pressed.

"But. I know she still held back on why she had gone out there that night. Why? Maybe that's why I don't think she's a liar. She could have made something up, told them she went out to check on Dolores Cardozo, to take her something, a whole bunch of things. But she didn't. She simply said it wasn't relevant, it was personal, and she wasn't going to tell them."

"But does she see that it makes her look bad?" Nell said.

"I don't know. But it seems important to her not to tell them why, even though I can tell it's messing with her head. I think her comment about not being sure what she did out there that night was said out of complete frustration." He finished his Scotch and looked up, this time smiling slightly.

None of them knew whether it was the Scotch, the heaping plate of food, or simply talking to people important in his life. But the combination seemed to have given Charlie new life. He sat forward in the chair, the weariness fading from his face. He seemed smug, almost, as if he'd figured out the secrets of the universe while devouring his uncle's grilled cod.

"Yeah, I'm convinced. I wasn't until you let me talk it all out. Family therapy. Good for the soul."

Ben chuckled and opened his mouth to say something, but Charlie wasn't finished.

"And who knows," he said, looking at Izzy, then the others, "being the superhero I am, maybe I can find out what the answer to that 'why' question is and stop the fuss. I'll take care of Kayla; you guys find the bad dude."

He stood and looked toward the doors leading into the house, then back toward his aunt. "What's for dessert?" he asked.

CHAPTER 18

Saturday was cloudy, a chance of rain in the forecast, and if it hadn't been one of the last days for the outdoor market, Nell might have found an excuse not to go.

Birdie had shown up early, wanting a cup of coffee before they left. Her groundsman Harold had brought her over and she seemed adamant they get out. "Fresh air," she said. Then she added, almost as an afterthought, "I'm meeting Kayla and the kids at the market. I've promised the children a treat. They've never had Harry Garozzo's St. Joseph's Day fritters."

"That's shameful," Nell said, nodding agreement.

She poured coffee into two mugs, and settled on one of the stools beside the oversized island.

"Three," Birdie said. "Izzy is coming, too."

"Izzy? What about the shop?"

"It will still be there, even if Izzy is not.

Mae's twin nieces are home from school for the weekend and helping out. They're going to decorate the window. They started early this morning. It's a vision and will surely get everyone in town excited about the knitting project. Bamboo trees dripping with hats and mittens, knit scarves fashioned into two baskets that they're filling with fall leaves. Even tiny little knit socks positioned up a winding, red brick road. Those girls are talented."

Nell imagined the sight. And she also wondered what else was on Birdie's mind. "Have you told Kayla about Monday's meeting?"

"No. In fact, I haven't told anyone about it. That's one of today's tasks. Chief Thompson and I decided to give it this week before we talked to the benefactors. I think Jerry was hoping the case would be solved by now and the whole thing would be a little cleaner. But nothing is solved. And with rumors beginning to circulate about Dolores's will, it's time to let the beneficiaries know. If we don't, we'll be hearing about people not even in it who are turned into instant millionaires."

"People, no doubt, who never laid eyes on Dolores Cardozo," Nell said.

"We're here," Izzy called, kicking off her

boots in the hallway. Cass followed her in.

"Cass," Birdie said in surprise. "I thought I heard those cowboy boots of yours. Noisy things."

"Isn't hearing supposed to dim at your age?" Cass asked with a smile. She took another mug from the cupboard and helped herself to the cream.

Izzy wore a soft alpaca poncho that she had knit during last year's long, cold winter. It was the color of the sea, with orange circles scattered around it playfully, slits for arms, and a fringe that touched her knees and moved in slow motion as she walked across the room. "Abby loves this poncho. She wants one just like it so we can dance together and have the fringe fly around us like butterflies."

They all knew that meant Izzy was probably nearly finished with it.

Izzy filled her own cup, then waited until everyone had their coffee. "Before we head to the market, I have a couple of things I wanted to say —" It sounded like a prepared speech, an announcement, and the other three looked at one another, then at Izzy.

Cass was about to tease her about the drama, then thought better of it and looked around the kitchen counter for a leftover bagel instead. "Go on. We're all ears," she said.

"Mae said the newspaper called the shop again, wanting to do a story. The editor called us the Seaside Knitters Society."

"That has an elegant sound," Birdie said with a smile. "I rather like it."

"Me too," Izzy said. "So we need to be thinking about doing the interview and being the elegant Seaside Knitters Society. You all seem to be ignoring this request."

"Not intentionally," Nell said.

"I know," Izzy said. "We have other things on our minds these days. But it'll be good PR for the knitting project. I'll tell her maybe we can meet over the weekend or next week — at least she'll stop bothering Mae."

They nodded and Izzy punched a reminder into her phone. "The other thing —" Izzy said, her smile fading. And then to everyone's surprise, her large brown eyes grew moist.

"Hey, what's wrong?" Cass said. She started to get up but Izzy stopped her, her palms out.

"No, it's nothing," she said. "I'm fine. Really. I don't know why I'm so emotional. It must be PMS or something." She took a quick, deep breath. "The other thing is, well, I wanted to talk about Dolores Cardozo."

They all waited while Izzy composed herself.

"It's about a dream I had."

"About Dolores Cardozo?" Birdie asked.

Izzy nodded. "I can tell Sam almost anything. He understands me inside and out. He'd listen to anything I had to say. But there are some things, I don't know, things like this dream, that I can only share with you guys. You'll get it."

They nodded, no one saying anything. They didn't need to. They'd all done the same thing as their friendship deepened.

"It was a real memory," Izzy began, "something that happened a while ago that I'd forgotten about, but it resurfaced last night, all tangled up in a dream. And now I can't stop thinking about her. And I'm feeling so sad."

"Was the dream frightening?" Nell asked. Dreaming about a murdered woman was closer to a nightmare, and not the kind she'd want her niece to be dealing with.

"No. It was sad and touching, but not frightening at all. The memory was of me, jogging with Abby, who was happily bouncing along in her Bob —"

Birdie's white brows lifted.

251

"Bob — that's our jogging stroller," Izzy explained. "We were out at Halibut Point and we spotted Dolores walking in front of us on one of the trails. She must have heard us behind her because she stopped walking until we caught up. That part really happened. Abby was infatuated with her and with her wonderful walking stick. Dolores seemed every bit as infatuated with Abby. She crouched down in front of the stroller, her fingers wrapped around the sides, and talked to her quietly, as if the two of them were old friends having a private conversation. I told her Abby's name, and she nodded, but she must have misunderstood and called her a different name. Shelly, I think she said. She touched Abby's face with the tip of her finger and it was magical. Like it was lit up at the end. Abby reached for it, wrapped her fingers around it and squeezed it tight, and then . . . then she told Dolores that she loved her."

Izzy's words caught in her throat. She cleared it with a drink of coffee and went on quickly, covering up the emotion. "I mean, you know how Abby does that sometimes, that little 'wuv you' that comes out of her like a sneeze. But Dolores — and this I remember now so clearly — Dolores got tears in her eyes. And then she leaned on her stick and pushed herself up straight, turned back toward the ocean, and went on walking until she disappeared in a mist."

Izzy stopped. She bit down on her lip, staring into her coffee mug.

They all sat in silence, not sure what to say or where Izzy was going with her story. Or if that was the end of it.

Finally, Cass leaned over and gave Izzy a hug.

Izzy gave a lopsided smile. "Goofy, huh? Most of that really happened. Somehow it took the dream to bring it back. Maybe not the E.T.-like finger, but meeting her on the trail that day, Abby's response, that happened.

"And that's the lady that someone brutally murdered. Maybe someone we know, someone who comes into the shop. I can't let go of that. . . . We can't, we just can't let that be."

They refilled coffee mugs and talked more about Dolores Cardozo, a woman they were coming to know better in death than life — and about the twists and turns that defined one short week in their lives, events and suspicions that were slowly building a resolve to get to know Dolores Cardozo even better. And to find out who murdered her.

"Getting to know her better is the only way her murderer will ever be found," Birdie said. "We need more memories, more dreams, Izzy." Her veined hand moved across the island to cover Izzy's. "We need to walk in Dolores's shoes."

"And carry her walking stick," Nell said.

A short while later all the coffee mugs were drained and they were about to head out when Cass brought up Charlie and his evening with the Stewarts.

A topic they'd left hanging when the deck lights had finally gone out the night before.

"We walked out to our cars together and he told me that he has this strange attraction to her," Cass said.

"That seems obvious," Izzy said, a hint of concern in her voice. "Passing fancies, as Birdie would say."

"Well, maybe not. Maybe he's attracted to her as a woman — and if so, that would be fine, right?"

"I guess," Izzy said. "And I suppose one can be attracted to someone else quickly. It happened that way with Sam —"

"Even though you'd known him since you were three," her aunt said.

They all laughed. Izzy had thought little about her older brother Jack's best friend.

254

Not until happenstance brought him to Sea Harbor as a visiting fine arts photographer. And then it had truly been immediate. Bing, like a light went on.

"Maybe it's just that I don't know Kayla," Izzy said.

Cass patted her friend's hand like a mother would, holding back the "there there," and Izzy laughed.

"I think it's more complicated with Charlie and this woman," Cass said. "He told me he's almost certain he's seen her before. Somehow that seems really important to your brother, Iz."

"Where would he have seen her?"

"It could have been a lot of places," Nell said. "Charlie traveled all over after leaving here a few years ago."

"That's true," Birdie said. "He told me about some of his travels last night. He called it a kind of pilgrimage. First, spending time with his parents. And then going back to some of the places and people who had been important in his life during those rough years. People who had helped him out, given him new direction. He has interesting stories."

"Where did Kayla live before she came to Sea Harbor?" Nell asked.

But none of them knew.

In fact, they knew very little about Kayla Stewart, a thought they carried with them as they rinsed out cups, turned the coffeepot off, and drove the short distance to the open-air market on Harbor Road.

CHAPTER 19

In spite of the chilly weather, the Harbor Green was filled with crowds of people bustling in and around the white tents and long tables filled with fall produce. In the distance, hot dog, popcorn, and pastry vendors vied with a high school band playing in the gazebo. It was as if the chill in the weather had pushed them all forward to a grand autumn, filled with pumpkins and Halloween costumes.

Nell looked across a heaping bin of leafy greens and spotted Elizabeth Hartley standing alone near a tent post. She mouthed to the others that she'd be right back and walked over to say hello. Elizabeth looked worried, like she could use a friend.

Before Nell got within speaking distance, Jerry Thompson walked over to Elizabeth's side, a bulging market bag slung over his arm.

How odd. Saturday or not, it wasn't where

Nell would have expected the chief of police to be in the middle of a murder investigation.

Her first thought was that maybe things were coming together for the investigation and Jerry could afford to get out and breathe some fresh air.

But Ben had talked to his friend just that morning. He would have hinted at it, if that'd been the case. Then, as she approached the couple, she saw visible proof that the investigation wasn't winding down. The strain on Jerry's face was palpable. His stance formal and inflexible, a rubber band stretched too tightly. The week since Dolores Cardozo had been found lying on the pine floor of her house must seem like a year to him.

Elizabeth welcomed Nell with a warm smile, relieved, maybe to have the company; Jerry was somewhere else, his eyes directed at things they couldn't see.

Elizabeth tapped his arm and his attention came back to the present, the old Jerry back briefly with a half smile and look that said he knew she understood. His world was not a very social one at the moment.

He excused himself, telling Elizabeth he thought they needed more leafy greens, and headed toward the crowd, his frame tall, his broad forehead filled with thought, his eyes alert and scanning the crowd.

Watching him, Nell realized immediately why Jerry had left a busy investigation to come to the Sea Harbor market. It wasn't that things were falling into place and he could relax for an hour.

Jerry was working. He'd often said that murder was the one crime in which society has a direct interest. *Listen to everyone.* Somewhere out there on the crowded Harbor Green, among the groaning tables of vegetables, kids throwing Frisbees on the edge of the green, and friends and neighbors and shopkeepers clustered together, sharing news and gossip and perhaps rumors of a woman's awful death — somewhere out there a murderer might be walking the aisles, stopping to test the ripeness of an eggplant or melon for purchase.

"It's not an easy time," Nell said to Elizabeth, who was also following the chief's movements, watching now as he was approached by a young man in jeans and a baseball hat. Jerry turned to him, spoke a few words, then walked on by himself.

"That's Richie Pisano," Nell said, watching the interaction. "He works for the paper. He's probably bothering Jerry about the case, trying to get a scoop."

Elizabeth nodded. "I've seen him around. But Jerry is used to it. He somehow manages to send them all away, always pleasantly, never offending anyone. I, on the other hand, would like to swat them."

Nell smiled, the idea of the headmistress swatting anyone being unimaginable. "These are long days for him."

Elizabeth was still following Jerry with her eyes, watching him watch their town. "Jerry says this is the quietest, leanest investigation he can remember. And he doesn't mean that in a good way."

"I suppose it's one thing when you have friends and associates of the deceased to talk to. People who even unknowingly might offer information. People who actually *knew* the person."

Elizabeth was nodding. "The police can probe only so far without pushing the limits of privacy. No one seems to know anything. And he's running out of *no ones,* people, like you said, who were connected to Dolores. And the few that there are — like Kayla Stewart — aren't being much help."

Kayla and Dolores. Both women with few discernible ties to Sea Harbor life. But ties to one another. Kayla was a regular visitor at the Cardozo house. *A delivery person,* was how Kayla described it when she was asked.

But Nell knew it was more than that. She knew Fiona wanted the two women to know one another. To like each other. It wasn't the way one would describe a relationship with a food delivery person.

She wondered now if they *had* liked each other, if Fiona's matchmaking had been successful. Or if it had backfired, and for unknown reasons, Kayla had developed a distaste for the woman. Maybe disliked her terribly. *Hated* her . . .

Hannah Swenson walked up, her face showing concern. "I'm walking into a web of worry, I can feel it. I don't mean to interrupt, but you both look as if a bottom has fallen out of something. Is there any way I can help?"

Elizabeth shook her head and welcomed Hannah with a smile. "You're not interrupting," she said, then changed the subject. "I'm glad you're here so I can thank you in Jerry's stead. You've been a wonderful support, Hannah. Thank you."

She turned to Nell. "Twice this week Hannah has dropped off casseroles at Jerry's house, somehow aware that the man forgets to eat when things are pressing on him."

A thoughtful thing to do. Nell hoped her smile covered up her surprise. It wasn't that Hannah wasn't generous and kind. But

Hannah Swenson had never impressed her as being a homebody, much less one who cooked up meals for folks in need. If Mary Pisano was right in her bit of gossip, one of Mary's own bed-and-breakfast caterers was recently employed part-time by Hannah to fill her freezer and cater her occasional cocktail parties.

"Okay," Hannah said with a kind laugh. "I can read your face, Nell, and I know we've talked about this. You know that my idea of preparing a meal is making a reservation at Duckworth's."

Nell chuckled. "Nonetheless, it was very thoughtful of you."

"And nice of Harry Garozzo to prepare it," Hannah admitted.

Elizabeth thanked Hannah again, assured her it didn't matter who cooked it, it was Hannah's gesture that counted. Then excused herself to both of them, heading off to find Jerry in the crush of people.

"Jerry is lucky to have her by his side," Hannah said, watching Elizabeth walk away.

"I think it goes both ways. Our chief is a good man," Nell said.

"A good man, indeed," Hannah said.

Nell looked sideways and caught a fleeting glimpse of envy on Hannah's face, and then it was gone. Hannah's own relationship hadn't been so amicable, she knew, an acrimonious marital split that left her alone with a son to raise. Izzy had talked about it at the time, the ugliness of it, the gossip among the knitting groups in the back room. Hannah's talk of affairs and cruelty.

"It must have been difficult raising Jason on your own," she said.

Hannah's answer was immediate. "My ex-husband gave Jason and me nothing. He was a fake and a failure, pretending to be wealthy, running around. Then running off for good. I am far better off now than when I was married to him, without a doubt and for all sorts of reasons. I've finally figured out how to take care of myself and my son and I do it better than he ever pretended to do." There was a note of pride in her voice.

The answer surprised Nell in its forcefulness, but its message was understandable. Bad marriages left baggage and emotions, and Hannah Swenson wouldn't be the first person who had to take charge of her life. And she seemed to have done exactly that, building a very comfortable life for herself and her son.

Nell was sorry she had brought up a painful topic for Hannah and she changed the subject, thanking her for her thoughtfulness to Jerry and Elizabeth. Then she excused herself and headed over to the Russell Orchard stand, where Cass and Izzy were helping Birdie fill up a cloth bag with apples.

"Where are you meeting Kayla?" Izzy asked Birdie, scanning the crowd for Sam and Abby.

Before Birdie could answer, a familiar shaggy dog bounded toward them, heading directly for Cass, then rising up and planting his furry paws on her chest.

"Oh, Sheppy, nonono." It was Sarah Grace, racing over to grab the loose leash and laughing delightedly at the spectacle. Christopher followed more slowly behind, next to his mother. Protecting her was how it looked to Nell. The thought saddened her. He was too young to assume that role.

In jeans and a sweatshirt that could have come from a junior clothing department, Kayla looked like a kid herself. Her bandage had been reduced to a small white square, and she'd tugged spikes of her dark hair down as far as she could to cover it.

She was clearly chagrined at the muddy footprints left on Cass's sweatshirt.

"These are our friends, Mommy," Sarah Grace announced happily.

Kayla stood a few feet back but looked toward Nell, nodding a hello.

Nell smiled warmly, then introduced her

to the others, moving from one to the other, from Birdie to Izzy to Cass.

Kayla followed the introductions, slightly wary, but meeting the eyes of each of them, acknowledging the connections as Nell said their names. Birdie, whom she'd talked to on the phone. Izzy — *You're Charlie's sister.* When Nell got to Cass, Kayla paused.

"Cass," she repeated. "Cass. You're the one who found Sarah Grace's clothes. He shouldn't have been there that night. He did that because he thought he was helping me out, saving me from a trip when I got home." Her voice was sincere, but defensive, the words coming out quickly. Then she stopped and looked at Cass again, more closely, her eyes narrowing. "It's you, isn't it? You were at the kids' school that day. . . ." Her eyes indicated what day it had been. The day she'd hung on a fence, her heart nearly broken in two.

Cass nodded. Then she softened the moment with a smile and a light tone. "Hey, Kayla, I didn't know it was you that day. Not then, anyway. I was out walking and stopped at the fence. I went to that school a hundred years ago. Hasn't changed a bit. I thought maybe I'd see the kids out at recess, check out the uniforms, make sure we got our money's worth in the Laundromat." She smiled crookedly. "If I had known it was you, I'd have told you right then and there what really great kids you have, responsible. I like 'em a lot. But then, well you must know how great they are. You raised them."

Kayla nodded a couple of times. Then she allowed a smile that changed her face — the edges softened, the wariness faded into a shadow, and her large eyes brightened. Accepting.

Christopher looked up at his mother, and when he saw her face, he smiled, too, as if permission had been granted.

"Now, you dear things," Birdie said to the kids, hunching over until they were eye to eye. "I told your mom that this is the day for a special treat. They have something at the market called a special market fritter. And I couldn't believe my ears when your mother said you'd never had one. Is that true?"

Sarah Grace and Christopher nodded, their eyes bright.

"Oh, my. From now on it will be our special tradition. You two and me. Are you in?" The two children giggled and nodded again. Shep slapped his tail on the ground.

In minutes Birdie had explained to them everything they'd ever need to know about the St. Joseph's Day fritters that her dear friend Harry Garozzo made in his deli practically every day of the year, even though St. Joseph's Day was March 19, the day the pastries were traditionally served. Harry seemed to ignore that small detail, saying St. Joe wouldn't care a bit.

"Zeppole di San Giuseppe-delizioso," she whispered into Christopher's ear with just enough of an accent and the squeezing together of two fingers, her eyebrows pulling together tightly, to elicit a lovely laugh from the dark-haired boy.

"How about we take the kids over to meet Harry and his fritters while you and Kayla talk?" Nell suggested.

Kayla looked surprised at the child-care offer, then worried, then looked sheepish at worrying. "Sure. Of course. Thank you," she said.

Birdie picked up two plastic cups of apple cider from the nearby Russell Orchard's apple stand and led Kayla over to a bench near one of the pine trees at the edge of the market.

Again, Kayla was uncomfortable, not at all sure why Birdie Favazza wanted to give her kids treats, much less talk to her. The words of Sister Fiona, though, rang in her ear. "Next to the pope," she had said, "there's no finer."

Birdie began with easy talk, telling her again about meeting Sarah Grace and Christopher that Sunday, and how responsible and sweet they'd been. "You are a good mom, Kayla," she said. "I see it in the sparkle in their eyes."

Kayla began to relax.

Then Birdie talked a bit about knitting, suggesting Kayla come into the shop some day, maybe join the young mothers' knitting group. "Izzy has the grandest toy room for kids, everything from trucks and dolls to mini foosball games."

And then she moved on to Dolores Cardozo. "You were friends, I understand," she said. "It's a sad time."

Birdie felt Kayla stiffen but went on, her voice unthreatening, as if talking to a friend.

"Sister Fiona mentioned that you had spent time with her, taking her meals. I envy you in a way. I'm just beginning to know her now, and from what I am learning, I think Dolores Cardozo and I could have been good friends."

Kayla relaxed slightly.

"Did you enjoy taking her meals?"

Kayla didn't answer right away. When she did, it was in a tone that made Birdie think what Charlie Chambers had said might be true: Kayla Stewart didn't lie. Not easily, at least.

"I have two little kids," she said, "so being with them is what is most important to me and what I like best. But doing the volunteer gig was something I told Sister Fiona I'd do. She made it easier, I guess, by assigning me to Dolores." She paused, then said with a slight smile, "Dolores scared the bejesus out of me at first. But then, well, then I didn't mind it so much. Dolores liked the food from the café."

"I don't blame her."

"Right. It's good food." After a moment or two, Kayla said, "I'll miss her. I will. She was a good lady. She was decent."

Decent. It made Birdie wonder if there had been people in Kayla's life who hadn't been decent. She let the comment settle between them for a while. Finally, she said, trying to keep her tone part friendly, part business, "I don't know if you know this, but Dolores left a will. And even though we didn't know each other, she made me executor of it. The will has shown us what her bankers already knew — Dolores wasn't poor, no matter how many free meals she enjoyed at the Bountiful Bowl Cafe." Birdie smiled, easing into the conversation.

Kayla sat with her hands in her lap. She

wiggled the toe of her boot into the dry ground, sending loose pebbles flying low in the air. Birdie watched and realized Kayla's posturing wasn't because she was anxious or nervous or excited, none of the emotions you would expect. It was simply that Kayla wasn't interested in executors or wills. Nor surprised that Dolores Cardozo had money.

"I don't mean to bore you with details, dear," Birdie said. "But you knew Dolores, and —"

Kayla interrupted in a low voice, "I knew Dolores wasn't poor. Not dreadfully poor, anyway."

Not like me, seemed to be insinuated in her words.

Kayla continued. "She kept money in the house."

"The house?"

"Her house. In her stove and cupboard, strange places."

"How did you know that? Did she tell you?"

Kayla was very quiet. She shrugged but didn't answer.

"Well, it doesn't matter. The reason I needed to talk to you was because, as executor, I need to contact the beneficiaries in her will. That means —"

"I know what that means," Kayla said.

Her tone was slightly defensive without being rude, and Birdie realized she had sounded condescending. Birdie was spoon-feeding an intelligent woman.

"I apologize, Kayla," she said. "I didn't put that quite right. I just wanted you to know that you're mentioned in the will. Monday we're having a meeting at the Danvers Bank to distribute it. We'd like all the beneficiaries to be there." She handed Kayla a card with Elliott Danvers's name, the bank's address, and her own cell number scribbled on the back, in case Kayla needed it. "Ben Endicott is an old hand at these things — he knows about the meeting and the will — and he said he'd be happy to give you a lift over and answer any questions you might have. I would recommend you take him up on it, although, of course, that is your decision."

Kayla seemed to be listening, as best Birdie could tell. She took the card and shoved it into her pocket, but when Birdie looked at her face, she saw that the connection between her and Kayla had been broken. Kayla was no longer listening. She was looking beyond her, and beyond the pine trees and white tents into the crowded area near the parking lot. Her face had paled slightly, her jaw clenched, and her eyes were filled with worry. Then just as quickly, Birdie saw a flash of anger in her eyes.

"If you would let Ben know, it would —" Birdie began.

But Kayla had gotten up from the bench. She checked her watch, then mumbled to Birdie that she had to go. Could she tell the others, and watch the kids for a few minutes? Ten minutes, that's all she needed.

And she was gone, disappearing into the crowd, her diminutive form lost among the muscled fishermen and families and townsfolk.

"What's going on?"

Birdie turned to see Charlie standing a few feet away. He walked around the bench and sat down beside her, but his eyes were on the crowd that had swallowed Kayla.

"Were you listening?"

"I just caught the end of the conversation. I wasn't trying to eavesdrop, but it seemed best not to interrupt. Where did she go?"

"I don't know," Birdie answered.

"I talked to the kids over at the Garozzo stand. They're all having a great time. Sam was there with Abby, too. They're hanging on to balloons and have enough carbs stuffed in them to last through the end of the year. Those fritters are poison."

When Birdie didn't answer, her eyes still

combing the crowd, he said, "Is Kayla okay? Iz said you needed to talk to her. If she's looking for her kids, she went in the wrong direction."

"No. She knows where they are. It was something else. She checked her watch like she'd promised to meet someone."

When she looked up, she saw the concern in Charlie's face. "I don't think the meeting was social," she said, her hands curled over the edge of the bench, pushing herself up. "She'll be back shortly."

Charlie shrugged. "Well, let's go back to the kids." He started to take Birdie's arm, then stopped and looked down toward the bench legs. He bent over, picking something up from the ground. "Did you drop these, Birdie?"

He held out an envelope, folded in half and smudged and wrinkled as if it had been scrunched inside a pocket. The letter was puffy, unsealed, and the flap, folded inside, created a gap in the sleeve.

"This was stuck to the envelope." Charlie held out a small piece of cardboard. "It looks like a Danvers Bank business card."

Birdie took the card. "Yes, that's what it is. I just gave it to Kayla. She shoved it into her jeans pocket. It must have fallen out when she stood up."

And so, no doubt, had the envelope. Charlie unfolded it, smoothed it out, and rubbed off the debris. There was no stamp, no address.

He turned it over and the gap in the envelope widened.

"Well, that's a surprise," Birdie said.

It wasn't a letter inside the wrinkled envelope. Instead, the edges of a thin stack of fifty-dollar bills, neatly bound with a rubber band, appeared through the gap.

Birdie and Charlie walked slowly back to the group. In their absence it had grown to include the young Danvers girls and Abby Perry, toddling around on a pair of orange Nikes that Sam had bought her. Daisy Danvers and Gabby had taken it upon themselves to take over child-care duties, ushering them all off to a patch of grass to bat around balloons with sticky fingers and run in wild circles singing songs along with the high school band. Sarah Grace had seemingly fallen in love with little Abby, and sat with her in the center of the noise, carefully braiding pieces of grass into her hair.

"Where's Kayla?" Izzy asked. She looked around. Somehow the possibility of Kayla leaving her children hadn't entirely been cleared from their minds.

"She'll be back in a minute," Birdie said.

But she appeared sooner than that, slightly out of breath and her eyes immediately darting around bodies and over heads, searching for her children. When she spotted them in the field, happy and safe, a mother's look of relief washed over her face. Her mind switched gears almost immediately and she looked around the cluster of adults standing nearby, searching for Birdie. She saw Charlie first, then the small silver-haired woman standing beside him.

They spotted her at the same time and Birdie began walking over to meet her, wanting to spare her any needless worry over the lost envelope.

"Kayla, dear," she said, "I wanted to be sure you got this. I think it fell out of your pocket when you left earlier. Charlie found it beneath the bench."

Kayla looked to Charlie, her brows lifting. "Hi," she said, puzzled at his presence. He handed her the business card and folded envelope.

"It's a little dirty but nothing fell out of it as far as I could tell."

Kayla uttered a hushed sound. It was followed by a thank-you too profound to be explained away by a lost business card. This time she shoved the two pieces of paper into a pocket on the small denim purse strapped across her chest. She closed the zipper tight and managed a smile and another thank-you.

Kayla glanced over at Sarah Grace and Christopher again, running her fingers through her short hair. "When I noticed it was missing, I ran back to the bench, but . . ." She let the rest of the sentence fall to the ground. "Well, anyway, you found it. Thanks. Both of you."

"Yes we did," Birdie said, and suggested they join the others, now cheering the children on as they raced after balloons, trampling the grass into a path that circled Abby and her adoring caretaker, Sarah Grace.

When the children began to fall in heaps, giggling and stretching out, finding animals in the clouds, Birdie suggested they all go over to the Artist's Palate Bar and Grill — just in case Christopher and Sarah Grace hadn't yet tasted the juiciest cheeseburgers in the state of Massachusetts. The children shrieked with joy, including Gabby and Daisy, who testified proudly to Christopher and Sarah Grace that the food really was the best in the state. Izzy added that the grill's outdoor patio would allow Shep to join them at the table — which left no room for refusals, not even from Kayla Stewart, who seemed bewildered by the group of strangers who were scooping up her children as if they had known them their whole lives.

Kayla watched Charlie Chambers gathering up her children and directing them to his car, and she felt a visceral crack inside her — a crack in her carefully constructed privacy. And she wasn't at all sure what to do about it.

CHAPTER 20

"Do we know Kayla any better?" Izzy asked. She'd piled several baskets of yarn on the table, a stack of Xeroxed patterns next to them.

Mae had taken a message the day before from the *Sea Harbor Gazette,* saying that they wanted to interview the knitters. "Knitters Society," Mae had said, lifting her chin and nose in the air. They had promised it wouldn't take long, so Mae had promised an hour, figuring it would be quiet since Seaside Knitting Studio was closed on Sundays.

The knitters were fine with it. An excuse to spend an afternoon surrounded by yarn and each other was not something they'd protest. Add in Adele's inimitable voice singing in the background and a glass of Birdie's Pinot, and they might even forget the kind of week that had absorbed them.

"Kayla is definitely a private person," Nell

said, mulling over Izzy's question.

The hamburger outing had been great fun for the kids, and Kayla had come along, her mood seeming to lighten up at the sound of her children's laughter.

Merry Jackson — the singer in Pete's band and owner of the Artist's Palate Bar and Grill — loved children. She had made her patio deck safe and welcoming, complete with smaller tables, booster chairs, kids' menus, and coloring pads. It was the perfect suggestion, especially for a crowd as big as theirs. The whole group had gone along with Birdie's invitation, unwilling to pull the happy kids apart — the Danvers, Charlie, Gabby, and the usual crew. Merry welcomed them effusively, claiming it was her best early Saturday crowd ever and made a big fuss over everyone.

"And how would that have happened?" Cass said. "With our noisy mob? She barely got a word in."

"I think she was relieved that it was a noisy mob," Birdie said. She pulled a ball of brick red baby alpaca yarn from the basket, rubbed it lightly against her cheek, and then began casting on for a scarf, warm and soft. Her movements were pleasingly automatic, her thoughts somewhere else. "She is very private. I admire her for coming."

"She went along with it because of her children. She could see that the kids were having a great time," Izzy said. "I might not know her any better after being with her yesterday, but I like her better. Those two cuties are the light of her life, and although it wasn't easy for her to be with a crowd she didn't know well, I thought she handled it fine."

"Charlie helped," Nell said. She held up one nearly finished sock, a top-down design with a heel flap and gusset. She'd knit it up in a bright blue and green Leicester wool — soft as cotton candy with plenty of stretch. It would keep someone's toes from turning blue come January.

"I think Charlie helped, too," Birdie said. "Kayla relaxed some when he was nearby."

"So what do you think, Cass?" Izzy asked.

Cass tugged at a strand of chunky yarn, finally pulling it free from the ball. She held up the pattern — chunky, dark gray mittens. "These are going to be huge," she said. "Perfect for some blustery fisherman. Or maybe Aunt Fiona."

They laughed. Fiona did have big hands, but they matched her heart nicely, and even Cass seemed to be appreciating her more these days.

"So?" Izzy said. "You haven't answered

the question. I saw you talking to Kayla for a while before we left the grill."

Cass gave it some thought. "She's smart," she said. "And thoughtful, even though she keeps you at arm's length. She's secretive and a little wary, sure, but mostly I saw the same thing you did, Iz. She loves those kids more than life. And what I really went away with yesterday was bike or no bike, I don't think she could kill anyone, much less Dolores Cardozo — a woman, according to Fiona, who liked Kayla. Never, not in a million years. Not someone who loves her kids that way. She'd never do anything to take her away from them."

Nell was touched by Cass's answer. Although she never talked about having children, she seemed to understand what a mother's love for her children was all about. She glanced over at a large canvas print of Izzy and Sam's Abigail Kathleen and nodded a silent thanks to the toddler. She was teaching Cass well.

The feeling was instinctive, and they all felt it, nodding along with Cass as they worked their needles. No mother would do something that would take her away from her children — maybe forever. It was unthinkable.

But once the emotion subsided and they

went back to knits and purls and working the cuff on a pair of winter socks, a glaring fact remained: Kayla *had* left her children one night. Alone in a house with only the dog, Shep, to bark away intruders.

And for reasons she refused to explain.

With her fingers working magic, Izzy had nearly finished the rib of her squishy hat when Nell wondered what time it was.

"Time, yikes," Izzy said. "I almost forgot."

"So who is this person who's coming over to make us famous?" Cass asked, frustration on her face. She had ripped out her cast-on row three times and now, nearly finished with the cuff, was worried it was time to do it again. A break was in order.

"Maybe Betsy Figlio," Izzy said. "Mae didn't say. In fact, she didn't say anything, except that she'd agreed to it for us. I think she was probably inundated with customers when they called."

"I don't think Betsy does much writing except for editorials," Nell said. "She's a good editor. Smart. Mary had insisted that Pisano uncles or cousins or whoever now owns the papers stop giving all the top editorial jobs to other Pisanos. It was getting incestuous, she said. Betsy has brought fresh life to the paper."

Birdie, having known most of the Pisanos in question chuckled and started to agree, when the jingle of a bell announced someone coming in the front shop door.

Izzy was up and heading that way but stopped before she got to the steps.

"Hey, guys. Is that Adele I hear? That's cool. I like her, too."

His red hair flew in different directions as he flew down the stairs. He held out one hand to Izzy. "You must be Isabel Perry? I'm Richard Pisano from the *Gazette*. Friends call me Richie."

"Well sure you are," Izzy said, grinning and taking his hand. "And you can call me Izzy. Come on in. Welcome to the Seaside Knitting Studio."

But Richie Pisano was already in, bounding over to the table like a kangaroo.

In minutes he had introduced himself to Cass, all the while admiring the thick library table, the baskets of yarn, the cat who was curled up near Birdie's knitting bag, and the three pleasant women staring at him, surprised at the familiar face, so like the one they'd seen for years on television reruns. And looking exactly as Mary Pisano had described him.

"I feel like I know you," Cass said, holding back a grin.

"Okay, sure." He grinned back. "From *Superman*? *Happy Days*? What?"

"Happy days? Oh, sure. *That* Richie. That works," Cass said and they all laughed.

"Good to see you two again," Richie said, turning his smile on Nell and Birdie.

Richie pulled out a chair opposite Birdie and set his iPad and a Coke he'd brought in with him on the table. He sat comfortably, at ease, as if he'd known them all of his life. The fading light from the alley window washed over his face, turning his freckles into late summer tan. He stretched out his legs, his hands clasped behind his head.

"It's really great to be here. Sorry if I was a pest, calling all the time. I think the lady who answers the phone was getting a little tired of me. But it works to be a pest. She finally said yes. Who is she, your agent or something?"

He paused for a breath and they laughed

"Anyway, you gals have a reputation in town so I was like a dog with a bone, wanting to be sure I didn't pass up a good thing." He smiled again, something that seemed to come easily to Richie Pisano. "The Seaside Knitters Society. That's what my editor calls you guys."

"Is that so?" Izzy said, sitting down next

to him. The name was beginning to feel comfortable.

"So, would you guys like to ask me any questions before we get started? Make sure you're comfortable with me?"

"It's not really a question," Izzy said. "I just want to be sure we're on the same page. We were surprised you wanted to do a feature on us — we're not all that interesting — but it's fine, as long as the project we're doing gets nice coverage. That's what's really interesting."

Richie chuckled. "Well, here's the thing. This town has more to offer than being a dot on a map. You just need to scratch your way through the surface and you see all sorts of stuff. You'd be amazed at what I've discovered. That's why I'm here."

"Well, now," Birdie said pleasantly, "that's interesting. I'm not sure how much surface there is to scratch but we'll see. You did a nice job writing about the food pantry. It'll be nice to have Izzy's shop and the knitting pro —"

"You liked the food pantry article, too?" Richie broke in. "That's great. I got lots of compliments on it. I met lots of great people doing that, hanging out over there, and I learned a lot. It helped me steer my ship, plan ahead, if you know what I mean."

"You learned a lot about the Bountiful Bowl, you mean?" Birdie asked. She frowned, expressing the confusion they were all feeling. Richie Pisano was a decent writer, apparently, but his conversation seemed a bit scattered.

"So, here's the thing, Miss Birdie. You have to follow the arrows, catch the way the wind is blowing. Everything leads to something else. You meet people, and they tell you things, lead you to other people, and in between all of that are other projects, more people, interesting tidbits. You collect 'em all. The secret is to just keep your ears clean and your eyes open — and then the whole town becomes an opportunity."

They listened politely, although Richie Pisano's enthusiastic explanation left them wondering what he'd been doing before coming in to the yarn shop.

"What kinds of opportunity are you discovering or looking for?" Nell asked nicely, trying to bring some sense to Richie's talk. "I agree that Sea Harbor is full of opportunity."

Richie leaned forward, his hands flat on the table now, his face serious as he gave the question more attention than Nell had intended. He seemed to be enjoying the chance to be the focus of all their attention.

Finally, he said, "My editor gives me that opportunity to be a better writer by letting me write these human interest stories. Absolutely. She says I'm good at it."

He seemed to blush slightly, but it was difficult to tell beneath the wash of freckles.

"But it also gives me the opportunity to meet people. I do research on people I interview — it's a big part of my work. I'm good at it. It's all so interconnected, you know? One person leads to another and another. It's this huge, widening circle, and in every ring of it there's something to explore, some kind of opportunity for me. You just have to open your eyes. Do you get it?"

There was silence as they tried to process Richie's thoughts. His grin was slightly off and Nell wondered briefly if he was putting them on and everything coming out of his mouth was a joke or one giant tease. Or if there was a point to anything he was saying.

Finally, she asked, "Can you give us an example of what you're talking about? She also said you were very thorough when you wrote the article on the Bountiful Bowl Café a while back. Is that what you're talking about? Did you find opportunities as you worked on other articles?"

Richie grinned. "Yeah, I've written good

articles for the local rag. Better than most, as far as I can tell. And as for opportunities, sure there were mega opportunities. You have to look for them is the thing. But if you do, you'll find them. You dig a little and there it is — a diamond in the rough."

Warming to his subject, Richie went on.

"I thought a few times folks were going to kick me out of those places, like the bank, the soup place, but you just have to know how to treat people and you'd be surprised what doors open. Case in point — the Bountiful Bowl Café. The nun introduced me to Kayla Stewart, and she let me ride shotgun with her while I was doing my research. I got to know Kayla really well. A lot *about* her, too. Interesting gal. You just have to scratch the surface, like I said. And that's when you find it, a diamond in the rough — that was Kayla."

Cass frowned and opened her mouth to say something, then closed it again.

"Are you and Kayla friends?" Birdie asked.

Richie nodded, smiled. "Sure. I know Mr. Endicott gives her rides sometimes. She's had some trouble with her car."

A strange segue, Nell thought. And how did he know Ben gave Kayla a ride? Was Richie Pisano Kayla's boyfriend or was he stalking her? She thought of Charlie, then

288

looked back to Richie.

"So you helped Kayla deliver meals," Izzy was saying. "Did you ever meet Dolores Cardozo while you were doing that?"

"Dolores Cardozo. Wow, now that was a surprise, right? Geesh. Poor lady. Dead. Terrible thing. I was on the graveyard shift that night. It was terrible. I went out to the Cardozo place with Kayla a few times." His fingers were drumming the table as he talked. Nervously, as if talk of murder wasn't why he was there. "But I never met the Cardozo lady. I saw the house from a distance — that was about it. Kayla was pretty proprietary about it all. She made me stay in the car. Dolores didn't like company, she said, and I guess the gal had a BB gun she'd use if people got too close."

"But Dolores didn't mind Kayla coming in?" Izzy asked.

"No, she liked Kayla. They'd talk. I waited thirty minutes one time, checked out the whole neighborhood while I was waiting for her. You know there's a quarry back there? It's cool." He looked down at his iPad and turned it on. "I should stop talking about myself and start asking you guys some questions, right?"

"I have a question first," Cass said. "Opportunities are pretty important to you. Why

289

are you writing about us? What opportunity could we provide — knitting lessons?"

They all laughed, Richie the hardest. Too hard.

Finally, he said, "Hey, you're the Seaside Knitters Society. Cream of the crop. The wonderful ladies who know everything about anything going on in Sea Harbor. Someone told me that you four together were about as close to the beating heart of this place as you could get. And that's where I want to be, too. Close to the heart, feel the beat. Right?"

It was nearly five when they walked Richie Pisano to the shop's front door.

After Cass's question and Richie Pisano's strange answer, the interview had morphed into questions Richie Pisano had carefully constructed, ones that had little to do with the yarn shop and the knitting project that dozens of people were generously participating in. The HMS project to warm the town.

Richie Pisano was more interested in the women organizing it, where they came from, what their husbands, living and dead, had done, what the women themselves had done before . . . well, as he put it, *before knitting*. And how Birdie Favazza ended up in that huge mansion up on the cliff.

The knitters would have none of it. Personal lives were personal. But they did give Richie the story about that Thursday night so long ago that they'd all met in the knitting shop, lured in by Nell's seafood pasta, and had begun a weekly, near sacred tradition that deepened their friendship into the richest colors of a Sea Harbor sunset. How Nell's amazing meals and Birdie's Pinot became as integral to the evening as the piles of soft, fleecy angora and sea silk and fine merino yarn. How they'd sit in front of a blazing fire and knit their hearts out — head-hugger hats for friends with cancer, a wedding shawl for Izzy's wedding, baby booties, prayer shawls, and now, during this glorious fall, how they were joining with all the knitters on Cape Ann to knit hats and mittens and socks and scarves to ensure that everyone on the rocky cape was kept warm and toasty during the robust, windy, and snowy winter to come.

By the time he left, the Seaside Knitters had written their own story for him, nearly word for word.

Richie, who seemed to have snoozed during parts of it, could take it or leave it.

"Was that just an hour?" Cass asked. They watched Richie climb into a bright red Jeep

291

and gun the engine.

"A long hour," Nell agreed.

"That red car clashes with his hair," Izzy said. "The guy has no fashion sense."

Birdie chuckled as they walked back down to the comfort of their knitting room. "I think a recap is in order. Perhaps over that extra bottle of Pinot Gris I brought in last week."

Adele was still singing and in minutes Izzy had the wineglasses out, along with a round of Camembert and plenty of crackers.

"How do you recap that?" Cass asked. "I think we got our story in place, but all that talk that came before it? What was that about? He's weird." She pulled her legs up beneath her on an overstuffed chair, making room for Purl to join her.

Izzy sat down across from her. She'd already finished one floppy winter hat and pulled out a ball of chunky purple yarn for the next. "See this yarn?" She untangled several strands of the cozy wool and cotton blend. "This color is called 'giggle.' That's what I wanted to do halfway through all that talk about *opportunity*. And then just when I thought I might embarrass him by laughing at his sincere monologue, I started to shiver. What he was saying was suddenly not funny."

"And what *was* he saying?" Cass asked without a hint of sarcasm. She shared Izzy's feeling.

"That's the thing," Izzy went on. "I'm not sure. But as personable as Richie Pisano tries to be, he's a little bit scary. He reminds me of a professor I had in law school. He could be charming, but he'd sometimes give these crazy lectures and we'd all walk out wondering what we'd just heard. And then we'd wonder if he'd done it on purpose, just to mess with us."

Nell's fingers were moving, her needles clicking as she worked on the second sock, a strand of bright blue yarn curling up in her lap. "He said he and Kayla are good friends."

"I don't like the idea that he might be Kayla's friend," Cass said, her words drawing smiles, even from herself. "What I mean is, well, I don't know what I mean. It's just a feeling. But the way he said it, how well he'd gotten to know her. Almost like he was bragging about it — all in that nice, friendly, smiley, Jimmy Olsen way. And then all that confusing talk about opportunity. What was that about? I was half sincere when I asked him what he hoped to get from us. It sounded . . . it sounded opportunistic."

They were quiet for the next few minutes,

letting the thoughts settle as Izzy spread Camembert on the crackers and passed them around.

She sat back and sipped her wine. "He went out to Dolores's house with Kayla," she said, taking the conversation in a different direction. "So he knew where she lived."

"He said he never got out of the car — but he knew there was a quarry nearby," Cass added. She looked over at Birdie. "You're being awfully quiet, Ms. Favazza," she said.

Birdie lifted her head, her fingers still playing with the plush red scarf puddling in her lap as it grew longer and longer. "Richie Pisano might be a fine young man, who knows? But he's not what I expected. I suspect his goals aren't exactly those of a cub reporter on a small-town newspaper. He's friendly enough, but that being said" — she looked over at Nell — "I saw your face when he talked about going out to Dolores's house with Kayla. That bothered you. Me too."

Birdie was pulling them back from jumping to conclusions, and she was right to do it. But it was an unusual time, and sometimes suspicions were okay as long as they looked at them from all sides.

"There's something about all his talk that

doesn't sit right," Nell said slowly. "And as he said himself, you have to follow the arrows. I think Richie Pisano knows more than he's saying."

"About Dolores?" Izzy asked.

Nell picked up her wineglass and drank it slowly. She didn't have an answer. None of them did. They were playing with emotions — their reaction to Richie — and with feelings that were scattered and unformed.

But a woman had been murdered. And she wondered briefly, thinking back on the odd interview and Richie's confusing talk, if murder itself might be thought of as an opportunity.

CHAPTER 21

The elegant bank board room was filling up with early arrivals, including many of Cape Ann's nonprofit directors and CFOs, surprised and happy to be included in however small a way, yet awkwardly wanting to express condolences to acknowledge their benefactor's death — a benefactor who was a virtual stranger to most of them.

But there was no one there to accept the condolences — not a daughter or son, a husband, or even a distant relative. In fact, there was no one with the name Cardozo anywhere in the Danvers Bank executive meeting room.

When Father Lawrence Northcutt walked in with Birdie, the popular priest was greeted with hugs and greetings and some relief, the kind a pastor can effect when there is both expectation and uncertainty in the air. He sensed the awkwardness and immediately assumed the role of accepting condolences.

"Dolores was a good person, a generous parishioner we will all dearly miss," he said, and then he spoke individually and in groups about a quiet woman who had already benefited their community — and would continue to do so, even in death.

And finally, when he had people's attention, he said, "Weddings and funerals are the two things that can tear families apart. You toss in inheritances and it can only get more complicated. I'm here to keep the peace." His smile was wide, filling his round face as people nodded to his words.

Marian Brandley, Danny's aunt, came up to Birdie with a huge smile filling her pleasant face. "Now tell me this, Birdie, how in heaven's name did I end up on this list? Isn't this one for the books?" Marian laughed at her own choice of words. Known as "Marian the librarian," the well-loved Sea Harbor head librarian was plainspoken, friendly, and known by every single Sea Harbor Library patron — which included the entire town. Between Marian and her brother, Archie, who owned the Sea Harbor Bookstore, they were unofficially considered Sea Harbor literati. What one hadn't read, the other had. The two also competed regularly as to who had been the biggest influence on Danny Brandley, the success-ful mystery author: his aunt or his father. What wasn't in contention, however, was their unabashed and loving pride for Danny and for each other.

"I was thrilled to see your name. And the library's bequest, too. Every single one of us should remember you in our wills. But it is curious when you scan through the list. I'm sure many people are happily puzzled at seeing their names on it."

Marian's smile was tinged with sadness. "I'm sure that's true. I knew Dolores, though not in one single way that should merit a mention in her will. I'll miss her. I loved watching that keen mind of hers pull things together."

"You noticed that in the library?"

"I did. She was one of my regulars."

"It doesn't surprise me that she was an avid reader, but I'm learning that she avoided crowds. And your library is always buzzing."

"Oh, she signed out books, sure, but her time in the library was spent sitting in her 'office,' as she called it. Not reading."

"Office?"

"One of those small computer alcoves in the research room. They're identical, but Dolores claimed one particular one had good karma. I believe firmly in good karma so I tried to make sure it wasn't in use when Dolores needed it — which was often, especially recently. Once or twice I even shuffled people about when I saw her coming."

"It's odd that she didn't have her own computer."

"They don't get good wi-fi out on Old Quarry Road — but lord, now we know she could have bought her own computer store." Marian chuckled. "Maybe she just liked my Colombian dark roast. I always kept some brewing in the back room for her. It was strong enough to make your hair stand up straight."

"Did you like her?" Birdie asked. Everyone in that room liked Dolores today, of course. But Marian was a straight shooter, kind and honest at once.

She considered Birdie's question, but not for long. "Yes, I did. Dolores was unique, a character, but a decent and very intelligent one. She was even good on computers. She knew her way around the Internet better than Google. Every now and then I'd help out a bit, but not often and usually just with system glitches."

"I'm having a hard time visualizing the Dolores who walked all over Cape Ann with her walking stick with the computer, Dolores. How did she use it? Was she secretly playing FreeCell and reading the *New York Times* like so many of my friends?"

"Dolores? Oh, good grief, no. Dolores came in to work. She was all business. Writing down figures. Calculating something or another. Checking ledgers, programs. This sheet and that sheet. The woman was a human calculator. She was very serious about it. I asked her about it once and she said she both loved and respected numbers. They were sacred and pure, and then she added gravely, 'And they should never ever be abused.' I had a brief fleeting feeling that I had just cheated on a math test and been caught."

Birdie chuckled but tucked the conversation away. From all she'd learned, Dolores Cardozo didn't speak frivolously.

Birdie joined Elliott Danvers on the other side of the room and the two looked over the short agenda, then chatted quietly, with one eye on the door, mentally recording each arrival. Chief Jerry Thompson came in, gave a small wave to Elliott and Birdie, and then followed Tommy to chairs near the back of the room. Beyond the open board room doors people hovered, peering in, then walking on. Bank personnel, Birdie supposed. And by now they probably all knew why the crowd was gathering. When she glanced into the lobby again, she was surprised to see a mop of red hair in the distance.

Richie Pisano was chatting with two young women near the door, but his eyes kept drifting to those inside the room.

Elliott had followed her look. "Our resident reporter. He's everywhere I look. Chumming it up with the staff. Flirting his way across the lunchroom. Hopefully, he'll have his story and be out of here soon. I don't want to offend the *Gazette*'s editor but I wouldn't mind at all offending this kid."

Birdie listened, then looked back to the lobby. The women had moved on, but Richie was still there. His hands were shoved into his pockets and he seemed to be recording attendance — and not especially happy with what he saw.

Kayla Stewart walked with Ben Endicott across the parking lot, his long strides slowing to match her own. Kayla looked up at the sleek glass building in the distance, identified by the tall letters spread across the second story: Danvers Family Bank. The bank building was on the north end of Sea

301

Harbor, anchoring a half circle of office buildings, all landscaped with small trees and pots overflowing with fall mums.

Kayla kept her eyes on the building, one foot moving in front of the other.

She hadn't wanted to come.

Instead, she wanted to turn the calendar back, to forget this was happening and travel back those months to late spring and early summer, to lazy days when she'd pack sandwiches and take the kids to Sandpiper Beach, where she would lie flat on the cool sand, letting Sarah Grace and Christopher bury every inch of her body except for her head and her arms. The kids' high giggles would spin around her, filling her whole being with joy. The days had been simple and easy. She didn't have extra money, but enough. A decent job, generous tips, good days. Happy days. Safe days.

Until they weren't.

But even then, there was a way. There was always a way.

But none of it had gone as she had planned. None of it.

The thought of Dolores Cardozo came to her suddenly. Unbidden and powerful and shattering, as if Dolores herself were standing at the door to the bank building, watching Kayla approach. Tears sprang to her eyes instantly, the cry in her heart as deep and mournful and silent as death.

"Kayla?"

The steady voice of Ben Endicott brought her back to the present. She looked up.

Ben was standing at the heavy glass door, holding it open for her. His face was calm, his manner easy, friendly.

Protective.

"We're here," he said. "It's going to be fine, Kayla."

Kayla looked through the door into the marble lobby. She placed a hand on the flat plane of her abdomen, pressing away the uneasiness.

"Shall we?"

Kayla nodded and walked slowly into the building.

Birdie scanned the group one more time. She stopped when her eyes settled on a familiar, well-built man standing near the bar that held the coffee and rolls. His coffee cup was balanced in one hand, a pastry in the other. Davey Delaney managed to juggle both of them, along with a conversation with Sister Fiona.

More of a monologue, Birdie decided. Fiona appeared to be half listening, her attention directed toward the door. Wondering where Kayla was, Birdie guessed. She checked her own watch. There was still time.

She looked back at Davey. But why was *he* here? According to his mother, Davey was now the top man at Delaney Construction, finally giving his father some well-earned rest. D.J. would never give up the reins entirely, everyone knew that, but at least he was giving his son a chance.

Birdie had known Davey Delaney since before he was born — and the rest of the family longer than that. They were decent folks, including Davey, although she knew from Ben that his volatile temper was often on display at city hall meetings. Davey would come with gloves on, ready to fight when he wanted zoning laws changed or some land reclassified, or a dozen other things that would profit his construction and development company.

But this wasn't city hall, and the Delaney Company wasn't a beneficiary.

And then it came to her. *Of course.* Davey wanted Dolores's land. Badly. Not the house — he would bulldoze that in a New York second. But he'd been fighting for that land near the old quarry for years. The Cardozo land.

· She thought of Joe Duncan and wondered if Davey was one of the riffraff run off by

Dunc's gun. The thought made her smile. Davey wouldn't be intimidated by the crusty neighbor, but the gun? Maybe.

Father Northcutt had seen Davey come in, too. He walked over to Birdie's side. He smiled wryly. "Our friend Davey just wants a heads-up to see who he needs to start sending flowers to so he can get his hands on that land."

Birdie's smile widened at his words, then broke into a laugh, joining Father Larry's deep-throated chuckle.

Davey Delaney was in for a surprise.

She shuffled her papers, looking around once more at several onlookers out in the lobby, more office staff with large curiosities. Mary Pisano's homage to Dolores had stirred up conjectures and a buzz about her estate, a riff in bars and coffee shops. But soon the double walnut doors would be closed and they'd have to wait a few hours before gathering at Coffees or the Gull for the newest wave of rumors.

Ben and Kayla were the last to arrive, just a minute before Birdie and Elliott walked up to a table podium at the front of the room. Birdie made sure her smile reached Kayla before moving to Elliott's side as he welcomed everyone to his bank and reminded them of the coffee and pastries in the back. He explained they wouldn't be there long — it was a simple reading of Miss Cardozo's will. He also welcomed anyone with questions in the days to come to contact himself or Birdie Favazza.

Birdie stood as tall as she could to see over the podium. She explained briefly how it all worked. The will would go through probate before moneys were distributed, but because Dolores Cardozo was not only generous, but a "financial genius," her last will and testament was clean and orderly — and could probably be used as a model for anyone studying estate law in the future.

"Dolores has made my job very simple," she said. "She paid for everything from funeral expenses to taxes ahead of time, leaving no debt." Birdie straightened her glasses and looked at the papers in front of her, then looked up and chuckled. "I mean, how many of you pay your utility bills *forward* for the entire year? And with such an exact calculation that she almost always hit the amount dead-on."

The crowd laughed.

Birdie gave a few more instructions and repeated that she and Elliott would be available to answer questions. There'd be packets handed out to each of them at the end. She was going to skip over the legalese at the beginning of the document so no one was tempted to snooze but suggested they all read it at their leisure when they got home.

The list wasn't as long as the number of people in the room indicated. Some directors had brought their CFOs along, and several individuals had come with a friend or partner. And then there were the uninvited. And the police, whom Birdie judiciously refrained from looking at.

Then she got right down to business, beginning with organizations.

The Bountiful Bowl Café was first on the alphabetized list, and although Father Northcutt and Sister Fiona knew they were benefiting, they both beamed, knowing they would now be able to fix the café's stove, handle the utility bills without worry, hire a manager, and then some.

The list went on, including Dr. Lily Virgilio's Free Health Clinic, where Charlie volunteered, and the adjacent Community Closet — which, thanks to the knitters' HMS project, would soon be filled with hundreds of hand-knit hats, mittens, socks, and scarves. Several small and obscure Cape Ann organizations that most of them had never heard of were not forgotten. The police dispatcher Esther Gibson's initiative to teach incarcerated women how to knit was not forgotten. Esther beamed from her chair in the corner of the room, lifting her eyes from a half-knit hat in gratitude. She'd be in Izzy's shop soon, buying baskets of yarn and needles and courting volunteers along the way. When it came to Marian Brandley's bequest, there was a ripple of applause. Dolores had set aside plenty for the library, but she had also rewarded Marian herself for a lifetime of promoting library use and assisting all those who entered her doors.

Although Birdie had read the will many times in the last couple days, the generosity of the testator continued to move her. Dolores Cardozo was defining generosity in a new way. Selflessly and silently.

"Goodness is everywhere," Birdie said with a catch in her voice. "And Dolores Cardozo seemed to know exactly where to find it."

It might not have been obvious to the recipients, but it was clear to Birdie and Elliott that Dolores Cardozo had not only singled out people doing decent, ordinary things, she had found them through careful *looking,* through attention to life around her.

And also through assiduous effort. Elliott had told Birdie that Dolores had examined the budgets of every one of the organizations; dissected mission statements and annual reports; paid meticulous attention to how moneys were spent, to anticipated expenses and needs — and she had quietly and invisibly probed into the leadership and of each group. In Elliott's opinion, her thoroughness was extraordinary; he wished he could have hired her for the bank's foundation. He had teased her once about being a ghost and listening in on board meetings and decision-making conferences. And she hadn't denied it.

"Yes," Birdie said at one point, removing her glasses and looking out at the gathering, "Dolores Cardozo was an amazing woman. One we won't soon forget. And you, each one of you, are footnotes to her life." Her blue-veined hands applauded those in front of her, and then she put her glasses back on and continued.

Some of the bequests were simply statements of names and amounts; others included wry notes. There were generous gifts to a teenager she'd seen stopping traffic so an old woman could cross a busy street; a woman who came to Dolores's house to wash her hair because she had noticed leaves and dirt in her pretty white hair when she'd walked by the salon one day; a craftsman from Maine who had made her precious wooden cane, carving the handle to fit the curves of her hand; Claire Russell, a fellow vegetarian, who made sure the soup pantry had plenty of organic zucchini and tomatoes at no cost; and a whole host of ordinary folks who had in some way affected either Dolores Cardozo's life or — even more often — someone else's.

Butchers and bakers and walking stick makers.

Birdie took a deep breath, soaking in the spirit of Dolores Cardozo. She examined the faces in the crowd, each with a story to tell. Each with emotions rising to the surface. She hoped Dolores was looking down on it all, seeing what she had set in motion.

Out of the corner of her eye, she spotted Davey Delaney, standing near the coffeepot, fidgeting.

Dolores's house and land were next on the list.

She read it with a smile in her voice: "I give my interest in my property and house at Eight Old Quarry Road, which was my residence my entire life, together with any insurance on such real property, to Sister Mary Fiona Halloran."

There was a slight gasp coming from pockets of the room, then some shuffling of chairs and soft conversation as people looked around for the nun who was now landed gentry, as some would see it.

Sister Fiona sat quietly in her chair, her thoughts unreadable. But a smile played at the corners of her lips. Her head was back, her eyes cast upward, as if she were enjoying a private and playful moment with her friend, Dolores Cardozo.

The reading of the will was nearly finished, one bequest remaining.

Many who were there thought the magnitude of the bequests already announced would deplete any Sea Harbor estate. Whatever was left would be trivial, a small trust, perhaps for a pet or her church. People began turning in their seats, talking with neighbors, readying themselves to call relatives — others to send happy texts to board members and staff. Everywhere there were smiles on the faces of good, simple people, surprised at their sudden fortune — and inordinately grateful.

Birdie ignored the background din, her heart growing heavy as she looked over at Kayla Stewart. Kayla sat still, her face unreadable, her eyes not leaving Birdie's face. Would this be a blessing or a burden she was placing on this young mother's shoulders? Dolores had planned for it so wisely, almost as if Kayla were her own daughter. She had appointed trustees to guide Kayla for several years — to help keep her inheritance safe — after which Kayla would manage on her own. But no matter how many protections Dolores had built in, her life-altering gift to the young mother of two could carry with it a burden of suspicion, a motive for murder, that Dolores Cardozo never anticipated.

Birdie cleared her throat and then began to read the words that would change lives.

"I give, devise, and bequeath the remainder of my estate, consolidated entirely into a trust fund of stocks, bonds, annuities, and other investments, to Kayla Stewart. . . ."

By the time Birdie finished reading the bequest, including the stipulation that she and Elliott Danvers would serve as trustees to the trust, people had moved on, excited at their good fortune, and with only a few of them aware of the significance of the final bequest.

But Kayla Stewart had heard every word of it, her face impassive, her body still, unresponsive.

Kayla Stewart — who had walked into the glass-fronted Danvers Family Bank an hour before without ever having had a savings account anywhere — walked out of the bank a short while later a wealthy woman.

CHAPTER 22

There was nothing Ben could say to stop the tears.

Kayla had climbed into his car and doubled over, and started to cry. It was a sound that would ring in Ben's head for days — an inconsolable heart-wrenching sound.

Finally, Kayla straightened up, accepted the box of tissue that Ben handed her, and fastened her seat belt. The tears had continued on the drive home, her sobs quieter, with slow breaths in between.

When they arrived at the house, Ben turned off the engine and sat quietly, waiting.

Kayla looked out the window, as if not sure where she was. Then she pulled herself together and sat back, her head pressed against the seat. She breathed deeply, steadying herself, pulling tissues from the box. Finally, she rolled her head to the side and looked at the patient man sitting in the driver's seat.

"I'm twenty-nine," she said. Her voice was hoarse, thickened by crying.

Ben smiled. One hand rested on the top of the steering wheel. "Old lady," he said. "But well preserved."

Although her lips tried to return the smile, the effort was blurred by a new stream of tears that rolled across her cheekbones, around a single dimple in one cheek, the rill collecting near her chin before it fell like raindrops. She reached for the door handle but her eyes were still on Ben.

Her hand dropped. "I thought I had it figured out," she said, her voice rough with tears. "My life. Sea Harbor. A good place, a good life . . . a good . . ."

She stopped, sputtered, searching for words. "What Dolores Cardozo did . . . what she did for me . . . it . . . the . . ." She stopped, the words never making it to a sentence and falling flat as she reached for another tissue and blew her nose. "Why?" she asked, her words muffled by the tissue.

"Why?" Ben asked.

Kayla met his eyes and held them. "Why is this . . . this gift from a kind and generous and wonderful dead woman, why is it killing me? Why is it turning into a curse?"

CHAPTER 23

Ben walked into the yacht club dining room and looked around. He was late for lunch, half expecting an empty room. But as always, there were those who lingered, resisting real-world responsibilities as they sat with a view of the sea and the club's signature sandwiches and salads, chowders or soups lulling them into two-and sometimes three-hour lunches.

Ben wouldn't be one of them — nor would the women he was meeting. He hoped they had waited for him.

He spotted Nell's waving hand and wound his way quickly to a table for four along the side of the room.

"Sorry I'm late," Ben said. "I had to answer some calls." He kissed the top of Nell's head and smiled across at Birdie and Cass.

A bowl of clam chowder sat at the empty place and Ben eyed it hungrily. He sat down and snapped his napkin onto his lap.

"I've told Cass and Nell about the bank meeting," Birdie said. "Now it's your turn with what came after. Is Kayla all right?"

"Frankly, I don't know. Charlie texted me wondering the same. I suggested he stop over there, just to make sure everything's okay. It's a lot to process and Charlie's a good listener."

"Birdie said her reaction was strange," Cass said. "I get it, all the thoughts that must be running through her head. When old man Finnegan left me all that money a few years ago, I wanted to kneel down and thank the lord for saving the Halloran Lobster Company. But in the next breath I wanted to run away. I knew what was coming. When your benefactor has just been murdered, inheriting brings a whole lot more with it than money."

Ben nodded and slowly spooned up his chowder.

"Izzy said she's already heard snippets about the will," Birdie said. "Rumblings in the shop. Esther Gibson came in and filled her in a little. I wasn't sure how many heard about the bequest made to Kayla, but Esther had. She was curious — and surprised."

"Everyone will be, I imagine," Nell said.

"I'm not sure Kayla was," Ben said, drawing puzzled looks.

Birdie stirred her coffee. "Well, she knew why she was there, that she was mentioned in the will. The enormity of it was probably a surprise."

"Sure. I don't mean that exactly," Ben said. He took another spoonful of chowder and smiled a thanks to Nell. The yacht club's wine-laced soup was not what she'd usually order for her cholesterol-conscious husband. She was indulging him, figuring comfort food might be in order, and he knew it.

"Are you saying she knew there was a trust?" Birdie asked. "I'm not sure how she could have known. In fact, even Elliott isn't sure yet about the exact amount of the trust. There are a few bank investments that haven't been calculated."

"But it's considerable?" Cass said.

Birdie nodded and then she turned to Ben. "Are you thinking Kayla knew about it ahead of time?"

Ben thought about the question, not answering it directly. Instead, he said, "Maybe. And maybe this is just a feeling I have that I should shake off."

"Before you shake, explain your feeling," Birdie said.

"All right, here it is. Imagine that you are

Kayla Stewart and someone tells you that you are included in a will written by a woman you did a few nice deeds for — taking her food, whatever. What would you think she might leave you in her will?"

Birdie considered the question, remembering Kayla's reaction when she'd talked to her at the market. It seemed appropriate according to Ben's hypothetical. "Something small. I suspected Kayla thought that, too. In fact, when I told her about the meeting at the market last Saturday, she wasn't very interested in it. I had trouble holding her attention. She had something else on her mind. I was concerned she might not even show up."

Ben chuckled. "So that's why you insisted I drive her over? I was the watchdog to make sure she got there?"

Birdie laughed. "Yes. And you are a splendid watchdog, Ben Endicott."

The waitress cleared the plates and brought fresh coffee and a plate of lemon bars. When she had walked off, Cass said, "Ben, something is going on in your head. You're not usually the suspicious type."

Ben poured a few drops of cream into his coffee. "You're right, and I'm not very good at it. It's an impression I had, that's all, nothing more. And it wouldn't hold up under much scrutiny. *Any* scrutiny, in fact. Besides, I'm hoping I'm wrong."

"But something made you think that way," Nell said. The irony of the situation didn't escape any of the women sitting around the table. Impressions were valuable and even sacred to them, something Ben sometimes warned them about. Impressions and emotions didn't convict people, he'd said more times than they could count.

"It was the way she reacted. I was sitting next to her through the whole reading of the will, close enough to feel any sudden movements, vibes. Kayla listened to everything in complete silence, not commenting or taking notes, as some others around us were doing. That's her way, I think. Quiet and attentive. She seemed almost invisible, or at least wanting to be."

He looked at Birdie and continued. "But when you finished reading the list of the beneficiaries and moved on to the trust — with Kayla as the sole beneficiary — she didn't move a muscle. No movements, not even an involuntary twitch. No changes in breathing, no gasps, no indication of surprise, nothing. Others reacted plenty to their good fortune — happy gasps, congratulations to one another, even some scattered applause when their favorite foundation or charity got a boost. But when Kayla heard that she was the recipient of a sizable trust fund, she didn't make a sound."

They found themselves nodding along with Ben's words. Imagining the scene. Then frowning. The image of a woman finding out that her life and her children's lives were about to change in a way other people might dream about was not what Ben was describing.

"Do you think Dolores might have told her before she died?" Nell asked. She spoke the words slowly, hoping Ben's answer would wipe that possibility off the table. Kayla's narrow shoulders were already carrying more than their share of suspicion in the Cardozo murder.

Ben took a small lemon bar and finished it before answering. He wiped the sugar from his hands. "That was my thought — no, my fear — too. Like Cass said, being named in the will of someone who has been murdered arouses suspicion. And when you add Kayla being at the scene, it moves her closer to the front of the line.

"But," he said, his tone a bit lighter, "I talked to Fiona on my way over here and she seemed relatively sure that Dolores wouldn't have told her. There wouldn't have been reason to, for starters, and she added that it wasn't the way Dolores did things. I wasn't sure what that meant, but I called Elliott Danvers, and he said the same thing. Dolores wanted her affairs kept private. They'd talked about it only days before she died. I don't think Fiona even knew about the will before Dolores died. And she was probably her closest friend."

"She may not have known about Kayla's trust, but Aunt Fiona told my ma that she and Dolores talked about the Cardozo land sometimes, ideas for its use. I doubt that part of the will surprised her."

"I suppose that means that Davey Delaney doesn't need to send Fiona roses?" Birdie asked.

Ben laughed. "Probably not, though it takes a lot to deter a Delaney."

"He's no match for my aunt," Cass said.

"So if not Dolores, then who could have told her?" Nell asked.

"Or when," Birdie said, the thought causing her to push away the last remnant of her lemon bar. Her appetite seemed to have taken a shift.

Ben had no idea. Birdie, Cass, and Nell kept their thoughts quiet.

"And again," Ben added, "this thing with Kayla is just an impression, not a fact. I hope she didn't know. But you know everyone in that room will probably be asked that question. Dolores was murdered. Money is the oldest motive in the books."

Nell watched Ben, seeing concern beneath the tired eyes. "There's something else, isn't there?" she said. "What did Kayla say about the will when you drove her home?"

Ben's reply came slowly, as if he himself didn't completely understand what he was about to say. He looked out the window at the billowing clouds, the stark white sail of a lone boat heading out to sea. Finally, he shifted his attention back to the table.

"I'm not sure how to answer that. I'll try, though, because I think Kayla needs our support and our help, although I'll be damned if I know what that is and how we do it."

And then he repeated what had happened once he and Kayla were alone in his car.

When Ben was finished, Nell and Birdie sat quietly, pulling apart his words and their own confused thoughts.

Cass got up and walked to the wall of windows framing the sea, her hands shoved in the pockets of her jeans, her own experience floating around on the edges of Kayla's. *A curse.* Cass understood.

Ben stood and rotated his shoulders, his head working out the kinks. He picked up the check and told Nell he'd bring fresh fish home for dinner, then headed across the dining room.

Nell watched him walk around the tables toward the hostess station, his steps slowed by thoughts of Kayla Stewart. She knew that he had a meeting over at city hall, he had said, but being this close to the *Sea Dreamer* would encourage a detour and she wasn't surprised when he walked out the side door and headed toward the pier instead of to his car. He'd go to the slip, if only to lean against the hull of the forty-two-foot sailboat — and his day would become calmer because of it.

Birdie suggested she needed something to clear her head, fresh air maybe.

No one resisted and they collected their sweaters and walked out the sliding back doors, across the empty patio, and down a set of stairs to the beach and the welcoming arms of ocean air and smooth sand.

"Hey, there. We meet again. Same place, even."

Hannah Swenson was waving and heading toward them from the opposite direction. She wore a sailing hat, shorts, and a T-shirt with *Seaside Initiative* silk-screened across it in rainbow colors. Her blond hair was loose today, escaping beneath the hat and blowing across tan and toned bare shoulders.

"I just saw Ben," she said. "From a distance. Just to wave."

"Down at the slips?" Nell asked.

"Yes, headed toward his boat, I think. He was deep in thought or I'd have stopped him to let him know I finally bit the bullet. I bought a small sailboat — not as fancy as his, but it's nice. I was checking it out today, hence the unusual getup." She looked down the length of her body. "Not my usual navy blue suit."

"But more comfortable," Birdie said. "You're a sailor? Is there anything you don't do, Hannah Swenson?"

"Oh, yes. Lots of things, Birdie. Confession? I don't sail. Crazy, right? But my son, Jason, does. This sweet dinghy will make the most wonderful early Christmas gift for him."

"What? Wow. That's putting it mildly," Cass said. "Lucky son."

"He works hard," Hannah said, pushing a silky strand of hair from her cheek. "He's a wonderful son. He deserves it."

"You look more relaxed than when we saw you the other day," Nell said. "This is a wild guess, but is the board retreat over?"

Hannah laughed. "It is. It's off my calendar for another year. Hurray. And it went well. I was able to announce a few new grants approved recently and the board promised to bring some heavy hitters to an event I'm planning. We may get the new office furniture we need. Better computers. Workshop leaders. The struggle for donations is always out there, as you well know, Nell. The bigger the donor, the better," she said.

"The only trick is finding them," Nell said with a smile. "It's the endless plight of a nonprofit. But when you do good things, the money will come in. It's worth all that begging in the end, right? I'm glad things are coming along. Good for you."

Hannah blushed slightly, dipped her head, then waved a good-bye and headed for the patio, her long, toned legs taking the steps easily.

The others turned and continued their walk down to the water's edge, the cool sea breeze ruffling hair and cooling their arms and faces, the warm sun soothing the chill away.

"Ma calls this feeling 'Baked Alaska,' " Cass said. "Cold and hot. Just like the dessert."

Nell chuckled, then realized Birdie was no longer beside them. She turned around.

Birdie was standing where they'd left her, watching Hannah Swenson disappear across the patio.

Nell frowned. "Birdie?"

Birdie turned around, scolding herself with a shake of her head, and headed toward them, kicking up sand as she hurried. "I'm sorry, dears. I was lost in thought for a moment."

"You're thinking about this job you've taken on, aren't you?" Nell asked. "You know the one — the job that was going to be simple and easy. But somewhere between *simple* and *easy* it took a turn. At least on the emotional front."

Birdie smiled. "No, honestly, Nell, managing Kayla's trust with Elliott will be a pleasure and a privilege. I like that family. And the fact that it will provide financial security for those beautiful children brings me joy. Actually, I was thinking about Hannah Swenson."

"She has a difficult job, that's certain, but Hannah is enterprising and it sounds like new donors are stepping up," Nell said.

Birdie nodded. "I was on the board a few years ago, before Hannah was director. The Seaside Initiative does good work. The excellent workshops that you did for them is a case in point. What happened to those?"

"The funding dried up for that project. That's the challenge of nonprofits. The Seaside Initiative relies on grants and the generosity of donors to run effectively."

Nell looked up toward the clubhouse. Hannah had disappeared from sight.

"Perhaps it's just the kind of day I've had that's making me acutely aware of the impact generous people like Dolores Cardozo have on nonprofits," Birdie said. "Wealthy donors are necessary to the life of those organizations."

Nell nodded. "That's certainly true. Donors are important for their survival."

Birdie nodded. "Hmm." She looked up toward the clubhouse again and this time she spotted Hannah, standing with a glass of water in her hand, talking with a group of women in tennis attire. "I had a question for Hannah. But it looks like she's met up with friends."

Nell looked up at the women, the attractive director in their midst. She glanced at Birdie, climbing into her thoughts.

"I'll ask her the next time I see her. We seem to be running into her with some regularity. Shall we go?"

She looped her arm through Nell's and the three women continued down to the water's edge.

CHAPTER 24

Izzy sat in the backseat of Nell's CRV. She was humming along to some eighties tune on the radio, one she couldn't identify. She watched the trees passing by the window. They were close enough to touch, their edges starting to turn, some already a brilliant orange or red. She opened the window a crack, breathing in the crisp fall smell as it floated around the car, creating welcoming images of bonfires and thick cotton sweaters.

In the back of the car, boxes shifted around. Izzy glanced over her shoulder. "I hope we have room for everything."

"We will," Nell said.

The Seaside Knitting Studio had free classes booked all day for those knitting for the HMS drive, helping knitters turn heels in socks and loop colorful lace designs into scarves. At Mae's urging, Izzy had agreed to take some of the completed items out to the Clothing Closet to free up space in the yarn shop's back room.

"Don't fret, Izzy. There's no mess too big for the likes of us," Birdie said. She sat in the front seat beside Nell, well into her third shale pleated scarf. She was working this one up in a brilliant blue wool alpaca blend. She fingered the little pleated pockets in the scarf and smiled at the pleasure a clever design and beautiful yarn created. The simple things in life.

Nell turned the wheel sharply to avoid a skunk meandering across the road. Worrying about a mess in a clothing center was a nice reprieve from the other messes facing them — the more complicated mess of wills and abandoned bikes and the murder of a generous woman who spent her life doing good things without anyone knowing about it.

Cass sat in the backseat next to Izzy. It was a workday for her, but Izzy had convinced her to take a break — they needed her brawn to move some boxes, she'd said. But mostly they'd all felt the need to be together, to sort through the uncertainty that hovered over them, begging for clarification. Muddled thoughts about an inheritance, two innocent kids, and a murdered woman who had, for reasons that were anything but clear, tried to make Kayla Stewart's life easier, her children's lives more secure.

"I think maybe Charlie is volunteering at the free clinic today," Izzy said, looking up ahead as the car slowly took the curves along the narrow road. She squinted at the sunlight filtering through the trees and slanting across the windows of the car.

"We'll look for him, then," Birdie said. The Sea Harbor Free Health Clinic was in the same wing of the Anja-Angelina Community Center as the Clothing Closet, both in comfortable quarters deemed to be even more comfortable and efficient once Dolores Cardozo's moneys were distributed.

They rounded the last bend in the road. The trees fell back and the land spread out in front of them, a clearing anchored by a magnificent lodge with pine walls, high ceilings, and tall panels of glass that brought the woods and sunshine inside the spacious rooms used to host many community events and parties. *A community center like no other,* the Chamber of Commerce boasted in vacation flyers.

Although located within the town limits of Sea Harbor, the lodge and natural reserve had the feeling of being far away from everything. It was a magnificent refuge, a place to escape with the sounds of wind and wildlife and ocean waves providing a background symphony.

It was a place to think.

Nell parked in the circle drive near the health clinic and Clothes Closet wing, and together they pulled the boxes out of the back and lugged them into the shop.

The clothing center was open today but empty of people except for Esther Gibson, the police dispatcher, who sat in an old rocking chair near one of the windows, letting the sun's rays warm her arthritic knees. Her cane was beside her on the floor and an open knitting basket sat at her side. "I was about to drift off, but for you, dear ladies, I'll keep these tired eyes open."

"It's very quiet in here," Izzy said, walking over and giving Esther a hug. "What did you do with everyone?"

"I ran them off." Esther chuckled. "I always snag this time to volunteer because I don't have to do anything but sit here and knit."

"Or snooze." Cass laughed.

Nell fingered a lacy dress on a mannequin near the window. Laura Danvers probably donated it, she thought, checking out the designer label. The whole shop was a fashionable boutique, complete with mannequins sporting T-shirts and jeans and dresses, small curtained dressing rooms along one side, and a vase of fresh flowers at the checkout counter. The only thing missing was a cash register or credit card reader. Everything was free.

"I love this place," Cass said as she dropped into a comfortable faded chair across from Esther. She pointed to the brilliant orange hat with snowflakes scattered around the rim that was lying on Esther's ample lap. "Esther, that is one cool hat."

"I brought in a bunch of these hats that my ladies knit up for the warmth project." *Her ladies,* they all knew, were women in the addiction center adjacent to the jail.

Esther reached into a box in front of her and pulled out another. A fluffy angora baby hat. "Isn't this the softest thing you've ever seen? Probably knit by someone who has a little one somewhere, just waiting for her mom to get back to her." Esther's voice was cheery, but the affection she felt for her ladies clearly informed her words.

"It must be wonderful therapy for the women," Birdie said. "You're a genius for starting this program."

Esther laughed. "Oh no, there's no genius in the Gibson family. The genius is all Sister Fiona's. Those Hallorans are smart, you know." Her eyes twinkled as she looked over at Cass. "And kind, too."

Cass's response was lost in the sound of heavy footsteps. They all turned their heads toward the door.

"Hey, I thought I saw a familiar car out there." Charlie Chamber strode across the room, his white medical coat flapping against his jeans.

Izzy looked at the jacket in amazement. It was covered with colorful doodles and cartoons, tiny faces and names in a child's scrawl. Then she gave her brother a hug. "Nice jacket. Did you spill spaghetti on it?"

"It's a collector's item, one of a kind," he said. "Patients' art. They doodle on my jacket with permanent markers. And no, you can't have it." He eyed the kolaches sitting next to the coffeepot. "You brought those for me, right, Esther?"

Esther's laugh came out in a rumble.

Charlie looked tired, Nell thought. He was worried about something, too. Of course he was. Although she didn't know exactly what his feelings were for Kayla Stewart, she knew there was a connection there that was strong enough to worry him.

He met her glance, read the concern on her face, and, as he always did, immediately disavowed it with an "I'm fine" grin. "So what are you guys doing out here?" He looked around at the boxes.

"What are we doing right this minute?" Birdie asked back. "Right this minute we are learning that Esther's knitting project with the women in the jail was masterminded by Fiona."

"Fiona? That's no surprise. That nun has her hands in everything," Charlie said. "Even Cass's love life."

Cass threw darts at him.

"Fiona brought some kids in today for their vaccinations because the moms were working," he said. "She's sitting in the clinic playing Old Maid with them right now." He helped himself to a poppy seed kolache and half sat on the deep window ledge. "Fiona may have stolen that knitting idea, though. I remember hearing about a program like that somewhere else in one of my travels. And Birdie's right, it's great therapy."

"Maybe Fiona started that program, too," Esther said. "She worked with women with addiction problems someplace before she came back to Sea Harbor. You all knew that, right?" Esther said.

Cass was quiet, slightly embarrassed that Esther knew more about her aunt than she did. She knew Fiona had been principal in several different places, wherever her order needed her to be. But knowledge of her aunt's work was scanty, mostly confined to letters that arrived at the Halloran Lobster Company asking for donations for some cause or another. Cass's dad had always supported his younger sister's charities, so Cass did the same.

Nell realized she didn't know much about Fiona's missions, either. Or maybe she did and had forgotten. Mary Halloran had mentioned once that her sister-in-law had come back to Sea Harbor after the place she was running ran out of money. But she hadn't expanded on it. And Fiona herself seemed much grounded in the present rather than talking about the past.

On the other hand, Esther was the kind of magical grandma figure who elicited talk and secrets from even hardened criminals. Perhaps it was the endless hours she spent at the jail, but whatever it was, it surprised no one that Fiona talked things over with her, and suggested the knitting program for the women's jail.

"Where was the program she was involved in?" Charlie asked. He licked a drop of filling from his finger.

"Somewhere out west. One of those states beyond the Mississippi. South Dakota, maybe?" Esther said. Then she shook her tight gray curls, as if scolding herself. "No, no, no. It was where they have the potatoes."

"Like grow them?" Charlie asked. "Idaho?" His brows lifted into a wayward hank of hair.

"That's it," Cass said. "Potatoes sounds familiar. Lots of corny jokes about potatoes."

"Idaho," Charlie repeated. He was listening intently, as if Fiona's coming home from Idaho, with or without potatoes, was somehow interesting. Important, maybe. "Idaho is quite a place," he said, and then concentrated on his kolache. He checked his watch.

"Are you leaving?" Cass asked.

"I want to catch Fiona before she leaves. I need to ask her why potatoes make good detectives." He grabbed a napkin and the last kolaches and headed toward the door.

"Why?" Cass knew she shouldn't ask, knew it before the word was out. She ignored Izzy's warning scowl.

"Because they keep their eyes peeled." Charlie grinned and disappeared down the hall.

With Esther's help, it took less than an hour to figure out where and how they'd display the knitted items, samples of each category displayed on tables, then hundreds more would be hanging on colorfully painted pegboards. The yarns alone would turn the Clothing Closet into an explosion of color. A winter of warmth was ahead.

The thought warmed them all.

Esther began packing up her knitting and making a move to leave. "No one will be coming in at this hour, I don't expect, but if you'd kindly lock the door when you leave and drop the key at the Free Health Clinic next door, I'd be grateful."

"Night shift?" Birdie asked, helping Esther into a heavy cable knit cardigan she had knit during long hours in the dispatcher's office.

Esther nodded. "Home first to check on the hubby. Then off to the station."

"May it be a quiet night," Birdie said.

Esther nodded. "I've had my excitement for the year."

"Of course you have," Birdie said.

"Were you on duty the night Dolores died?" Izzy asked.

Esther nodded.

"Did you know her?"

"I knew her well enough to know she was a good woman who didn't deserve to die that way."

"She recognized the good you do, Esther," Birdie said, smiling. "Not only the bequest, but her comments about the knitting project were lovely."

"Yes, they were. Somehow Dolores heard about the program — probably from our Fiona. And then low and behold she turned up at the station one day, walked all the way over from her house near the old quarry. Can you believe that? Just this skinny woman with a giant walking stick. And not sweating a bit as far as I could tell. We got on, the two of us. Maybe it was comparing my cane to her walking stick that did it. But she didn't come for talk; she came because of the knitting program in the jail. She asked me lots of questions about it, where the money came from —"

Esther laughed at her own words, and the others laughed along with her. They all knew where Esther got the money to buy the yarn and needles and the food and drink she'd bring along to the ladies in the jail. She got it from her own paycheck and from pleas to Sea Harbor's policemen, and from any friends, including those in the room right then, who happened to ask her how it was going.

Few could say no to Esther Gibson.

"And now, low and behold, we have this big pot of money at our disposal. The boys at the station cheered when they heard the news, thinking incorrectly that they'd be off the hook to donate." She looked at Izzy. "You can bet I'll be buying up a storm in the shop, Izzy."

"We'll be ready and waiting." Izzy handed Esther her cane.

The others went back to moving boxes while Nell walked Esther out to her car, ignoring the police dispatcher's insistence that she could get there just fine by herself.

Nell held the center's heavy wooden door open while Esther and her cane made it through, then down the steps. As they approached the pickup truck that Esther and her husband shared, Nell paused before opening the door. "Esther, I'd like your opinion on something."

"Well, dear Nell, you know I have plenty of those." She opened the door herself and threw her cane into the cab, then leaned one elbow against the open door.

"It's about that new reporter. Someone told me he's been hanging around the station, so I'm assuming you know him."

"Richie. That's who you mean. Mary Pisano's cousin so far removed she sometimes forgets which relative bore him. A plucky lad. He's everywhere, isn't he?"

"He seems to be."

"At first his charm got to me along with

others at the station so we allowed him to hang around, drinking coffee in the break room, taking pictures now and then. He was funny, mostly polite and very talkative. But once that top layer wore off, we discovered the young man could be pretty full of himself. It's probably not his fault. Who knows what kind of a childhood he had? So much begins there, in those early years."

"Do you think he was hanging around the station waiting for a crime to happen? Hoping maybe? Something to write about?"

"Oh, no, dear. I don't think that. I have come to suspect that Richie Pisano has agendas that don't have much to do with journalism. If truth be known, I think Richie is more interested in being rich than being a journalist. Perhaps he was aptly named. But that might be me watching too many TV shows. No matter, we all soon tired of his comments, his poking around, the personal questions. He told me recently he was on a quest to research the wealthiest people in Sea Harbor. Who says that sort of thing?"

Nell frowned. "I agree. That's a bit odd. When did he say that?"

Esther pulled herself up into the cab and sat back in the driver's seat, catching her breath and thinking. "Well, that's a good question. It was before Dolores died, I think. I remember because he mentioned Dolores that day, too. Wondering what we knew about her. We all wondered how he even knew her name since few people did."

She closed the door and started up the engine, her jaw set, upset all over again at Richie's impertinent questions and comments. She leaned on the window frame, the flesh of one round arm hanging over the edge, and looked at Nell. "Some of my guys in blue said he reminded them of some television character, Superman's friend or someone like that. He reminded me of one, too. Remember the old *Leave It to Beaver* show?"

Nell nodded.

"He's Eddie Haskell."

When Nell walked back inside the center, she spotted Charlie down the wide hallway, just outside the free clinic waiting area. He was leaning against the wall cradling a mug of coffee. But he wasn't drinking it. Instead he was staring out the window opposite him, his face a collage of emotions.

Nell walked over to his side.

Charlie seemed not to notice.

"Charlie," she said softly, trying not to startle him.

But she had. Coffee sloshed over the side of the cup, rivulets joining the colorful artwork covering his jacket.

"No one will even notice," Nell said, pulling a tissue from her pocket and blotting it up. "In fact, it looks perfect on top of that little head some child drew. A lovely blob of tan hair."

Charlie smiled and set the mug on a table.

"Ben told me he sent you over to see Kayla after the reading of the will," she said. "She was quite emotional, he said. I hope she's all right. I suspect that's what's on your mind?"

"She's on my mind, sure. And yeah, Uncle Ben told me about her reaction to the whole thing. She seemed anguished, he said. *Anguished.* It doesn't compute. But in a way it does. She's a smart woman. She knows she's in the middle of a murder investigation — and she has two beautiful kids she thinks about constantly. I guess Uncle Ben thought maybe she could use a friend."

"He said she seemed burdened. I hope she was able to share it with you, somehow lessen that emotion. You're good at that, Charlie."

He waved off the compliment but admitted that for some strange reason, she did seem to talk to him more openly. "Some-

342

times she tells me to get lost, but other times, she loosens up. It's as if we're kindred spirits in some odd way. So I went by, but I didn't get a chance to talk to her. So I don't know what she's thinking."

"Was she working?"

"No, she was home. I parked across the street and started to get out of the car, but then I saw movement through the door. She wasn't alone."

"Fiona, maybe? I'm sure she was concerned about her, too."

"No. It was a man. They were standing on the other side of the screen door, in the front hallway."

"Who was it?"

He shrugged. "It was shadowy and the guy had his back to me." Charlie picked up his mug again, the coffee cold now, and drank it down in a single swallow. "I saw his car, though. It was parked right in front of her house." He looked back out the window.

Nell looked out, too. It's what one did at the park. Lose your thoughts in what surrounded you. Long, late afternoon shadows falling across the lawn and parking lot. A flock of gulls flying in wide circles near the path to the beach, and closer to them leaves dancing across the parking lot.

Peaceful. Untroubled. Not at all matching

her nephew's face. "Charlie, what is it?"

He shrugged. "Something's not right over there, Aunt Nell."

She agreed. Kayla Stewart was a mystery. And without anyone planning it, she had become *their* mystery. Charlie's, Ben's, Cass's, all of theirs. Their responsibility, in some undefined way.

"What kind of a car was it?" Nell asked. Something was niggling at the back of her mind. An uncomfortable itch.

"One of those old Jeeps. It might be the same one I saw careening around the corner that first night I went over there. You know what I mean — canvas top, no door. I had one in high school."

Was it red?" Nell asked.

She felt Charlie's nod before she saw it.

"Yeah. Blood red."

CHAPTER 25

Birdie was the one who suggested that she and Nell take some of her housekeeper Ella's muffins out to Joe Duncan and his wife, Marlene. When Danny Brandley heard they were headed to the Cardozo neighborhood, he asked to go along.

"I knit," he reminded them as he climbed into the back of Nell's car. "That gives me some credentials to tag along with you two."

"Not to mention the lure of a murder scene," Nell said.

He'd never be turned away, of course. Danny was one of Nell and Birdie's favorite people. Nor would they mention that his knitting expertise had been stalled on knit stitches for two years. The plethora of plain-looking scarves his generous father wore all winter were proof and added questionable doubt to his assurance that purling was just around the corner.

"Now tell me why we're going out to the

Cardozo place?" Danny asked, settling in.

"We're taking Ella's blueberry muffins to a neighbor. The muffins are still warm. And they're magical."

"In what way?" Danny eyed the Tupperware container sitting beside him. He quietly pried open a corner of the container.

"In every way, you'll see. Now close the muffin lid, please."

Danny laughed. In his mind, Birdie was the one who was magical. "Are you a witch?" he asked. "I could use a witch in one of my mysteries."

"A witch, hmm." Birdie pondered the thought and told him she would let him know.

"I haven't seen that old quarry since I was a kid," Danny said, watching the small Sea Harbor neighborhoods fall away. The road grew narrow and winding, lined now with copses of hemlock and maple trees, clumps of shadbush and catbrier squeezed in between. Every now and then a small house was visible behind unkempt foliage.

They drove in comfortable silence, around the bends in the road and up and down hills. A light breeze and warm, plentiful sunshine filled the car. "Ah, peace," Birdie said. "Nature has its way of feeding our spirits, clearing our minds."

From the backseat, Danny felt it, too. He nodded, his thoughts moving like his stories sometimes did, unplanned, unpredictable, revealing. Or not. He leaned back, closed his eyes, and thought of Cass crawling out of bed that morning. She'd gotten up early to watch the sunrise. He had heard her get up and watched from the bed as she stood at the windows, watching the light come up over the water — pinks and purples, light blue and gold. Soon after, she had brought him coffee in bed. And then she took it away instead and crawled in beside him.

Later she'd laid her head on his chest, thick black hair rubbing against his skin, and she had talked about Sarah Grace and Christopher Stewart. About their mother, who tightly guarded secrets, her life tangled up, but who had two children whose whole lives — their psyches, their thoughts, their dreams and values, their livelihood — depended on her, on what she did and what she said and how she said it — and on who she was. And she had no one to help her on that journey.

He'd held her and listened, letting her talk it out, knowing Cass wasn't talking about Kayla Stewart, her responsibilities, and her two sweet kids. She was talking about Cass Halloran.

347

"Danny?" Birdie said, once the easy silence had run its course. "Are you still back there?"

"It depends." Danny stretched his feet out as best he could and brought himself out of his thoughts. "What's up?"

"I'm thinking about our friend Charlie Chambers."

"That sounds ominous. Cass and I had a few beers with Charlie last night."

"I know you did. That's why I'm wondering about him with *you,* and not with Joe Schmoe."

In the privacy of the backseat, Danny grinned again. Maybe Birdie really was a witch. "So we're wondering together."

"Yes. All three of us. Has Charlie mentioned that reporter to you?"

"The guy with the red hair, you mean. The one that seems to be a friend of Kayla Stewart's, or at least has been hanging around her house. That one?"

"Have you met him?" Nell asked.

"Funny you should ask — yeah, I have. He was also at the Gull last night. Hanging out with some guys. He'd had a few."

"What was your impression?" Nell asked.

"Same as Charlie's and Cass's. He's pretty full of himself. At first, we were kind of invisible to him. For a while he was too busy talking to notice us. So we just sat at the bar and eavesdropped."

"He seems to be climbing the journalism ladder, or at least hoping to," Birdie said.

"Maybe. But he'll never get there. I was a journalist for more years than I want to remember, and our friend Richie isn't very good. Cass showed me a couple articles of his. If he's on a ladder, it's the bottom rung. He's writing about people we know and love, like Gabby and Daisy and Lambswool Farm, and that's why people think he's good. But a real journalist? Nah, no way."

Danny was right, and they knew it. Sometimes trying to be kind clouded the truth. "So he didn't talk about his job last night?" she asked.

"Only to say how good he was. And then some garbage about how being a journalist gave you entry into all sorts of things. 'Opportunities,' he said, and when he mentioned the word, Cass almost choked on a fried clam. I was afraid I'd be doing the Heimlich on her."

Nell and Birdie laughed, fragments of Richie's yarn shop monologue echoing in the car. Esther Gibson's assessment — that Richie was more interested in being rich and the concept of "opportunity" — began to take on new overtones.

"We were listening for Kayla's name in the conversation, but if he talked about her, we didn't hear it. Not until they were about to leave. He went to pay the tab — flashing big fifty-dollar bills around, by the way — and noticed us. Or noticed Cass, anyway."

"And?" Birdie turned her head toward the backseat.

"And he turned on the charm, albeit the charm was a bit slurred. He even hugged her, much to her chagrin. She introduced us, Charlie, too."

"Did Charlie say anything?"

"No, but Richie looked at him hard, like he recognized him, and he said something like, 'Hey, you know my friend Kayla, doncha? Great gal, our Kayla,' and some more gibberish. Charlie didn't say a single word, just stared at him, and finally Richie's buddies pulled him away."

"So he *is* a friend of Kayla's," Nell mused. "Or at least claimed to be."

"Well, there's something there."

"Between Richie and Kayla?" Nell asked.

"Yeah."

"Something romantic?"

"Cass says absolutely not, that there's no way that could be true. But you know Cass. She's attached to that family in some Cass-like way, and she doesn't like the reporter guy. So in her head, at least, they can't be anything more than acquaintances."

"And Charlie?" Nell asked. "What does he say?"

Danny shrugged. "He's kind of in a strange position. And Charlie isn't pushy, though I could tell he didn't like the guy any better than Cass did. In fact, I think he was worried about it."

"We talked about it a little yesterday, connected some dots. He told me about a car he spotted at Kayla's," Nell said.

"He mentioned that, too. He went by to see Kayla again yesterday; it was before we went out last night. He had some excuse or another — I think he took something over to the kids, but we could tell he was worried about her. Her reaction to the will was strange and he wanted to help. She seemed relieved to see him, he said, but then it looked like she was about to cry again so he kept the conversation light."

"I called her, too," Birdie said. "I wanted to set up a meeting with her to explain all the details of the will provisions, but she became so sad, and then she asked for some time."

"Time?" Nell asked.

Birdie shrugged. "The poor girl is worried about something. Whether it has to do with

Dolores's murder or something else is yet another mystery. And it sounds like Charlie didn't get very far either."

"No. The kids were around and he could tell she was getting emotional. So he tried to change the subject, but picked a bad one. He brought up the reporter. Casually, he said."

"And —" Nell asked.

"It worked to stop the flood of emotions. She switched from sad to mad, claiming she had more important things to do and maybe he should leave. And that was that. He felt like he'd been slapped, he said."

The sight of a wild turkey ambling across the road slowed down both the conversation and the car. The turkey stopped at the edge of a thicket, stared back at them, then started back the other way.

Nell made a wide circle around it, wondering if turkeys were smarter than people gave them credit for. This one seemed to be enjoying some game he was playing with her. She tapped the horn for good measure, not wanting to end the poor bird's life, and drove on down the road.

"We're close now," she said, rounding another curve in the road where the land spread out, a deeper woods visible in the distance and one house close to the road, the other tucked back closer to the woods.

Nell turned into the drive that wound up to Dolores Cardozo's land and brought the car to a stop near the mailbox, just as she had done before. She pointed out the old quarry to Danny first, hidden behind the woods, then Dolores's house.

Danny looked over at the tree with the gnarled branches. The one where Kayla had parked her bike that night. Then he looked back to the house, bathed in sunshine today. "It's so normal," he said. "Murder is unspectacular." He looked over the flat and plain yard, then toward the woods just steps away, and beyond the house to the curving, bending road. Lots of places to disappear.

"So fill me in," Danny said as Nell turned off the engine. He unsnapped his seat belt and leaned forward, his arms on the back of Birdie's seat. "What happens now? I guess we put those muffins to their magical use?"

Birdie reached up and patted his hand. "Patience, Danny. We brought them, and now he will come."

Nell laughed as Birdie's sentence ended right on cue.

First they heard the slam of a door. Then Joe Duncan appeared on his small porch, his shotgun tucked beneath one arm, his binoculars hanging from a cord around his neck. He lumbered down the steps and across his small yard, headed their way.

The image of a flying cormorant was barely visible on his baggy sweatshirt, the seabird's long hooked bill hidden beneath smudges of dirt and something that looked vaguely like spaghetti sauce. He drew closer, his body hunched over, his small eyes squinting as Nell opened the door and climbed out of the car.

"Oh, it's you folks again," he said.

Birdie walked around from the other side with Danny beside her, carrying the muffins.

Birdie introduced Danny to Joe, wiping away his wary look with the fact that Danny was a famous mystery writer. And he also loved birds.

Nell held back a smile. She'd never heard Danny mention birds, but as Birdie no doubt suspected, the fact carried some weight. It wiped the wariness from Dunc's eyes and the gun nozzle slipped into a downward tilt. They all hoped the bird topic would be dropped before Danny's knowledge of feathered vertebrates was put to a test.

"Dunc, call me Dunc," the grizzled man said. "Are you here to give me news of my land?" He tilted the bill of his baseball cap toward Dolores's house.

Their confused looks nudged Joe to continue.

"The land." He swept his free hand in a wide semicircle. "It's ours. Just haven't gotten the word yet." He glanced back at his own house.

"Your land?" Danny asked.

He nodded, a few long gray hairs coming loose from his baseball hat and sticking out straight.

Just then the front door of the Duncans' house slammed again and they looked over to see a round-faced woman with blue-white hair standing on the steps, grasping the railing tightly. She wore an apron over her dress, and her hair frizzed wildly about her face.

"Yoo-hoo," she called, one hand waving in the air. Then she began descending the steps in slow motion.

"That's my Marlene. She'll want to meet you folks. Can you come across the road with me? Marlene doesn't like to leave our place."

They looked over at Marlene. She wasn't carrying a gun, which pleased them greatly.

"Of course," Nell said, and they followed him across the road and up a short walk toward the steps.

"This is Marlene," Dunc said proudly.

Marlene stood smiling on the walkway.

"My name is Marlene Duncan," the woman said, as if Joe hadn't spoken. She leaned forward, two pudgy hands reaching out to shake theirs, making a sandwich out of them. She moved from one to the other, scanning each face slowly and carefully, not letting go of each hand until she was satisfied. Finally, she stepped back and the smile returned. "Joseph told me about you visiting out here."

"Yes, and now we've come back," Nell said.

"Your husband was kind to give us some time when we were out here last week," Birdie said, looking from Marlene to the muffin container in Danny's hands. "So we brought some muffins as a thank-you to both of you. It's been a difficult time for you and perhaps something sweet will help. They were made this morning and are quite delicious."

Marlene and Dunc looked at Birdie with surprise, and then were effusive with thanks.

Birdie glanced at Danny, along with a lift of one white brow. *Magic muffins.*

"While we're here, if it's not disturbing your day too much, I wonder if we could ask a question or two —"

Joe Duncan's thin brows pulled together but Marlene shushed him as she breathed in the smells of cinnamon and butter and blueberries. "Of course you can," she said brightly, a lopsided smile creasing her face.

"Is it about the Cardozo murder?" Dunc asked.

Marlene's smile disappeared. She looked up, the muffins briefly forgotten. Her high voice came out in a staccato rush. "I don't want to talk about that. Stop it, Joseph. Right now. Stop it." Her hands slapped together as she stared over at the house, as if the murderer might still be in it, lurking behind the curtained windows, watching her. "Blood everywhere," she said with a frown.

Marlene looked shaken and her husband stepped closer to her side, one arm moving around her shoulders. He scowled, upset. "It's been hard on her, all the commotion. All the noise."

"Of course it has," Nell said. She looked at Marlene. "The police are working very hard, Marlene. They will solve this soon. It must be difficult for you, living so close, and having a neighbor die like that." She rested one hand on her arm and could feel the tension ease away. "Were you and Dolores Cardozo friends?"

Marlene's smile returned, slightly crooked now, and aimed directly at Nell — two women chatting over tea. Her head moved in small shivers, up and down. "Oh, Dolores. Yes. Yes. She loved to walk, you know. Everywhere. I'd sit in my rocking chair and wave to her as she walked by. Every day. Rain or shine. She was so healthy, not pudgy like me." She blushed slightly. "When she'd come back from her walk, she'd wave back to me. One hot day I made some lemonade and I waited for her to come by. When I saw her, I invited her up to the porch and she came."

The words were said with a childlike joy, as if the popular girl had agreed to sit with her at lunch. "We sat together while she drank a glass. She said it was the best lemonade she had ever tasted. And I told her I loved the slipcover on her sofa. It was the same color as mine."

"I'm sure she was a good neighbor," Birdie said.

She frowned, as if processing Birdie's comment. "I was a good neighbor to her. She knew that. I wasn't a bother, not like some of them. She would be upset with the people coming to look at the land. Peering in her windows. Trucks trampling her grass. They frighten me. The noise, you see." She covered her ears tightly and grimaced at the imagined intrusion. "Dolly was always quiet. She never made noise."

"So what kind of questions do you have?" Dunc asked, his arm still resting on Marlene's shoulders.

"I'm just wondering about the people who might have bothered Marlene, coming around here," Birdie said. "I know that the food pantry workers brought food out, but they wouldn't have been a bother, would they?"

Dunc was nodding his head as Birdie spoke. "Oh, sure. They came often. No bother there, although Marlene thought the car sometimes made a rumble."

"Did you ever meet the woman who brought the food?" Nell asked. "A young, dark-haired woman. Very nice."

"I saw her when she'd drive up in her old car. We'd be sitting right here on our porch, Marlene and me. We never talked to her, though. She was here to see Dolly, not us. We know to mind our own business. We stayed on our porch."

Marlene's blue-white hair nodded with his words. "The black-haired woman," she said.

"She was a skinny thing," Dunc added. "Had all those rings in her ear."

"It must have hurt," Marlene said, rubbing her own ear.

Birdie and Nell exchanged a look. Dunc may have politely allowed Dolores Cardozo and her visitors their privacy, but seeing someone's ear from his porch would have been a feat for Superman. Not to mention the color of Dolores's slipcovers. Dunc's binoculars must have worked overtime, doing his walking for him.

"It was nice of her to come all the way out here alone. Dolores must have appreciated her," Nell said.

"Don't rightly know. Like I said, we didn't talk much. But the gal would stay in there for a while sometimes. Talking, we supposed. Or we wondered if maybe she cleaned the house for her, but she never took rags or buckets or anything in. Just the white bags with the food. Big blue letters saying it was from the Bountiful Bowl Cafe."

"She didn't always come alone," Marlene said, her tone scolding. She looked up at her husband as if he'd made a terrible error in not telling all the details. "You should have told them about the fellow, Joseph. There was that fellow."

Joe Duncan nodded patiently and smiled at Marlene as if he were extremely grateful for her help. He looked at the others. "My

360

Marlene's right, she doesn't miss anything. I nearly forgot, but she remembered. There was the fellow who came a few times. Hair as red as that mum back there in Marlene's pretty pot. I nearly forgot about him."

"I called him Carrot Top," Marlene said. "And when I looked through the bins at him, his hair looked like a burning bush."

"I suppose he helped carry the food in for Kayla. Like a gentleman," Danny said.

"Nah, never, lazy galoot. But I don't think she wanted his help anyway. She waved her hand that first time, like motioning for him not to come in. He didn't like that — you could tell — but he stayed back. The first time anyway."

Again Marlene was miffed at the lack of details coming from her husband. "Here's what he did the next time. He'd wait for her to disappear around the back of the house. She always walked around to the back. There's a kitchen door back there. And then he'd sneak out of that car like he had good sense. Moving in the shadows, all the way up to that tree near the corner of the house." She pointed over to a giant pine tree, its branches brushing against the roof. "He stood there, crouched over, spying on her through the window. His face all surprised the first time. Then he went from window to window, even looked into the bedroom. He was sneaky, that one."

"He scared Marlene," Dunc said. "She didn't like him poking around her friend's house the way he did. Strangers aren't welcome here."

Marlene settled her body into Dunc's side, wrapping one arm around his waist. She smiled up at him. "But no more, right, Joseph?"

"Right, darlin'," he said.

"No more?" Nell asked.

"No more noise. No more bother. Like I said, the land is ours," Dunc said.

Marlene's smile grew until it filled her whole round face. "Ours. Dolly promised me that day we had lemonade together. I told her about the noise. How it made me nervous. How it was hard to think. She told me not to worry. This land is our land, she said. And she'd keep the noise away."

Dunc nodded. "Yep. She knew Marlene was special. She told me we didn't need to worry about the noise. We'd keep it away. None of those big boxy stores. No sirree, not on our land. No one loves the quiet like we do. Dolly loved it, too." He scratched the side of his head, looking over at the house. "Sure sorry Dolly had to leave us, though. We'll miss her."

He looked down at his wife and smiled. "There'll be no more noise, Marlene. Dolly promised."

CHAPTER 26

Izzy was frowning as Birdie finished relating the saga of Marlene and Joe Duncan to the others. "Are you saying you think Dunc might have killed Dolores to get the land?" she asked.

It was what they had discussed with Danny all the way back into town the day before, then continued it over a glass of iced tea and turkey sandwiches on Birdie's patio. Marlene was challenged in some way — and her husband was obviously her loving protector. That they all agreed on. Yes, he could have murdered Dolores to ensure the integrity — as Joe and Marlene saw it, anyway — of the land.

"I left a message for Elliott after we talked," Birdie said, pulling a bottle of wine and several soft drinks out of a carrying bag. "It's such a strange story and I wondered if Dolores ever mentioned the land in connection with the Duncans. Maybe originally she had promised them the land when she died. But it's clear from the will that the land is now in Sister Fiona Halloran's hands. And we know from Cass that she and Dolores discussed uses for the land. So it doesn't sound like she planned to give it to Dunc and Marlene, at least not recently."

"Perhaps Fiona's religious order will build a retreat house out there and Marlene will still have her quiet," Nell said.

"But there'd be cars. The lady doesn't seem to like them." Cass had heard the story twice now, a longer, detailed version from Danny the night before. "Danny says that fear of loud noises is real. It's called phonophobia or something. In serious cases it can cause panic and anxiety — all sorts of things."

"Maybe that's why she never leaves the house," Nell said.

"I know Danny isn't a policeman, but he probably studies more murders than most people. He's always on the lookout for the perfect suspect. He said Joe Duncan would probably be in that camp."

"He could be a suspect," Nell said. She peeled the foil off the meat loaf pan and set it on the warming plate. "But to kill for *quiet*?"

"No, to kill to protect his wife," Cass said.

She moved closer to Nell and leaned in to smell the flavors rising on the steam. *Wine and sweet caramelized onions. Bacon and savory tomato sauce.* She whispered her undying love for Nell, then stepped away from the food to think more clearly. "Danny said the guy looked like he would do anything for her. He said the lady never leaves their yard. Her husband is her whole world."

"And people have certainly killed for less." Izzy carried a basket of biscuits over to the coffee table. Of the four of them, Izzy was most aware of what little motivation sometimes led to murder. She had seen it firsthand as a lawyer when she had defended some of those very people. And she still saw it sometimes in unwelcome dreams.

"Joe Duncan had access," Birdie said. "With those powerful binoculars, he probably knows every inch of Dolores's house. I only hope the dear lady didn't know how little privacy she had. I agree with Izzy that the motive is sound enough. He clearly loves Marlene and he seems to take his job as her savior seriously."

"But he already had what he wanted — what Marlene wanted. They had the quiet they craved while Dolores was alive. He didn't need to kill for it," Cass said, playing devil's advocate, a role they would toss back and forth many times.

"Unless he thought she might sell? Change her mind —" Birdie said.

"Which she obviously did," Nell said.

"That's only if you buy the Duncans' story that she considered giving it to them. Sounds a little crazy to me," Cass said.

"So Marlene and Dolores were friends?" Izzy asked. "If so, I can't imagine he'd want to kill his wife's friend."

Birdie gave the question thought while she filled her plate. "I think Marlene made friends with Dolores in her mind. And Dolores was kind enough not to shatter the illusion. I don't think they sat in each other's kitchens and chatted."

Nell agreed. "That's more logical. Just like Marlene coveted quiet, I think Dolores coveted her aloneness. And I can't imagine what they would have had in common. But Dolores was kind, so she wouldn't have been rude to Marlene. From all we've heard, Dolores's connection to others wasn't through companionship but through acts of kindness and her long walks, communing with nature. Maybe that's all she needed."

"Almost like a contemplative nun," Birdie said.

Birdie uncorked the wine and carried it

over while they settled themselves in the cozy corner of the room. Norah Jones's husky voice followed them, a comfortable companion in the background.

Once I was seven. . . . Izzy hummed along as Norah began singing one of little Abby's favorite songs, and her thoughts turned automatically to a sleeping toddler cuddled in her crib a mile away. Warm and safe.

Purl curled up next to Birdie on the cracked leather chair near the fireplace, rubbing her head against Birdie's soft knit slacks, and the others sank into the remaining chairs, the cushions shaped to their bodies after years of Thursday night knitting. Years of friendship.

"To friends," Birdie said as glasses were lifted and forks unwrapped from napkins. With plates on laps they dug into the tangy meatloaf, appreciation lighting their faces.

For a while the music and food absorbed them, senses satisfied and spirits soothed. It wasn't until Nell poured more wine that she gently brought Kayla Stewart into the room.

"There was a police report made that may involve Kayla," she said. "Charlie was upset when he heard. He's heading over there tonight."

They looked up from their plates.

"What kind of report?" Birdie asked.

"It's probably nothing, but there's a chance it could be connected to why Kayla went out to the Cardozo home that night. She still hasn't told the police why she was there. Yesterday Ben was talking to a neighbor who's an aid at Our Lady of Safe Seas School. She mentioned that she'd heard something about one of the Stewart kids."

Mention of a child got everyone's attention.

"That's crazy. One of the kids was mentioned in a police report? What is that about?" Cass's voice had an edge to it, as if she was fully prepared to refute it immediately, whatever *it* was.

Nell put down her fork. "It was disturbing, so Ben called Jerry Thompson right away, hoping to stop a rumor before it grew legs. Apparently Christopher Stewart was buying school lunches for himself and little Sarah Grace, and when he went to pay, he pulled out a fifty-dollar bill. A couple more fell out of his pocket."

There was silence.

Cass broke into it. "Since when is having a fifty-dollar bill a crime?"

Nell continued. "The cafeteria lady was only concerned that Christopher might lose such a large amount of money so she walked with him up to Sister Fiona's office, suggesting they keep the rest of the money in the principal's desk for safekeeping until it was time for him to go home. But as sometimes happens, things careened out of control when the security guard — a man who apparently would much rather be on the police force and is following the Cardozo case as if he's going to singlehandedly solve it — saw the money and called the police."

"Because he'd heard about Dolores keeping fifty-dollar bills in her house," Birdie said softly.

"Yes."

Izzy sighed. "That's not good."

"Ben says the irony of it is that after talking to people who had any contact with Dolores, the police discovered she gave out fifty-dollar bills like candy, rewarding random kindnesses — people along the trails who picked up trash, a teenager helping an older man shovel his walk — kind of like she did in her will. And somehow she did it invisibly, although after her murder, recipients of the surprise bills came forward, suspecting for various reasons that she was probably the one who did it."

"So now Kayla has to go and tell Jerry Thompson why she has fifty-dollar bills?" Cass said. "I have a fifty-dollar bill in my wallet right now. Am I next?"

But she knew how hollow her words were. Cass's bike wasn't found leaning against a tree the night Dolores was killed, nor did she suffer a wound leaning over a dead woman's body.

Birdie took a drink of wine, then a deep breath, and then she told them for the first time how she and Charlie had found an envelope Kayla had dropped at the market last weekend. "It was none of our business," she said, "so we simply gave it back to her and never mentioned it again. Although we didn't try to pry, the envelope had buckled and we could see what was inside."

"Fifty-dollar bills," Nell said.

Birdie nodded. "Neatly bound with a rubber band. Kayla was relieved when we gave it back, as if finding that envelope had somehow saved her. From what, we weren't sure. She was nervous — but definitely relieved to have it back. Maybe simply because it was grocery money, food for her children."

"It's strange, though. Who sends kids to school with fifty-dollar bills?" Izzy asked rhetorically.

"Sometimes the odds are stacked against you," Nell said. "And this seems to be one of those times."

"It can be easily explained away," Cass said. "If Dolores handed out money the way you described, Nell, who's to say she hadn't handed some bundles to Kayla? Aunt Fiona said they were friends, they liked each other. And Kayla did favors for Dolores by delivering food to her."

Izzy looked at Cass. "I could have used you in the courtroom. Good argument."

"I'm practiced at arguing," Cass said, a slight smile lifting her concern. "I'm not sure why those kids have gotten to me the way they have. I think of Kayla handling this all alone and it really gets to me. I look at Danny and think how lucky I am. No matter what comes our way, I have someone there who will fight the lions with me."

"I think of that, too," Izzy said. "Maybe that's why we feel so involved in this."

"Sure it is," Cass said.

"But we're basing it on emotions. That isn't going to convince the police," Birdie said.

"So what will?" Cass said.

Birdie put her napkin on her plate and sat back. She spoke with the same resolve that those sitting around the table felt. "Finding the murderer. Crawl inside Dolores. She did more than walk around Cape Ann. She had a life. She spent hours in the library, for example. She had a brilliant mind, and people with brilliant minds usually use them. And she was a genuine humanitarian. Dolores walked into people's lives as silently as a cat burglar, but with kindnesses. So what if one of those lives was touched by Dolores in the opposite way? We have lots of walking to do."

Izzy stacked up the empty plates as she talked. "Wanting the land is a motive, for sure. Dolores didn't want to sell it to the people pounding her door down. She probably made them angry. But that scenario is flimsy. Contractors have other ways of getting what they want without resorting to murder."

"Like sending roses. You joked about this, but Davey Delaney actually did it. He sent Aunt Fiona roses! Two dozen, long stemmed. Ma took them and put them on the altar at the church."

They laughed.

"Neither the Delaneys nor the other investors and builders were secretive about wanting the land, and that's not something a murderer would broadcast," Birdie said. "They wasted a lot of the city council's time pleading their case. To then go and murder Dolores doesn't seem to be a way to go."

"Let's set them aside for now," Cass said.

"What about red-haired Richie. He might have discovered the hidden money in Dolores's house when he rode out there with Kayla."

"Joe saw him watching Kayla and Dolores through the windows. He knew the inside of the house, that's true," Birdie said. "And if he didn't see the money Dolores kept around her house, maybe Kayla mentioned something to him as they rode back into town. It was a curious thing, money stored in cookie jars and around the house. Something you might mention in conversation."

"But how would killing her have played into that?" Izzy asked.

"Maybe a simple robbery gone bad?" Cass said. "That would fit his profile. I don't think the guy is brilliant. He could have gone out that night to steal the money — remember his talk about opportunity? Maybe this is the kind of opportunity he was talking about. And then Dolores came in from a walk and surprised him, and he killed her."

"And then Kayla showed up, and he knocked her out so he could escape?" Izzy wondered.

They mulled over the possibility, unable to come up with little to refute or substantiate it. Richie would stay on the list. "He's done something," Cass said. "I don't know what it is, but he figures in all this. There's something about Richie Pisano that smells bad."

Like dead fish could have come next. But the lobsterwoman was polite enough to hold the words back.

"And I don't think we can cross Joe Duncan off either," Birdie said.

"You said he's a birder," Izzy said. "Birders aren't killers. They protect."

"They protect birds," Birdie said quietly. "Humans might be a different story. I'm not sure how fond Dunc is of humans. And he might have spotted loose money in the house with the binoculars."

Nell looked up. She had taken out her knitting and was stroking a silky skein of Bluefaced Leicester yarn. "Maybe we need to check further into the will, just to see if there's anything there. Find out what Joe was talking about."

Birdie nodded, scribbling a note on a yellow piece of paper. Loose ends that needed to be tied off.

Izzy watched her shove the pen back into her purse. "And I will try one more time to teach you how to take notes on your phone."

Birdie smiled sweetly and reached across the table, patting Izzy's hand. "I'll make a note of that. Now back to walking in Dolores's shoes. . . ."

They sat together comfortably, the way of old friends, knitting needles moving to the tempo of a conversation about a murderer as if it were the norm — and not the awful shaking up of lives.

"Dolores walked through town, along the shoreline, through the woods. In her quiet, nomadic way, she probably knew as much or more about our town than any of us. All those footsteps. Just think about it," Nell said, working the short rows of the heel of her sock.

Nell's imagery was effective, expanding their thoughts. Walking in Dolores's shoes meant more than walking trails with an ornate walking stick. It meant moving into her solitary life, dissecting her thoughts and her motivations, looking at her life and into her soul with a magnifying glass, and finding therein the reason someone wanted to end her life.

It was all there, waiting for her to show them.

CHAPTER 27

Charlie was the first one to arrive, his hair looking more shaggy than usual, his brown eyes tired. He gave his aunt a giant hug and settled on an island stool in the kitchen, watching her whisk together a grilling sauce for the fish.

"My mother never taught me how to cook," he said, flipping the top off a bottle of Heineken.

"That's because your mother wasn't very good at it."

"But you came from the same gene pool, had the same mother. What happened?"

Nell laughed. "My sister is an expert at teaching high school math. I wouldn't know a hypotenuse if it bit me." She set a cutting board and knife in front of Charlie, then added an onion and handful of mushrooms. "Chop," she said, putting an empty bowl in front of him. "Small little squares. Now tell me how things are going at Glenn Mackenzie's family practice. Are you enjoying working there?"

Charlie held the onion with one hand and sliced it in half. "Glenn is my idea of a perfect family doctor. He knows his medicine, but he's also terrific at relating to patients. He even charmed Kayla Stewart when we took her stitches out."

Nell finished grating the lemon zest into the sauce, pushing the remaining fragments off the tool with the pad of her finger. "Kayla is ever present these days. She's been on my mind a lot. And other people's, too. Cass especially."

"I know. Cass thinks those little kids are great. Yeah, it's touch —"

He concentrated on his chopping, but Nell could see that he wanted to say more. "Did you see her last night? And Christopher? Poor little guy, just trying to pay for a lunch and ending up in the principal's office."

"Chris is fine. Fiona probably gave him a lollypop. I took all of them down to the pier while it was still light. Pete was there doing something to one of the lobster boats and he let the kids run along the deck. The kids'll be okay."

"And Kayla?"

"Kayla? She hasn't talked to the police

378

again, that much I know. But I don't know how she is. I honestly don't. It's a mess, though. You wonder what shoe will drop next. I asked her about the money Chris took to school. She said it was a mistake. They were all rushing around that morning and she told him to take some dollar bills out of her purse for their lunches because she hadn't had time to make them. He took the wrong bills."

"That could easily have happened."

"It *did* happen." Charlie scraped the onion chunks into the bowl. "I believe her. It's exactly what happened. But it doesn't explain why she seems to be so flush with fifty-dollar bills, I suppose. I'm sure Birdie's told you about the envelope we found."

Nell nodded. "Did you ask her about the money?"

"Sort of, in a roundabout way, kind of joking about it. And her answer was equally as vague. She said, 'I work, you know.' "

"And that was it?"

"I think she was about to say something else. She got real quiet and looked at me for what seemed like a long time, her eyes combing my face as if trying to read something there. Acceptance maybe? Trust? Her mouth even opened." He began chopping the handful of mushrooms Nell had set on the board. "And then it shut again."

"So maybe she wants to let you in but just isn't ready yet."

"Could be. I threw a ball with Christopher for a while before leaving. She sat on the steps watching us, braiding Sarah Grace's hair. She seemed to be okay with the company. She didn't mention the money again, or whether the police had contacted her."

"Do you think she took money from Dolores? Could that be why she was going out there that night?"

"To steal, you mean?"

Nell was quiet.

Charlie took a deep breath. "No. I haven't known her long, but she wouldn't steal. I'm sure of it. I think she went out there that night because it was important to her to talk to Dolores Cardozo about something. Why she doesn't want the police to know what it was is beyond me. Fiona is as confused by it as I am."

Outside the sound of voices and slamming car doors told them their time for quiet talk was almost up.

Nell checked the clock, then looked at Charlie. His brows were pulled together and he was looking out the back window toward the ocean, searching for something. "What is it, Charlie?"

He looked at Nell, then picked up his beer, shaking his head. "It's nothing." He took a long swig. "No, it's not nothing. It's something. It's this eerie feeling I have that gets stronger by the day. I feel this almost visceral connection with Kayla. And maybe because of it, a kind of responsibility. I care about her. And it's all intensified by the fact that I think I have met her somewhere. Or at least that I've seen her before. But I can't put it together and I can't get it off my mind. It's driving me crazy."

"You've been many places," Nell said.

"That I have. And I am willing to bet she has, too."

"Have you asked her?"

"She never saw me before in her life, she said, and she's quite sure the circles we ran in didn't intersect."

Nell smiled to herself. She whisked the basting ingredients one more time and set the sauce aside. "They say we all have a double somewhere. Maybe you saw her double?"

That made Charlie laugh, and he finished off his beer, just in time to greet a noisy stream of people filling up the house. Abby led the parade, toddling full speed over to her uncle, who picked her up and swung her around.

Ben came in from the deck, where he and Danny had been piling coals into a perfect searing configuration for the fresh tuna steaks. The fact that it had taken them nearly an hour meant world problems had been solved and beers drunk while the coals turned gray.

Ben greeted Don and Rachel Wooten and suggested Don help Danny uncork some wine. He kissed Abby on the top of her curls and wound his way around Birdie, Cass, and Izzy to the kitchen sink and Nell. He pulled her aside and spoke quietly. "I forgot to tell you earlier, but I ran into Fiona at the fish market. She looked tired and worried, so I invited her to join us tonight. Friday night therapy on the rocks, I told her."

Nell looked up at Ben and smiled. "You're a good man, Ben Endicott. That was a nice thing to do."

"I thought so."

Fiona had come onto both their radar screens over morning coffee. It was Ben who mentioned the affection she had for the family, and how they sometimes forgot that she and Dolores Cardozo were actually friends. Fiona was burdened with worry over a family she cared about, and going through personal loss at the same time. Not an easy coupling.

Hopefully, she'd be able to relax on the deck for a few hours. It had worked its magic many times before.

The Brewsters had arrived with Jane's now-famous peanut butter coleslaw and newsy tidbits from the Canary Cove Art Colony: a new exhibit opening up, several new artists looking for gallery space, and another benefit that Hannah Swenson had talked them into doing for the Seaside Initiative.

Rachel listened as they moved out to the deck.

"I don't see Hannah for weeks, and then I seem to run into her every day," Nell said to Rachel.

"She's a busy lady, I guess."

"Who is?" Don asked, offering wine and martinis as people gathered.

"Your ex-sister-in-law," Nell said.

"No on no," Don said. "It's several branches of the tree away from that." He set the empty drink tray on a table.

"She told us about her son," Birdie said. "Law school. Apparently Hannah's son — your nephew? — is quite an achiever."

"He's not actually my nephew. He came with Hannah, as it were, who married Tim

Wooten, a cousin of mine, I forget which number. Once you get past first and second cousins I get befuddled. Like what would my dad's nephew's kids be? Or my dad's brother's nephews? Are they my cousins?" He waved it off with a bewildered look and a laugh, then took a long swallow of his martini. "Anyway, it wasn't the happiest of unions from what I hear. I think Hannah is the kind of person who needs to be taken care of — and in a nice manner, if you know what I mean. Tim looked the part — handsome and showy in sports cars and golf club memberships he finagled out of someone."

"Well he must have left her comfortable," Izzy said. "For which I'm grateful. Hannah has excellent taste and buys my most luxurious yarn."

"And one of those great new condos over near the point," Jane said. "We had a meeting there. I told her I'm moving in."

"That's interesting," Rachel said. "Hannah must be good at making ends meet, though I never saw that side of her. And she does have good taste. But there wasn't any money at all in the divorce settlement. Like Don said, Tim was one of those charming, handsome guys who looked rich, and I think that was what Hannah thought, too. But . . ." She let the sentence fall away, uncomfortable with the discussion.

Don wasn't as discreet. "The guy was a likeable deadbeat who liked beautiful women," he said. He caught Rachel's look. "Well, he was. So my wife is right — the divorce didn't make Hannah's life easier. But she's smart. She got herself a job, and maybe she's good at handling money — better than she was at handling Tim anyway."

"Who's good at handling money?" Cass walked out carrying a tray with cheese sticks, olives, and a bowl of sweet gherkins.

"You, my love," Danny said, walking over and wrapping an arm around her. He cuddled her close and kissed the top of her head. "You're good at handling me, money, lobsters, you name it."

"Not all at the same time, I hope," Rachel said. "Lobster claws are vicious."

Their laughter was interrupted by a familiar voice coming through the open French doors. "Is this where the party is?"

The words carried the hint of an Irish brogue.

"Aunt Fiona?" At the sound of the voice, Cass spun around, out of Danny's arms. The look on her face said she was fourteen and had just been caught in a dark alley kissing the paperboy.

Fiona stepped out on the deck, smiling all

around and breathing in the tantalizing grill odors. "I am definitely in the right place." She waved at her niece.

"We're so glad you could make it," Ben called over from his spot at the grill. He wiped his hands on his chef's apron, walked over, and greeted her with a hug. "You know everyone here, right?"

Greetings came quick, friendly and with familiarity, and in minutes Fiona had told everyone present to drop the "sister." She was among friends.

And they did, welcoming her into the group as comfortably as if she'd been there every week.

Nell stood near the door with Charlie, a basket of chips and dip in her hand. "Our dear Fiona doesn't meet a stranger, does she? She's a good woman."

Charlie watched the nun circulate the group, her greetings friendly, her eyes attentive, her smile open. "What's Cass's problem with her aunt?" he asked.

"Cass doesn't allow people to interfere in her life, especially her love life. Occasionally Fiona tries to do it, I think. But it's what family does sometimes. Besides, I think Cass is mellowing. There's something different about her these days."

Charlie leaned back against the door

frame, absently stabbing the olive in his martini with a toothpick, but his eyes were on Cass. They had become good buddy-type friends, maybe because they were so similar in some ways. He didn't like people interfering in his life either. Except that's exactly what he was doing to someone else's life. Not interfering maybe, but peeling it like an onion to see what was underneath.

Across the deck Fiona approached her niece and they moved a few steps away from the group, standing beneath the branches of the old maple tree that guarded the deck and the picnic table. Whatever the conversation, the nun showed little disapproval, only sincere attention as she leaned in to hear what Cass was saying to her.

Nell was watching them, too. "Cass is talking about the children," she said.

Charlie nodded. There was no need to name which children. *Sarah Grace and Christopher.* It was another way in which he and his friend Cass were alike. For whatever reason, they were both becoming tethered to Kayla Stewart and her kids. Irrational.

"Fiona cares a lot about that family," Nell said.

"Do you know why?" Charlie asked. "I've been wondering about it. I asked Kayla, but she mumbled something about nuns being like that. It's their job, she said. But I didn't buy it. Fiona has hundreds of kids over at that school. Why are these two so special?"

"I asked her once," Nell said. "The answer must have been vague because I don't remember it. But Cass's mother said her sister-in-law has been like that since Kayla arrived late last year. 'A mother hen,' Mary Halloran called her. She talked Don Wooten into hiring Kayla at the Ocean's Edge, and even helped her find a house. Maybe she does it for others, too, and we just don't hear about it."

"Maybe," Charlie said. He chewed his olive, then drained the glass and offered to pass the basket of cheese sticks around. Besides, he'd never had a chance to ask Fiona his potato riddle.

"Go for it." Nell laughed and went back inside to bring out the chilled tuna.

Fiona didn't seem surprised when Charlie walked over to her. She suggested they sit on the deck steps and get a glimpse of the water while there was still enough light left. The ocean was just visible over the tops of the trees, and in an hour it would all be black, as if swallowed up by the sky.

Charlie grabbed a beer from the cooler and followed Fiona across the deck. She settled herself on a step, her legs bent and her sneakers resting on a lower step. Charlie sat down next to her, each of them comfortable with the quiet moment. The music and voices were a pleasant hum in the background.

Charlie spoke first. "My sister lived here for years before I even visited her. I didn't know this kind of place existed."

"It's beautiful, that's for sure. And Izzy and Sam seem very happy here. But Sea Harbor is a small place. That brings both challenges and comfort. Probably in equal doses. I was fine leaving Sea Harbor, but I'm happy to be back."

"Where did you go?"

"Different places. My order had grade schools in the Midwest — probably close to where you grew up. I was in Kansas City for a few years, and then to a school farther west."

"Idaho?"

She nodded without comment.

"Teaching?"

"At first, but it was a small town, schools consolidated, and mine closed. I moved into a different field after that. I taught in a correctional institution for a while. And then became involved in helping women in different ways. It was a good opportunity for me. Stretched me in good ways. Sometimes you have to leave home to find yourself and reach your full potential, even if you're in a religious order, like I am. But when my project ran out of money, I came back home. And that was fine, too."

Charlie took a deep breath. "There's some weird serendipity going on here. I ended up in Idaho for a while. And that kind of happened to me, too. I was a college dropout, a messed-up ski bum. Then it got worse and I really catapulted myself off the deep end. But somehow the land of potatoes straightened me out."

"Potatoes can do that." Sister Fiona looked over at him for the first time. She smiled.

It was the same kind of smile Charlie had seen on Cass. Compassionate and kind — but protected, just in case someone might think her "soft."

"When were you there?" Fiona asked.

"Long time ago. A dozen years maybe. I had dropped out of college and roamed around. I ended up in a little off-the-map kind of place not too far from Boise. Beautiful place."

Fiona was watching him closely. "Ten or fifteen years ago? That was before I knew Idaho existed. But I'm sure the mountains were still there back then. The rivers."

"The potatoes," Charlie added.

Fiona laughed.

"I circled back through there two, three years ago to see an old friend, to thank her for some things she did for me. Like save my life." He shrugged, his lips lifting into a crooked smile.

Fiona was listening with full attention now, her brows pulling together as if she was piecing things together in her head. She sat back against the wooden step and looked over the trees at the disappearing ocean, the black sky settling down for the night. "That can happen, you know. Lives can be saved, even in Idaho. Besides the mountains and potatoes, they've got themselves some good angels over there."

It was Charlie's turn to stare.

Fiona kept her gaze above the treetops, her voice quiet but clear. "Angel Martini. Your name hadn't connected before, Charlie. Nor should it have. It's not an uncommon name. Charlie Chambers. I'm guessing that it was you, anyway. Angel mentioned someone to me; it was after this guy had come back to see her. She was touched that he'd come back, and happy that he wasn't dead — she said it could have gone either way with that guy for a while.

She didn't call the guy Charlie, though; she called him Chambers." She turned her head and looked at him.

Charlie shook his head. "She called me lots of names. That was one of the nicer ones."

Fiona laughed. "Angel had a way with words."

Charlie leaned back against the step, smiling as if he'd been visited by an old friend. "Wow. So you knew Angel."

"I still do. She's there in Idaho, working on programs at the Y to keep kids out of trouble. Angel and I worked together some. She was tough and wise for her age."

"Tough? That doesn't begin to touch Angel."

Fiona laughed. "She has a way about her. She made me realize the true value in volunteering and it worked well with my own project."

"Your own project?"

Sister Fiona leaned forward, starting to say something. Then, in the next breath, she held back, as if uncertain about what it was she wanted to say. Instead of speaking, she reached up with one hand and wound her fingers around the railing, pulling herself up and looking back toward the grill area, where people were getting up from their chairs and moving around, cleaning up glasses, picking up appetizer plates. Ben and Nell were ushering everyone toward the long table, announcing that the tuna steaks would get cold if they didn't hurry.

Birdie stood near the table, pointing out empty places. Her glass was raised, ready to toast her friends.

Charlie followed Fiona over to the table, where baskets of rolls, pots of butter, and a winding river of small candles anchored nature's table runner of autumn leaves.

Once they had all touched their glasses to Birdie's familiar toast — *to friends, to family, to life, and to gratitude* — the feast began in earnest with the passing of dishes, the crisscrossing of conversations, the laughter and the cheers of triumph for another Endicott dinner on the deck. Charlie looked around at the sea of faces, this coterie of friends and family who were quickly being woven into the fabric of his life.

It wasn't until his eyes settled on Fiona, seated between Rachel Wooten and Uncle Ben, candlelight reflecting off her strong-boned Irish features, that Charlie began to rerun their conversation, a conversation he'd begun with the one person he thought might have some insight into Kayla Stewart. Maybe the only person who could explain her perplexing and frustrating behavior — her fears, her secrets, and her refusal to accept help from those who wanted nothing more than to help clear her of suspicion of murder.

Charlie knew from the look on Fiona's face when he had approached her that she was aware of what he wanted to discuss. She knew it was about Kayla. She knew he cared about her. She had welcomed the conversation, taking him away from the mainstream chatter on the deck — to talk about Kayla Stewart.

But not once was Kayla's name mentioned.

So why, Charlie wondered now, why had he felt Kayla Stewart sitting right there between Fiona and him the whole time?

CHAPTER 28

"Walking in someone's shoes can be uncomfortable, especially when they don't fit," Birdie said. She stopped on the trail and stared down at her sneakers.

"Perhaps you, we, all of us have Dolores's shoes on the wrong feet," Nell said, then frowned at her own analogy, not sure of where she was going with it. But she was glad for the chance to stop. The momentary rest felt good. The trail they had taken was beautiful, but circuitous, and longer than they'd expected.

Ahead of them, they saw Cass stumble. "Be careful up here," she called over her shoulder, one hand on Izzy's arm while she regained her balance. "There're lots of gnarly roots crossing the path." She began to lead the way again, pushing aside tangles of bittersweet and catbrier.

"I think the old quarry should be just ahead," Birdie said. "I remember coming out here years ago with Sonny, long after the quarries had closed for business and the rains and springs had filled them with water. This one became one of the safer ones in which to swim."

They'd planned a Saturday hike in Ravenswood Park over in Gloucester — an easy hike up to the lookout for an aerial view of the city. Their hopes were it would magically clear their heads and bring things into focus. Not to mention offer much needed exercise and fresh air. But when Cass suggested a hike around the old quarry near Dolores Cardozo's house instead, they had all jumped on the idea. They wouldn't get an aerial view, but maybe the land itself would release some of its secrets and help them get closer to Dolores, to hear her secrets, to feel her connection to Kayla Stewart, who was now mired in the messy aftermath of her death.

Perhaps walking her land, softened by her own footsteps, would be the same as walking in her shoes.

The trail took a sharp left and they shouldered their way through a bramble of thorny bushes, the reward coming just minutes later as the woods suddenly fell back, a curtain lifted, and the old quarry appeared before them.

"Wow. I remember this. We came out here as kids, too," Cass said, her voice soft with memory as she looked over the blue-black water held in its perfect pool by endless walls of granite. "We'd jump off that ledge right over there." She pointed to an outcropping where a stone ledge provided perfect access to brave kids wanting to jump into the water. "It was a respectable twenty-five-foot jump. My show-off brother soon called it a baby leap — although to this day my mother doesn't know about it — and he took off with his macho friends for the Klondike quarry, an eighty-foot plunge, and never came back here again."

Izzy and Nell shuddered.

"Maybe it's because we're not natives of the area," Nell said. "But I can't imagine it."

"No, it's because you're sane," Cass said. She walked over to a large flat table of granite, found her footing, and climbed up. "This is more my speed these days." She settled herself cross-legged on top. Nell and Izzy followed.

Birdie walked over to the edge of the quarry, cautiously looking over the edge. "There's something surreal about it all. Imagine having this in your backyard, as Dolores did. It's magical. So beautiful."

"There's a trail that circles the quarry," Izzy said. "It's great for running. Every now and then I'd see Dolores out here. She could probably walk every inch of this quarry blindfolded. Always with her walking stick, always calm, composed."

Birdie looked behind the ledge, back through the woods. She pointed to a small trail. "That one may lead to her house."

They all looked over, imagining a slender white-haired woman, her long ponytail moving between narrow shoulder blades, walking the paths.

Cass reached out a hand and Birdie took it, climbing up onto the flat boulder.

"So we've walked her walk, at least some of it. Now what was she thinking as she circled this quarry?" Birdie asked. She settled down next to Cass, pushing her sunglasses to the top of her head. "What was important to her?"

"We know she walked right into people's lives, intimately, whether they knew she was there or not," Nell said, nodding, encouraged as their jumbled thoughts smoothed out, just like the water below.

"I know we're repeating our thoughts, but that's okay. Slight nuances can spin a fact in different ways," Izzy said. "One thing, though, moving forward: if we think Kayla is innocent, we need to distance her from all this, set her connection to Dolores aside so we can think outside that box and move on to a murderer. Someone we might have seen yesterday or today or tomorrow. Someone walking around our town."

Izzy's comment sat there for a minute, spread out on the wide granite surface like butter on warm bread. One sentence stood out among the others.

If they believed she was innocent.

But did they?

There was silence. Even the water was still, the only sound coming from birds in the distance and a slight rustling of the trees circling the quarry.

Finally, Izzy spoke again, clarifying her own statement. "Yes, we believe Kayla is innocent of Dolores Cardozo's murder."

Izzy, the lawyer among them, speaking from a courtroom and in that same tone of voice. "Our belief isn't based completely on emotion or the fact that Charlie is involved in that family's life, or that the Stewarts have triggered something in my best friend —" She looked over at Cass, then turned away just as quickly. She was all business now.

"It's a combination of everything. Sure, it's what Cass said, that Kayla would never

ever do anything that would separate her from her children. But it's also based on facts — her small frame, for example. How could she hit Dolores hard enough to kill her, a woman at least six inches taller than she? And there's her own injury. It would be difficult to inflict that on yourself, and even if she had tripped and hit the table, it wouldn't have been enough to cause that degree of damage. And there's the amnesia, authenticated by a doctor.

"Moreover, unless someone can prove she knew of her inheritance ahead of time, there's no known motive. Is she a suspect? I suppose so. But getting a conviction? Right now the case would be full of circumstantial evidence, most of it flimsy. A long shot."

But even long shots were disturbing — they all knew that. When a town was desperate to put a murderer behind bars so they could declare their streets safe again, long shots became shorter.

Izzy unzipped her backpack and pulled out a large paper bag with grease stains already spreading through. The smells coming from the bag were a welcome, brief diversion.

Cass stared at the bag. "Iz, you're the absolute best. When you said you'd bring sandwiches I was expecting Abby's leftover peanut butter and jelly." She inhaled the garlic, vinegary onions, and sopressata aromas of Harry Garozzo's deli specials.

"I know the way to your heart, Cass," Izzy said, pulling the sandwiches out of the bag.

Cass unzipped her own pack, pulling out four bottles of water. She passed them around and took the first sandwich from Izzy, unwrapped it immediately. With a tip of her finger, she scooped up a dab of Harry's secret and sinful sauce — a rosemary-laced whipped lardo that Cass sometimes dreamed about.

"Why you aren't as big as a house is a mystery, Catherine," Birdie said, shaking her head.

They attacked their sandwiches in silence, the sun warming the stone and their bodies, their minds mulling over the thought of Dolores Cardozo walking around the quarry, perhaps sitting in the same spot now littered with sandwich wrappings, apples, and water bottles.

Birdie wiped off her hands and took a long drink of water, looking over at the path that probably led to the Cardozo home. Maybe the route the murderer had come and gone along. "The Duncans claim Richie Pisano looked in the windows of the house while Kayla was inside," she said. "Richie claimed he only saw the house from a distance. Why?"

Izzy painted the possible scenario again: Richie robbing the place, Dolores walking in on him. "Dolores wasn't the type to play victim. She fought back, was killed, but before he could gather up the money, he heard someone coming in, so he hid in the bedroom or somewhere."

Cass nodded, liking the story. "Maybe he escaped down that very path."

"Motive, means, opportunity," Izzy said, the last word drawing wry smiles. Richie was fond of opportunities.

"Ben mentioned that the police have talked to him," Nell said. "Mary Pisano told me he seemed rather proud to have been questioned."

"That figures," Cass said. "But Mary also said work for Richie may have meant nosing around the police station and hospitals. Even if he was working that night he could easily have taken a detour to load up on fifty-dollar bills —"

"But would he have drawn attention to himself, then, by posting that announcement in the paper?" Nell asked. "And they didn't find any prints that would place him there."

That quieted them while they mulled it

over, finishing lunch. They stuffed the remaining litter in a bag. But Richie Pisano stayed there in the mix, not discarded. Not yet.

Birdie shifted her small body on the granite, working out the kinks. "I think Dolores knew the person who did this to her. Most victims do. And I think the murderer had a reason for killing her. We've come to know Dolores as kind and generous. But those traits don't often lead to murder. Unless . . ." Birdie wrinkled her forehead, trying to find the rest of her thought.

"Unless someone was jealous, or Dolores had done someone an injustice — at least in that person's mind. Something they didn't think fair," Nell offered.

"Other than money, what could it be?" Izzy asked.

"Well, let's start with money," Birdie said. "Dolores's generosity. Her final will and testament. Sometimes murder isn't complicated, just like Dolores's will wasn't complicated."

Nell agreed. "Let's assume that those in Dolores's will didn't know about her bequests. At least for now. So killing her to receive the money sooner wouldn't be a motive," she said.

They agreed halfheartedly. Murder for

money was an easy motive and difficult to let go of — even though imagining Claire Russell or Father Northcutt or the woman who washed Dolores's hair as murderers was equally difficult. And none of them wanted to put Kayla back in the mix.

"Joe Duncan. Motive, opportunity —" Cass said.

They thought about Dolores's neighbor with the binoculars and the rifle — Joe Duncan — wanting to protect his wife from change, from noise. From other people.

Nell climbed off the rock, her feet finding solid ground, her thoughts on the man who had been so pleased with receiving home-baked muffins. "Joe claimed he was in town during the possible time of Dolores's murder."

Birdie took Nell's hand and followed her down to solid ground. "I stopped by to see Elliott Danvers yesterday but he was in meetings. He needs to know about Joe's claim on the land. If there is one, anyway. That poor man. He clearly loves his wife. I suspect his life isn't always easy."

Cass slid off the rock. "Which is why Danny thinks he might have snapped. If he really thinks he's going to get possession of all this land now that Dolores is dead, he'd have a pretty solid reason to make it happen."

"If the police thought he was a strong suspect, they would have checked his alibi," Izzy said.

"Except for the fact that there's leeway in the exact time of death. If Kayla's memory is accurate, she would have gotten out here a little after dusk —" Cass said.

"While Joe was conveniently in town," Birdie said.

"Maybe." Izzy scooped up the empty water bottles and slid off the rock. "So many 'ifs.' "

"Back to Dolores's final will and testament," Nell said. "We need to stretch ourselves as we explore Dolores's life. What about people who weren't in the will, people who maybe thought they should be and somehow found out they weren't going to be?"

"Like nonprofits?" Birdie asked.

"Maybe."

"That would give them a motive — anger, maybe," Birdie said.

Cass shook her head. "No, that's too far-fetched. If the money were owed to them, it would be one thing. But would someone really murder another person because they didn't receive money that they weren't really owed in the first place? Especially a non-profit person. Aren't they all nice?" Cass looked over at Nell.

"Of course we are." Nell chuckled. "But who knows what people will do? I agree with Cass, though. It's far-fetched."

It seemed almost ridiculous when they turned it this way and that, the facets of a motive turning garish, or disappearing entirely.

Until Birdie reminded them, "Murder is a *human* thing. Who knows what goes on in another's mind? What emotion can build up or actions be misinterpreted?"

"That's where we go astray, isn't it?" Nell said. "We want everyone to be nice and kind and generous — and nonviolent. But someone *was* violent."

"No stone unturned then. That is how we need to look at this. I will check in with Elliott about the deed to the land, but there's something else I want to get from him. He's kept records of Dolores's giving, going back a few years. It's worth looking at. I'm not sure why, but there might be something there that would point us in a new direction." Birdie mentally recorded the task, her bobbing head clicking items in place.

"What's up with Dolores spending hours

in the library?" Izzy asked. She wiggled into the straps of her backpack and started to follow Cass around the rock to a new path.

"Marian Brandley said she came in to use the computers, not to read. She also made sure I knew that Dolores wasn't playing games like some of my old lady friends do over there. She was working, Marian said."

"Working," Cass repeated. She pushed a dead branch to the side of the path as the others followed her into the woods. "Working on what?"

"Figures, numbers. She loved numbers, their purity." Birdie paused, trying to remember something else the librarian had said. She smiled as her memory cleared. "Dolores told Marian that numbers needed to be respected and shouldn't be abused." Izzy laughed. "Don't ever look at my unbalanced bank account."

"I need to pick up some books I have on hold at the library," Nell said. "I'll see what I can find out."

They walked on through the sweet-smelling woods, sunlight filtering through the trees, guided along the path by an invisible woman.

A short while later Cass called back that they were getting close to the trailhead, though she wasn't sure which one. In minutes they stepped out of the cool woods and into a pool of sunlight. They were near the far edge of Dolores's yard, her house in the distance and the Duncans' visible across from it.

"I hadn't realized how deep these woods are," Nell said. She looked down the road to Dolores's house. From where they stood, it looked cold, desolate, without the heart and warmth a living person had so recently breathed into it.

"It looks lonely," Birdie said.

"Hey, what's that?" Cass asked, pointing to a moving spot in the distance, near the edge of the Cardozo house.

They all squinted, trying to bring the blur into focus.

"A deer?" Izzy wondered, taking a few steps down the road.

But the movement wasn't the quick, agile gait of a doe or fawn. Instead, as their eyes adjusted for the distance, a round figure with frizzy, silvery blue hair came into focus. It was just a quick glimpse, but a distinct one. Then she disappeared around the back of Dolores Cardozo's house, the strings of her apron flapping in the breeze.

CHAPTER 29

Nell dropped Izzy off at the yarn shop, Cass at her office, and, finally, Birdie at her home to meet with the banker. Elliott Danvers had promised to drop by to talk about Dolores's donation records. Birdie promised him an even exchange — Ella's lemon bars in exchange for the records. He assured her he was getting the better deal. There wasn't anything new in the records.

Nell checked the time as she drove out of Birdie's circular drive and headed back toward town, her mind playing with the different images of Marlene Duncan.

The woman who never left her place. There'd been no doubt in Birdie's or Nell's mind who the figure scurrying around the Cardozo house was. Even Cass, who had never met the woman in person, recognized her from Danny's vivid description. "He's a great writer, you know," she had added with a lifted brow.

Birdie had chuckled. "And this just may be something for one of his books. What an odd thing to lie about. Agoraphobia or whatever it is. What was that other fear Danny mentioned?"

"Fear of loud noises," Cass had said.

"I wonder if Joe is aware of Marlene's shenanigans."

Thoughts and words and suppositions had collided as they drove back into town, none of them making complete sense.

It was Birdie who had remembered Marlene talking about the color of Dolores's couch. It was the same as her own, she had said proudly.

Spying through the binoculars, though, could have been the source of that information. But it didn't explain the fleeing figure all of them had just seen. Nell put thoughts of Marlene aside and concentrated on Harbor Road traffic. She waved at Harry Garozzo, taking a break outside his deli, his apron displaying the day's specials in vivid red and orange spills. At the next stoplight, she turned left, driving up the gentle hill to the Sea Harbor Library.

Built in the mid-1800s, the stone building with its steeple and pointed roof looked more like a small church than a library. It was one of Nell's favorite places in all of

Sea Harbor. Its grassy lot was bordered by a stone fence and a meandering walkway that led to the two welcoming wooden doors.

Directly across the street, the police station and courthouse commanded a large hunk of public property but generously offered overflow parking spots to library patrons. Nell found a place and got out of the car, glancing back at the police department and adjoining jail. She imagined Esther Gibson taking her break from the dispatcher's office and visiting her "girls" as she called the female inmates. She'd be sitting comfortably in the middle of them with baskets of yarn and needles at her side. Then, with fingers lifted and yarn looped around them, the lesson would begin, just as it did when she so patiently taught the children in Izzy's shop. Nell could almost hear Esther's singsong voice guiding the women with the childlike verse as they looped their yarn around fat needles, learning directions for the first stitch:

In through the front door
Around the back
Out through the window
And off jumps Jack.

And just like that, the first stitch was complete.

Nell stood in the middle of the lot, the simple rhyme gluing her to the pavement as it raced through her head. *In through the front door . . .*

And in the middle of it was Dolores Cardozo. Dead.

Is it the front door we need to go through to find the killer? Or around the back? Out through the window?

She shook away her confusion and crossed the street quickly, nearly colliding with a biker heading down the hill. She hurried up the library walk and through the double wooden doors into the safe and calming library.

The building wrapped her up in the familiar, comforting smells of childhood — of old books, polished wooden floors, and generations of readers whose presence lingered in the wood paneling of the tall-ceilinged rooms. Nell took a deep breath and smiled.

"Nell — over here."

Nell looked into the main room of the library, the half-moon walnut desk, and into the welcoming wave of Marian Brandley. She stood near the checkout area, now almost totally automated, but it was where

Marian stood to talk with anyone who wore a question mark. No matter their interest, Marian had the perfect book for them to read. Nell's stack of books sat waiting on the shelf nearby.

"I spotted your reserved books and thought you might be by today," Marian said. "And I'm glad — I was hoping to see you."

"It must be karma. I wanted to see you, too. I hear congratulations are in order. Birdie told me about your good fortune."

"Yes. That was gracious and surprising and generous of Dolores Cardozo. Totally undeserved by the way; this is my job, for heaven's sake. But I'm even more thrilled with what she's left to the library. It's a huge bequest that will help us with so many things, all the things Dolores probably noticed in the endless hours she spent in here: better lighting, more computers, new study carrels. The list goes on. She's been on my mind a lot. I think that's why I was hoping I'd run into you or Birdie. I've been wanting someone to talk to about everything that's going on. A generous good woman — murdered."

"That's kind of why I'm here, too — trying to understand Dolores's life a little better. To know her better. And just maybe, if we all put our heads together, to remember some forgotten conversation or something — *anything* — that might help us understand why Dolores died in such an awful way."

"It makes absolutely no sense to me, Nell. None. It's a travesty." Marian glanced around, making sure staff and volunteers were meeting patrons' needs. She motioned toward a door behind the desk. "Let's go in here."

The strong smell of coffee greeted them in the comfortable and cozy staff lounge. Marian walked over to a kitchenette counter and poured two cups of the very black coffee from a carafe, then handed one to Nell. "Break time. I need to get off these feet. I swear by afternoon they're two sizes bigger." She settled herself in an overstuffed chair and kicked off her shoes, motioning for Nell to join her.

About Nell's own age, Marian Brandley was tall and slender and rarely stopped moving, which was one reason she was so trim and fit and looked ten years younger, big feet or not.

"This is the coffee Dolores loved. She drank it by the gallon when she was in here working."

Nell sat down across from her and glanced

at the pot of thick black brew. "In her death, I'm getting to know her — and now I know she loved the world's strongest coffee. The more I learn, the more I think she and I would have been good friends."

"Sure you would. I liked her, too. I didn't really know her that well, though I helped her on the computer now and then. Mostly I got to know her by observing her, watching her mannerisms, her reaction to things. Maybe that's the way we get to know many people."

"What did you observe? What was Dolores like when she was here?"

Marian gave the question some thought. She crossed one leg over the other, cradled her coffee mug on one knee.

Nell poured a heavy stream of cream into the coffee, watching expressions play across Marian's face. "If there's anything we can unearth that will help rid Kayla Stewart of the awful pall of suspicion hanging over her, it would be —"

"Kayla?" Marian looked up. "Yes, it's awful what that young woman is going through. I saw two ladies whispering about her this morning when she brought the kiddos in for story hour. They're normally nice women, but this is a difficult time. People are grasping. And in their grasps, they can sometimes be cruel."

It was what Nell dreaded. "Does Kayla come in here often?"

"Regular as a heartbeat. She and those two lovely kids. She's a wonderful mother. You notice things like that as a librarian."

"I'm sure you get an eyeful," Nell said.

"Yes. Mostly I see nice, sweet interactions. People are inherently good, I think, but people parent differently. Kayla was very hands on, sitting on the floor with her kids, pulling book after book off the shelves. I never once saw her glance at a phone while she was with the children. She adores those two. And as for the rumors insinuating she might have been implicated in Dolores's death? It's simply people desperate to end this nightmare. But it's hurtful and absolutely unfair."

Marian's face was flushed, her calm librarian's voice still intact but her eyes ready to take on some invisible foe. "I will be the first to vouch for Kayla. Not only do I like her, but Dolores did, too. And Kayla liked her. I'll swear to that. And you don't murder someone you like."

It was a thought they all wanted to believe but it wasn't true. Sometimes people did murder people they liked. Nell set her coffee mug down on the table. "How do you know that they liked one another?"

"Well, I just knew. For one thing, Kayla could coax a smile out of Dolores without even trying. And it changed that woman's face, transformed it into the warm, affectionate person we now know she was. I knew them separately, of course — Kayla from all her library visits. Those little guys walking out of here with books piled high in their arms, acting like it was Christmas every Saturday. And of course I knew Dolores because she was in here all the time. Then, some weeks ago, Kayla and the kids had come in for a kids' movie we were showing — *Charlie and the Chocolate Factory,* I think. They were coming out of the children's theater at the same time as Dolores was coming through the front doors. I was at the desk, about to wave hello to Dolores, when I saw her looking at Kayla — she saw Kayla before Kayla saw her, I think, and I had to look twice. Dolores's face changed. It lit up, like a spotlight was on it, especially when she saw the children.

"Then Kayla saw her and went over immediately. Unusual in itself. Kayla was smiling, the way you do if you see someone you care about but in an unexpected place. The kids followed their mom.

"Dolores leaned over, one hand on her

walking stick, and spoke quietly to each child in turn. The kids seemed mesmerized, and the older one, Christopher, must have asked something about the stick because Dolores held it in front of him so he could see it close up. She showed him the handle and let him touch it. He wrapped his small fingers around it, laughing. And Dolores laughed right along with him.

"Frankly, I was the one mesmerized at this point. The interaction was so intimate. I know I'm probably imagining it, but from where I stood, I thought I saw tears in Dolores's eyes. Happy ones. Dolores must have figured out that Kayla came on Saturdays, and I saw them together a few more times after that. Dolores liked those kiddos."

Nell hung on every word, the scene playing out in her head, frame by frame. She remembered Izzy's telling of meeting Dolores one day when she had Abby with her. A similar tale of Dolores' affection for kids. "That's a lovely story. Thank you for sharing it."

"I thought it was lovely, too."

"So this Dolores was different from the one you saw other times?"

"Yes. And Kayla was different, too. I suspect she is very warm underneath, but she usually stands slightly apart from the other moms, as if protecting herself. But there was a sincere warmth there when she was with Dolores."

"What was Dolores like when she was here alone?"

"She was one of the most focused women I've ever met. I'd have gotten through college in two years instead of four with her kind of attention span. It wasn't that she shunned other people. Dolores was always polite and pleasant. But she exuded a vibe that told everyone around her that she was busy, and that whatever she was doing was serious business and demanded concentration."

"Do you know what she worked on here? Birdie mentioned figures, accounting kinds of things?"

"Yes. Of course I don't know too much, only what I learned from her. Internet privacy is important here. We have software in place to protect anyone who uses our computers. Library cardholders' activity is gone as soon as they log out. And at the end of the day, the servers are cleaned of the day's activity. It's important that everyone who uses the computers understands that their searches and words are safe."

"That's a good thing to know —"

"But you're disappointed. I know you too

well, Nell. At times like these it might be helpful if we could somehow crawl inside Dolores's mind — or at least her search history. It might help."

"That's it exactly, Marian. Even knowing the sites she visited might give us a glimpse into her life."

"Well, here's the thing. Although the library provides security measures, Dolores was sometimes open with me about her searches, especially if she had a question about something. She wasn't trying to hide anything. Like I told Birdie, she was both an accountant and an auditor. She was interested in how companies used their money, how it was spent, the financials, and so on. Now we know why — it makes logical sense. The organizations she gave to had to toe the mark. I suspect she didn't suffer fools gladly."

Nell smiled. That was probably an understatement.

"She spent hours on this work. I'd watch her writing down numbers, taking notes, frowning, then smiling, then simply looking like an accountant. Serious, you know?"

"But you didn't know at the time what she was looking for?"

"Not completely. And I try not to guess people's motivations when they use our computers. I'm just happy that people — especially seniors — are interested and keeping their minds sharp. But I was around Dolores so often, and she'd say little things now and then, that I came to understand she wasn't just examining financial records to keep her mind sharp, like doing crossword puzzles. She was interested in how nonprofits were run. She'd talk to me sometimes about how important it was to be good stewards of other people's generosity. She probably based some of her own giving decisions on that."

"That seems wise." As a former nonprofit director, Nell had experienced groups being run in a sloppy manner. Often it was simply because they weren't careful, or maybe for monetary reasons they hired people not entirely qualified for the job. It was rarely malicious; most often, it was simply a result of carelessness. But it happened.

"A tightly run institution was important to her. I was acutely aware of that one day when she reacted in an uncharacteristic way. Uncharacteristic for her, anyway. She was usually so calm and genteel."

"What happened?"

Marian got up and refilled their coffee mugs, then sat back down. "It was recently. I think it might have been the last time she came in here. Something she was doing on the computer was frustrating her that day. Sometimes she was so quiet I didn't know she was in here unless she spoke to me. But that day I was sitting nearby, helping someone with a computer problem, and I could almost feel her tension. She had her ever-present calculator and a copy of the newspaper — one she'd brought in with her — next to her.

"Every now and then she'd glance at the newspaper, grimace slightly, then go back to the computer or the calculator or scribble numbers on a yellow pad, then double-check them against the computer, then jot more numbers down. Others probably didn't notice anything strange because they didn't know her. But I knew something was wrong.

"Finally, she turned the computer off with such force I was worried about the keyboard for a minute. Next thing I knew she lifted her cane and stomped it on the floor with a bang. Dolores's face was flushed, and at first I thought she was having a stroke, but I soon realized that it was plain old anger — something I've been known to express when people scribble in library books, but I had never seen Dolores get angry. In someone else, it might have seemed to be an angry ripple — an 'oh, damn' kind of thing — but in sedate Dolores it was like a tsunami. Her eyes flashed and everything about her tightened, even the skin over her high cheekbones. When she saw my worried face, she took a deep breath and released it slowly, her eyes closing briefly. In a minute or so, her reaction had been softened to one of disappointment. But a serious disappointment. She assured me, however, that she was fine. She simply had some things she had to take care of that were difficult and unpleasant. But then, well, then everything would be fine."

"What do you suppose the anger — or the disappointment — was about?"

"I'm not sure."

Nell tried to fit what she was hearing into what she knew about Dolores. "Was that it?"

"Almost. She told me she was going to go for a long walk and nature would help her put things in their proper order. It never failed her, she said, even when people sometimes did. And then she'd do what needed to be done. She managed a smile — sort of — to let me know she was okay, and suggested I should try long walks, too. It was the answer to many things."

"Do you have any idea what she was upset about?"

"Not specifically. My cousin was an accountant, and he'd be upset for days when the numbers on his ledgers didn't line up right. He'd act like the world had ended. Maybe Dolores was like that. Something was off kilter with one of the organizations. And it ruffled her need for things to be in order."

Nell nodded. But somehow Dolores's response — at least as Marian described it — seemed rather extreme for numbers being slightly off, especially for small nonprofits. It could easily happen. Nell wondered if Marian was being kind — or if she had missed something.

Marian slipped back into her shoes and got up, her eyes on the wall clock. "I guess I'd better get back to work — or I'll have to fire me. It's almost closing time."

Nell got up, too, and walked with the librarian into the main library. She said her good-byes, then headed toward the outer door, stopping halfway there. She turned and walked back to the desk where Marian was already busy on the computer.

"Marian, this may sound like a silly question. In fact, it may well *be* a silly question. You mentioned Dolores brought a newspaper in that day. And she referred to it somehow?"

"Yes. She stared down at it, her pencil in her hand. Angry, though I don't think she was angry at the newspaper. It was what she was figuring out on the screen. Or maybe it was both?"

"Did she take it with her?"

"No. But I think she meant to. We have the daily newspaper here if she wanted to read one — but for some reason she had brought her own. I think she forgot it because her departure was so abrupt. I found it on the floor later."

"So it was thrown out?"

Marian frowned. "Hmm, maybe not, now that you ask. I'd forgotten all about it until now. I hung on to it for a while in case she needed it the next time she came in. And then, well, then she died and an old newspaper was the last thing on my mind. It might still be in here." She pulled open a cluttered drawer in the desk and rummaged through some lost reading glasses, a tangled mess of earbuds, and finally pulled out a newspaper, folded over to an inside page. She held it out. "This is it."

"May I take it?" Nell asked. "I'm not sure why, but I'm curious why she brought a newspaper in with her."

"Of course. It's you or the recycle bin."

Nell knew she was grasping at straws, but she took the folded newspaper and tucked it under her arm. A yellow sheet of scrap paper poked out from the fold, numbers scribbled on it, but Dolores had left that, too. Sometimes the devil was in the details. In a matter of thirty minutes she had become closer to Dolores. Her death was more personal and intimate now. How did the chief of police handle such emotions when dealing with crimes, sometimes looking into the suspicious deaths of people he knew or cared about? Were emotions a hindrance or did it make you work harder? She couldn't be sure, not even for herself.

Once in the car, Nell dropped the newspaper on the seat beside her, started the car, and only then glanced down at the folded newspaper. It was an inside page that showed on top. A mix of neighborhood news: a fire over on Cedar Road, a teenager winning an award, a man arrested for selling illegal lobsters.

Down at the bottom, a small headline caught her eye:

NORTH SHORE DYNASTIES
SUPPORT CAUSES

And right below it, the reporter's byline: *Richie Pisano*

CHAPTER 30

The ladies' Sunday night out had been
Ben's idea, including making the reserva-
tions at the Ocean's Edge himself, although
he'd conspired with Danny and Sam for the
special touches.

At first Nell thought the idea might have
been connected to tickets to a Sox game
someone had offered Ben, but she mis-
judged her husband. Ben was going to stay
home, eat soup, and pay bills; Sam planned
to have a special evening with Abby, who
was pretending her daddy was Lightning
McQueen and she was Mater, pushing the
tow truck up and down Sam's back; and
Danny was relaxing at home watching old
West Wing episodes on Netflix.

The three men had agreed a relaxing night
out might ease some of the tension cloud-
ing the women's faces. Coping with puz-
zling inheritances, the fate of a vulnerable
mother, and the heavy dark cloud created

by an unsolved murder was taking its toll. They'd been pulled into the morass in a personal way, far more personal than Ben liked.

It was becoming an obsession, he had said over coffee that morning, expanding his point as Nell buttered the toast: "It doesn't matter that the police say it wasn't a random crime. It's still murder, Nellie. Someone who kills once knows he has the power to do it. And if that person feels threatened, who knows what he might do?"

Nell knew Ben was right, yet for reasons that escaped her, she wasn't afraid. She had left the library the day before weary but with the certain feeling that they were closer to knowing why Dolores Cardozo had lost her life. And instead of fear, she was beginning to feel the outer reaches of peace, albeit one shrouded in sadness. Nothing about murder brought joy. Especially when it was so close to home.

The library visit had brought to the surface what they'd been inching toward. A different path and opening the door to a different room in Dolores Cardozo's remarkable brain.

It left Nell once again assured that Kayla wasn't complicit in a murder. Someone else was. Someone with more ties to Sea Harbor than the recently settled woman and her children.

"Meet at my place first," Birdie had texted to all of them. "Cocktails at sunset in Sonny's den before we go to dinner." They all thought it was a brilliant idea. Loose ends were better tightened in privacy. And Sonny Favazza's den was the perfect place.

Birdie, Izzy, and Cass were already comfortable in the round paneled room that still carried the sweet scent of Sonny Favazza's cherry tobacco. Or at least that's what Birdie claimed. Maybe it was all in her imagination, she admitted, but it didn't matter a whit. Sonny was there in the room with her, and had been all these years, ever since an undetected heart weakness took his physical body away. Usually the closeness she felt brought her joy and the intimate nearness of his spirit.

But for a few days now, Sonny had perplexed her, a feeling she expressed out loud.

" 'Perplexed,' can that be a verb?" She looked up as Nell walked into the room.

"If it works for you, I say go for it," Cass answered from across the room. "Whoever thought that 'googled' could be a verb?" She and Izzy were standing in front of one of the six-foot windows, the entire town of Sea

430

Harbor spread out before them. They never tired of the view. It worked a kind of magic, putting lives and loves — and even murder — into perspective. And it was why Birdie had suggested they meet there first.

"So Sonny is perplexing you? That requires an explanation." Nell poured herself a drink from a pitcher with lime slices floating on top.

"Gimlets," Birdie answered before Nell asked. "Ella says they're good for solving difficult and thorny conundrums."

"Well, good, then. But back to Sonny?"

"Here's the thing. Sonny somehow had a role in Dolores appointing me to be her executor. I know that. And I don't know if it has anything to do with her murder, but it's a dangling thread so we need to find out." Birdie's clear gray eyes were bright, the thought of her Sonny joining them to solve a mystery a lovely one, perplexing or not. She took a drink of her gimlet.

Cass settled into a soft leather chair. "Then let's get to it. Let's solve this thing, all parts of it. But first things first. Did Elliott Danvers bring Dolores's records to you? Maybe that will help explain your role, Birdie."

"Yes, he did. The list of her giving goes way back." Birdie pointed to the file of printouts on the low round table in front of her chair. "We also talked again about her appointing me executor. Elliott only remembers Dolores mentioning my name once, and that was tacked on to Sonny's — Sonny and Birdie Favazza, like that. At least that's all he could remember. She had come in for a meeting with him and it happened to be on the anniversary of the day her sister died. Her usual reserve was softened, Elliott said, no doubt moved by the memory."

"I forgot she had a sister," Izzy said. She settled into a wingback chair, her bright silk blouse melting into the colorful print and her long legs, slim in skinny jeans, crossed at the knee.

"I did, too. Michelle was about ten years younger than Dolores and she died young. Dolores brought up the fact that the Danvers Bank was built on the same land that the old factory occupied — the one Sonny's family owned and where Mr. Cardozo had worked for years. I never made that connection but now I remember the old building, Sonny's office. Dolores was reminiscing how she and Michelle used to come into the office with their dad on weekends and play around his desk. It was the same office she eventually worked in."

Izzy sat up forward in her chair. "Michelle? That was her sister's name?"

Birdie nodded.

"I had a friend in grade school, Michelle Wittchen. We called her Shelly."

Nell was the first one who remembered Izzy's sweet story. "Your part dream/part memory, Izzy. Dolores kneeling down in front of Abby when they met in the woods."

"And she called her Shelly," Izzy said, her voice hushed and her eyes smiling.

The tender story brought quiet for a moment, and then Cass brought them back to business.

"So Dolores mentioned your name to Elliott. What else?" Cass asked.

"It was more about Sonny, but Dolores knew I was his wife, Elliott said. I was riding on his coattails. Dolores talked about how kind Sonny had been to her family — especially to her and Michelle when her parents died. She repeated something Sonny had said to her one day, something she never forgot and that touched her deeply. Elliott didn't understand it at the time but he remembered it. Sonny told Dolores that he had fully intended to save two lives, but he had only been able to save one — and for that he harbored deep regret."

They were all quiet for a moment, Sonny's words filling the room.

"No wonder he's perplexing you," Cass finally said. She looked over at the laptop on Sonny's old leather inlaid desk. "May I?"

Birdie nodded.

"She opened up to Elliott on the anniversary of her sister's death?" Izzy asked.

"Yes. She went on to say that her gratitude to Sonny Favazza knew no bounds — and she promised him that she would pay it forward."

"Pay it forward. . . ." Izzy tried to put the words into context. "Well, that I understand. Maybe that began her path of giving."

"Maybe. Elliott thought Sonny's personal files might shed more light on it if I needed to know more. He wouldn't have used the company funds for helping individuals. So Elliot and I ransacked his personal file cabinet over there." Birdie pointed across the room to a dark wooden cabinet, and then a brown folder on the table.

"Life before computers," Nell said with a smile.

Birdie nodded, her eyes on the old files as if Sonny himself were holding them, sitting there beside her, one arm around her shoulders, dropping a kiss now and then. "I'm not sure I need to know more than that. From what Dolores told Elliott, we know

Sonny helped her financially. That should be enough. The amount doesn't matter."

"It explains why Dolores would appoint you as executor. But what's not clear is what he meant by saving lives," Nell said. She watched Birdie retreating into her memory. Not only were they all learning about Dolores Cardozo, but Birdie was hearing her husband's words, learning about his role in a life that she hadn't been privy to before.

Birdie pulled the typed sheets and banded canceled checks from the brown folder. "These are around the years that Antonio Cardozo worked at the factory and after, when Dolores was hired on. Sonny was neat and very exact."

Antonio Cardozo's name was typed at the top of a sheet, the family members listed below it. It took only a few minutes to learn how Sonny Favazza had walked into the Cardozo family after Antonio and Anna Cardozo had died in that freak car accident one icy December night, leaving two daughters, one with the formidable task of raising the other.

"Hold on a minute," Cass said, her head lifting. "I found something. Listen. It's an obituary from a New Hampshire newspaper."

Michelle A. Cardozo passed suddenly in the New Hampshire Correctional Facility for Women. Cardozo was twenty-one. She leaves one sister, Dolores Cardozo, of Sea Harbor, MA.

They stared at Cass.

She pushed a handful of hair behind her ear. She read it again, more slowly this time.

"Her sister was in a correctional facility —" Izzy said.

"And passed suddenly." Birdie's voice was hushed as she pondered the euphemism.

Cass looked down and read the last line that confirmed their thoughts. " 'Donations in her memory can be made to the Agency to Prevent Suicide in Youth.' "

"Suicide and jail," Nell said, the combination unraveling a devastating chapter in Dolores Cardozo's life.

It took little time for the file in Birdie's hands to reveal Sonny Favazza's efforts to help save that second life. Through bonuses and finally a trust, he had assisted Dolores financially in raising a child who seemed doomed to a life of addiction. Canceled checks showed payments to rehab centers across New Hampshire, to therapists and hospitals. To a private school for troubled youth and the best addiction doctors in

New England.

"Oh, dear Sonny," Birdie said out loud, looking around the room to be sure he heard her. She looked upward. "But you can't always save everyone, my love."

Footsteps in the hallway drew their attention away from the drama spinning out in the room.

Ella Sampson appeared in the doorway, apologizing for interrupting. "You have company, Birdie," she said.

Standing just behind her were Gabby and Daisy Danvers, and behind them, a larger woman standing in the shadow.

Sister Fiona took a step inside the door, explaining her presence. "I was bringing the girls home and we spotted the cars in the drive. Gabby suggested I come in to say hi." She looked down at the papers, the computer on her niece's lap.

"We helped Sister Fiona teach some of the diners at the Bountiful Bowl Café how to knit scarves for the HMS project. Wait'll you see the stack of things for the clothing center, Izzy. You won't believe it. It's way cool."

Izzy started to thank the girls, but in the next minute, Gabby and Daisy were gone, up to Gabby's third-floor room to do whatever preteens did when they escaped adult company.

Fiona walked further into the room. Her corduroy pants were decorated with scraps of yarn, and the knit sweater she wore, bearing a smiling lobster on the front, belied the serious expression on her face. "Truth is, Gabby didn't suggest we come up to say hi. I did." She sat down in the one remaining chair. "It's been busy at the school, but I wondered how all of you were doing."

"We're wondering the same, Fiona," Birdie said.

"It's hard," she said. "Dolores was a friend. I miss her every day."

"Of course you do," Birdie said. "We're glad you came up."

Nell watched a range of emotions pass across the nun's face, not the least of which was grief. In the aftermath of Dolores's tragic death, the fact that Fiona had lost a friend had largely gone unnoticed. Of course she was grieving, an emotion lifted to unnatural proportions by the way she died.

"Dolores was a lovely woman who certainly didn't deserve this." Nell offered Fiona a tissue. "There aren't many words to ease the loss of a friend."

Fiona took the tissue and nodded, her round face grateful.

"Murder is a strange and awful beast," Birdie said. She motioned for Fiona to sit. "And so terribly human."

Fiona looked into the glass Nell handed her, swirling the liquid against the sides, a whirlpool that seemed to match the emotions on her face. Finally, she set it down and nodded. "What's that we say? To err is human, to forgive . . . divine? But it's difficult to take that second step until we know whom we're forgiving. Someone killed my friend. How can they bear to let others suffer because of their silence? And why did they do it? It's so difficult to understand the taking of another's life. No matter what reason. No matter the person."

"The motive could be very simple," Birdie said. "And very human. Exploring Dolores's humanity may help us find that person." She looked intently at Fiona. "That person *will* be caught, Fiona. This will end."

The conviction in Birdie's voice surprised the nun, and she managed a small smile. "And then we shall grieve in peace."

"Yes, we shall." Birdie sat back in the chair.

"Kayla must be grieving, too, in her own way. We sometimes forget that," Nell said.

"Sure she is. But there's more than grief going on inside her. And I'm not sure what it is. This unsolved murder is a horrendous thing and Kayla is tied to it no matter what. And I feel responsible for it — I knew Kayla needed a Dolores in her life. Even more, Dolores needed a Kayla. I just knew it right here," Fiona placed a hand over her heart. "Charlie and I talked about it today. He came by the cafe to carry in some supplies for us." Fiona turned and looked at Izzy. "Your brother understands life in a way that I wouldn't have expected. Insightful, he is."

"He's been around the block a few times. Maybe that's part of it," Izzy said. "But you're right. Charlie's compassion is sincere. He's turned into a sensitive guy."

"He thinks Kayla's stress is rooted in protecting her kids. Something is threatening that and he doesn't think it's related to Dolores's murder. At least not directly."

"That's vague," Izzy said.

Fiona agreed. "But I think Charlie and Kayla have had more late-night talks than any of us realize and he's trying hard to figure it out. He says she's complicated — I agree with him there — but in some ways he thinks she's naïve. She knows she didn't kill Dolores Cardozo, so Charlie claims that in her mind it's a given that she won't be convicted. So she isn't afraid of being put in jail."

Nell found some relief in knowing that Kayla didn't lose sleep worrying that the police might show up at her door, even though her rationale might be naïve and her comfort premature.

"If she isn't worried about being arrested, what do you think she's afraid of?" Izzy asked.

"I don't know. Charlie is determined to find out. He's getting close, he says."

Nell tried to pull apart the strands of thought tangled in her mind. Two roads diverging in the woods. Her head told her they needed to travel both. She looked over at Birdie, who was looking down at Elliott's records of Dolores's giving history. She was thinking the same thing.

Getting close. One path leading to a murderer. And one to a mother trying to protect her children.

Nell looked back to Fiona. "What did Charlie think of the café? It's an amazing place."

"It is that, but now that you ask, I don't have a clue what Charlie thought of it. Gabby and Daisy showed him around and then left him to wander on his own. I saw him in the kitchen staring intently at the bulletin board as if it held the secrets to the universe instead of the menus for the week and other things people tack up there. The next thing I knew he was heading for the door at high speed, shouting a good-bye over his shoulder, and disappearing up the stairs as if his pants were on fire."

"Maybe he had an emergency at the family clinic," Cass said. "Or the free health clinic. Poor guy seems to be on call twenty-four hours a day."

"Maybe." Fiona fidgeted in the chair, her wine untouched, her expression still bothered. "I'm sorry to keep barging in on you like this."

"No, no, you're not barging in," Cass said. But her voice was gentle and there was a smile that started in her eyes. "And we're not sorry, either, Aunt Fiona. All of us are thinking the same thoughts, feeling the same wretched sadness, and trying to get our lives back to normal. Better to do it together than apart. Heck, you're not so bad to have around."

Nell looked over at Cass. There was something different about her these days. But she knew better than to ask about it, for fear of it disappearing. In the middle of all the uncertainty around the town, Cass seemed . . . well . . . settled, somehow.

Fiona was touched by her niece's words, too, but in true Halloran fashion, she

442

acknowledged them with a brief cough, a pat on Cass's hand, and a change of subject.

"So" — she glanced at her watch and rose from the chair — "dinner with your mom tonight, Cass. I'd better get on over there. She eats earlier and earlier. Next thing I know we'll be having pork chops for breakfast."

Birdie looked up. "Fiona, before you leave, there're some things about Dolores that confuse me, and you knew her better than any of us."

Fiona stayed standing, her look wary. She wrapped her fingers around the top of a tall chair.

"You seem somehow protective of her — her life, her background."

"She was a private person," Fiona said. "She'd hate people talking about her. I respect that, so I don't."

"You knew she had a sister, right?" Birdie asked.

Fiona nodded. "Sure. It was in the obituary. I'm not sure how Mary Pisano unearthed that, but none of this matters now, does it? Her sister was at the center of her life, always in her thoughts. She devoted her life to her after their parents died. The girl died young and it broke Dolores's heart."

"Do you know how she died?"

Fiona seemed surprised at the question. "No," she said. "She told me once that her sister was a troubled person. She ran away in her teens and got into drugs. Dolores didn't like talking about it. I think she thought she had somehow failed her sister."

Cass leaned forward in the chair, the computer still open on her lap, the blue screen lit with a faded newspaper obituary. She looked at Fiona and told her about Michelle Cardozo's death.

Fiona released a lungful of air. She shook her head slowly. "How awful for Dolores. No wonder she was so understanding, so helpful to kids who had problems."

"Sonny Favazza helped both Dolores and her sister," Nell said. "He set up a trust for the two girls after their parents died, and he tried to find help for the sister for years after that."

Fiona listened, putting the pieces in place. "Dolores never mentioned that."

"And then Dolores herself set up one for Kayla," Izzy said.

"There are obvious themes weaving through this story," Birdie said.

"That explains why Dolores chose you to manage her will," Fiona said.

"Or, more accurately, why she chose Sonny's wife," Birdie said. "I'm a stand-in for someone she trusted deeply — and I'm very happy to play that role. Her parents were killed leaving a company party. It's what Sonny would do. But what I can't figure out is why Dolores helped the Stewart family the way she did. I mean specifically. Was there something about that family that set them apart?"

They all looked up at Fiona.

She had loosened her grip on the back of the chair and started walking toward the door. She paused for just a moment. "It's simple," she said. "She was just paying it forward."

They listened to Fiona's footsteps fading away as she wound her way down the wide staircase, her words trailing after her.

The phrase echoed around the room, taking on different shades of meaning. Paying it forward was clear. But it still wasn't clear why Kayla Stewart had been singled out. And they all knew the nun now walking out the front door had held something back.

Finally, Nell broke the silence, glancing at the grandfather clock in the corner. "It's almost time for our reservation, and we haven't gotten to Elliott's printouts. I think it's critical that we do. We don't want these getting in the way of Don Wooten's Sunday night chef's special."

Izzy began spreading the sheets out on the table as she talked and stepped into her orderly lawyer mode. "Nell's right. Kayla and Dolores's relationship is interesting. And Sonny's involvement with the family, especially his attempts to help Dolores help her sister, is generous and wonderful. Beneath her worry Kayla is grieving this woman just like Fiona is. All this is good for us to know because we care about the people involved. But there is more we need to know about Kayla, things she is holding tight to herself for reasons that probably seem legitimate to her."

She paused for just a moment, looked around at her audience. "But right now that might be a distraction. Maybe Charlie can go down that road for us. But to find out who murdered Dolores Cardozo, we need to follow some other path. We're on it, I think. All we need to do is stay the course." She grinned. "There. That's what I think."

"Yes," Birdie said, smiling broadly at Izzy. "Thank you, Isabel. You have brought us focus."

"So shall I start?" Nell asked, then responded to the nods by filling them in quickly on her visit to the library and what she'd learned about Dolores's studious and exact approach to the charities she sponsored. "She knew everything about every organization who received money from her. And probably about those who didn't. And that's something these records will tell us more clearly."

Birdie had organized the sheets, one for each year since Dolores had retired and begun helping Sea Harbor in a myriad of ways.

"This is interesting," Cass said, pointing to the columns on one of the sheets. "It's like the *New York Times* best seller list, which, by the way, Danny has been on for every single book. He's quite remarkable, you know." She smiled as she said Danny's name, a goofy kind of smile was how Izzy explained it later to Sam. Not Cass's usual look.

"Cass, you're getting soft on us," Izzy said.

"I'd call it something else," Birdie said wisely, looking into Cass's deep blue eyes.

"Aw, come on, you guys," Cass said, brushing off the teasing. "As I was saying, look at the lists carefully. They not only list each organization and the amount received, but indicate if it's a new beneficiary or, if old, how many years it's been on the list."

Izzy held up a sheet she was looking at. "And at the bottom, she boxes those who were removed from the list that year."

Birdie leaned over and scanned the sheet. "But it doesn't say why."

They tried to imagine the reactions from organizations when Dolores sent out her annual anonymous donations. The haves and the have-nots. Some small organizations could be in dire straits, even fold, if they didn't make the grade. And the anonymous factor meant the directors couldn't even wine and dine the mysterious benefactor to gain favor.

"Maybe it's that group at the bottom that we should start with," Nell said. "Let's each take a few sheets, study them, look for anything suspicious, patterns, and we'll get together tomorrow to see what we've come up with." She flipped through several print-outs, pulled out one in particular and slipped it, along with two or three others, into her bag. Izzy had spoken a stark truth in getting them to focus, even when doing so might be unpleasant down the road.

It had brought about a definite shift in the room that they all felt. Loose ends were still there, but once you had a focus — someone or something you were headed toward — it was far easier to tie them off.

Cass had felt it, too, and looked at a few of the lists. "It won't take long to go through these and it's interesting. I for one feel a desperate need to get this settled so I . . . so *we,* so all of us, can get on with our lives."

Izzy looked over at her. Nell was looking, too. Cass's words were cryptic, slightly mysterious.

"Stop looking at me," she said with a small laugh. "All I'm saying is that there is more here than numbers. I can feel it."

"We just have to find it," Nell said.

"And we will," Cass said definitively. "Maybe we already have. We just need to put on our glasses."

"And remember," Izzy said, "we agreed it's a long shot that some nonprofit director would murder a benefactor because of not receiving a donation for the organization. There has to be more to it. Think about it. Would you — would anyone — kill Santa Claus because he didn't bring the present you wanted?"

They laughed — and welcomed the lightness it brought into the room.

And they purposefully ignored the fact that people had probably killed for far less.

CHAPTER 31

The late September night was nearly perfect. A crisp, cool breeze blew in off the ocean and a full moon spilled its light on the Ocean's Edge Restaurant, warming the porches and decks and large thick windows.

The owner himself held open the door for the four women coming up the steps.

"Ladies, we've been expecting you," Don Wooten said with a slight bow, as if greeting royalty.

Nell gave him a hug and laughed as she looked over at the crowded bar and the dining area beyond. "Us and how many dozen others?"

"Nope. Just you four are special tonight. Ben said you needed a night away from it all. We're here to see that you get it. Your table is almost ready, my special friends." He left them with a smile as he turned to greet a new group of diners coming up the steps.

They moved toward the bar, a long curved slab of mahogany that ran along the front of the restaurant. Nell stood back for a few moments, looking into the restaurant proper, the white-clothed tables and curved booths. She wondered if Kayla Stewart was on duty, but the busy bar area blocked her view.

There was no sight of her, but as she looked over to the hostess station, she spotted someone else. Joe Duncan stood talking to the hostess, his arms cradling a large white bag. He noticed her watching him, nodded solemnly, then turned and headed toward the front door. Don Wooten held it open, greeting him warmly. He said something to Don that brought a laugh. Don patted him on the back and sent him off with a warm good-bye.

Nell walked over to Don as the door swung closed. "That was Joe Duncan, right?"

"Sure was. My most faithful diner."

"He eats here every Sunday? Alone? Those looked like a lot of leftovers he was carrying."

Don laughed. "No, he doesn't eat here ever, alone or otherwise. Every Saturday night of the year he comes in to get fried clams, the lobster penne, and a chocolate mousse. Every week without fail. He takes it home to his 'bride,' as he calls Marlene, and they eat together by candlelight." Don shook his head, smiling. "Tonight was Marlene's birthday so he came in again, even though it's Sunday. She gets two candlelight dinners this weekend, one with a cake. Dunc's a character. It took him a while to warm up to us, but now he sits at the bar and has a beer while we get his dinners ready. He talks the bartender's ear off. Or mine."

"I've met Marlene. She's housebound, Joe said."

"Well, sort of. More property bound, than house." Don chuckled. "But old Dunc came up with a way around it, a way to expand her horizons at least a little and get her some exercise. Marlene thinks they own the Cardozo property now and he lets her believe it, so at the least he can get her out walking around the quarry and prowling around the old Cardozo house. She needed exercise, he said, and with this plan, she's already lost five pounds. Joe checked it all out with Sister Fiona, since she's the rightful owner now. She told him to go for it. Dolores believed in exercise, the good sister told Joe. She'd be tickled with Dunc's clever solution to the problem."

Don looked out again as Dunc moved slowly to his car. "He's a good man," he said. "He was in here the Saturday night Dolores Cardozo was murdered. He had had a few extra at the bar that night and I ended up driving him home — though he told Marlene some story about his truck having problems, blaming the delay on Shelby Pickard. He told me later that maybe, had he been home on time, he'd have heard something, seen something — even been able to save Dolores. It chewed him up for a while."

Nell listened carefully to every word, holding back her surprise. She felt relief and sadness at once: sadness that they had met Joe Duncan, talked to him a couple times, but hadn't looked deep enough. They hadn't seen that a thoughtful and kind man lived behind the binoculars and the rifle. It pleased her more deeply than she would have expected.

It wouldn't hurt to walk in all kinds of people's shoes now and then.

"Yoo-hoo, Nell," Birdie called over with a wave. "Come, dear."

The bartender had set wineglasses in front of them and was filling each with Prosecco, but it was the man in the middle of her friends that Nell noticed more than the sparkling wine Don had ordered for them.

"Charlie," she said, surprised.

"Aunt Nell." He stepped over and hugged her.

"Are you meeting someone? Can you join us for dinner?"

He shook his head, a shock of hair falling across his forehead. Nell refrained from pushing it back or suggesting her nephew get a haircut. Then she noticed the set to his jaw. "What's wrong?"

"Nothing, things are okay. I had a little free time so I came by to see Kayla. She's somewhere around here, but the babysitter said she gets off soon. I'll see if she needs a lift." He drummed his fingers on the surface of the bar next to an empty beer bottle and craned his neck to see over Nell's shoulder.

"My gallant brother," Izzy said, but she said it softly, aware that Charlie wasn't in a teasing mood. Nor was he being gallant.

"I'm assuming Kayla is all right," Birdie said. The tone of her voice was the same that had coaxed worry out of all of them at one time or another.

Charlie managed a half smile, looking around as he talked. "Yeah, sure. I think so. I finally realized something about her that had been niggling me for days. I need to talk to her about it, is all. It'll be fine."

At that moment the muscles in his neck knotted. He took a quick, audible breath and glared at a man who had walked into the lounge area.

Richie Pisano, a wide smile on his face, lifted a hand in a wave as he spotted the women. He walked their way.

Nell glanced at Charlie. She put one hand on his arm, suddenly unsure of the emotion in his eyes. "Charlie?"

"I'm okay. I don't like the guy, is all," he mumbled. "I'm out of here."

He slipped away before they could say anything, and in time to avoid one moment with the reporter, who was now greeting the four women as if they were longtime friends.

"I thought I saw Charlie boy over here," Richie said, his voice upbeat. He laughed. "Hope I didn't scare him off."

"Charlie's hard to scare," Izzy said with clipped pleasantry.

"Hey, I was just kidding. Charlie's a good dude. We're friends." Richie laughed again and made small talk, much of it describing several events he was covering and writing about, including another charity event that included the who's who of everyone. "Awesome" was his evaluation.

Standing slightly behind him, Cass rolled

her eyes.

Birdie filled in the pause. "I suppose meeting important and wealthy people is a chance for you to make connections, Richie. Perhaps provide career opportunities."

"For me?" He laughed. "Nah. I don't need them. I've got a good thing going — or will soon."

Nell swore he winked before stepping out of her direct sight, allowing a group headed for the bar to pass in front of him. She cringed.

At that moment, while Richie remained invisible, Kayla Stewart walked over and greeted them, telling them their table was ready. Her voice was warm and welcoming, a smile easing her usual somber look. She seemed clearly happy to see them.

Birdie gave her an unexpected embrace. At first she looked surprised, then pleased.

But in the next second Kayla's lips pressed tight together. The smile was gone, and along with it, all warmth. Her body was rigid.

"Hey, there," Richie Pisano said, moving back into their circle. "I checked with the hostess. She said you're off soon? Cool. I'll give you a ride home. We need to catch up."

Kayla turned back to the women waiting for their table and forced a smile to her face.

"Mr. Wooten picked the best table in the house for you," she said. "Please follow me."

By the time they'd wound their way through the dining area to a candle-lit table with a view of the sea, Kayla's shoulders had loosened slightly, her walk gaining back a semblance of assurance.

But it was clear to all four of them that Richie Pisano was not her boyfriend, not her lover, not someone she wanted to drive her home.

A small arrangement of peach roses, lemon leaf, and seeded eucalyptus leafed out in the middle of their table, along with a white card poking out from sprigs of fall berries.

"I guess Don meant what he said about making the evening special for us," Izzy said, pulling out the card. She read the names on the card. Then looked up with a smile. "It's from Ben, Danny, and Sam."

Cass took the card from her. Her face reddened slightly. "Except it's Danny's handwriting. I spotted him in that new florist's over in Canary Cove when I drove over."

"Our Danny?" Birdie said. "That fellow is turning into a lovely sentimental man, just like my Sonny. I see it in his beautiful eyes and gestures like these."

"His eyes?" Cass chuckled. She leaned in

to smell a peach rose and to hide a blush of pleasure on her face. Then she happily sat back as a plate of Oysters Rockefeller in half shells was placed in front of each of them. Sprigs of watercress and green onion were sprinkled between the shells.

"Is it the end of the world?" Izzy asked. She sighed. "If only life were plates of Oysters Rockefeller delivered by candlelight. And sweet men sending us love and flowers."

"It can be. For tonight anyway," Nell said. She looked up as a shadow fell across the table.

Kayla had returned, this time with her name tag off and a light jacket covering up her crisp white waitress blouse. She stood near Birdie's chair, apologizing to all of them for interrupting. And then she directed her full attention to Birdie, a worried look now replacing the brief sight they'd had earlier of a more relaxed Kayla. "I need to apologize for not answering your phone calls, and, well, for not meeting with you, Birdie. Please know I'm totally grateful for your kindness and your offer to help with this . . . this will business. This mess. It's just . . . it's just that I'm not sure how to fit it into my life. You know. Like, safely."

Birdie listened carefully, her eyes holding

Kayla's and giving her permission to say whatever was on her mind or in her heart, and with whatever time it took to do it. In the distance, soft classical jazz floated around the softly lit room.

"So, I want what's best for my children," Kayla said, her voice choking a little bit. "I want them to have a different kind of life, you know, like from mine. But sometimes it's complicated. You get that, right?" Her eyes began to fill, but as if turning off a faucet, she managed to stop the tears.

Izzy and Cass were listening, but their eyes were watching a figure standing yards away in the shadow of the kitchen doors.

Richie Pisano's stare never wavered as he watched Kayla's back.

And not far beyond him, behind a line of tall plants that separated the dining room from a smaller bar that serviced the outdoor deck, Charlie Chambers sat on a stool, drinking a beer — and watching the whole thing.

Kayla seemed to have suddenly run out of words. She straightened up, then gave them a subdued good-bye, turned, and walked quickly across the dining room.

Richie Pisano moved to her side, car keys dangling from his fingers. They disappeared through the service entrance.

When they looked over to the bar, Charlie was gone, too.

"Drama," Cass said.

"Strange," Izzy added. "Charlie probably gave up and went home. He's not one for confrontation."

Nell nodded, a slight worry line crossing her forehead. Then she reminded herself, not for the first time, that her nephew was a grown man. A smart and wise grown man.

"Did you understand what Kayla was saying, Birdie?" Cass asked.

"I'm not sure," Birdie said. "I think she's saying that this inheritance may hurt her life. But Dolores had put things in place to help her with that."

They concentrated on the oysters, wondering about the power of money.

"And what's with Richie the reporter showing up like that?" Cass asked.

"That's strange," Izzy said. "And a little creepy. I was relieved to see that Charlie saw it, too. Maybe he can do something about it."

Cass reached for a warm sourdough roll and pulled off a piece to soak up the lemony wine butter pooling on her plate. "I don't know if it involves Richie, but Charlie definitely had something bothering him tonight."

Nell looked around the restaurant, half expecting Charlie to reappear and assure them Kayla would be okay. "Speaking of Richie, I nearly forgot something that I think might be important." She reached down and pulled the folded newspaper from her bag, the creases beginning to fade out some of the newsprint. The scribbled yellow sheet fell to the floor as she unfolded the newspaper. Nell picked it up, glanced at it briefly, then folded it back into her purse and explained to the others where the newspaper had come from. "It's clear that this is the article that was irritating her. You can see pencil pokes in the column and the headline is circled. But why? And why had she taken it to the library with her?"

They passed the article around, scanning it quickly. It wasn't earthshaking, or even that interesting, as Nell pointed out. The elegant fund-raiser had been held at the new hotel in Gloucester with several North Shore agencies represented. Some directors had given talks, detailing the needs of their agencies and the ways their donations were used. Mary Pisano and Hannah Swenson had helped plan it, apparently, and Hannah had welcomed everyone with a talk and her plans for improvements to the Seaside Initiative — things that would enable them to help even more North Shore nonprofits. But Richie had seemed more interested in the who's who of wealthy guests than the efforts of the nonprofits.

"Richie should have stopped with a description of the hotel and left the guests alone," Birdie observed.

The list of wealthy patrons detailed in the article was impressive — but the reporter had presented it in an offensive manner, sure to have riled feathers.

"Good grief. Who characterizes a group by adding up their net worth? Do you think that's what Dolores was upset about? Richie's offensive writing?" Cass asked.

At first, that was exactly what Nell had thought. But in that moment, as Cass asked the question and pointed out the obvious, she read some things she had missed and she changed her mind.

Richie Pisano's inappropriate reporting wasn't what had bothered Dolores Cardozo that day; it was something else he had written. She saw Don Wooten approaching the table and slipped the article back into her purse.

Don carried a bottle of wine he had chosen from the cellar, along with his recommendation for dinner: a small brioche filled with warm truffled lobster, and the chef's special salmon, bathed in a cardamom and ginger sauce.

Nell sat back and smiled. She looked around the table at the faces she so loved.

The evening, the candlelight, the warm embrace of friendship needed to be savored tonight. And the article burning a whole in her bag needed a small amount of time to ripen and grow into its own.

She would give it that. And give in to the magic of the ladies' night out that three kind men had arranged for four women they loved.

CHAPTER 32

Charlie wondered briefly about how it would look to a bystander — the nurse practitioner from the town's well-respected medical clinic moving as quiet as a cat in the dark. Spying.

Yep. That's what you're doing Chambers. You're spying.

Following Richie Pisano's Jeep to Sandpiper Beach had, at first, been strictly an impulse action. He had seen the look on Kayla's face as she walked out of the restaurant. She was angry — but she was also afraid. It was the fear that got to him.

He drove around the bend that brought the ocean in sight and spotted the red Jeep immediately, parked toward the far end of the narrow gravel parking lot that straddled the beach. Several other cars angled along on either side of the Jeep, facing the waves. Music poured out the windows of one, the bass vibrating in the salt air.

The bright moon illuminated the Jeep as he drove by. It was empty. Charlie pulled into a space a few cars down. At this end of the beach an outcropping of boulders created a climbing playground for kids in the daytime. At night their shadows were ominous, hiding folks not wanting to be seen.

He walked slowly, picking his way across the spike grass and rocky sand toward a narrow opening between two boulders. He heard them before he saw them.

"We're a match made in heaven, Kayla," Richie Pisano was saying, the ocean breeze pushing his voice toward the rocks. "What you've given me is pittance. Nice, but hey, the world is our oyster now. We'll be rolling in it soon. Think of your kids, Kayla. Don't forget the kids."

Charlie climbed closer until he could see Kayla's long shadow in the sand, detailed by moonlight. Her hands were balled up at her side, her body so still he wondered if she was breathing.

And then he heard a loud, angry voice, unleashed, rising over the crash of the waves. Strong and forceful and clear.

"You're a miserable thief. Don't touch me. It has to stop. I'm through."

The words swirled up around Charlie. *Don't touch me. . . .*

In minutes — or maybe it was seconds — the former football player was over the mound of granite and had pummeled the redheaded, freckle-faced reporter to the ground, one fist meeting a cheek with forceful certainty. And then another.

"Charlie, stop!" Kayla screamed into his ear, but all Charlie could hear was the echo of her voice commanding the man now lying on the ground to not touch her.

It was when the tears came, when Kayla sobbed, that Charlie moved away from him and turned to comfort the woman with tears streaming down her face. He wrapped her in his arms, one eye on the man on the sand.

Richie pulled himself up, his fingers lightly probing the bruises on his face. Blood streamed from his nose and over his chin, collecting on his shirt. One lip puffed up like a balloon. He looked over at Charlie, his injured mouth twisting into a grin. "Not a good move, Charlie boy. You'll regret this. You want a police record, too, just like our Kayla here?" He laughed, then looked at Kayla and nodded as if they were caught up together in some secret web of understanding. "See you, babe. Soon."

And he was gone.

Charlie walked Kayla to his car. They sat

in the front seat looking out, the ocean stretching out in front of them, the full moon creating brilliant, rippling pathways across the water. For a long time they said nothing.

Finally, Charlie spoke, his voice even and calm. "I saw a newspaper photo of you today at the soup pantry. The old Kayla with long, wavy black hair. That's when it clicked. I remembered where I'd seen you before."

Kayla didn't move, tears still streaming down her face.

But Charlie sensed her surprise. He went on. "You were working with kids on a playground in Idaho, doing the same community service I had done at that same place years before, assigned there by the same rehab program that had helped me get my life back. And yours, too, I suspect."

Kayla took the tissue Charlie handed her, her eyes wide, focused on the moon, but she listened to every word.

He'd gone back to Idaho to thank an old friend a couple years ago, he said, and he had seen her there, playing with the kids. Her hair, rich and dark and flowing over her narrow shoulders, had made her stand out, be noticeable. He'd asked his friend about her because she looked so young, but also tough. Strong. And he recognized the look on her face because he'd been there himself. The look of ongoing recovery, of breathing fresh air and waking up to the world.

"Your friend was Angel," Kayla said, her voice hushed.

"Yes, it was. Angel. That's where you met Sister Fiona, too. It wasn't until I saw the photo that I put it all together. That big-hearted nun brought you here with Sarah Grace and Christopher because it would be a good place for the three of you. You'd leave your past behind and begin a new life."

Kayla began to cry again. A low unbearably sad sound that filled the car and Charlie's heart.

He sat quietly, his eyes focused on the waves.

Finally, Kayla sank back into the seat, and in time, she began to talk, filling in the gaps before Charlie even asked. Her defenses were gone. There wasn't any fight left.

"It's over," she said.

Charlie listened to every word, picking up bits and pieces until he knew more about her than maybe she knew about herself.

Richie Pisano had wanted a story, and he found one as he hung around, prodding and plotting, asking questions, at first out of curiosity. An ambitious reporter looking for gossip or scandal. Something attention worthy. Then probing deeper when he spotted an opportunity, an old woman with money all over her house and a young woman with ready access.

She had mentioned Idaho to Richie once, and he called newspapers, explored public records, traced Kayla's life all the way from Sea Harbor back to jail.

And then he put it all together in a package and blackmailed her.

He'd not tell a soul, keep her past life a secret, he promised her, her kids free of the scandal that would ruin them if this small town knew their mother had been in jail, in rehab, in a dark place. Even giving birth without knowing who the dads were.

All she had to do was get him some of Dolores Cardozo's money now and then. Loose change, he called it. He'd seen it himself. The demands grew and the ante was upped when Richie spotted Dolores Cardozo in the Danvers Bank one day while he was researching a story there. So he snooped around and listened to private conversations until he discovered that Dolores Cardozo was one rich lady.

It'd be simple, he told Kayla. All she had to do was ask for it, tell Dolores a kid needed an operation or something. Cardozo was crazy about Kayla, he could tell. One lump sum was all he was asking for. And then he'd leave her alone. He promised. But he was in a hurry, had some debts of his own to pay off.

"I couldn't take it anymore," Kayla said. "I knew it would never end. So I went out that night to tell Dolores everything. What I'd done. What Richie had made me do. And I'd beg her forgiveness and ask for her help."

Charlie filled in the rest himself.

It might have ended there. Except Dolores Cardozo was murdered.

And in her will, Kayla Stewart would receive more than even Richie Pisano dreamed possible. Having lost her own sister to drugs and suicide, she considered Kayla her second chance. She would do everything in her power to save her.

She would be sure that Kayla and her children had a good life.

An irony of awful proportions. Kayla's trust was music to Richie's ears, manna from heaven. He'd plant himself in Kayla's life permanently — and there was nothing she could do about it.

Charlie finally allowed himself to look over at Kayla. Her face was red with tears, her breathing finally slowed. Her face utterly sad.

And, in Charlie's eyes, excruciatingly beautiful.

CHAPTER 33

Ben wasn't home when Nell came in carrying white cartons of leftovers. He'd be happy whenever he did get in and discovered a midnight snack to beat all midnight snacks. She checked the clock. It was almost midnight — late for Ben, and the scribbled note he'd left in the kitchen told her little.

Had to go out for a bit. Don't wait up. Hope the evening was great. See you in the morning.

Nell made herself some sleepy tea and carried it upstairs, the sheets of paper in her other hand. She took a quick shower, got into her pajamas, and slipped into bed, counting on the comfort of downy pillows and a soft duvet to ease the task ahead.

Then she put on her reading glasses, spread a line of typing sheets across the comforter, and began to read.

She was especially interested in the last couple years. Agencies who benefited, and those who didn't. And those who had benefited at one time and were then discontinued. Some small organizations had received money two or three years in a row and then disappeared from Dolores's list. It didn't surprise Nell nor did it reflect poorly on the organization. It was the way of nonprofits and of society's needs. Sometimes they were replaced by bigger groups, ones that could fill the same need more efficiently. Some simply lost steam.

She noticed Jake Risso's name in the box at the bottom and frowned, then looked closer. The Gull Tavern owner? Jake was a good sort with a big heart but Nell couldn't imagine him even toying with the idea of starting a charity. Nor did she remember talk of it. Every second of Jake's free time was spent in his old fishing boat. She circled his name and scribbled a note beside it before moving on to the next.

With a pencil in hand and a finger leading her from one line to the next, she worked her way through the list, circling some numbers or names, drawing arrows here and there, and finally gathering all the sheets into a pile, putting them on the nightstand, and leaning back into the pillow.

She thought of Birdie, Cass, and Izzy, imagining them doing the same thing, their minds gathering information and wanting to shut it out at the same time. Wanting to come to the end of the road, and hoping somehow to find a rainbow there, not a murderer. But the rainbow would have to wait.

A blanket of sadness settled between her body and the comforter.

She wondered if Dolores had had the same feeling as she had put it all together. Good people doing bad things. And to what end?

But Nell herself could guess the answer to that. And she suspected Dolores Cardozo had, too.

Ben was already downstairs when Nell finally awoke the next morning. It was midmorning. Nell couldn't remember sleeping that late since graduate school when study sometimes turned her night into day. Now it was uncomfortable, as if time had a different meaning when one got older. She hadn't heard Ben come in the night before and wondered for a second if he'd ever come to bed.

But the wrinkled sheets and pillow on the floor told her he had been there, at least for a while. She had tried to stay awake until he got in, but the long day had won out and plunged her into a fitful night of disconnected dreams. From the looks of the bed, Ben had had a long night, too.

She showered and dressed quickly, then followed the smell of strong coffee down the back steps and into the kitchen. Ben's coffee was magical. It began the day right. And she hoped it would end right, too, although she had no idea at that moment what the word *right* might mean.

Ben was at the sink, staring out into the backyard. He wore slacks and a button-down shirt.

A meeting? Nell frowned. She couldn't remember his plans for the beginning of the week. The past days seemed to have been lived from moment to moment rather than calendar reminders. "Ben?"

He turned around quickly as if he'd been suddenly pulled back from some other world. His lids were heavy. Nell wondered if he'd gotten any sleep at all.

"What's wrong? Where were you last night?"

He managed a semblance of a smile and poured her a cup of coffee. "Last night, my love, I was at the police station, getting one fellow out of jail and putting another one in."

And then he explained the call he'd gotten from Charlie — and where their nephew had gone after Nell had seen him at the Ocean's Edge Restaurant the night before.

Ben called Sam, who got a neighbor to stay with Abby, and the two went down to the station together.

Richie Pisano had meant what he'd said to Charlie. His spite got the better of his judgment and he reported an assault, telling the police where they might find the guy who'd messed up his face. The police had picked up Charlie, still sitting in his car on Sandpiper Beach with Kayla Stewart still wrapped in his arms.

But Richie Pisano had made one grave mistake. He had counted on Kayla remaining steadfast no matter what happened. She was bound to him. Protecting her kids from scandal and shame was the rope that held her in its firm grip.

Richie Pisano was wrong.

With Charlie Chambers beside her, Kayla told the police everything they needed to know — the whole sad story of the last few months — how he'd found out her past and used it against her. She explained that she'd gone out to see Dolores Cardozo with hopes she would help her pay Richie off and banish him from her life. But instead, she had found her friend lying on the floor, dead.

It had taken less than an hour for Chief Jerry Thompson to put everything together and send Tommy Porter to pick up the redheaded reporter. He was sitting in the Gull Tavern nursing his injuries with beer, pleased with himself, at least until he saw the police car parked at the curb, a light spinning on top.

Nell's mouth opened and closed several times while Ben talked, but not a single word came out. She was stunned, her heart filled with anguish for the young woman who had lived under that awful cloud. For the pain Richie had caused. And for all sorts of things she hadn't had time to process.

"What will happen now?" Nell asked.

Ben checked his watch. "It may take a little time to figure it out, but we're going to go over it today. I'm headed to the station to meet briefly with Jerry — as you'd expect, his mind is going in different directions. This thing with Richie Pisano has shaken up a lot of things for the police, not the least of which is the Cardozo murder. He had been seen at the Cardozo house. And he was known for spreading crisp fifty dollar bills around town. He was definitely a suspect.

"But whatever happens with Richie now it will include protecting Kayla and her children's privacy, which is what Kayla herself has been trying to do, although in a misguided way."

Nell understood why Kayla had been silent about it all. She wasn't willing to risk tearing apart the only semblance of ordinary life she had ever been able to build for her children.

Ben held Nell close, then kissed her soundly, grabbed his keys, and headed out to his car.

It was only after Ben left and she glanced at her phone that she saw the list of text messages. And it was then she realized she hadn't said a word to Ben about the records Elliott Danvers had given them. About the suspicions, about Dolores's careful screening. But maybe it was just as well. There were still holes in their suspicions. Questions that still needed logical, sound answers.

She read through the texts. Izzy, Cass, and Birdie were headed to the yarn shop, ready to add up numbers right along with Dolores Cardozo.

Nell was relieved. Cass was excellent with this sort of thing, Birdie was wise, and Izzy's mind was logical and clear. Maybe one of them had seen something she hadn't. Part of her hoped so. The other part wanted this to be the end of it all. Finally.

She slipped on a light jacket, then assembled her printouts in order, the ones with arrows and circles and highlighted boxes on top. She glanced down at one of the sheets.

Jake Risso's name popped out of the box. *Jake and Marie Risso.* And then the name: Healthy Eating for Kids. It was an old project from some years ago, before Jake's wife died.

She texted Izzy to say she'd be there after a quick stop at Jake Risso's Gull Tavern, and she headed out the door.

Jake was wiping off an empty bar when Nell walked in. Surprised, he hurried around it and greeted Nell with a hug. "What's up, Nell?"

"Got a minute for a couple questions?"

"For you I have a week of minutes. Always." He grinned and motioned Nell over to a table in the corner. "What's your pleasure? Beer? Wine?"

Nell laughed. "It's a little early for me, Jake. All I need is you. I learned recently that you and your Marie used to manage a small nonprofit and I have a couple questions about it. I think it involved kids and cooking?"

Jake's hands went up in the air, a smile filling his whole face. "Sure you have questions. Like how could old Jake teach kids to plant and cook? Hah, you know it was my Marie. She was a saint. Everyone loved her cooking, so it was a natural. And that little garden she had out back?" He looked down at his rotund middle and shook his head. "I don't eat so well since she passed."

"So Marie taught kids to cook?"

"Yup. She taught them how to garden, too, then cook the good things they grew. Mostly kids who didn't have much. They used the kitchen in the back. It was a great time."

"It sounds terrific. How did you fund it?"

"We put a little into it. 'Seed money' we called it and laughed since most of it went for seeds. Some of my regulars donated, too. But then Marie wrote some grants or whatever it is you do to make it more official for the tax man. Then we got lucky and got one big chunk of *scharole.* Marie was thrilled." He looked around as if someone might be eavesdropping on something that had happened years before.

"And then what happened?"

Jake looked embarrassed. "Well, after Marie died some wait-staff here tried to keep it alive, just because Marie had loved it, but you know how that goes. And then, well —"

"Then that yearly contribution stopped coming?"

Jake met her look. "Yeah, it did, but it was almost a relief. Especially when it was explained that the effort wouldn't really die. It'd just be better."

"You knew why the contribution stopped?"

"Sure. She explained it all."

"Who did?"

Jake took a deep breath, then let it all out, the burst of air ruffling a napkin on the table. "Okay, it don't matter anymore, I suppose, now that the good lady is gone and people know she was rich. Ms. Cardozo, she was the one giving the funds for our project. Maybe you already know that since you're askin'. She wrote a letter telling me she'd like to move the funds. There was a new program doing the same thing at that club for boys and girls. She was so smart, she knew to the penny what we were spending on ours and said maybe The Boys and Girls Club could combine our effort with theirs and make it more efficient. Consolidate, she said. And maybe they'd set up a scholarship over there in Marie's name. Or maybe a bench in the garden with her name on it. And they did. I go sit there sometimes and can feel Marie's smile."

"She explained it all," Nell said quietly, processing her own thoughts.

But Jake heard her. "Sure she did. She sent me a letter, then came to see me, too." He chuckled. "She said she'd walked past my bar for years and had yet to taste my special brew. This was her chance. So we sat back there in the kitchen, drank a fine one, and she explained it all again. That's when I knew where the money was coming from each September — her fiscal year. She paid everyone that courtesy, she told me. Always sent a letter explaining her decisions. What she said made sense. I run a business. I know that sort of thing. It was the right thing to do."

So Dolores's generosity wasn't completely anonymous, at least not to people who stopped receiving it. But she didn't just cut people off without notice. Nell felt a twist inside of her as another piece of the puzzle fell into place, the thud so loud she was sure Jake must have heard it. She slipped her purse strap over her shoulder and got up to leave.

At the door she looked back at Jake, his face now filled with memories of his wife, Marie, seeing her out there planting seeds with the kids, teaching them about good food. "There's one thing that puzzles me, Jake. No one in this town seemed to know Dolores Cardozo was wealthy until she died. But people like you who had at one time benefited from her wealth — you knew. Secrets like that aren't kept easily in small towns. Why didn't you tell anyone?"

For a brief moment Jake looked at her as if she had asked him something absurd, like if he loved the Red Sox or fishing. And then he laughed, stood up himself, and headed back to the bar, calling over his shoulder, "Because, Nellie, m'dear, she asked me not to."

Izzy's shop was closed for regular business, but the store was bustling, people coming in with bags of knit items and leaving empty-handed.

"The last day for donations for the HMS drive," Mae explained to Nell, as she directed someone from a Brownie troop to a box marked SOCKS. "Can you believe it? Look at this room of riches." She pointed to boxes lining a wall. "Not to mention what's already out at the clothing center."

Each day there were more hats and socks and mittens and scarves, some in boxes and bags left at the yarn shop door before Mae came in to open up each morning. All colors and softness and kinds of yarn — merino and cotton and soft fuzzy angora. Everyone would be kept warm during the harsh winter to come. Like prayer shawls, the winter warmth project would help both ends of the body and both ends of the giving spectrum, the givers and the receivers. And in Sea Harbor, sometimes the two were the same.

"It's great, Mae. And so are you. What would Izzy do without you?"

"That's the question of the day." Mae laughed and sent Nell on to the back room and out of her way.

There were a few more boxes in the knitting room, too, marked neatly and ready for final items.

Izzy sat at the long table finishing telling Birdie and Cass about Kayla, Charlie, and Richie Pisano. They looked up when Nell walked over, their expressions of sadness and shock matching what she'd felt earlier that day.

"That awful young man," Birdie said with unusual venom in her voice. "Using that young woman the way he did. Shame, shame, shame."

But their shock was tempered with regret when they reflected on the last weeks. All those small signs they wished they'd noticed. They *knew* that Kayla was suffering, that something in her life was terribly wrong; why hadn't they figured it out?

"Because we were focused on a murder," Birdie finally said. Their attention was misdirected. The small signs would have been interpreted differently as they somehow tried to connect them to Dolores's murder. "And we still are," she added.

Nell pulled out a chair and sat down. "Birdie's right. Kayla and the kids are in good hands now — Chief Thompson will make sure Richie's threats are buried. The awful cloud of suspicion is finally lifted and Richie will be punished appropriately. I have no doubt about that. Ben said we will know more soon but it's all being taken care of."

Birdie agreed. "Gratitude is in order, not regrets."

Gratitude. Celebrating the present. Yes, Birdie was right. Nell took the mug of coffee Izzy handed her and wrapped her fingers around it, reluctant for a moment to move away from Birdie's wise advice.

But there was still a murderer out there somewhere, and even though Kayla might be free of police suspicion, it wouldn't be lifted completely until someone else was behind bars.

She looked down at a yellow pad in front

of Izzy and the printouts next to it. Numbers and boxes and names and figures. The thorny issue of Dolores Cardozo's paperwork was there in front of them, begging for attention.

"So what went on at the tavern?" Cass asked.

Nell repeated the conversation she'd had with Jake and how he had honored Dolores's privacy. "It was so simple for him," Nell said. "Dolores asked for anonymity. And he agreed. Honorable and simple."

But it was the letter itself that was important — the fact that Dolores didn't just cut people off and leave them hanging, wondering why annual monies they'd counted on had suddenly stopped coming. She explained why, graciously, kindly, intelligently. And she helped them decide the next step if there was one. Dolores Cardozo was exceedingly fair.

Birdie had made several calls to acquaintances whose names appeared in the "box," as they were starting to call it, and had heard the same story: they had each received a serious but gracious letter explaining why the funds had been discontinued and applauding the group for the good work it had done. "And they all honored Dolores's request to respect her privacy."

Izzy took a deep breath and fiddled with the papers she had pored over that morning. "So we now know that all the names in all these boxes on all these sheets are people who knew Dolores had stopped funding them. And they knew why."

Nell expressed what they were all thinking. "It's the recent ones that are important."

They were quiet for a moment, aware that they were speaking in code, reluctant to mention real names, names of people. A person.

Izzy picked up Nell's list. The one that Dolores herself had put together just weeks ago. September, the beginning of her fiscal year. One group in particular had received money from the Cardozo fund for years, but it had stopped this year. "Instead of money, a letter had come," Izzy said, as if reading a play.

Nell picked up her coffee mug again. She was suddenly chilled. "Explaining why."

The silence that followed was heavy. The names seemed to take on their own life. But there was only one that mattered.

Nell had taken out the newspaper article Dolores had stabbed with her pencil. Cass took it from her and started to unfold it. "How weird it would be if that awful twerp of a reporter actually helped reveal Dolores's murderer."

But an article wasn't proof, they knew.

A yellow sheet of scrap paper fell from the fold as Cass smoothed out the cheap newsprint. "Hey, what's this?"

Nell looked at it. She'd almost forgotten about it. "It's a piece of scrap paper Marian found with the newspaper that day. She saved it in case Dolores needed it."

Cass was silent, her eyes moving up and down and across the sheet of scribbled numbers. "She was adding up numbers, expenses against income, salaries, donations. It doesn't say what organization she was checking but it's similar to what our accountant does — though not on scrap paper. It's a check to make sure everything lines up and there isn't any discrepancy. It wouldn't be too hard to find out what group had these expenses."

Nell took the sheet and looked at some of the items on it. She frowned. Then checked the article again and passed it around to the others as the words came together, telling a story that even Richie Pisano hadn't intended to tell.

It wasn't proof.

But it was the beginning of proof.

And Izzy was right. People normally

wouldn't murder Santa Claus because they didn't get the present they wanted. But they might if Santa told them why they weren't getting it.

And while their coffee got cold, they outlined their imagined details of the sad and terrible murder of a woman they had come to respect and appreciate and like.

In the distance the hum of voices rose and fell as knitters came and went, showing off their projects to each other, then gently placing the hats, mittens, socks, and scarves in their proper place. Mae appeared now and then, quietly adding new items to the boxes near the back room fireplace.

Nell stepped over to the window to call Jerry Thompson. Then she tried Ben, leaving brief messages for both. They needed to talk.

Back at the table Cass was running her finger over a header that appeared on each annual list, right above the year:

The Dolores Francesca Maria Cardozo Fund
2014 . . . 2016 . . . 2017

"An elegant name for an elegant lady," Birdie said, looking over Cass's shoulder.

Mae walked down the steps again, her arms full, a scarf dangling from her fingers. Nell hurried over and relieved her of a few items about to fall.

489

"These just came in. It may be the last of the group donations," the shop manager said.

Nell fingered the soft scarf on the top of the pile. Then she handed the rest back to Mae and unfolded the scarf, letting the silky yarn flow over her hands. She walked over to the table. "Look at this gorgeous piece. It's qiviut, I think."

"Yes," said Mae. "Beautiful, isn't it. It takes everything in me not to sneak it into my bag."

Izzy took the scarf from Nell, frowning and about to speak when a voice floated down the steps to the knitting room. "You dropped one, Mae," Hannah Swenson said, walking down the steps.

Then she looked around and spotted the others, her tan face lifting into a smile. "What a great surprise," she said, walking over to the table. She looked around and smiled happily at each of them.

Birdie offered her a cup of coffee while Izzy and Nell commented on the gorgeous scarves Hannah had brought in, their praise coming too quickly. "I can't quite believe you're donating these," Izzy said.

"It's the warmest fiber in the world, did you know that?" Hannah asked.

"And you're paying for every strand of

warmth," Nell said.

"Well, no matter. It makes me feel good to donate it."

"I hope whoever gets it appreciates the luxury item they're wrapping around their neck," Birdie said.

Hannah looked over at her, a note of pride in her voice. "I will know. That's what matters."

Hannah walked closer to the table, holding the coffee mug in both hands. "What are you all doing in here? Finishing up your projects for the drive?"

She looked at a basket in the middle of the table, filled with needles and place markers, a pair of scissors. But there wasn't any yarn or half-knit mittens or patterns anywhere. It was then Hannah noticed the printouts — and at closer glance, the words at the top of each.

The Dolores Francesca Maria Cardozo Fund

The knitters were still, making no attempt to cover anything up.

Hannah's voice changed and color drained from her face. "What are those? What are you doing?"

No one answered.

Hannah looked at each of them, at the sheets of paper and the circled names and numbers. She took a step back and focused on Izzy, sitting at the end of the table.

"Izzy," she said, her voice shaky. "You have a daughter. I have a son."

Izzy nodded and the others listened, not sure where Hannah was taking them.

"You'd do anything for your little girl. Anything. That's what we parents do. Sacrifice. Jason needs so much. The best schools, clothes —"

"Sailboats?" Cass asked. "A trip to Europe? A mother with expensive clothes, a hip condo?"

She stared at Cass, not answering.

"Dolores figured out what you were doing," Nell said quietly. "I thought it strange that you made the same appeals, fund-raiser after fund-raiser, for the same things. Furniture, plumbing, new shades and lighting and adequate space for workshops. More staff. Laudable things. But the furniture and shades and lighting never happened, the donations funneled in other directions." In *Hannah's* direction, they now knew.

"And then you asked for those things yet again, as Richie Pisano detailed in his newspaper article a few weeks ago." Birdie held up the already yellowed clipping.

"I don't think you understand how this all works, Nell. Dolores Cardozo didn't understand. I got her letter terminating her annual donation. That was okay, that was fine. I am enterprising and have wonderful connections. But then . . . then she had the audacity to tell me why she was doing it.

"So I went out to see her, just to explain why it happened, to explain that I had a son to support. Bills. To make her understand that I wasn't a thief. My son was going to Harvard Law School, I told her."

Her voice turned hard as she revisited that Saturday. "I didn't care about her money, her measly annual *gift.* But she insisted that she had to report the discrepancies she found, the small blips in the accounting records she'd fine combed her way through."

"Small blips?" Nell said. "Hannah, what you were doing wasn't small. You were stealing donors' money. Lots of it."

Hannah still wasn't listening. "It probably wasn't even legal for Dolores to go through my records the way she did, and I told her that. 'They aren't your records,' she said to me, as if she were the judge, teaching me something. And she accused me of stealing, of fraud. Of all sorts of things. . . ." Her voice trailed off and she looked over their heads as if explaining something to herself. "I knew then that I couldn't convince her. I knew she was going to send me to prison. And that couldn't happen. How would . . . what would it do to Jason?"

A slight sound from the top of the steps turned their attention to Mae Anderson, standing still, her face ashen and her arms full of mittens and hats.

Behind her, Jerry Thompson and Tommy Porter stood quietly, listening, their faces sad.

Uncovering a murderer was never a time to rejoice. Not even when the nightmare was finally over.

CHAPTER 34

It took over three hours and more than a half-dozen people sitting around the well-used conference table in the Sea Harbor police station to determine Richie Pisano's fate.

It was early on a chilly Friday morning, with a breeze coming through the single window that someone had gratefully opened a crack to move the stale air around.

Richie was there, happy to be in civilian clothes after two weeks in jail clothes, with several lawyers from his father's prestigious New Hampshire law firm lined up in chairs beside him. His father was at the far end of the row, disassociating himself as best he could from the adult son he was having to deal with again. Chief Jerry Thompson, Tommy Porter, and an attorney for the department sat opposite them. Ben Endicott was there, too, with Kayla and another attorney well versed in blackmail cases.

Conferring with Ben and the attorney, Kayla had agreed not to press charges against Richie Pisano, but only if he agreed to certain terms, all spelled out in an airtight document that he had to sign. Any infraction of the terms would send him to jail for what could be a very long time. He was not ever to talk to Kayla Stewart again, or to approach her for any reason, in any way, or to divulge to anyone personal details about Kayla or her family or her life. Nor was he allowed to return to Cape Ann.

Richie was also committed to three years of community service in some tiny town in a remote corner of New Mexico, one chosen by his father for its distance from New Hampshire, where he and his wife lived. Richie had done a couple of other undesirable things, all of which were coming to the surface and all of which the Pisano family was eager to bury as deeply as they could.

When it was over, all the parties approved of the course of action, although some more than others. Charlie Chambers, who waited out the proceedings at the school playground with two children and a dog, would have preferred to wipe the man off the face of the earth.

"He was lucky," Ben said later that morning. "Kayla was mature and thoughtful and did him a favor in agreeing to it all."

They sat around the kitchen island, Abby playing in the toy corner of Nell and Ben's family room. They all needed to be elsewhere — it was a day packed full of activities. But for the first time since Hannah had been led away, they felt a kind of joy inching its way back into their lives.

"Why did Kayla agree to it?" Cass asked. She was in Charlie's camp, thinking sending Richie to Timbuktu was a more desirable outcome.

"Because it was the path of least notoriety. It wouldn't make the papers like a court case would. He would be out of her life more completely, more solidly than if he'd been put in jail for a dozen years." It was Danny who spoke, his eyes on Cass, one arm around her shoulder.

"It all centers around Kayla doing the best thing to protect her kids," Izzy said, moving closer to Sam. "Protecting those we love."

"Yes," Nell said. "Of course it does." She watched Izzy's head turn, her eyes on a curly-haired toddler a few feet away, playing with a Lightning McQueen car.

"A claim Hannah Swenson made, too," Nell said. The contrast loomed large as they considered what the woman had done in the name of her son.

"When did you begin to suspect her, Aunt Nell?" Izzy asked. "She floated in and out of my head a few times, but the connection seemed vague until this week. And then it began to come together in vivid colors."

"I think it was when we started examining Dolores's giving. You were the one, Izzy, who convinced us all it was unlikely for someone to kill a benefactor because they didn't make the cut. So I wondered what other reason there could be. I had some connection with Hannah and the Seaside Initiative, remember, and I knew what the needs of the Seaside Initiative were. I also knew that somehow, in spite of her healthy donation pool, some basic needs hadn't been met — things she was asking donors for, then not initiated when the money came in. I just didn't put it all together until there was a reason to. And then, learning how carefully Dolores chose the groups she helped, some of those observations came back."

"Dolores's anger that day makes perfect sense now," Birdie said. "She realized Hannah was using good people's money — money intended for other good people — for her own needs, whatever they were."

"Even if she hadn't been heard confessing, an accountant going through everything would quickly have discovered the theft." Ben got up and carried the coffeepot around, refilling cups, but Cass and Danny declined. Cass stood and stretched.

"Things to do?" Izzy grinned.

Danny grabbed his jacket and grinned back. "We're busy folks."

"I don't know why any of us are sitting around like this," Nell said, her voice rather stern. "It's Friday after all."

Cass laughed. "Friday. Sure. Dinner on the deck." She looked through the window. "Outside, right?"

"Absolutely," Ben said. "Talked to the weather gods myself. This might be the last good one, so we're going to make the most of it."

"I think we can manage that," Birdie said. "I feel a vibe that says we'll have a crowd tonight. Who knows, I may even dance."

Ben bowed slightly and asked if he could be the first on her dance card.

They all felt the vibe. The coming together of friends as they moved out of a dark, angry and fearful place. Together they'd make the world bright again.

"So scat, all of you," Nell said, her eyes shining. She'd keep them all right there for the rest of their lives if she could. But if they didn't leave, they couldn't come back. Nor could she get the house cleaned and things ready for Friday night on the deck. And there was plenty to do.

She smiled, then picked up her Abby and together they waved them all away. Until they came back.

CHAPTER 35

Cass stood on the bedroom deck of her house. It was just up the hill from the Canary Cove Art Colony. She loved this house. Warm, simple, and open to the sea. A small island in one direction, the bustle and lights of the harbor in another. And everywhere in between was the ocean she loved.

She was a water child. Like her father. Strong, fluid — and moody. But mostly what she felt right now was fluid. Time didn't stop for people; it just kept going.

It didn't stop for a mother like Kayla with two beautiful kids, wanting to block out bad things and sit on the beach with her kids, feeding gulls and jumping waves and making time stop. But it didn't. So you had to move with it. You had to love the days you were given and move on to the next. She wasn't sure at all why the Stewart kids had gotten to her, and why they — not Aristotle

— had made her examine her life. But they had. And she wanted to make it worth living.

The sun was slowly sinking, the harbor lights reflecting off the water like slender dancers. Cass felt a sudden urge to dance herself. Dance? She laughed and walked back inside, closing the double doors behind her. She'd danced once today already. Maybe that's exactly what she'd do, dance her way across the Endicott deck.

It had been an amazing day already. It might as well end with dancing.

Charlie had called early that morning. He was taking Christopher and Sarah Grace to the playground, occupying them while Kayla had her meeting with Ben and the police.

"Grab Abby and join us," he'd said. "The kids would love it."

So she had. She loved Izzy's brother and being with him this morning seemed the right thing to do. After the playground, they'd walked down to the pier and found Pete fiddling with his guitar on one of the Halloran lobster boats.

In no time, Pete had balanced himself at the bow of the lobster boat and begun to play old jazzy tunes, while the kids frolicked and danced along the dock, hair blowing and hands grasped in circles until Cass finally collapsed in laughter, a pile of kids on top of her.

And then she'd scooped up Abby and headed to Ben and Nell's to meet the others. To have coffee. To be sure Kayla was going to be fine.

The ping of her phone now pulled her back to the darkening sky and she walked across the room to her dresser. She knew before checking that the text would be from Izzy. It was the fifth one in the last hour. Come now! it read. You won't believe tonight's dinner.

Cass shook her head. Everything was urgent for Izzy, but Cass had a few things to do, including picking up Birdie on her way to the Endicotts'. Friday nights were special, sure.

Birdie and I will be there soon, she texted back. We wouldn't miss it.

Another ping. Another text. Cass laughed out loud at Izzy's persistence. But this text was from Birdie, suggesting that if Cass was stuck in the Laundromat again — like that night a lifetime ago — perhaps she should find another ride to tonight's Friday night dinner?

It was Birdie's gentle way of saying, "Pick me up, Catherine. Now."

Cass texted Birdie back that she was on her way. She hurried down to the kitchen and picked up her bag. *Keys, keys, where?* She spotted them on the counter, wrapped her fingers around them tightly, and headed for the door.

Another ping. *Geesh, Izzy, I'm coming!*

But this time it was Danny.

Her Danny. And instead of words he'd sent another smiley face to her phone, a dopey one that made Cass laugh. The gifted writer Danny Brandley was sending her a dopey face.

She loved it. And him. And she had let him know that before he'd left the house a short while earlier. He'd had a grin on his face when he'd walked out the door, looking remarkably like the one she was staring at on her phone.

She'd watched him through the window as he'd headed toward his car. He'd looked up at the sky, thrown his hands in the air, and given a cheer.

She had heard him, through the crack of an open window. He'd turned around, knowing Cass would be watching, and waved, blown a kiss, and shouted that he'd see her soon.

Ben was grilling up something special, he'd said.

She looked down at the emoticon again, grinned, and checked her watch. And then she yelped.

She really *was* late now. Nell had said she, Izzy, and Birdie should come early. Ben was going all out, grilling lobster with an amazing orange sauce. With Pernod, Nell said. They'd love it.

There would be a merry crowd, one looking forward to ending days of unrest for some, sadness and fear for others.

Minutes later Cass was in the car, her foot to the pedal and headed toward Birdie's house. The window was down and her hair blew wildly while a sliver of a moon appeared above the horizon, guiding her way. The night was about to begin.

Charlie Chambers met them at the door when Birdie and Cass walked in. "Izzy's upstairs. She wants to see you both. *Now,*" he said. "Gads, what a taskmaster my sister can be. She's being weird tonight."

In the distance Cass spotted Danny. He glanced over and grinned at her, looking again like the goofy emoticon he'd sent her earlier.

She started to follow Birdie upstairs, and then glanced over the railing at a face in the distance, smiling at her. A slight wave followed.

Kayla Stewart stood alone near the family room fireplace.

Charlie brought Kayla — what do you know. Great. Her first Friday night on the deck. It seemed significant, somehow, that it was tonight. Not far from Kayla, Christopher and Sarah Grace were laughing as Gabby and Daisy taught them a silly dance. She smiled back at Kayla and started to turn, then saw out of the corner of her eye that Kayla was coming her way.

"Cass?" Kayla's voice was hesitant, her green eyes huge.

"Hi, Kayla. I'm glad you're here," Cass said. "Ben's Friday night dinners are the best."

"I wanted to thank you," she said quickly, as if hesitation might doom what she had to say. Her smile was still there, but her eyes, large and luminous, glistened with emotion.

"Thank me?"

She nodded slowly. "You cared about Chrissie that awful night. You cared about our lives, the kids and me. You and your friends started it all. The whole thing — everything. The road to making it all better. My kids are safe now. And happy." She looked over as Sarah Grace's giggles reached the stairs. "I am too — or at least on my way. And it's because of you. Thank you."

She reached out and gave Cass a quick, light hug.

But the feeling it left with Cass was profound. She gave her a quick one back, then blinked away the moisture in her eyes and said with a shrug, "Hey, Kayla, no problem. That's what we do here."

Then she turned and bounded up the stairs, Izzy's voice calling her from above.

Ben had fastened the front door open with a ceramic lobster, then corralled Charlie and Sam into helping with martinis and uncorking wine. The kitchen island was already filled with platters of appetizers, and plates, and outside the deck was a sea of festivity, with small candles on the old picnic table, pots of fall flowers everywhere, and drinks flowing.

Gabby had decided they needed lights tonight and climbed up into the maple tree with Daisy standing below, handing her strands of tiny white Christmas lights.

"Festive enough?" she asked Sister Fiona, who smiled her agreement. After the weeks they'd had, celebration and festivity were good in whatever form. A glass of wine would be, too, and Fiona took the one her sister-in-law, Mary Halloran, handed her. They'd both come at Father Northcutt's insistence. They deserved a night off, he said, and dinner on the Endicott deck was the perfect place.

Fiona spotted Kayla just inside the door. Charlie was at her side, teasing the kids about something and making Kayla a part of the noisy crowd. She hadn't wanted to come, but Charlie had insisted, and Fiona could tell she was happy she had. Watching the smiles on Christopher and Sarah Grace's faces as they spun around the deck with Daisy and Gabby left no room not to be.

"Where's Nell?" Jane Brewster asked Ben. She carried a bouquet of flowers out to the deck.

Ben looked around. "Nellie? I saw her a few minutes ago. Seems we're more folks than usual tonight. Maybe she went out for more beer." He grinned and Jane frowned back at him. "Ben Endicott, what's up with you?"

But Ben disappeared before she got an answer.

Pete Halloran had brought his guitar and was leaning against the railing calling Gabby and Daisy to his side. "Hey, you two. Tell me what songs you know," he said, and they quickly settled down on the steps with him, arranging a whole medley.

"Where're Izzy and Cass?" Fiona asked no one in particular.

Birdie seemed to have disappeared, too.

Finally, Ben walked over to Pete, who had been joined by his Fractured Fish bandmates, and suggested some music would be in order. He'd give them the sign.

After ushering everyone out to the deck and quieting folks down for a toast, he gave the sign. With the amplifier doing its job, the Fractured Fish tuned up, Pete strumming, Andy on the drums, and singer Merry Jackson flicking the microphone as the crowd looked their direction and the music began.

At first they just strummed and drummed, Merry humming along, but at Ben's nod, the chords took shape and Merry and Pete began singing, their voices full:

Every day, it's a-gettin' closer
Goin' faster than a roller coaster —

The guests began looking around, unsure if they should be quiet and listen or settle back and enjoy the martinis and the wine, the food, the company.

It was Mary Halloran, Cass's mom, who

suddenly broke into smiles that filled her small Irish face. And then, with tears streaming down her face, she rushed over to Archie and Harriet Brandley, Danny's parents.

"Look," she said, pushing them around until they faced the doors to the house.

They looked.

And then they looked again, at three women standing in the open French doorway.

Izzy and Birdie and Nell, arms linked, dressed in simple black dresses with colorful knit scarves, lacy and loose, floating freely from their shoulders. They smiled all around and then began walking, clearing a path through the center of the deck as the band sang on. Smiling at each other. At their guests. And at the Fractured Fish as they took the music up a beat.

Then Mary Halloran's tears began to flow in earnest.

Heads turned and the crowd shuffled noisily, everyone standing now and looking around.

Then Cass and Danny appeared in the doorway, their hips touching and their hands twined tightly together. Danny in slacks and a white shirt open at the collar, Cass's dark hair flowing loose over a simple black silk dress, a single peach-colored rose in her hand.

The crowd hushed as they realized a wedding was about to happen, and they parted like the sea to give Cass and Danny the room they needed.

Cass paused when she neared her mother, now hanging on Sister Fiona's arm for balance and composure. Cass handed her the rose and gave her a kiss. And then she wiped a tear from her mother's cheek before she and Danny continued on their way, over to a spot near the old maple tree, where Father Northcutt was waiting, his prayer book in hand and a blessing on his lips.

As the short ceremony was about to come to a close, Ben walked up beside Nell and wrapped her close. "Away with the sadness," Ben whispered in her ear.

Nell nodded, and at that moment, Cass motioned to her brother, and the band began to play again — big, full, and happy sounds. It was the song she'd picked for her Danny, the words going all the way up to the moon.

A song about dreams and love and living.

The band sang and the crowd clapped. Arms waved.

And Danny and Cass began to dance, their hands reaching for the sky, their hearts full and their voices singing about the best day in their lives.

The crowd joined in, singing and clapping and promising right along with them that they wouldn't look back.

There was a new day ahead.

No limits, just epiphanies.

ACKNOWLEDGMENTS

My village of help and support and inspiration for *Murder Wears Mittens* is varied and wonderful, person after person after person. And to each of them I offer great thanks.

Caitlin Taggart at the Johnson County Library, Corinth branch, helped me understand the levels of Internet security in place for patrons using library computers. Without her guidance I might have allowed the Seaside Knitters to shamefully and illegally invade Dolores Cardozo's library computer account, not a good move for our admirable women of Sea Harbor. In addition, I owe a thanks to the library systems in our dual state areas — Kansas City Missouri (particularly the Plaza branch), and the Johnson County Kansas libraries (with applause to my Corinth neighborhood branch). They've provided me a frequent home away from home, my office and my refuge during the writing of the Seaside Knitters Society mysteries.

The folks at Kensington Publishing — especially my editor, Wendy McCurdy, and also Norma Perez-Hernandez, who have welcomed me into the Kensington fold graciously — and made me feel like I've been there a long time. I'm looking forward to getting to know the entire staff who have helped bring this book to life.

The pattern in the back of the book was designed by Adrienne Ku, a talented designer who generously allowed me to reprint her pattern for top-down socks for my readers. (And who provided helpful tips for Nell as she maneuvered her way around the heel.)

My forever gratitude to Nancy Pickard, who spent a huge chunk of her Christmas vacation reading this book and offering invaluable suggestions, advice, insight, and encouragement (along with Godiva chocolates, André's lunches, and healing doses of humor at just the right moments). And my thanks as always to Mary Bednarowski and Sister Rosemary Flanigan, who are my perpetual springboards for all kinds of murderous ideas — as well as reminders of the goodness in everyone.

And my husband, Don, who's always there

with ideas and hand-holding, and who
doesn't mind (too much) eating frozen dinners for endless nights in a row.

SIMPLE SKYP SOCKS
BY ADRIENNE KU

Abbreviations

K — knit

K2tog — knit 2 stitches together

N — needle, N1 = needle #1

P — purl

P2tog — purl 2 stitches together

R — round/row

RS — right side

Skyp — slip 1 stitch purl-wise with yarn in back, knit 1 stitch, yarn over, pass slipped stitch over the last two stitches (k1 and yo)

Sl1 — slip 1 stitch purl-wise

Ssk — slip 2 stitches individually knit-wise, knit these 2 sts together through back loops

St/Sts — stitch/stitches

WS — wrong side

Yo — yarn over

Materials

Sport weight yarn: The designer used Blue
   Moon Fiber Arts, Socks that Rock Me-
   dium weight yarn (380 yards, 5.5 oz.) in
   Lagoon, 1 skein.
US Size #2 double point needles (or size
   needed to obtain gauge)
Stitch marker (optional)
Tapestry needle
Gauge — 7 sts = 1 inch in stockinette stitch
Size — Men's X-Small [Small, Medium
   Large]. 7″ [8″, 9″, 10″] circumference

Pattern

Cast on 48 [56, 64, 72] sts, join in the
round being careful not to twist sts. Place
marker to indicate beginning of round.

Cuff

R1 — (K2, p2) repeat to end of round.
Repeat R1 for a total of 10 rounds.
Purl 1 round.

Leg

R1 — (K6, p2) repeat to end of round.
R2 — (K2, Skyp, k2, p2) repeat to end of
round.
Work R1-R2 a total of 24 times (or to
desired leg length).
Work R1 once more to 1 [0, 5, 3] sts before

end of round. Small size only (56 sts) — remove stitch marker, knit 1st st of next round.

This will be the new beginning of round (row). Remove end of round marker when you come to it while working the heel flap.

Heel — Flap

The heel flap is worked back and forth over the next 24 [28, 32, 36] sts. Place remaining 24 [28, 32, 36] sts on a stitch holder or scrap of yarn to be held for the instep.

R1 — (Sl1, k1) repeat to end of row.

R2 — Sl1, purl to end of row.

Work R1-R2 11 [13, 15, 17] more times. (12 [14, 16, 18] slip sts along side.)

Heel — Turn

R1(RS) — Sl1, k13 [15, 17, 19], ssk, k1, turn.

R2(WS) — Sl1, p5, p2tog, p1, turn.

R3 — Sl1, k6, ssk, k1, turn.

R4 — Sl1, p7, p2tog, p1, turn.

R5 — Sl1, k8, ssk, k1, turn.

R6 — Sl1, p9, p2tog, p1, turn.

R7 — Sl1, k10, ssk, k1, turn.

R8 — Sl1, p11, p2tog, p1, turn.

X-Small size only

R9 — Sl1, k12, ssk, turn.
R10 — Sl1, p12, p2tog. (14 sts rem.)

Small Size Only

R9 — Sl1, k12, ssk, k1, turn.
R10 — Sl1, p13, p2tog, p1, turn.
R11 — Sl1, k14, ssk, turn.
R12 — Sl1, p14, p2tog. (16 sts rem.)

Medium Size Only

R9 — Sl1, k12, ssk, k1, turn.
R10 — Sl1, p13, p2tog, p1, turn.
R11 — Sl1, k14, ssk, k1, turn.
R12 — Sl1, p15, p2tog, p1, turn.
R13 — Sl1, k16, ssk, turn.
R14 — Sl1, p16, p2tog. (18 sts rem.)

Large size only

R9 — Sl1, k12, ssk, k1, turn.
R10 — Sl1, p13, p2tog, p1, turn.
R11 — Sl1, k14, ssk, k1, turn.
R12 — Sl1, p15, p2tog, p1, turn.
R13 — Sl1, k16, ssk, k1, turn.
R14 — Sl1, p17, p2tog, p1, turn.
R15 — Sl1, k18, ssk, turn.
R16 — Sl1, p18, p2tog. (20 sts rem.)

All Sizes

Sl1, k6 [7, 8, 9] sts (to middle of heel), place marker to indicate new beginning of round.

Gusset

Set-up round —

N1 — K7 [8, 9, 10] sts, pick-up and knit 12 [14, 16, 18] sts along edge of heel flap plus 1 extra stitch between heel flap & instep. (20 [23, 26, 29] sts.)

N2 & N3 — place 24 [28, 32, 36] held instep sts on needles 2 & 3. Work R2 of Instep Stitch Pattern (below) across these stitches.

N4 — Pick-up 1 extra stitch between instep & heel flap, pick-up and knit 12 [14, 16, 18] sts along edge of heel flap, k7 [8, 9, 10] sts. (20 [23, 26, 29] sts.)

R1 — N1 — K to last 3 sts, k2tog, k1. N2&3: Work R1 of Instep Stitch pattern. N4: K1, ssk, k to end.

R2 — N1 — Knit to end. N2&3: R2 of Instep Stitch Pattern. N4: Knit to end.

Repeat R1-R2 until 12 [14, 16, 18] sts remain on N1&4. (48 [56, 64, 72] sts.)

Ex-small
R1 — (p1, k6, p1)
  3×.
R2 — (p1, k2,
  skyp, k2, p1) 3×.

Small
R1 — K1, p2,
  (k6, p2) 3×, k1.
R2 — K1, p2, (k2,
  skyp, k2,
  p2) 3×, k1.

Medium
R1 — K3, p2,
  (k6, p2) 3×, k3.
R2 — K3, p2,
  (k2, skyp, k2, p2)
  3×, k3.

Large
R1 — K3, (k2, p2,
  k4) 4×, k1.
R2 — K1, skyp,
  (k2, p2, k2,
  skyp) 4×, k1.

Foot

Continue working sole stitches in stockinette stitch and instep stitches in pattern until foot is 1 1/4 [1 1/2", 2", 2 1/4"] shorter than desired length.

Toe

R1 — Knit.

R2 — N1 — Knit to last 3 sts, k2tog, k1. N2: K1, ssk, knit to end. N3: Knit to last 3 sts, k2tog, k1. N4: K1, ssk, knit to end.

Repeat R1-R2 until 24 [28, 32, 36] sts remain.

Repeat R2 until 12 [16, 16, 20] sts remain.

Knit across N1.